THE GEMINI
DECEPTION

What Reviewers Say About the Elite Operatives Series

"Baldwin and Alexiou have written a barn burner of a thril[ler] [in *Dying to Live*]. The reader is taken in from the first page the last. The tension is maintained throughout the book wit[h] rare exception. Baldwin and Alexiou are defining the genre of romantic suspense within the lesbian genre with this series. You'll find yourself rushing to purchase the first three books in the series if you haven't already read them, or, if you have read them, wishing the authors would write the fifth in the series faster."—*Lambdaliterary.org*

"Okay, I admit it: I am a fan of adventure/spy/thriller mysteries and always have been. So of course I have been lured into the web of the Elite Operatives series because as a kid, I was always imagining myself in the male leads of the spy thrillers I read. Baldwin and Alexiou clearly had the same fantasy. [They] have established a formula for this series that works: short, staccato chapters set in different locales that unfurl the plot layer by layer and then they develop into solid chapters where the main characters…begin to reveal themselves. The authors manage to take two plot themes that have been done and done again, meld them, and turn them into a solid, convincing, compelling page-turner that is quite satisfying."—*Lambdaliterary.org*

"*Dying to Live* is a chest-grabbing, throat-closing, sleek, sexy, thoroughly enjoyable white-knuckle ride of a thriller. Baldwin and Alexiou prove once again their deft understanding of the genre puts them eye-to-eye with the best in the business. Buckle your seatbelts!"—Amanda Kyle Williams, Author of *The Stranger You Seek* and *Stranger in the Room*

"Baldwin and Alexiou have given their fans a gripping read that's difficult to put down! *Dying to Live* has a complex plot with a pandemic created by an arch villain, and a rescue from Columbian guerrillas. This is a thoroughly enjoyable read, and I can't wait for their next adventure!"—*Just About Write*

"*Missing Lynx* puts the thrill in thriller. In true thriller style, Baldwin and Alexiou take their women around the globe… from Vienna, all around the U.S. Southwest, on to New York, down to some of the most dangerous parts of Mexico, on to China and Vietnam and back to the Southwest. Quite the wild ride. A dark, edgy, often grisly tale, *Missing Lynx* has the grit and pacing of a Bourne saga, but with highly engaging and thoroughly challenging female characters. Not for the faint hearted."—*Lambdaliterary.org*

"Kim Baldwin & Xenia Alexiou just get better and better at coming up with tightly written thrillers with plenty of 'seat of the pants' action. *Missing Lynx* is a roller coaster ride into the seamier side of life and the bonds which bind humans into trying to better the world. This is a book which grips the reader until the final page!"—*Just About Write*

"Unexpected twists and turns, deadly action, complex characters and multiple subplots converge to make this book a gripping page turner. *Lethal Affairs* mixes political intrigue with romance, giving the reader an easy flowing and fast-moving story that never lets up. A must-read, even though it has been out for a while. *Thief of Always*, the duo's second, and equally good book in the Elite Operatives series, came out earlier this year."—*Curve* Magazine

By the Authors

The Elite Operatives Series

Lethal Affairs

Thief of Always

Missing Lynx

Dying to Live

Demons are Forever

The Gemini Deception

By Kim Baldwin

Hunter's Pursuit

Force of Nature

Whitewater Rendezvous

Flight Risk

Focus of Desire

Breaking the Ice

High Impact

Visit us at www.boldstrokesbooks.com

THE GEMINI DECEPTION

by

Kim Baldwin & Xenia Alexiou

2013

THE GEMINI DECEPTION

ISBN 13: 978-1-60282-867-4

THIS TRADE PAPERBACK ORIGINAL IS PUBLISHED BY
BOLD STROKES BOOKS, INC.
P.O. BOX 249
VALLEY FALLS, NY 12185

FIRST EDITION: APRIL 2013

___

CREDITS
EDITOR: SHELLEY THRASHER
PRODUCTION DESIGN: STACIA SEAMAN
COVER DESIGN BY SHERI (GRAPHICARTIST2020@HOTMAIL.COM)

My eternal gratitude and respect to my invaluable friend Kim. Thank you for pointing me in this direction and for being there every step of the way. I am always there for you, no matter what. With only one book left in the series, I can sincerely say it's been an honor, a privilege, and a hell of a fun ride. Can't wait for our next project!

Mom, Dad, and Sis. You are my biggest support and comfort. Thank you for everything.

May, you have made my world a richer place to write in and about.

Claudia, thank you for doing all that you do for me in Holland so that I can live my dream in Greece. You're the world's best "wingman."

And as always a very big thank you to my wonderfully tolerant friends. Esther, Nicki, Dennis, and Steven, you were there from the beginning to constantly support and encourage me, and I will always be grateful. Last but never least, a big bow of appreciation to all the readers who enjoy the stories and make writing one of the most rewarding things I've ever done. YOU ALL ROCK.

Xenia Alexiou 2013

Acknowledgments

The authors wish to thank all the talented women at Bold Strokes Books for making this book possible. Radclyffe, for her vision, faith in us, and example. Editor Shelley Thrasher, your insightful editing of this book is deeply appreciated. Jennifer Knight, for invaluable insights into how to craft a series. Graphic artist Sheri for another amazing cover. Connie Ward, BSB publicist and first-reader extraordinaire, and all of the other support staff who work behind the scenes to make each BSB book an exceptional read.

We'd also like to thank our dear friend and first-reader Jenny Harmon, for your invaluable feedback and insights. And finally, to the readers who encourage us by buying our books, showing up for personal appearances, and for taking the time to e-mail us. Thank you so much.

My dear friend Xenia, working with you on the Elite Operatives Series has been one of the most fun and rewarding endeavors I've ever undertaken, and I'll long cherish the countless happy memories of writing, laughing, reading, and signing together. Here's hoping we do many more projects together once book seven is finished.

For Marty, my family for more than forty years. Your enduring support has been a critical factor in any success I enjoy.

Mom and Dad, I miss you both so much, and know you're watching out for me. And for my brother Tom, for always saying yes when I need a ride to the airport.

I also have to thank a wonderful bunch of friends who provide unwavering support for all my endeavors. Claudia and Esther, Pattie, Linda, Kat, Felicity. You are family, and near or far, I hold you always close to my heart.

Kim Baldwin 2013

To my nephews Alexi and Dimitri
May you always listen to your heart, follow your dreams,
and chase your passions.
I love you guys,
Xenia

You may be deceived if you trust too much, but you will live in torment if you don't trust enough.

—Frank Crane

PROLOGUE

Durham, North Carolina
Late January

When Ryden Wagner woke from the final surgery, even the massive doses of painkillers pouring through her IV couldn't completely eradicate the pain in her face. Still groggy, she skimmed her fingers over the bandages that covered her straightened nose and higher, new cheekbones. The swelling was so bad she had to view the sterile room through half-open eyes, but she could see she was alone.

She'd been in the private clinic for more than a month and during that time had undergone a series of procedures to radically change her appearance; this latest was the final alteration. A chin implant came first, then dental work when that was healed, followed by Lasik eye surgery to allow her to finally shed her thick, black-framed glasses. Yesterday, a stylist had come in and cut several inches off her hair. The man had dyed it as well, from light mousy brown to a darker brunette, but Ryden only knew that from the snippets of hair that fell into her lap. They still refused to let her anywhere near a mirror.

Horrific circumstances had gotten her here, and her unremarkable but satisfying life was about to radically change.

She would miss her work at The Bloom Room, the flower and candle shop where she worked in suburban Philadelphia. Not the day-to-day mundane tasks of cutting and trimming endless roses and arranging bouquets, nor the chatty interactions with customers she had to endure when the shop's owner was occupied, for she was by nature a loner who loathed small talk. Ryden would miss seeing people's reactions to the ornate candles that were the outlet for her creative side. At home, she spent most of her time dipping and sculpting the unique creations. Most who bought them at the shop or online declared them far too beautiful to ever touch a match to, and that response never failed to warm her.

The nurse who'd been tending to her came in, white shoes squeaking loudly on the faded linoleum, and smiled when she saw her awake. "How are you feeling?" She checked the nearly flaccid bag hanging from the IV stand.

"Sore," Ryden replied, "and thirsty as hell. Can I have some water?"

The nurse gave her some ice chips, and as she sucked on them gratefully, she once again explored the unfamiliar landscape of her mouth with her tongue. Porcelain veneers now covered most of her teeth, obliterating the big chip in front that had been with her since the orphanage, when a bigger kid had punched her.

The lawyer who'd brought her here had explained very little of what she was in for next, only that she would undergo extensive training after the operations to prepare her to impersonate someone for a few weeks, perhaps months. Then the threat of prison would be behind her, and she could resume her life.

Three days later, the nurse and doctor came in for the long-anticipated unveiling. She would finally be allowed to see her new self. An unfamiliar woman several years older than Ryden accompanied them. The stranger's makeup and hair, pulled back in a severe bun, were flawless, and her clothes and jewelry shrieked money. When she introduced herself, her hazel eyes held no hint of warmth.

"I'm Tonya." The woman extended a well-manicured hand in Ryden's direction. "I'll be your tutor during your recovery."

"Ryden. How's it going?" She returned the weak handshake before reaching for the remote to the TV on the opposite wall. She'd been watching the inauguration of Elizabeth Thomas, the first female president. A liberal Democrat from Maine, Thomas had served in the U.S. Senate for ten years before her narrow win in the elections nearly three months earlier. Though Ryden muted the sound, she kept the set on, intending to return to the broadcast once her visitors departed.

The doctor reached for a pair of surgical scissors on the tray beside the bed and snipped the sterile gauze wrapped around her head. Then he carefully peeled away the bandages beneath. "You're a fast healer," he told Ryden, leaning back with a satisfied expression. "The rest of the bruising will be gone in a few days." Turning in Tonya's direction, he added, "Some of my best work. The scars will be virtually undetectable." He smoothed his thumb lightly over the twin worry lines in Ryden's forehead, above her nose. "We can get rid of these with a little Botox."

"Can I see?" Ryden asked impatiently. The doctor glanced at Tonya, who responded to the query with a slight nod, never taking her eyes off Ryden. Her expression gave nothing away of what she thought of the doctor's handiwork.

The nurse departed, and Ryden returned her gaze to the television while waiting for her to return. The new president was just taking the oath of office. Though Ryden had no real interest in politics, she had voted for Thomas and was glad to see a woman finally take control of the Oval Office.

When the nurse returned with a small hand mirror, Tonya intercepted it and waited for the nurse and doctor to leave before she handed it over.

Ryden cautiously lifted the mirror to her face and gasped aloud. She looked back to the TV, then the mirror—back and forth another two or three times before she finally was able to speak. "Oh, my God." The realization of who she'd been manufactured to double was chilling. What had she gotten herself into?

Ryden snapped out of the trance when the TV clicked off but was unable to tear her gaze from the bruised but stunning stranger in the mirror. "I look just like—"

"The president," Tonya said. "And very convincingly, might I add. The eyes are still wrong—you'll need to wear brown contacts—but otherwise, you're perfect."

"I was never told—"

"Security reasons. We couldn't risk you backing out or talking. But from here on, you belong to us. To the government."

"What happens when my commitment to you is over? I mean, I'll still look like her," Ryden said.

"When that time comes, we will make new alterations."

"To my face…again."

Tonya nodded.

"Damn," Ryden muttered. "The president's double."

"Lesson number one: no more profanity," Tonya said. "And as far as the world is concerned, you *are* the president."

CHAPTER ONE

Philadelphia
Five weeks earlier, December 16

Ryden set the half dozen matching bridesmaid bouquets she'd been working on into the large glass-walled cooler and stepped back to admire her handiwork. The compact arrays of tiny pink tea roses, baby's breath, and delicate greenery weren't what she would have chosen, not that any weddings were in *her* future, but she knew the bride-to-be would be delighted.

"What do you think, Shadow? Meet with your approval?" she asked the ebony shop cat as he leapt onto the counter and purred to be petted. The name was apropos. Since she'd rescued him from the city animal shelter, the stray rarely left her side, except to chase down the occasional moth or bug that caught his eye.

Movement out of the corner of her eye made her glance toward the shop window. Tim Lauden was waving at her, and she had to force herself to keep from rolling her eyes. He was later than usual; normally he stopped in around lunchtime and it was now just an hour before closing. Magda Pagoni, the owner of the shop, was unpacking a fresh shipment of poinsettias in the back.

"Got caught up at the office," Tim said when he walked in. "Hope all the good stuff isn't gone."

"It's all good stuff," Ryden replied. "What varies is taste."

"Of course." Tim leaned over the counter, ostensibly to study what was left of the loose flowers in the bottom tier of the cooler, and Ryden took a step back. He was a friendly guy and she even tolerated the occasional chat with him, but his insistence at flirting with her was at times overwhelming, and so was his tendency to get too close to her. She had little patience for any invasion of her personal space.

He'd come into the shop two months ago for the first time to buy flowers for his mother, who was hospitalized for minor surgery. Though the woman had long since recovered, Tim continued to stop by at least once a week and had become a valued customer. He never ordered a ready-made bouquet, instead choosing something seasonal in stock—something that would take Ryden time to put together.

She had begun to wonder what he did with the flowers once he left the shop, since his visits were clearly now just an excuse to see her. Tim was in his mid-forties, with a perpetual five-o'clock shadow, receding hairline, and a beer belly that protruded over his belt. From their chats, she'd gleaned that he spent most of his time watching television, usually war documentaries on the History Channel. Ryden had no illusions about her own attractiveness; she considered herself average at best. But if Tim was the best she could do, then no wonder she'd rather be alone.

Magda, who'd caught on to Tim's intentions immediately, tried to play matchmaker by making herself scarce during his visits. Although Ryden had made it clear that she wasn't interested in him or in anyone else, for that matter, Magda's winks and meaningful smiles never ceased. Her intentions were as well meaning as all of her other attempts to get closer to Ryden, but as she did with everyone else in her life, Ryden kept her employer at arm's length. She had no close friends, only colleagues and acquaintances.

"The roses look beautiful today," Tim said. He was always very courteous and the perfect gentleman, but Ryden despised idle conversation, and most of their interactions lately had consisted of inane exchanges about the weather or flowers. Having been raised in foster homes where no one really cared for her opinion, or thought it silly if not meaningless, she had become accustomed to keeping her thoughts, dreams, and talents to herself. Now, as an adult, not only didn't she feel the need to share, but she viewed everyone who showed any interest in her as an intruder who could potentially ridicule or reject who or how she was.

"Yup."

"And oh, my..." He stepped over to the table where her candles were displayed. She'd added several this morning with Christmas colors—red and green, silver and gold. "Look at all the new ones."

"Made 'em this week."

"You really are very talented."

Ryden blushed every time he commented on her work. She hated herself for feeling flattered, especially because she knew all Tim wanted was a date. "Yeah, well," she stammered. "I try."

"You should show these to specialty shops. I know some." Tim hoisted one of her larger pieces toward the fading sunlight streaming in through the window so he could better see the delicately sculpted detail work. "I'm sure they'd sell like crazy, and who knows? Maybe someday you could have your own little place."

"Yeah, maybe. Though the economy being what it is, I doubt candles are the next big must-have item on everyone's spartan shopping list."

"You never know."

"So, what kind of flowers would you like today?"

"Why won't you let me help you?" Tim asked. "I know people who might be willing to invest."

"Nah. I'm fine where I am, but thanks all the same."

Tim was being pushier than usual, and all Ryden wanted was to close the shop and go home. She was tired and hungry and couldn't wait to start work on her candles. "What'll it be, Tim?" she asked again, trying to sound polite.

But he was apparently determined to linger, asking endless questions about every type of flower they had and taking forever to make up his mind. By the time she could start to put the bouquet together it was closing time. Magda wished them good night with the usual wink on her way out.

Ryden handed the bunch to him ten minutes later. "Well, I need to close up, so—"

"Let me walk you home."

"Thanks, but…I prefer you didn't."

"Maybe next time." Tim smiled.

"Yeah, maybe." She walked him to the door and opened it. "Good night then, and thanks."

"Think about my offer, okay?"

"Sure, will do." Ryden practically shut the door on his ass and sighed with relief.

Fifteen minutes later, she'd taken care of the cash and prepped everything for the next day. She was about to lock up when she got an eerie feeling that someone was watching her. She'd never been afraid of walking alone at night, or pretty much anything else; if she'd survived five foster homes and bully foster siblings, she could handle anything. But right now, something was making her skin crawl.

"You're imagining things." Talking aloud to herself was an old habit, the result of living alone all her adult life. For some reason, she found it comforting, especially when she was stressed.

She scanned the street carefully before she latched the door to make sure she was alone, just in case she needed to go back inside. All the other shops around were shuttered tight, the street devoid of pedestrians. When she didn't detect any sign of movement, Ryden locked up and walked briskly down the block. She was about to chalk it up to paranoia when the eerie feeling returned. "You're overreacting, scaredy-cat, and need to cut down on Fearnet." But she started to walk even faster, occasionally looking behind her. By the time she'd reached her apartment, she was out of breath.

Ryden slammed the door shut behind her and locked it, then went to the window that overlooked the street. Peering through a slit in the heavy curtain, she waited to see if someone was lurking outside. When she'd seen nothing suspicious after ten minutes, she made her way to the kitchen to defrost dinner, but the uncomfortable feeling of being watched stayed with her all night. Even her candle making didn't stop the uneasiness; she occasionally got up to hide behind the curtain and check the street.

At two in the morning, Ryden sat down to watch TV, hoping it would calm her nerves, but she could concentrate on the sitcom about as much as she had on her candle making. She went to check the street one last time before she went to bed, and it was only then, at three a.m., that she got the first confirmation she hadn't been imagining things.

A faint flicker in one of the long shadows in the park across the street became the silhouette of a man. "Tim? Is that you?" Could he be stalking her? She fished a pair of cheap binoculars from the chaos of her junk drawer and focused on the image. She couldn't make out the guy's face but was certain from his tall, hulking build that it couldn't be Tim. After a minute or two, he sank back into the shadow of a tree and disappeared again. Without bothering to undress, Ryden turned the TV back on and settled down on the couch with a blanket to watch a *Dawson's Creek* marathon.

Martin Graber stepped into the phone booth and impatiently dialed the number. He couldn't wait to tell the Broker he'd hit the money pot. His hands shook from excitement as a male voice answered on the first ring. "It's Marty," he said. "I need to talk to the Broker."

Her icy voice came on the line seconds later. "And?"

"Good news," he reported. If this didn't gain her respect, nothing would.

"About time," the perpetually unsatisfied voice replied.

"It wasn't easy." He felt inflated and confident he'd done a great job. "But we found a match. She's—"

"I want to see her tonight. If she's a fit, the transformation can begin."

"We need to get her first," Marty replied. "But she's the best candidate so far. An astonishing resemb—"

"Did I or did I not ask you to let me know as soon as you had the right woman?"

"Yes, you—"

"I don't remember asking you to bother me until you *had* her. I am once again stressing the word *had* and not *found*. I don't have time for useless pronouncements."

"It's not that simple," Marty said. "We can't just abduct her. Not if we want her to do what you need."

"Of course not, you fool. You have to make an offer. One she can't refuse."

"She won't bite," he said. "Not from what we have on her so far. Goody Two-shoes. Straight as they come."

"Everyone has a price."

"She's not into money. She doesn't make much, but her bank account shows donations to all sorts of causes—animal shelters and rescue groups, mostly."

"I'm rolling my eyes. Can you guess why?"

Marty hesitated, terrified of saying the wrong thing. Tougher men had died at the hands of the Broker for lesser reasons. "I checked her background. No relatives, grew up in an orphanage and, later, in foster homes. No ties with any of them. Single and no colleague or anyone in her life who matters enough to pressure her with. No drug abuse, no promiscuous behavior. Nothing. Not even a DUI." He was satisfied with himself for being thorough.

"What does that leave you with?" the Broker asked, her calm tone more ominous than ever.

He needed an answer, even a remotely relevant one, but nothing came to him, and as the seconds ticked away he began to feel numbness in his brain. He tried to concentrate on a rock at his feet and found himself praying to it for an epiphany.

"Again," she said evenly, "*everyone* has their price. Even if they don't know it yet."

Marty snapped his fingers. "You want me to…set her up," he said hastily. He knew he sounded like an eager child whom the teacher had just helped find the answer, but he didn't care. He was sure it was the right answer all the same.

"Bloody eureka."

He wiped his sweaty forehead and kicked the rock away.

"Do you think you can manage that?" the Broker asked.

How he hated her sarcasm. If he wasn't scared shitless of the bitch, he'd tell her to stick her fucking head in an oven and light a match. "No problem." He tried to sound confident. "Wouldn't be the first time."

"Let's hope not," she said. "Because the next time you call, it'd better be to tell me she's ready to cooperate."

"Sure, you can—" The phone disconnected. As usual, she'd hung up on him before he was done talking. Marty slammed the receiver back on its hook. "Cold bitch."

Houston, Texas

TQ, known to many in the criminal underworld simply as the Broker, disconnected her call and began to pace restlessly through her lavish penthouse apartment at One Park Place in downtown Houston. Her home was an extraordinary showplace for many of the world's rarest and most valuable antiquities and art—nearly all of them stolen—but no one aside from her two trusted servants had ever been inside the private museum she called home. And even they didn't know about her safe room, an impenetrable fortress accessed through secret panels in her bedroom and office.

She found it both soothing and motivating to skim her hands over the myriad ancient pieces that comprised her collection, for they represented the only two things she valued: power and money. She had plenty of both but was forever plotting ways to acquire more. Her influence extended to the highest offices in countries the world over; she had blackmailed or bought presidents, prime ministers, and more than a few royals, and she was rarely denied anything she set her mind on.

Her latest illegal acquisitions had been given prime real estate in her spacious four-thousand-square-foot apartment. Rembrandt's "Storm on the Sea of Galilee," one of several masterpieces stolen from the Isabella Stewart Gardner Museum in Boston more than a decade earlier, hung above her bed. The other recent addition, a gold burial mask more than three thousand years old and smuggled out of Luxor, Egypt, had its own crystal display case in her office.

But tonight, even those treasures failed to calm her restlessness. A looming impediment to one of her primary interests had to be dealt with, and soon. And it seemed as though the success or failure of her plans rested on the shoulders of Marty Graber. Alas, among all the men she had sent to find the match she requested, it was the low-level thug who could barely carry on a conversation who'd claimed to have found her.

But while Graber seemed incompetent at times, she knew better. He'd worked for her in the past, and although he frequently needed things spelled out for him, he always came through. Finding this woman was impressive and reason enough to allow him to continue to serve her.

She had plenty of men and women working for her, all of them available twenty-four hours a day, seven days a week. None had ever met her in person. Since she'd decided to disappear more than a decade ago, the only way to reach her had been through an untraceable mobile number. Even Dario hadn't known where to find her.

TQ sighed at the memory of her brother. *Idiot.* If she'd ever come close to feeling affection for anyone, it was her only sibling. Not because they were related—because that was never reason enough for her to feel anything except contempt for her parents—but because of his dedication to her. She doubted he actually loved her. She was certain, however, that he respected her, and not out of fear like the rest, but because she took care of him.

Without her, Dario would have been lost, a whore-visiting drunk with a meager inheritance to live on: a negligible sum he would have spent on brothels and booze within months. It was all the poor idiot could come up with to compensate for his physical limitations.

TQ had built an empire with her deceased husband's fortune and name, one that allowed her to employ her brother and make him a very rich man. Because of her, Dario could afford the best rehab clinic for his alcohol addiction, live-in help for his disability, a trio of bodyguards, private jet, and enough money to live like a king.

But that very lifestyle had been his downfall. He'd overindulged in the one addiction he never had any interest in trying to master: prostitutes. Unfortunately, the fool was stupid enough to fall in love with a common whore, one who had betrayed him and cost him his life.

Even though several weeks had gone by and TQ was never one to dwell on the past, she still got infuriated at her brother's naïveté. His hard-on for that prostitute had blinded his judgment and, worse, had brought her existence to the attention of what she suspected was a private law-enforcement or security organization.

She'd never had to deal with any such private entity before because she paid good money to those who mattered to keep that from happening, so the fact that they'd learned about her brother and his involvement in her business still bothered her.

Oh, well, she thought. She couldn't do anything to alter that, and after all, should these entities ever come after her, all she had to do was call her connections in either the CIA or FBI. She wouldn't lose any sleep over the matter.

Her only lingering interest in the whole affair was that Jack woman—the bitch who'd killed her brother. Though she'd tried to track her down, Jack was as elusive as she was. The woman had no connections to anyone high up that she could influence, and though they apparently had plenty of acquaintances in common—Jack had worked for many of the powerhouses in the underworld—none knew how to reach her.

If finding that woman was the last thing she ever did, TQ would die happy. But would she torture Jack to death or into submission? Despite the fact she wanted to seek justice for her brother, she had a begrudging respect for the woman who had earned the nickname Silent Death. Her reputation was well established as a very capable and ruthless killer who respected discretion and always delivered fast results.

But other matters demanded her attention before she could concentrate further on tracking down her brother's killer. Elizabeth Thomas posed an immediate and deeply concerning threat to the only thing that really mattered to TQ: her money. Why did vile, meddling women all of a sudden surround her? The newly elected president had vowed to shut down one of her two primary businesses: the illegal-weapons trade. TQ was also a key player in the global selling of black-market human organs, and she considered both concerns vital to the world economy, primarily her economy. She'd just invested several million on weapons destined for sale to various countries—including the U.S.—and she wasn't about to lose out just because the new president happened to be a woman who wanted to prove herself more capable and more ethical than any male before her.

Even aside from the new president's agenda, TQ derided the

election of the first female to the Oval Office. She viewed politics as a man's world—past, present, and future. Not because men were better at it but because they were testosterone-fueled monkeys who needed to pound their chests, claim power, and play war, regardless of how much it cost or how the wars got funded. In her mind, men weren't concerned about children or women getting killed or whether the sons and fathers of their country died. They wanted power and they wanted to win, and the rest was merely collateral damage.

TQ understood the sentiment. She, too, valued power more than any single or collective life, and she was well positioned to exploit it. She knew power in any form was born of money, which in turn bred corruption, and the rich were divided into two inseparable categories: those who practiced their power on stage and the ones behind the scenes who helped them launder their riches. TQ was in the latter category and reveled in the knowledge that so many influential people depended on her to keep their secrets and make them look good. When it came right down to it, she was the one with true control. She was a necessary evil, and as long as she was necessary, she was God.

TQ leafed through her private phone book, containing the names of movers and shakers on both sides of the law, as well as the more obscure individuals who did her dirty work. Most were people whose numbers were impossible to find, although a few of the underworld figures practically handed out business cards because they were either too arrogant or too stupid to be careful. Russian mob boss Yuri Dratshev fell somewhere in between.

She reached for the phone. "Time to deal with the president," she said aloud as she dialed the unlisted number to Dratshev's Manhattan Beach, New York mansion. She'd previously avoided contact with the Russian disease of a man; he was vulgar, uneducated, and without any decorum. But though she despised him, he had much to lose as well should the president get her way, and he had some of the best warlords on his side. If they combined forces, something he'd always begged for because of TQ's reputation, it was only a matter of time before this ridiculous weapons agenda ended up on the massive pile of unkept political promises.

"I'm looking for Yuri Dratshev," TQ said loudly, to be heard over the blaring sound of the TV in the background. She didn't own a set herself—they were annoying, misleading contraptions deliberately designed to numb the mind.

"This is him," came the heavily accented reply.

TQ rolled her eyes. Second-generation immigrant and he still couldn't speak the language correctly. "Good evening, Yuri. You haven't had the pleasure of meeting me in person, though I know you've wanted to."

"Who the shit are you?" the Russian mob boss replied. "I don't need to meet anyone. How did you get my number?"

"Is this a secure line?" she asked.

"Yes, line is safe," he replied dubiously. "Who is this?"

"My name is TQ."

There was a long pause, then a clicking in the phone line and the maddening blare of the TV stopped. "Now it is a secure line," Dratshev finally said. "What a pleasure."

"I'm sure."

"Finally, we meet."

"I wouldn't go as far as a meeting," TQ said, "but I do have a collaboration plan in mind."

"I would very much like business with you," Dratshev said. "Big business, yes?"

"Big, yes."

"I am all hears."

"The expression is 'ears,'" she said patiently, trying hard not to second-guess her choice. "But that aside, we have a certain problem in common."

"You mean guns."

"Indeed."

"That bitch is a big problem."

"Problems are like a cancer," she said. "They become a big problem and spread only when they aren't dealt with on time."

"I like the way you think."

"Good."

"So you see where I'm going."

"You have a cancer?" Dratshev asked.

TQ rubbed her eyes tiredly at his inanity. "No, I'm fine, thank you. The cancer that's spreading and needs to be stopped is the president."

"Ah, yes. The bitch."

"I want you to help me stop her so we can continue with our very profitable enterprises."

"How?"

"I'm going to need your best men to orchestrate an attempt on her life."

"Attempt?"

"Yes, just an attempt. You are to kidnap her and keep her in your possession until I instruct you to return her to me."

"How will my people get the president?" he asked. "She is very much guarded all the time in her white house."

"Leave that up to me. I will tell you where and when. All you have to do is make it look like a genuine attempt on her life."

"So the country will have no president. How does this change something for us?"

"Again, leave that up to me."

"You have a plan."

TQ was tempted to use an expression she never had, one completely out of character. She wanted to say, *Duh, you Russian idiot*, but refrained. "I do."

"But you will not share."

"It's to both our interests I don't, if you know what I mean."

"Your plans stay secret and I know nothing that can implisate me."

"Implicate. That's correct."

The Russian laughed. "Always careful. But you understand, this means big money to make it happen. My people will want big money, too. I have the best people who work for me, but they must be persuaded."

"I don't waste money, Yuri, but have you ever heard any rumors involving my lack of generosity for a job well done?"

"Good rumors. You pay good money."

"Then don't waste my time with pointless comments. Time, like money, is something I hate to waste." The conversation was draining. She sighed. "Get your people together and I'll get back to you with what you need to know."

"I know just the right person," Dratshev said, "but I hope I can find her."

"I want to believe your ability to help me does not hinge on one individual's talent."

"No, but she is the best."

"Make it happen or find a new best if you have to."

"No problem for me."

"Oh, and Yuri…if I so much as hear a whisper of a rumor from you or your men concerning our plan, I will eliminate you and your wife. And I'll make your daughter wish she'd become another trophy on that psychopath's wall." She knew the reference would have the desired impact. Yuri's daughter Nina had been the only person to escape serial killer Walter Owens, better known as the Headhunter because he'd cut off the faces of his victims to make macabre masks. TQ laughed when Dratshev didn't immediately answer. "Okay, Yuri?"

"*Da*...yes," Dratshev promised with a tremble in his voice. "Not one whisper."

CHAPTER TWO

Porto Carras, Greece
Next day, December 17

"Which one's yours?" The man who spoke was of average height and build and was fairly attractive, with a neat, short haircut and piercing blue eyes. He wore the conservative dark suit that was standard fare for his profession, and Agent Shield wore the feminine equivalent—a crisp white blouse and navy suit tailored to fit her lean, five-foot seven-inch figure. Standing side by side against the wall by the curtains, they provided, as always, the perfect balance between subtlety and warning.

Others of their ilk occupied similar positions around the perimeter of the banquet hall, watching the dignitaries. The lavish state dinner at the Porto Carras Grand Resort in northern Greece was the final event of a three-day international conference on global warming, so there was at least a pair of bodyguards for every major figure seated at the long table.

Shield adjusted her earpiece. "Francois Legard," she replied in a low voice, never taking her eyes off the French prime minister as the waiter poured him a glass of wine. *Not bad*, she thought, noticing the thickness of the gold liquid and the label. Wine was Harper Kennedy's passion, and regardless of where she was, whom she was with, or whether or not she was on a job as Shield, wine never escaped her attention.

The only other interesting entity at the table was the incoming American president, the first female to hold that office. Elizabeth Thomas wouldn't even be officially sworn in for another few weeks because of a court-ordered recount, but the outgoing president had invited her to represent the U.S. at the conference. To all appearances, the woman looked calm and in control, but Shield picked up on the minor nuances that transmitted her newness and nerves: she listened too attentively and fidgeted with her napkin, albeit discreetly.

At forty-three, Elizabeth Thomas was poised to soon become the youngest U.S. president since JFK, and that meant all eyes were on her, not only because of her age but because she was such an attractive woman. Her short brown hair was a bit too stern and immaculately coiffed for Shield's taste, but like anyone in the president-elect's position, she probably didn't have a choice in the matter. Beautiful, powerful women appealed to Shield because they had something to say and didn't feel the need to decorate every sentiment with three adjectives. Plus, she found something sexy about their dominant composure, which usually carried over into bed.

"He seems decent," the agent beside her replied, his accent placing him somewhere from the American Midwest. Like Shield, his eyes constantly scanned the room.

"I guess. When it comes down to it, they're all the same."

"I know what you mean. My name's Joe, by the way." He made no move to offer his hand, as that would have drawn attention to them. They were communicating so discreetly, in fact, that others in the room were unaware they were even talking.

Shield didn't feel the need to share her own name. Instead, she checked the time and tapped the watch with her finger.

"Bored?" he asked.

"Numb."

"How long have you been sitting?"

"Legard?"

"In general."

"Twelve years, give or take." In her peripheral vision, Shield caught him lifting one eyebrow.

"Long time," he said.

"I guess."

"For the French?"

"For whoever."

"But you're with the French SS, right?" he asked.

"I'm not with anyone."

"Oh. You have a bit of an accent, so—"

"Private security." It was bad enough that the protection jobs had become tedious and tiring. She despised occasionally having to put up with conversations like this—trivial niceties about absolutely nothing.

To most, she sounded American, but to those who, like her, had been trained to pick up on details, she clearly had a slight accent. He was wrong to peg her as French, though. She'd been stationed in Italy for two months at the age of twenty-three while on her first assignment with the Elite Operatives Organization and had fallen in love with the country. Though it took a while to convince EOO chief Montgomery Pierce to agree to base her there, he finally gave in, and she'd spent her off time the past dozen years at her villa in the mountains of Tuscany.

Joe mumbled *all quiet* discreetly into the transmitter in his sleeve. "I see. You don't say much, do you?"

Shield shrugged. "Not if I can help it."

He smirked and ignored the hint. "I'm with the American president-elect."

"That's nice." They both knew Shield was aware of whom Joe was sitting, but the never-ending need to point out the obvious seemed ever present and ever irritating at functions like this. Shield glanced at Thomas. Maybe some of her irritation had to do with the fact she envied Joe. If she was going to be taken away from the country she loved and halted from doing what she wanted most, then the least she could do was have someone interesting, or at least novel, to guard.

Joe must have read her mind or her eyes. "Not as interesting as you might think," he whispered conspiratorially. "Europeans have a certain taste for…intrigue that Americans don't. And definitely not this one."

"Because European officials are all extramarital affairs, booze, and wild parties?"

"Well, they do seem to have a rep for—"

"They're just not as concerned about hiding their missteps," Shield said. "Or they're not as proficient as the CIA at covering them."

"You have a point there."

"I know."

"This one's all work and no play," Joe said of his charge, his tone one of disappointment.

"She's new and has too much to prove for too many reasons. Add that to the fact that she lost her husband a couple of months ago and she has every reason."

"Never talks to anyone who's not family or an official," Joe went on. "I've been with her for four months, and I've never so much as gotten a *hello* or *how are you* from her. All she does is nod."

"Why waste words unless you have something to say?"

"Because it's polite."

"It's also fake, since she clearly could care less about how you are."

Joe smiled. "Fair enough." He remained blissfully silent for a few minutes, then, "Hey, what time do you get off?"

"Why?"

"I'm free around ten. What do you say we grab some beers somewhere and talk?"

"I have no interest in any of the three."

Just then, the dignitaries at the table got up, and all the bodyguards—even those in the kitchen and powder rooms—sprang to high alert. Some remained in their positions, while a few made their way to the table. Still others, she knew, were securing the entrance and exits, while the rest positioned themselves in the parking lot.

Joe and Shield both started toward their subjects, who were engaged in a quiet discussion off to one side.

"Three?" Joe asked, clearly confused by her response.

"Men," she replied as they neared the two political leaders.

As they waited discreetly a few feet away from the pair, Elizabeth Thomas glanced over at them, and her gaze lingered on Shield for several long seconds. That wasn't unusual since she was the lone woman agent in the room, and the president was a strong proponent of getting more women into male-dominated professions.

Soon after, the politicians ended their chat and separated. She just had to see Legard to his car now, and then she was free to return to her beloved Tuscany.

Philadelphia, Pennsylvania

"There you are," Marty said to himself when he saw the guy get out of his car and head up the steps to his front door. "Get comfortable, pal." Marty knew his boss wanted results, and if he wanted to get paid, and, more importantly, keep the Broker happy, he'd better be quick about it. He watched his target go inside and then obsessively checked his watch until exactly twenty minutes had elapsed. "It's time."

He waited a few more seconds, until the street emptied, to get out of his sedan. Marty walked casually up the steps to the door and looked around one more time to make sure no one was in view before he pulled the automatic from the back of his waistband. The house was ideally situated for his purposes, set back from the street and with tall hedges that helped conceal his presence from curious neighbors.

The guy inside had barely opened the door to his knock when Marty jammed his size-ten loafer into the gap. "I need to talk to you about a friend." He pointed the gun at the man's stomach and, with his other hand, pushed him inside.

"What the—"

"Do what I say and you'll be fine." Marty followed him in and locked the door.

"What's going on? Who are you?"

"I want you to help me with a certain friend we have in common."

"I'm sure we don't have any friends in common, so get the hell out of my house before I call the police." Despite the man's bluster, beads of perspiration dotted his forehead and his pupils were enormous.

Marty punched him, gun in hand, in the gut. "If I say we do, then we do."

The guy bent over in pain, trying to catch his breath. Marty grabbed him by the hair and lifted his face. "You okay?" he asked in a bored tone.

"I have some money hidden in the bedroom," his target managed between coughs.

"Good for you, although if you refuse to cooperate, you won't need it."

"What do you want?" the man asked.

"Like I was saying before you fucking interrupted, we have a common friend." Marty grabbed him by the collar and dragged him roughly toward the couch. "Have a seat." He shoved him so the man fell back against the cushions. "I won't hurt you unless you make me, Tim."

"Okay." Tim looked both confused and terrified at the realization his intruder knew who he was.

"Her name is Ryden," Marty said. "She's the florist you've been jerking off to."

The man's pupils grew even larger. "What about her?"

"I need you to call her and ask her over."

"Why?"

Marty bent over so his face was only a few inches from Tim's. "Because I say so." His tone was calm, but the smile that followed was feral.

"I hardly know her. What's this about?"

"I want to talk to her."

"I can tell you where she works."

"I know where she works, stupid. I want her here." Marty snatched Tim's phone from its charging station on the coffee table and threw it at him. "Make it happen."

"Look, I don't know what she's done or why you want her," Tim said, "but I guarantee you I had nothing to do with it."

Marty punched him in the stomach again, hard enough to get quick compliance. He deliberately avoided Tim's face or anywhere that would leave a bruise. "Just get her the fuck over here."

Doubled over in pain, Tim rasped, "How?"

"This is what you're going to do. Call and ask her to deliver some flowers. Tell her you're sick and can't do it yourself."

"What if she can't?" Tim asked. "Or won't?"

"It's her fucking job."

"I'll…" Tim coughed. "I'll try."

Marty dialed the florist's number and put the call on speakerphone before handing it to Tim. "One wrong word," he said, pointing the gun at Tim's head as they waited for someone to answer, "and you're screwed."

A female voice came on the line. "Bloom Room. This is Ryden. How can I help you?"

"Hi, Ryden. It's Tim. Listen, I can't make it in today, so I was wondering if you could deliver?"

A brief hesitation on the other end of the line, then, "What's wrong?"

"Stomach problems, I think." Tim was clutching his abdomen, and Marty had to smile at the guy's unintentionally witty reply.

"Um…Tim, listen. You're a nice enough guy and all, but you gotta understand, I'm not interested. So, if this is your way of getting me to your place, then—"

"It's nothing like that, Ryden. I—"

Marty shoved the end of his gun hard into Tim's stomach.

"I'm really…not well." Tim's tone was convincing, with good reason. He looked like he was on the verge of throwing up or pissing his pants.

"Have you seen a doctor?" Ryden asked. "You don't sound too good."

"Doc said I need some bed rest. I think some flowers will help make me feel better, too."

"Um, yeah…okay. I can be there in an hour."

"Hurry…" Tim shrank back against the couch when he caught Marty's scowl. "I mean, that's great."

"Do you have any preference?"

"No, it's up to you. You know what I like."

"I'll see you later. Get some rest."

Tim disconnected and gave the receiver back to Marty with shaking hands.

"You did good." Marty stuck the phone in his jacket and sank into the armchair opposite the couch. "Looks like we've got an hour to kill." He leaned back and made himself comfortable. "So, how's life?"

Before Tim could answer, the doorbell rang. Marty scrambled back to his feet. "Who you expecting?" he asked in a low voice.

"My ex-wife."

"Fuck." Marty pulled Tim up roughly and pushed him toward the door. "Go answer and no bullshit. Same drill. Tell the bitch to go away."

As Tim stumbled forward, Marty stayed on his heels, his gun pointed at the back of Tim's head. He hid himself behind the door and motioned for Tim to open it.

"Hi, Rhonda. I know we've got things to discuss, but today's not good." Tim's words poured out in a rush. "Looks like I came down with some stomach thing, and—"

Before he could finish, a forty-something redhead trailing cheap perfume pushed past him and into the room. "I don't care what bug you've got crawling where," she replied, half shouting the words. "You're late again with this month's—"

When Marty slammed the door shut, Rhonda wheeled around and found herself looking down the barrel of his gun. She went ashen and froze.

"Plant your ass on the couch." He waved the gun in that direction. "One more word out of you and it'll be your last. Got it?"

When she hesitated, her eyes glancing about for escape, Tim grabbed her by the elbow and pulled her across the room. They sat side by side, Rhonda clutching Tim's hand so hard he winced.

"Loud-mouth bitch, aren't you?" Marty said as he settled back into the armchair, enjoying the sudden change in her demeanor. Her eyes were about to pop out of her head, giving her a vaguely owlish look. "Used to have one of 'em myself," he added, looking empathetically toward Tim. "Always bitchin' about something." Glancing at his watch, he saw they had forty minutes more to wait. Plenty of time. "Now, where were we?" he asked Tim. "Oh, yeah. You were going to tell me about your life."

"I have to make a delivery." Ryden shouted so Magda would come take her place at the counter. "I'm going straight home after that." She'd chosen a mix of wildflowers to cheer up Tim. They were colorful and would keep well but weren't too pungent for a queasy stomach.

"Who are they for?" Magda asked as she emerged from the back room.

"Tim."

"Ah." Magda nodded knowingly with a mischievous smile. "Your Tim."

"He's not mine, and I'd really appreciate it if you stopped insinuating otherwise."

"All I'm saying, dear, is that he's a nice man with a decent job, and he's smitten with you. You're the only reason he comes in every week, you know."

"I do know, and I don't care," she replied.

"You didn't seem to mind his rather prolonged visit last time. I even saw you smile."

"Oh, my, could it be I'm desperately in love with him and am subconsciously playing hard to get?" Ryden sighed. She didn't know why she bothered to even reply. Magda wouldn't get her sarcasm any better than she'd get any of the dozen other ways she'd tried to dissuade her from matchmaking. "Anyway…whatever, I better get going."

"See you in the morning." Magda smiled. "Have a fun time with Tim."

Although she liked her boss, at times like this Ryden wanted to throw her in the stem cutter. The only way to end the debate, at least for now, was to shock Magda's conservative sensibilities. "You know, I might just stay there all night. Hell, maybe even all week. Hide in his apartment and have wild passionate sex till I need resuscitation and then go back for more."

Magda blushed. "Ryden!"

"See you." Ryden winked at her and left.

Not long after, she arrived at the address they had on file for Tim, a ten-minute walk from the flower shop. It was a two-story, single-family home in a quiet neighborhood, nearly obscured from the street by tall greenery.

She was about to ring the bell when she noticed the door was ajar. She rang anyway, and when no one answered, she pushed the door open another few inches. "Tim? You there?"

When no one replied, she cracked the door a little farther and stepped just inside the threshold. "Tim," she shouted, much louder this time. "Are you okay?" Still no answer. She started to worry. He hadn't sounded well on the phone. What if he'd been so violently ill he'd passed out…or worse? Perhaps, she considered, he'd been rushed to the hospital and the paramedics hadn't shut the door properly.

She couldn't just leave. "Tim, if you can hear me, I'm coming in." She stepped into the living room and placed the flowers on the coffee table. Tim wasn't the tidiest guy, but aside from the open door she didn't see anything unusual to prompt her niggling sense of alarm. She glanced into the kitchen and dining room, and everything seemed okay there, too. Perhaps she was just being paranoid. Maybe the memory of the guy who'd been following her the other day had stuck with her more than she cared to admit. Tim had probably just stepped out to the pharmacy for some medicine.

Just to be completely sure the poor bastard wasn't home and in pain, she'd do a quick check of the bedrooms upstairs. If he wasn't there, she'd leave a get-well note with the flowers and go. She'd never intended to charge him, anyway. These were on the house because he was such a good customer.

Convinced now that no one was home, she hurried up the stairs to ease her conscience and be on her way. She walked down a long hall, bypassing an office and then a kids' bedroom—bunk beds, toys and baseball gear on the floor, posters of athletes and racecars on the walls. Tim had never mentioned having children.

At the end of the hall, she knocked on the only closed door. "Tim, it's me. Ryden." She waited several seconds, her ear to the door, before trying the knob.

The bedroom's heavy curtains were closed so it was too dark to see much, but the ambient light streaming in through the sides of the windows allowed her to make out a silhouette on the bed. "Tim, are you all right? she asked louder. No response, and the figure didn't move. "Shit," she mumbled. Tim was either an extremely sound sleeper or something was very wrong. Skimming her hand over the wall, she found the light switch and flicked it on.

She blinked a few times, so shocked she was unable to fully register the scene before her. When she finally realized the magnitude of the horror, dizziness washed over her and she had to fight to keep upright. "Oh, my God."

Tim was naked and facedown on the bed. Countless stab wounds all over his back explained the widening pool of blood on the sheets and floor.

She was going to be sick. With her hand over her mouth, she ran headlong for the adjoining bathroom, only to trip over something on the floor just inside the dark room. Scrambling to her feet, she inhaled a vaguely metallic scent and was aware her hands were wet as she reached for the bathroom light switch.

She was standing over another naked body, this time that of a woman she didn't recognize. This victim had also been stabbed, but she was lying on her back. Blood still oozed from her wounds onto the tile.

"Jesus fuck." Ryden realized for the first time that the killer might very well still be in the house, and her urge to vomit vanished, replaced by the need to get the hell out of here as quickly as possible. She bolted down the stairs and out of the house, not stopping until she reached the middle of the street. Breathing hard, she reached for her cell phone, only then seeing the blood on her hands, jeans, and jacket. She was shaking so much it took three tries to successfully dial 911.

CHAPTER THREE

Later, Ryden would have no clear recollection of the police arriving or be able to say how long it took them to get there. But not long after they did, a tall plainclothes cop who introduced himself as Detective Johnston took her back into Tim's house and asked her to sit in the living room. Two uniformed cops and another in a suit stood by watching her, and she could hear more moving around on the upper floor.

The detective sat down beside her and pulled out a small notepad and pen. "Let's start at the beginning. Tell me everything you remember from the time you arrived here until you called 911. Take your time. You never know what kind of detail might be important."

As Ryden told him the story, more cops arrived—a quartet from forensics, she guessed, since they immediately began gathering trace evidence and dusting for fingerprints. One of them, a woman about her age, was summoned to take Ryden's prints once she'd finished relaying what she could recall.

"I need to take samples of the blood on your hands as well as samples from under your nails," the forensics tech told her as she pressed Ryden's fingers one by one onto an ink pad and then a white card. "And we'll need your jacket and jeans for evidence."

"My clothes?" Ryden asked. "What for?"

"They'll be returned to you," the detective said. "We'll take you home when we're finished here, and a female officer will accompany you inside to get them. It's just standard procedure."

While the tech swabbed samples of the blood on her hands and under her nails, the detective went to consult with the other plainclothes cop, who'd spent much of the preceding minutes on his cell phone. When Johnston returned to the couch, he had new questions for her. "How did you know the Laudens?"

"Laudens?" Ryden repeated. "Was that Tim's sister?"

The detective studied her face. "You didn't know her?"

"No."

"Ex-wife," he said. His gaze drifted to the mantel over the fireplace, behind where she was sitting, and Ryden turned to see what he was looking at. Among the photographs was one of a much younger Tim and the redheaded woman she'd tripped over. Other photos told her the couple had two boys. That explained the kids' room—apparently the couple shared custody.

Over the course of the next half hour, she was asked to recall everything she knew about Tim. She started from his first visit to the flower shop and ended with his phone call asking her to deliver the flowers that rested on the coffee table in front of them.

Then the detective started in on her, asking her about her life, work, family background, and marital status. By the time she was done, Johnston and the other complete strangers in the room had more information about her than anyone she'd ever known. Ryden had about as much need to talk about herself as she had interest in other people. The shock of her experience was rapidly turning into weariness under the endless questioning. She hadn't eaten anything since that morning and was beginning to feel weak and dizzy. She could see Johnston's mouth move but couldn't register what he was saying.

"Foster homes never work out," she said.

"Excuse me?"

"What'll happen to the children?"

He looked surprised. "Relatives usually rise to the occasion."

"Yeah. Relatives might work."

"We're almost done, ma'am." He sounded concerned.

Ryden just wanted to get the hell out of there. She needed the safety of her home and a stiff drink of anything. The cop asked her something else, but she didn't hear that, either, too distracted by a sudden flurry of activity by the stairs. Two men with MEDICAL EXAMINER'S OFFICE written on their windbreakers came down carrying someone in a body bag. She wanted to look away but couldn't. She wanted to run but didn't.

The detective droned on.

"Excuse me, what?" she asked.

"I said, you can't leave the state until we have more answers."

"I didn't intend to, but…I had nothing to do with this."

"We're pretty sure you didn't, ma'am," Johnston replied, "but we might have more questions for you."

"Yeah, sure. I understand." She didn't expect to hear from them again because she didn't have anything to add to what she'd already told the detective. She knew next to nothing about Tim except his taste for flowers. "Can I go now?"

"Yes. Officer Walker will see you home."

She was driven the short distance to her apartment, where she handed over her bloodstained jeans and jacket. Once the officer had gone, she went directly to her shower almost on autopilot. She stared blankly at the red suds as they disappeared down the drain, wanting to believe she was stuck in a bad dream, but the blood washing off her body told another story.

Next afternoon, December 18

Ryden sat in the back room of the flower shop drinking her third cup of coffee as Magda waited on a customer. She'd slept little because of yesterday's events, and this day had started out poorly, too. She'd spent nearly an hour searching for the wallet she seemed to chronically misplace, before finding it at the bottom of the laundry hamper. And her late start had thrust her into the worst of rush-hour traffic.

When she'd described what had happened the night before, Magda had told her to take the day off. She would have gladly accepted, too, if Magda wasn't just as, if not more, shaken by the events. They worked silently for most of the day, with Ryden disappearing now and then in the back to collect her thoughts and emotions.

She couldn't believe Tim was gone, that this mild-mannered man had fallen victim to a crazy killer. The distant ringing of the little bell that hung above the entrance to the shop startled her out of her thoughts.

"Ryden," Magda called out, "it's for you."

She sighed wearily as she got to her feet. God, she was exhausted and certainly in no mood for small talk with customers. She hesitated at the doorway, shocked when she saw who was waiting for her at the counter—Detective Johnston and the other plainclothes cop who'd been at Tim's house. "Something wrong?" she asked.

"We have a few more questions and would like to look around, if you don't mind."

"Look here?" Ryden asked. "What do you expect to find here?"

"We'll tell you when and if we find what we came for," the detective answered.

The realization that they were here to look for evidence chilled her. Surely they couldn't possibly believe she might be implicated in the murders. "But…like I said, I had nothing to do with any of this. I could have been lying dead next to them if I'd walked in a few moments earlier."

"Ms. Pagoni, we have a search warrant." Johnston produced the document from his suit pocket and handed it to Magda. "So, the sooner we can start looking, the faster we can get out of your way."

The situation was turning more surreal by the moment. What kind of evidence must they have, to have convinced a judge to allow them to search the flower shop? Ryden's heart started pounding. "Jesus. This is crazy."

The detective tilted his head toward a couple who'd come in to buy roses and were currently rubbernecking the goings-on with interest. "Please see your customers out," he told Magda, "and lock the door."

Magda complied with a dazed expression, still clutching the search warrant. When the other cop pulled her aside and said, "I need to ask you some questions about Ms. Wagner," Magda looked as though she was about to faint.

Ryden started toward her, but Johnston stopped her with a hand to her elbow. "Please, follow me." He led her into the work area in the back and closed the door.

"Will someone tell me what's going on?" Ryden asked.

"Please, take a seat over there while I look around." He indicated the cluttered worktable against the far wall. Though still outwardly polite, Johnston sounded different than he had the night before. At the house, he'd been patient and kind, treating her as the shaken near victim that she was. Today he was abrupt and stern, and he looked at her with suspicion, not empathy. Something had definitely happened to alter his perception, but what?

As she took a chair, he pulled on a pair of latex gloves. "Don't touch anything, please."

He went immediately to the large pegboard where their various tools hung and pulled one of the curved cutters from its hook. Examining it closely, he measured the blades with a small tape measure and then sprayed it with a small vial of liquid aerosol he pulled from his pocket. Ryden guessed it was the stuff she saw on police shows used to detect blood. One by one, he worked his way down the rack of tools, giving each the same scrutiny.

"What exactly are you hoping to find?" she asked.

"I'll know when I see it." Once he'd finished with every tool on the wall, he methodically searched the drawers of Magda's desk, then the rack of florist supplies—peering into boxes of vases, foam, and wire, and sorting through the stacked rolls of paper and cellophane they used to wrap bouquets. He was being very thorough, and the fact that he was coming up empty was beginning to reassure Ryden the ordeal would soon be over.

"Where's that lead?" he asked, indicating the only other door in the room.

"Just the toilet."

"I'll be right back. Stay—" He headed toward it but stopped abruptly as he passed by, his gaze focused on something behind her. "Please get up and walk away from the table."

She turned to look as she rose and stepped aside. All she could see were a few florist magazines and the haphazard piles of irises and birds of paradise that had been delivered twenty minutes earlier.

But Johnston's keen eye had caught the small hint of orange peeking out from beneath one of the magazines—the handle of her favorite curved cutters. They were the only tool in the room she'd paid for herself. She had small hands and disliked the standard ones that Magda used.

As he pulled them from their hiding place, she said, "There they are. I don't know why they're not in their usual place. Magda never uses mine."

Ryden was always very compulsive about hanging her tools back on the panel where they belonged. She couldn't stand to waste time searching for anything. She'd looked for the cutters this morning, but only very briefly. If she hadn't been so out of sorts from yesterday's events, she'd have turned the place upside down trying to find them, but instead she'd grabbed another pair.

Johnston ignored her comment. He peered closely at the tips, measured the blades, and then sprayed them with the aerosol. The metal points turned a bluish white.

Ryden had seen enough cop shows to know what it meant. "Is that blood?" she blurted as her heart began to race.

He didn't answer as he placed the cutters in a plastic bag and sealed it. Turning to her, he said, "I'll need you to come to the station with me for further questioning."

"What? Why?"

"Stand up, please." He removed a set of handcuffs from his belt. "You have the right to remain silent…"

A buzz in Ryden's ears replaced the rest of what he said. As though trapped in some out-of-body experience, she saw herself being handcuffed and taken to the front of the shop, where Magda stared, mouth open, as she was led to a waiting police car.

Chapter Four

Ryden's first couple of hours in the 15th District headquarters of the Philadelphia Police Department passed in a blur. After taking mug shots and fingerprinting her again, Johnston allowed her one phone call to arrange for an attorney before further questioning. She had to make it count, but she didn't know anyone well enough to ask for help or support. She ended up calling Magda, who was too hysterical to really listen and needed more comforting and reassurance than Ryden had the strength to offer. The only thing Ryden did manage to convey to her was that she needed a lawyer, and a cheap one, since she had virtually no savings.

She was then taken to a holding cell to wait: a windowless room, roughly twelve feet by ten feet, with benches on two sides and a tiny steel sink and toilet. The only other occupant at the moment was a fifty-something blonde named Ruby, who looked so bored and comfortable in her environs Ryden suspected she'd been here on several prior occasions. Aside from her name, Ruby offered little else about herself, including the reason for her current incarceration.

Ryden was happy not to have to make conversation with the woman, though she wondered whether she'd been put in with another murder suspect—one who'd actually committed the crime she was accused of.

Ryden lay down on one of the benches and stared up at the ceiling. The single bulb that gave the room a yellowish cast was too high to reach and protected by a plastic and metal shield. Their keepers were certainly thorough in preventing prisoners from having any means to injure themselves.

She couldn't grasp the bizarre predicament she was in, and no matter how hard she tried to come up with a reasonable excuse for this obscene development, she kept returning to the one devastating fact that no one would believe or even listen to her. Somewhere deep inside, she wanted to trust that the real killer would turn up; she would be released, apologies made, and her life would return to normal. It was just a misunderstanding, she told herself. Justice would prevail because justice always…

She couldn't bring herself to finish the thought. If time and experience had taught her anything, it was that life was nothing but a string of undeserved events. But as unfair and hard as her life had been, nothing could have prepared her to be suspected in a double homicide. She couldn't harm a bug, never mind an innocent man and his ex-wife, leaving two kids orphaned in the process. Sure, she'd always been pretty indifferent and distant when it came to people and her social life—some had even called her antisocial. But murder?

"No. No, it's not possible," she murmured to herself. She stood and walked to the front of the cell. "None of this is real." She grasped the bars. The metal was so cold in her palms, she shivered. "I didn't kill anyone."

Ruby guffawed from behind her. "Neither did I, honey. It was self-defense."

Before Ryden could react, a portly cop jangling a heavy ring of keys appeared in front of their cell.

"Hey, Smitty," Ruby called out. "Got another innocent one here."

The cop snorted derisively and leered at Ryden, his gaze lingering on her breasts. "Whatever you say, sweetheart."

Ryden let go of the bars and stepped back. "Please, you have to believe me."

"I hope, for your sake, your lawyer can make the investigating detectives believe you." He unlocked the door. "Come with me. He's waiting."

At least Magda had managed to get a lawyer down here.

The cop handcuffed her and led her to a small, bare room, devoid of anything except a table, two chairs, and a well-dressed man in his fifties. He stood as Ryden entered. "Ms. Wagner, I'm Sean Swartz, your attorney. Please, take a seat."

She didn't know much about labels or fashion, but she could recognize when someone reeked of wealth. Swartz didn't look like he worked pro bono or charged minimum rates. He wore a tailored navy suit with a starched white shirt and silk tie, his hair was stylishly clipped, and his leather loafers were immaculate. He even smelled expensive—his subtle musky aftershave a stark departure from the cheap shit that most of the guys who came into the flower shop and local bar wore—and the Rolex on his left wrist undoubtedly cost more than she earned in a year. In short, the guy looked more like a power-hungry corporate attorney than the cheap lawyer she'd asked for.

She hesitated to sit across from him, afraid the act alone would deplete her account. "Did Magda mention my finances?"

"I'm well aware of your financial status. You don't need to concern yourself with that."

"Don't be so sure." Maybe she should have been more specific with Magda about her savings.

"You have bigger problems to worry about, Ms. Wagner," Swartz said. "Let my fee be the least of your concerns. We'll work out an arrangement."

Ryden finally sat down. "I don't know where to start."

"I've been briefed on your case and have read the police report. You really don't have to say much."

"I don't understand. Granted, I've never had to deal with murder accusations and lawyers before, but far as I know, you need my side of the story. The truth."

"You claim you didn't kill the Laudens. That's all I need to know for now. We'll get into details when the time is right. I'm here to advise you not to answer any further questions. You need to exercise your right to remain silent, because the cops already have enough evidence against you to take to the grand jury."

Ryden couldn't believe what she was hearing. "What evidence could they possibly have?"

"The tool they found at your shop was the murder weapon. It fits the medical examiner's findings of the wounds inflicted on the Laudens, and the blood on it was a match for both victims. You even admitted in Detective Johnston's presence that it was yours."

"That can't be possible. I didn't kill them."

"It's only circumstantial evidence, but very damning," Swartz replied. "And your employer told the detectives you were going to the Lauden residence that evening to see Tim, who'd been in to flirt with you several times. She intimated there might even have been some romantic element developing between you. It's enough for the grand jury to indict you on two charges of first-degree murder. If convicted, you'll be given a minimum sentence of life without parole, and you easily could receive the death sentence because of the gruesome nature of the crimes."

Ryden collapsed back against the chair, a wave of hopelessness overwhelming her. She knew murder cases often took months to go to trial. Even if she was set free in the end, her future was bleak. "Well, then, that's that. I'm going to rot in a cell."

"No, you won't." The attorney got up, went to the door, and knocked on it.

"What do you mean?" she asked. "Do you know something?"

"Like I said, Ms. Wagner," he replied just as the cop opened the door, "we'll talk details when the time is right. First, we have to tell the detectives you're not going to give them any more information and get you out of here. I have a car waiting outside."

A half hour later, they emerged from the jail to find a driver standing curbside in front of a black Lincoln Town Car. He looked like he could have played for the Philadelphia Eagles.

"We're going to my office," Swartz said as they got in. "Would you like something to drink?" The car's minibar was stocked with only the best scotch, bourbon, and brandy, and though she rarely drank, she was tempted, given the circumstances. She declined, however, determined to keep her wits about her.

"I'd like some answers instead," she told him as they pulled away from the curb. "Like, why the hell is such an obviously affluent lawyer taking my case, knowing I have limited funds?" She had a million other questions, but that was at the top of the list.

"All in good time, Ms. Wagner. I'll explain everything, including our course of action, as soon as we're alone."

They rode the rest of the way in silence and parked in front of a glass-and-steel office building on the opposite side of town from her apartment. Instead of dropping them off, the halfback of a driver got out and walked with them into the building, though he waited outside the plush suite of offices emblazoned with a gold plaque that read S. SWARTZ, ESQ.

The outer reception area was impressive enough, but Swartz's twenty-second-floor inner office confirmed Ryden's assessment that the attorney usually represented only the wealthiest of clients. The room was bigger than the whole flower shop, and its floor-to-ceiling windows provided a magnificent view of the downtown skyline. Swartz's polished cherry desk and matching credenza sat at one end of the room, and a cozy sitting area—with expensive teak and leather couches, Tiffany lamps, and original oil paintings—filled the other.

She couldn't have felt more out of place. As Swartz directed her to one of the couches, she imagined she looked as ragged as she felt, dressed in faded jeans, tennis shoes, and wrinkled sweatshirt.

He sat across from her, all business. She watched patiently as he set his briefcase on the coffee table between them and removed a thick file. Her name was typed neatly in one corner. "So…" He flipped the file open. "Here we are."

"Do I start by telling you I'm not guilty?"

"No." He shut the file. "I start by telling you," he said, as he threw the folder into the wastebasket beside his seat, "that I know for a fact you're innocent."

"Yeah, but…" Ryden paused when she realized what he'd just said. "You what?"

He unbuttoned his blazer and loosened his tie. "Let me start from the beginning. Please refrain from dramatic reactions and spontaneous sentiments until I'm done and you've taken a few moments to grasp the situation."

She sat back, flabbergasted. Did this man know who the murderer was? Could he be her get-out-of-jail card? "I'm listening."

"I know for a fact you didn't kill the Laudens, because I know who did."

She jumped up. "That means you can tell—"

He raised his hand to stop her. "Please, Ms. Wagner. Sit down."

Ryden smiled, feeling almost giddy. "Sorry."

"This individual killed the Laudens to set you up. The killer was hired to make you look guilty."

It took several seconds for her to absorb what he was saying. "Why?" She tried to remain calm so he wouldn't tell her to stop asking questions.

"You were made to look guilty because someone wants you to work for them. This person, however, requires discretion, dedication, and complete cooperation."

"Two innocent people were killed."

He shrugged. "It's unfortunate, but—"

"But? There's actually a but?" She didn't know whether she should feel terrified at the power of whoever was responsible or disgusted. "What kind of people are you?"

"When my client wants something, my client gets it."

"You lost me. All this is because of a job offer? Couldn't they just ask?"

He sighed. "Please refrain from commentary and try to concentrate on what I'm saying."

"Fine."

"Have you ever heard of doubles?" he asked. "People so impossible to tell apart you can't distinguish the difference? So identical they can be used as decoys?"

Was he being rhetorical now? What the hell was he going on about? Doubles, decoys...what was next, unicorns? This conversation was making less sense by the second. She hesitated, not knowing whether she should answer.

"Do you understand my question?"

"Of course. I'm not an idiot. I just didn't know if I was allowed to answer." She bit back her irritation at being spoken to like a child.

"And?" he asked patiently.

"I get TiVo. I know some VIPs use them."

"Indeed." He smiled and leaned forward, watching her reaction. "My client wants you to double someone."

Ryden got to her feet. "Let me see if I understand you correctly. Two people died, and I was set up for these murders..." She started to pace. "By someone who wants me to impersonate somebody?" She turned to him. "Do you have any idea how absurd this all sounds?"

"I'm not done." He gestured toward the couch.

"No, I have no interest in sitting down. As a matter of fact, I have no interest in any of this. I don't see how I, of all people, ever got involved in this weird-ass conspiracy. I want you to pick up that phone and tell the police what you know, and then I want to go home and forget this past week ever happened," she shouted.

"That's not an option," he replied evenly. "Not one you want to entertain, anyway."

"What's that supposed to mean?"

"Should you refuse to cooperate, not only will I make sure you go to jail, I will also provide eyewitnesses before the grand jury. Witnesses who will seal your fate and make sure your lengthy life in prison is ended only by a lethal injection."

"What witnesses?"

"There's the one who saw you wining and dining with Mr. Lauden, another who saw you leave his home early in the morning in a condition of dishevelment—postcoital state, if you will—and yet another who'll testify he saw the victim welcome you at the door the night of the murder."

"Lies. All lies." She paced some more and paused by his desk. Ryden couldn't stand unfairness. She didn't know whether to cry or throw Swartz's heavy paperweight at his head; she wanted to do both.

She just wasn't sure about the order. She pulled her hair instead. "Why me?" she yelled.

"I already told you why. You fit what my client needs. Although, after having met you..." He looked her up and down like she was a leper. "I honestly don't see the connection. That aside, should you agree to these conditions, and after of course you complete your...term with my client, you'll no longer have to worry about prison."

"Who the hell is your...client? Let me talk to him."

"You might as well ask to speak to God."

"So, if I refuse to do this, I go to jail."

"The death sentence." He sounded satisfied.

"What will I have to do?"

"Once you agree to the terms," he replied, "you will be further instructed on what is required of you."

"Who am I supposed to double?"

"I'm not at liberty to discuss that. You must understand, this is all highly confidential. So much so, even I don't know the details."

"Will it be dangerous?"

"All decoys must take certain risks. It's why they exist, after all. But I can assure you, any dangers this job might involve pale compared to those of top-security prisons. And I can guarantee you, you will be sent to the worst there is."

"How long will I have to be this...this double?"

"It's my understanding it won't be longer than six months."

She started to pace again. What were the chances this was all a bad joke, or a case of mistaken identity? *Yeah, that's it.* A spark of hope ignited. "Are you sure you have the right—"

"Yes."

"But I'm a nobody."

He nodded. "You are."

"But I don't even—"

"Ms. Wagner, I need an answer. Are you going to work for my client, or are you going to spend the rest of your shortened life in prison?"

Ryden sat back on the couch. Life in prison and the death sentence, or six months of being an impersonator. Were those really her only choices? "How do you know I won't run? Or—"

"Should you be foolish enough to breach contract, reveal your real identity, or do anything contrary to your duties, you will be terminated."

"Fired?"

"Killed."

"What?" she yelled.

"It's still the better option. Maybe you haven't quite grasped the severity of your situation, Ms. Wagner, but you are already the proverbial dead man walking. Whereas, if you take the job and do as instructed, you'll be free to start a new life."

"New life?"

"The grand jury will most certainly indict you, probably within the next few weeks. But the work will necessitate that you be unavailable for your trial, so you'll be a wanted fugitive. My client will provide you with a new identity and a quarter of a million dollars so you can relocate wherever you want."

She let the figure sink in. Money had never been a priority, but if doing this meant she would be on the run from the law, she'd need the help to disappear. "I don't know if I can do this. What if I can't?"

"You will be taught what you need to know."

Ryden stared blankly at the view of the skyline for what seemed like hours. She'd lived all her life in Philadelphia and would miss the city. "When would I have to start?" she finally asked.

"I need an answer before I can disclose that." He got up and walked to the door.

Clearly Swartz wanted her decision right now, but did she really have any choice to make? Right now, she could see only one answer, and she was pretty certain it would be the same even if she had a month to sleep on it. She finally got up. "I'll do it."

"Very well," he said, and locked the door. He pulled out his phone and dialed. "She'll do it," he said, and hung up.

"Now will you tell me when I start?"

"You already have," he replied. "Someone will pick you up very shortly."

CHAPTER FIVE

New York, New York
Two months later, February 22

Jack Harding left the Colorado home she shared with Cassady Monroe very early in the morning, on a quick excursion to her New York apartment. She was booked on a flight back in just a few hours. She'd put off going to her old place to pick up some clothes and personal items because she was afraid she'd return to find Cass gone again. Part of her knew her lover was alive and safe, but the other dark part of her feared she'd wake up one morning to find it was a lie. Jack awoke every night to reach for Cass, just to make sure it wasn't all a dream.

Cass had been through so much the last couple of years Jack couldn't understand how she was still so keen on working for the Elite Operatives Organization as Agent Lynx. On her first solo assignment, she'd nearly died at the hands of serial killer Walter Owens, and the previous October Andor Rózsa, the madman who'd killed millions with his deadly Charon virus, had held her captive. For three weeks, Jack believed Cass had been killed in the explosion at Rózsa's lab, and in her terrible grief, she'd contemplated suicide.

Ever since Cassady's resurrection, Jack had vowed never to let her out of her sight again. This was one of the few times they'd been separated longer than a few hours, and she was doing her best to conceal her worry. Jack hated to acknowledge she needed or even missed anyone, but when it came to Cass, she not only admitted her feelings, but she reveled in the fact that Cass knew how dependent Jack was on her.

They both knew Cass would eventually get called back into action, but so far, Montgomery Pierce had left her alone and they had taken full advantage of their undisturbed reunion. Jack had also used every opportunity to get Cass to leave the EOO, but so far, no argument had worked. Cassady continued to believe in the organization's cause and that she was fulfilling her destiny. Every time she said that, Jack despised Pierce even more. She hated him for what he'd done to her and how thoroughly the organization brainwashed the EOO ops.

When Jack's cell phone rang a couple of blocks from her apartment, she checked the caller ID and smiled. "Miss me already, baby?"

"That, too," Cassady replied.

"What else?" Jack stopped walking and her heartbeat accelerated. "You're okay, right?"

"Of course, baby. Are you at the apartment yet?"

Jack relaxed and continued down the street. "Almost. I have to get through the polyester nightmare coming my way." She sidestepped the group of elderly tourists in track suits. "So, what's up?"

"I was wondering if you want to go out for dinner tonight."

"Why?"

Cassady laughed. "Because I want a break from cooking, and you can't keep coming up with excuses to keep me indoors."

"Wanna bet?"

"Jack, it's time we left the house. And you know I'm going away next week, anyway. You can't keep me cooped up forever."

Jack had been trying to forget the fact that Cass had a violin solo scheduled with the Boston Symphony, her first musical engagement in months. "Yeah, about that."

"Yes?"

"I don't see why I can't be there. You know, watch you rehearse and all that."

"Jack?"

"Yeah?"

"No."

"Why not?"

"Because the rehearsals are only for a week and you'll be at the concert anyway. And that aside, you'll scare everyone if you're there the whole time."

"Huh?"

"You keep standing guard over me like I'm a flight risk. People notice, you know? And besides that, honey, I know you love me and I adore you, too, but I need my old life back. Your overprotectiveness is a reminder."

She knew Cass was right but wasn't sure she was ready to take any risks.

As if reading her mind, Cass added, "Stop being paranoid, baby.

No one's out to get me."

"About dinner…what if I cook tonight?"

Cassady chuckled. "Honey, the last time you cooked, the oven went up in flames."

"I'm almost sure it wasn't my fault and I said I was sorry."

Cassady laughed. "You really are a beautiful kinda different."

"I prefer it when you call me Special Edition." Jack laughed, too. "So, what can I cook for you tonight?"

"We're going out."

"I'll cook naked," Jack offered.

Cass replied after apparently mulling over the offer for several seconds. "I guess you deserve one more chance."

Jack laughed again. "Good thing you didn't accept the bet," she said, satisfied.

"Naked, with nothing but my floral apron."

"You can't be serious."

"Those are my conditions."

"That's ridiculous." Her eyes bled from the image in her mind. "You can't possibly expect me—"

"I'll make reservations at that little Italian—"

"Okay, I'll do it," Jack mumbled.

"Excuse me, what?" Cassady asked mirthfully.

"I said, fine." She must really love this woman.

"And I get to take one picture."

"No way. No way, Cass."

"Maybe we can go for a drink after dinner."

"One picture. And no one ever sees it," Jack hurriedly added.

"We have a deal."

"Boy, am I whipped or what?" Jack said to herself after they'd disconnected.

She was almost at her apartment when she heard someone call out, "Ms. Jack!" She turned to find the owner of the dry cleaners she'd always done business with, a short Turkish man named Mustafa. He not only cleaned her clothes, but he also passed along messages when one of her underworld clients wanted to contact her. "I have a message for you," he said.

Jack hadn't received any notes from him in well over a year. Ever since she'd stopped taking hit jobs and changed her life, she'd stayed away from any previous connections to the mob bosses and other criminals she'd worked for. She had no idea if any of them had tried to reach her because she'd abandoned the landline Mustafa used to contact her and deliberately avoided the dry cleaners.

She had always been very careful about how she was contacted. The cell phones she used on the job were disposables. Clients could find her only via a three-step process of intermediaries. They would first contact a man Jack never associated with, who in turn would pass along the message to a second intermediary she simply called Pigeon, a skinny black guy who was gayer than the whole of 1920s Paris. Pigeon would go to the dry cleaners and write the number of whoever was looking for her on her laundry ticket. Mustafa would then reattach it to her clothes and call her to pick up her laundry. If the Turk knew what the messages were about, he never let on to her or said anything to anyone else, as far as she knew.

"I haven't dropped anything off," she said.

"I know." Mustafa shrugged. "I tried to call you, but you never answer. I thought you moved away." He was aware Jack lived in the area because she was usually quick to pick up her messages, but he never knew precisely where.

"That's right."

"Here." The Turk shoved the laundry ticket into her hand and turned to go back to his shop.

Jack didn't look at the stub before she stuffed it into her pocket. "If my friend drops by again, tell him I died," she called after Mustafa.

"About time," he replied, and disappeared inside.

Jack went to the kitchen the moment she got to her apartment. Determined to burn the stub, she pulled it from her pocket and grabbed the matches she kept on the counter for the gas stove. She could have tossed it, but she was in the mood for a dramatic ending. She was about to torch the message when she saw the number written on it. It didn't ring a bell, but what Pigeon had written beneath it did. BIG MONEY.

Yuri Dratshev, the Neanderthal of a Russian mob boss, was trying to reach her. The last time she'd taken a job from him was to find Walter Owens, the serial killer who had once kidnapped Dratshev's daughter, Nina. Nina had managed to escape, but when Owens resurfaced years later, Dratshev sought Jack out and agreed to pay her three-million-dollar price tag to deliver his head on a platter. Jack did the job and even let the mob boss keep the last half of the payment. She had her own reasons for wanting Owens dead; his last kidnap victim was Cassady. After that job, she'd vowed to stay away from her previous life and everyone in it.

She was about to burn the stub when something stopped her, perhaps morbid curiosity for what was going on in the netherworld. She shoved the number back into her pocket and set about gathering up what she needed so she could get home to Cassady.

Philadelphia, Pennsylvania

Ryden still did a double take every time she looked in a mirror, unable to recognize herself now that the transformation was complete. Once the swelling and bruises were gone and she'd gotten the contacts that changed her green eyes to dark brown, her resemblance to the president was uncanny in its perfection. She was at least grateful that the person she'd been chosen to double was a striking, elegant-looking woman and not someone with looks even more plain-Jane average than those given to her at birth.

Training her to emulate Elizabeth Thomas convincingly, however, was proving much more time-consuming and difficult than even the surgeries themselves. After a month of practice, she wasn't doing too bad mimicking the president's slight Maine accent and patterns of speech, but her own vocabulary was radically different than that of the Harvard-educated Thomas. Thomas used a lot of big words Ryden didn't even know the meaning of, and never cursed—something she herself did with even more regularity than she realized until Tonya kept correcting her.

Learning Thomas's mannerisms was difficult as well. It was more about learning what *not* to do than about perfecting what *to* do. The president practiced excellent etiquette—no elbows on the table, no interrupting people when they were talking, and so on, things Ryden seemed to do constantly without thinking. She also had to break her tendency to run her hands through her hair or raise her voice when she was frustrated or stressed, and instead adopt Thomas's calm, reserved demeanor in every crisis. Ryden gestured constantly with her hands when she was talking, something Thomas rarely did.

The hardest thing to master, however, was Thomas's erect posture and the way she walked. Ryden had lived her life in tennis shoes whereas Thomas wore high heels, and she looked as ungainly and awkward as she felt even after weeks of practice.

The single plus in the whole situation, if there was one, was that she was eating like a fiend and they were providing her with all of her favorite foods. She had to gain a few pounds to better match the president's weight, and since Ryden had always had a fast metabolism, that meant she was consuming four or five big meals a day.

She heard a car door slam outside—Tonya had arrived for today's lesson—so she switched off the video she'd been watching, a compilation of recent public appearances by the new president. Ryden had seen so many hours of footage she had at least a solid understanding of Thomas's viewpoints on nearly every subject possible, and she'd grown to admire the woman's poise and ability to quickly articulate her thoughts and opinions. She'd first thought it impossible to ever match the president's eloquence, but Tonya had assured her that once she was put into position, someone would script everything she would say in public. The one thing going for her was her excellent ability to memorize.

"How are we today, Madam President?" Tonya said by way of greeting when she came through the door. Ryden hadn't heard her real name since Tonya and two men in suits had driven her, under cover of night, from the private clinic to a secluded home outside Arlington, Virginia. Tonya came and went, but the two men remained to make sure she didn't leave or try to contact someone.

She had already corrected her slouch at the sound of Tonya's approach. "I'm very well, thank you. What is my schedule for today, Tonya?" she replied in Thomas's Maine accent.

Tonya smiled her approval. "One of your first public appearances will be at a formal dinner, so we're going to dress you appropriately and teach you the proper utensils, glasses, and so on for each course." She glanced at her watch. "But first, your patron wants another update on your progress. She should be calling any moment."

Patron. Tonya always called her that, but Ryden thought of her as the bitch who'd set her up and gotten her into this predicament. She'd learned the sex of her mysterious blackmailer a couple of weeks earlier, when the woman had first checked in via Tonya's cell to see how the lessons were going.

She still knew nothing else about the woman. Not her name, or location, or even why she was doing this. Ryden only knew her voice and attitude: icy, ruthless, and terrifying. The first time she'd called, Ryden had asked why she'd been singled out for this nightmare, and she literally begged to be set free.

The woman just laughed. She'd calmly told Ryden that she was in far too deep to back out now, and any premature exit from this plan would result in her sudden and gruesomely painful death.

When Tonya's phone went off, Ryden jumped. Tonya put the ice bitch on speakerphone.

"How is our student doing?"

"Since we spoke last, she's mastered all the names and faces in her briefing list," Tonya reported. "And is well familiar with the full agenda we've given her. We're down to the final small social niceties and protocol she'll need to master for official functions."

"Excellent. We're set to make the substitution in two days," the reptilian voice replied. "Madam President?" Whenever ice bitch used the formal address for Thomas, it always sounded somehow condescending.

"Yes, ma'am. I'm here," Ryden replied, careful to perfectly mimic Thomas's accent and intonation.

"Of course you are, dear. Where else would you be?" Her laughter was as chilling as her voice.

Washington, D.C.
Two days later, February 24

The crowd amassed at the historic Jefferson Hotel for the posh Democratic National Committee fund-raiser included a host of Hollywood celebrities, but Elizabeth Thomas was still the star of the event. After two hours of nonstop handshakes and picture taking with top contributors to the party's coffers, she slipped out of the cocktail-hour preliminaries to change for the four-thousand-dollar-a-plate formal dinner. The hotel manager had provided her the expansive Thomas Jefferson suite on the top floor for just that purpose.

As Elizabeth stood in front of the elevator, surrounded by five Secret Service men, she wondered how she'd ever get used to how guarded she had to be at all times. Her only private moments since her election were in the bathroom, bedroom, and on the rare occasions she asked to be alone with a family member. And even then, the Secret Service stood guard outside. She hadn't even had much privacy during her husband's funeral four months earlier.

She'd known her new life as president of the United States would come with plenty of sacrifices, and she hadn't minded making them. Ever since she was a little girl, she'd realized it was her destiny. Not so much because she had been groomed and raised in the political arena—

her father had also represented Maine in the Senate—but because she sincerely wanted to make a difference. Her ideas for a better America would rub some the wrong way, but as with all new laws and initiatives, it was just a matter of time before the dust would settle and people came to accept the changes.

The elevator arrived and one of her guards stepped in to make sure it was secure. Exaggerated, she thought, but they, too, needed to follow protocol.

"Madam President." He gestured for her to enter, and the remaining four men who surrounded her followed her inside. One pressed the button to the eighth floor, and they all stood solemnly staring at the floor indicator above the sliding door.

Elizabeth heard a noise right above her, and in an instant, two of her guards were at her side, hovering over her and shielding her with their bodies, while the other three pointed their guns at the ceiling.

"What's happening?" was all she had time to ask before the lights went out and the sound of bullets surrounded her. Dull, almost distant reports—they were using silencers, she realized, as she was abruptly and roughly pushed to the ground, facedown. Her two nearest men covered her, their weight oppressive. Barely able to breathe, and unable to see what was happening, she felt her heart roar in her chest. Seconds later, in a momentary lull of the gunfire, she heard the sound of something heavy drop next to her.

"What's going on?" she shouted, and squirmed under the weight of her guards, which had become increasingly unbearable. Dead weight, she realized with a panic. They weren't moving at all.

The shooting stopped, but Elizabeth didn't dare move. "Is it over?" she whispered. She was trembling, and her pulse boomed in her ears. No one answered, but she could hear heavy breathing, and suddenly the weight on her lessened and she could move a little. Thank God. At least some of her men were apparently okay, and she was still alive.

Then the weight crushing her was gone entirely, but it was still pitch-black in the elevator. Still too shaky and out of breath to get up, she rolled over onto her back. Immediately, a bright beam of light pointed directly in her face blinded her.

"Be quiet, and lie still," a voice behind the light commanded, and Elizabeth was surprised to realize it was a woman's voice. Her heart began to beat even faster.

The figure was hovering over her. Elizabeth tried to push her away, but the woman pinned her down roughly.

"Help!" she shouted, but the assailant quickly covered her mouth.

"I *said*, be quiet, or I'll shoot you right now."

Elizabeth froze and let herself be pulled up. The beam of light shifted as she rose, allowing her to see more clearly. Though she still couldn't make out the woman's identity—she was dressed all in black and wore a ski mask—she could see that all five of her guards were dead, each of them shot in the head.

She glanced up to where the initial sound had originated and saw that a metal ceiling tile was missing. The masked woman immediately blindfolded and gagged her, then tied some kind of harness around her.

Elizabeth wanted to kick, punch, try to scream through the gag for help, but she was afraid she'd end up on the pile of dead bodies. The woman bound her hands and feet, and removed her wedding ring. Seconds later, she was being lifted. She could do nothing to stop it; it was impossible for her to move much at all.

"Go," she heard a man say as she was being pulled up.

"Jesus, are they dead?" a female voice replied.

Ryden had never imagined any operation could happen this fast and be this well organized. One guy had deactivated the elevator and lights, while another two individuals were lowered down the shaft with a wire. They had shot the Secret Service agents through the roof of the elevator, with the help of devices attached to their heads. She assumed they were some kind of infrared or other high-tech gadgets that helped them see their targets through the elevator ceiling, like she'd seen in spy movies.

Seconds later, she was lowered down the shaft herself in a harness and came face-to-face with the gagged and bound president of the U.S. going up. They were wearing identical clothes. The masked woman who was waiting in the elevator positioned Ryden on the floor and gave her the president's wedding ring to put on. Ryden thought she would lose her lunch at the sight of dead men scattered on the floor. No one had said anything about people being killed. After tossing Thomas's purse beside Ryden, the masked woman shoved the bodies of two of the dead agents over her and disappeared back through the hole in the ceiling.

The time elapsed between the start of the attack and when the elevator began moving again, this time with Ryden in it, was only about a minute. Had the Secret Service agents not been wired, no one would have known something was wrong.

Ryden heard the panicked shouts and screams as the elevator slowed, then stopped. She closed her eyes and crossed her fingers. *Please give me the strength to do this.* The rustling of people on the other side of the door told her the show was about to begin. She opened her eyes and began to struggle as it slid open.

A voice shouted, "Clear!" and the bodies of the dead agents were being lifted off her. Soon after, another voice shouted, "She's alive! The president's alive!"

CHAPTER SIX

Bibbona, Italy
Next day, February 25

Harper Kennedy lifted her glass of red wine in a toast. "See you on the other side, buddy." She rested the shovel against a tree by the grave and took a sip, swallowing hard as she realized another decade had gone by. Angelo had been her second companion since she'd moved to Italy, but he was not the first dog to bear that name.

Harper had inherited the vineyard she loved, together with her first dog, from Pepo, short for Giuseppe. Pepo couldn't imagine the vineyard or his life without his Weimaraner. He'd started the winery in 1953, when Angelo the first was just a pup. Pepo came to love that adopted stray so much he'd labeled the wine after him: *Il Grigio Angelo*, The Gray Angel.

When she had first come to Italy on assignment with the EOO thirteen years earlier, Harper had never imagined she'd find not only a home but also a job she loved. She'd run into Pepo, already nearly eighty, at the local village café. They had started out talking about every Italian's favorite topic and one Harper could relate to—politics—but the chat soon turned more personal. Ordinarily, Harper hated polite conversation and never volunteered much, but she surprised herself by opening up to Pepo about her hopes and dreams. She told him about her love for the country and how she never wanted to leave but had to find a job. It took but a few hours for them to become friends, and soon Harper moved into a small cottage he'd built next to his farmhouse. His only request was that she help out around his vineyard.

Before long, she couldn't fathom her life away from Tuscany or grapes. The work thrilled her and gave her a satisfaction nothing and no one ever had. When Pepo passed away and left her his sixty acres, she relished the challenge of making it her own and within five years had taken the vineyard to another level. She'd found investors who believed in her vision and the wine, and with the funds she expanded the vineyard and improved the earth, flavor, bottles, and label. She poured money into marketing and distribution, and soon she had taken Pepo's popular local wine and turned it into an internationally renowned label now going for almost one hundred euros a bottle.

The Bibbona region, eighty kilometers southwest of Florence, was ideal for producing quality wines. The silty soil was rich in minerals and the weather was moderate, with a minimal variation in temperature during the long growing season. Harper's estate was also ideally situated, facing west, which gave her grapes optimum sunlight and exposure to the gentle sea breezes.

She'd also renovated the two-hundred-year-old farmhouse, which had a glorious panoramic view of the Mediterranean. Built of stone, with dark wood beams and floors, the two-story structure now had an updated interior and modern conveniences, as well as a large gun safe where she kept her weapons. Outside, where she spent most of her off time when the weather was pleasant, was a large stone terrace with a massive brick fireplace that she and Pepo had built together.

Harper walked the short distance home and built a fire in the fireplace, like she did every evening, and relaxed before it with a glass of her own wine. Normally, Angelo would lie at her feet and she would occasionally pat him and talk to him about what needed to be done the next day, but now she quietly stared at the flames and listened to the trees rustle in the soft wind.

When Pepo had fallen gravely ill five years ago, he told her he would always be with her in the wind and in the leaves. Now, every time Harper heard that sound, she imagined him watching over her, giving her strength when she was tired and praising her when she managed to come back home in one piece.

Although the EOO held its operatives to strict privacy regulations concerning their work and involvement in whatever they were hired to do—they all were raised to conceal their identity—Harper had confided in Pepo. Living as closely as they did, it hadn't taken him long to realize something was different about her. She would disappear for weeks at a time, sometimes returning beaten and broken, at other times distant or angry. At first, he thought it had to do with family matters, until she told him she didn't have a family. Then he thought it involved a man, until she told him she was gay, and finally, when he thought it concerned health issues, she sat him down and told him the truth, or at least part of it. Harper didn't mention the EOO, but she did tell him she worked security for an international private contractor.

Pepo vowed to never ask anything about her work or her physical or mental state when she returned from assignments. From then on, he would seat her by the outdoor fireplace, pour her a glass of wine, and talk about vines. Harper came to love him like the father she never had and considered him her family. When he died, a small part of her died with him, but she knew he would live on in the wine.

She heard a sound in the far distance, too brief to make out precisely what it was. She didn't get up, but she did grab the shotgun at her feet. Here, up in the mountains, she would regularly spot a wolf, and although she'd never had any problems with the animals, other villagers had been attacked. She listened a while longer, then smiled and set down her weapon. "Hey, you missed the ceremony," she said without turning around.

"I'm sorry," Monica replied as she bent to kiss Harper's shoulder. "I couldn't get away from work."

"I figured."

"Are you coping?"

"I'm fine." Harper tried to smile as the attractive blonde came around to face her. "You know how it is."

Harper had met Monica three years earlier on a flight back to Italy from the U.S. Monica was in the olive-oil business and had her own production factory. They spent the whole flight talking about the differences between the tree and the vine and the similarities between the business aspects of selling. What had started out as a friendship soon turned into a sexually open relationship, and both were content with that status since neither had the time nor interest in anything serious or binding. Harper had come to care a lot for her but actually cared about their friendship, not the sex.

"I assume it won't be long before a new Angelo comes running to greet me." Monica sat on her lap.

"It wouldn't be right to leave the vineyard without a Grigio Angelo."

"We can go look together, if you want."

"It's something I do alone, you know that." Harper massaged Monica's shoulders and Monica leaned back into her. Maybe a good night's sex session would help her out of the funk she was in.

"I just thought you might want company."

"I do, but not for picking out a dog." Harper kissed Monica's neck.

Monica turned her head and kissed her. "Why don't we go inside?"

"What's wrong with here?"

The woman glanced around as if to make sure they were alone. "Nothing. Nothing at all," she replied with a grin before attacking Harper's mouth with her own.

Harper's cell phone vibrated on the table next to them. She never had the sound on because she hated the meddling, annoying contraption. She checked the caller ID and sighed. "Give me a second, okay?"

Monica reluctantly got up off her lap. "I'm going to get a glass of red. How about you?"

"Sounds great." Harper took the call as soon as Monica was out of earshot, answering, as she always did, with her code number to verify her identity. "Shield 29041971."

"You're babysitting."

Harper appreciated the fact that EOO chief Montgomery Pierce didn't waste words. "How exciting." She didn't try to conceal the irritation in her voice.

"You sound tired."

"I sound bored. Bored numb with self-proclaimed VIPs. All of them, without exception, think they're especially important to the human race. Meanwhile, they're either as deep as puddles or as pleasant as a rash."

Pierce didn't laugh. "I assure you, this one's different."

"As in a whole new kind of skin condition."

"As in highly significant."

Harper arched an eyebrow. "Where are you sending me?"

"Washington, D.C. 1600 Pennsylvania Avenue."

"The Castle."

"Be here ASAP for the briefing."

"Is this about the attempt on POTUS?"

"Correct. Still bored numb?"

"Less so. I'm on my way."

Southwestern Colorado
Next day, February 26

Shield hadn't been back to the EOO headquarters southwest of Colorado Springs in six months. She'd gotten all of her recent protection assignments through intermediaries, since they'd all been brief details guarding dignitaries throughout Europe. Her plane was delayed, so she floored the rental car in order to make the briefing on time.

The sixty-three-acre EOO complex, set high in the snow-capped Rocky Mountains and adjacent to the nearly half-million-acre Weminuche Wilderness Area, looked much like a private boarding school except for the high razor-wire-top fence that surrounded it and other obvious and not-so-obvious security enhancements. The Elite Operatives Organization was still as virtually unknown to the world at large—with a few exceptions, Interpol being one of them—as it had been in its infancy more than sixty years ago. Its remote location helped shield it from outside scrutiny.

An array of squat red-brick dormitories and classrooms dominated the campus, but once Shield was admitted by the guard at the gate she headed toward the massive Neo-Gothic administration building, where Montgomery Pierce's office was located, along with those of the two other members of the governing trio. Once she'd passed the retina and hand ID scan required to get inside, she rode the elevator up to the conference room where they held all their briefings.

She had spent nearly half her life at the compound, from the time they'd adopted her from an orphanage in Australia at age six until she began taking missions seventeen years later. Like the rest of the ops, they gave the infant Harper the surname of a U.S. president and provided her with the best education possible. But she held no fond memories of the place. Her formative years had mostly been filled with weapons training, survival exercises, hand-to-hand combat drills, and other similar pursuits, not the normal fun of childhood, and she'd made no enduring friendships here. The ops were discouraged from making close attachments either inside or outside the organization, though many had disregarded that directive. Harper, however, did feel a sense of responsibility and gratitude toward the organization that had given her a higher education and the opportunity to discover and love Italy.

The dozen men and women gathered in the conference room were all ETFs, members of the organization's Elite Tactical Force, comprised of seasoned agents who had the training, skills, and resourcefulness to handle almost any situation. Most had specialties: Fetch was skilled at infiltration and hostage rescue, Chase was a top-notch tracker, Domino's marksmanship with any kind of gun was unparalleled, and Reno could hack into nearly any computer in the world.

When Shield joined them, the other ops were admiring a photo of

Domino's new daughter—who'd been born to her partner, Hayley.

Allegro, their breaking-and-entering expert and a close friend of Domino, was the only one not making a fuss over the redheaded infant, probably because, as their resident cutup, *she* was usually the center of attention at such gatherings. "I don't know why no one is congratulating me," Allegro complained. "I'm the godmother, you know. That kid's future…" she pointed to the picture, "will depend on me."

Domino quickly stuffed the snapshot into her back pocket. "The hell it will."

The other ops laughed. Montgomery Pierce tried to keep a straight face, but as was often the case when it came to Allegro, he didn't entirely succeed.

"I saw that." Allegro pointed to him. "You're taking their side."

"You're not exactly the…classic role model."

"Typical. It doesn't matter what I do, you always hammer on the small things," Allegro replied. "Say what you want, all I hear is blah blah blah."

"I'm sure you'll be a wonderful example." Joanne Grant, the Director of Academics and the second member of the EOO's governing trio, chimed in. "The rest of you, stop goading her. That goes for you, too, Monty."

Several of the ops chuckled at her comment. They all knew that Grant and Pierce, both in their sixties now, had become romantically involved and were living together. Though they still refrained from publicly acknowledging that fact, in deference to the no-close-attachments directive, their affection for each other was clear.

Pierce cleared his throat. "Everyone take a seat so we can begin." He went to shut the blinds, a habit whenever anything important was to be discussed, then took his chair between Grant and Director of Training David Arthur, the third member of the governing trio.

"You are *so* negative," Allegro replied, and took her place at the table. She turned to Domino. "No christening invitation for him."

Pierce pretended he hadn't heard. "By now, you all know about the attack on the president. Since all five of her guards were killed, we've been asked to provide additional security for her while the Secret Service conducts an internal investigation to determine how this could have happened." He turned to Shield. "You'll be assigned as Thomas's primary or SAIC—Special Agent in Charge. The Secret Service Presidential Protective Division will fill out the rest of her detail but will be under your direction."

"I imagine Director Alexander hasn't entirely embraced this development," Shield said. The head of the Secret Service was well known for maintaining rigid control of his department and had always resisted any effort by others to dictate how it was run.

Pierce nodded. "The request for our involvement came via a joint missive from the vice president and chief of staff. In light of what happened, Alexander really doesn't have a say in the matter." He gestured toward their crack computer op. "Reno will be your main contact, should you need any intel. The rest of you can consider yourselves on standby to provide additional support. Questions?"

When no one replied, he withdrew a folder from his briefcase and slid it across the table toward Shield. "A copy of the Secret Service's file on Thomas. As you know, the White House Communications Agency has assigned her the code name Beacon, but in your communications with us, we'll be using Lighthouse. The file also has your credentials and flight documents. You're booked to D.C. in three hours."

Chapter Seven

The White House, Washington, D.C.
Later that day

Ryden swiveled in the cushy leather chair, away from the massive Oval Office desk to face the three large south-facing windows behind her that overlooked the Rose Garden. The sun was just setting, so the external security lights popped on, illuminating the grounds. Two days after the switch, she'd so far done a very convincing job deceiving the world and those close to Elizabeth Thomas. But she was already exhausted. They hadn't told her exactly how long she would have to play president, but she felt every bit the imposter she was with every minute that passed. For some reason, she'd thought it would get at least slightly easier over time, but forty-eight hours later, her nerves were raw and the headache wouldn't go away.

The toughest moment had been when she appeared on TV that morning in the press briefing room, to show the world the president was still alive and well. She wasn't ready for a full-blown press conference with impromptu questions she might not know how to answer, but she'd delivered a statement that she was uninjured by the attack and vowed that justice would be served. No one would stand in the way of a better America, and so on. The most difficult part for her had been in praising Thomas's Secret Service agents for their courage and sacrifice, and extending condolences to their families.

Kenneth Moore, Thomas's special advisor and her contact within the White House, had scripted every word that came out of her mouth. The whole operation to switch Ryden with the president would not have been possible without him. He had fed her mysterious employer the dates and location of the Democratic Party fund-raiser even before it was publicly announced, and he had been the one to pass on the president's every move and details about her wardrobe, including her ensemble the day of the exchange.

Moore knew virtually everything about Elizabeth Thomas, since he was her right hand the same way he was now Ryden's. He'd been with Thomas since her early days in the Senate, so Ryden couldn't imagine what had prompted him to turn on her. She wanted to feel confident knowing he was there to tell her what to say and when, but the guy simply terrified her. With black beady eyes that constantly observed her, and a thin face and lips, he looked like a giant, dangerous rat. When they were alone, he prefaced most comments by leaning close to her ear and saying, "So far, so good. Keep it that way and you'll live." She'd tried to pull away earlier today before he got too close, but he'd grabbed her by the hair. She already loathed him so much she now wanted to hurt him more than she did her anonymous employer.

He'd met with her earlier to tell her the Secret Service had appointed a new special agent as her primary bodyguard, one who would be with her at all times—even within the White House, where the Uniformed Division usually provided security. He didn't say that this new bodyguard was in on their conspiracy, but he implied as much when he pointedly reminded her that several other entities within the White House were watching her and would report back to him any slips or attempts to reveal the deception.

Ryden jumped when the phone rang. She swiveled around and answered. "Yes?"

"Your appointment with the Secret Service is in five minutes," Ratman said. "Meet me in the Cabinet Room."

Ryden straightened her clothes before she opened one of the four doors leading out of the Oval Office. Though it was her first visit to the adjacent Cabinet Room, where the president routinely met with her cabinet secretaries and advisors, she knew which seat was hers. Not only was each leather chair around the large oval table outfitted with a small plaque designating who sat where, she'd been supplied with floor plans, virtual tours, and pictures of all the rooms in the White House during her training.

Ratman and the two people present stood when she entered. One was a pleasant-looking middle-aged man she recognized from her briefings with Tonya as Frank Alexander, the Secret Service director. The other was an attractive woman probably in her mid-thirties—four or five years younger than Ryden, and at five-seven or so, a couple of inches taller than she was. She had blue eyes, full lips, high cheekbones, and shoulder-length light-brown hair with blond highlights. With a lean, athletic build and skin bronzed from long hours in the sun, she was a striking woman in her classically tailored black suit.

"Good evening, Madam President," the man said.

Ryden shook his hand. "Good evening, Director Alexander."

"We're all very sorry about what happened."

"Please." Ryden lifted her hand to stop him. "I'm sorry about your men. They gave their lives to save mine."

"It's what we do, but yes, we were very sorry to lose our friends and colleagues."

"I can't imagine how their families must feel."

"It's always hard to break such news." He looked away, still clearly upset. "Their families will be well compensated and looked after."

"A small but necessary comfort, I'm sure."

"Indeed." Alexander turned to his right. "Let me introduce you to agent Harper Kennedy."

The agent took a step forward and extended her hand. Ryden reached for it guardedly as the Ratman's words rang loud and clear in her ears. She could be one of *them*.

"It's an honor to meet you, Madam President." Kennedy's hand was rough and firm, more the hand of someone who did manual labor than a woman who stood guard. She looked Ryden in the eyes as if trying to see past her.

Tonya had taught Ryden to never look away during introductions, and so far she'd done a good job even with those closely associated with Thomas, but the intensity of this woman's stare made her feel exposed, susceptible to the lie she was living. The woman furrowed her brow and for a second Ryden swore she saw her sniff. Had Kennedy met the president in the past, and did she somehow smell different? Ryden finally pulled her hand away and the woman let go.

"I will be your SAIC—Special Agent in Charge—from now on," Kennedy said. "That means I will be with you at all times, including the places men aren't allowed."

"Isn't that a bit extreme?" Ryden asked.

"With all due respect, Madam President, your attackers proved to you, us, and the world that organized terrorism is a real threat, one that can strike at any moment. We want to ensure you are constantly protected."

"But I was protected when these people attacked. I'm alive because your people made the ultimate sacrifice. Because they did their job."

"Yes, and now your attackers know that. They also know what to do differently. These people…" Kennedy paused, and those intense blue eyes bore into Ryden again, "got past our security, which means we failed. Maybe next time you won't be so lucky. Our men saved your life, but they failed at their job. We will not allow that to happen again. If that means twenty-four-hour protection, regardless of the situation or location, then that's what I will do."

"What makes you so sure you can handle a situation like that on your own?"

"Because I have thirteen years of experience with similar situations." Kennedy sounded arrogant and Ryden didn't know if she liked that. She sure had a lot of overconfidence for someone who looked like she belonged in the *Sports Illustrated* swimsuit edition.

"Madam President," Alexander said, "Kennedy here is indeed one of the best in her field. She is highly trained and skilled in surveillance, guarding, martial arts, and various forms of combat. Her instincts are unparalleled. She comes highly recommended."

"Recommended by whom? I thought she was one of your people." Ryden knew she was pressing her luck. Ratman had said to stick to the script so that she didn't say something stupid or unconventional, but she couldn't help herself.

"We have contracted her," the Secret Service director replied.

"In other words, she's on loan," Ryden concluded.

"From a very prestigious private organization. I presume you've already been briefed about the EOO—the Elite Operatives Organization?"

Ryden hadn't, but the tone of the question made it clear that Thomas probably *had* been, so she nodded. "Why doesn't she work for you if she's so good?"

Ratman shot her a warning stare before he jumped in. "The president is understandably still very shaken up. She wants to make sure her new guard is qualified for this job."

"I would want that, too," Kennedy said. "I'm…on loan, Madam President, because I'm not for sale."

"I see." Ryden had hoped Ratman's implication about the new guard was just to scare her, but now she was convinced it was true. She was certain her mysterious employer had deliberately hired an outsider for this position to keep close tabs on her.

Ryden turned to Kennedy. "Does that mean you start as of now?"

"As of tonight," her bodyguard confirmed. "I will be staying in the bedroom next to yours."

❖

Houston, Texas

"And how is Madam President today?" TQ hadn't yet contacted Yuri Dratshev since the kidnapping, presuming that if anything whatsoever went amiss she would have been immediately notified. She'd spelled out to the Russian mob boss several conditions regarding his part of the plan: he was to use only a handful of his most trusted men, who would be told to keep the president somewhere safe and secure, under heavy guard and well fed. They were not to know who had hired Dratshev or why the operation took place. And they were to keep their faces hidden whenever they were around her, not that they needed to be reminded of that. Considering who their captive was, they had to be well aware of the consequences should something go wrong.

"They tell me she is scared and quiet," Dratshev replied. "She tried to negotiate with money and the usual bullshit."

"You did a good job, Yuri. Your men will be paid well once this is over."

"I know, I told them. They will do a great job, you don't worry."

"Oh, I'm not. I'm sure they want their boss and his family to live a long, happy life."

"If they don't," Dratshev said, "I will kill them myself."

"Now, concerning this ridiculous legislation against us…" TQ stopped when she heard another voice coming through the line. Irritated, she spoke louder than usual. "Who is that?"

"Where?"

She could almost see the idiot turn around to look. "I hear someone."

"Oh, I am listening to my messages."

TQ rolled her eyes as Dratshev let the recording drone on. She was about to tell him to turn it off when she realized she recognized the voice, or thought she did. No. It couldn't be. She sat up in her chair and listened more intently. "Who was that?" she asked when the recording ended.

"Old friend. She works for me sometimes," Dratshev replied.

"When did she call?"

"It is an old message. I'm not regular."

TQ would have corrected him, but she was too undone by the

voice to even get aggravated at his lack of proficiency in basic English. "Play it back and get me closer to the speaker."

"Why?"

"Because I said so!" She didn't routinely shout, but then again, her reactions in general had been atypical since her brother's death. So much so, in fact, she wondered whether she'd actually felt something for the inadequate fool.

A few seconds later, Dratshev said, "Here it goes."

"I got your message," the woman's recorded voice said. "FYI, I stopped taking jobs, but curiosity got the best of me when I saw you were trying to reach me. Anyway, assuming I still care in a few days, I'll try again."

That's her. TQ was certain it had to be the woman she'd vowed to find. "What's her name?"

"Who knows?" Dratshev said. "No one uses a real name. This woman is mysterious but…very good. The best in the hit business."

"What name does she go by?"

"With me?"

"No, with my grandmother. Of course with you."

"In the business, they call her Jack, or Silent Death."

TQ almost gasped at the confirmation of her suspicion. "Where can I find her?"

"You want to find her?" Dratshev laughed. "No one finds her." He laughed again. "She finds you, if she feels like it."

"Are you too stupid to realize I could have you extinguished like a bug for laughing at me?" How dare he make her feel naïve or stupid for thinking she could find this arrogant bitch? TQ could find or buy whomever she wanted.

Dratshev's laughter ceased abruptly and his voice was appropriately apologetic. "I don't want to offhand you."

"It's offend, and you have, and this is how you are going to make up for it. You are going to find this Jack and bring her to me."

"But—"

"Do it!" she shouted, and hung up. She walked to the bar and poured a glass of whiskey, downing a good measure of it in one long swallow. Returning to her desk, she idly tapped the glass with her finger. The mere voice of that woman had brought back feelings of helplessness and anger. The first was a feeling long foreign to her and one she'd promised she'd never allow anyone to make her feel. The second was what sustained her.

She was going to find Jack, no matter what or whom it took, and she was going to make sure the bitch knew just how badly she reacted to being made to feel vulnerable.

She snatched the letter opener off her desk. She was going to personally torture that— Someone knocked on the door. "What?"

One of the two maids entered. "Your bath is ready, madam."

"You're two minutes early."

The maid's eyes widened in horror as she checked her watch. "My mistake, madam. My watch is running fast."

"Come here."

The young woman approached cautiously and stopped in front of her desk. Without hesitation TQ stabbed her in the eye with the letter opener. "And that's nothing compared to what I'm going to do with you, Jack," she whispered as the maid fell to her knees and screamed in pain.

CHAPTER EIGHT

Shield waited outside the Cabinet Room while Elizabeth Thomas and Special Advisor Kenneth Moore met privately for a half hour after her introduction to the president. When the two came out and went in different directions, she fell into place a couple of steps behind Thomas. Even here, she was on high alert to any hint of danger. During the journey to D.C., she had studied blueprints of the White House, so she knew they were headed to the second-floor private quarters, where the president's bedroom occupied the southwest corner.

Shield had been given the so-called Living Room, an adjacent suite with its own bathroom. Used by several presidents and first ladies as a separate bedroom, in recent years most chief executives employed it as a private study or family living space, but Thomas hadn't yet designated a function for it.

Shield stopped in front of the president's door. "Madam President, should you need to leave your room for any reason, please knock on the paneled door that joins our bedrooms or call my room."

Thomas brushed off the request. "That won't be necessary. Besides, I have two men on guard at my disposal."

"Those men have been replaced by me. I am your primary." Shield had already stated that a little while ago. Maybe the president was too preoccupied to recall everything that happened to her, but surely she'd remember an important mention that concerned her well-being. Perhaps she was just still too new at this to know what primary implied.

"Correct me if I'm wrong, but you were hired to protect me during public appearances."

"As well," Shield said. "Maybe you haven't been informed, but the job of a primary involves constant security."

The president hesitated. She sounded strangely reluctant when she replied, "I…I am aware. I simply don't want you to intrude on my privacy."

Shield observed her a few more seconds before she said, "Very well then, Madam President."

Only after Thomas had entered her bedroom did Shield go to hers. The room was everything she expected a presidential suite would be: luxuriously appointed and well equipped with all modern comforts, but she missed her earthy, wood-beamed bedroom. Others might have been impressed with the canopied four-poster bed, wondering which presidents or influential guests had slept in it, but she gave little thought to such matters. As a matter of fact, she found the massive thing so suffocating she felt as though she were being buried alive.

Fifteen minutes later, she lay in bed wearing navy pajamas, which she'd purchased to wear during guard duty just in case someone barged in or she had to move fast and didn't have time to change. At home she slept in nothing but boxers. She could only hope the ongoing investigation into the assassination attempt would lead somewhere so she could soon return to her home in Tuscany. Sitting POTUS was admittedly more interesting than most jobs she'd gotten recently, but at least with the others she was always back home within days or weeks. If nothing ever came of this investigation, she could be stuck here for Thomas's entire term.

And what was up with the president, anyway? Thomas didn't appear at all happy to have a permanent private guard. If anything, she seemed irritable and distracted. Sure, the attempt on her life and five dead guards were enough to throw anyone off their game, but she didn't even acknowledge having seen Shield in Greece. Despite her get-more-women-into-male-dominated-fields rhetoric, maybe Thomas would have preferred a male guard like most VIPs did. People were under the general misconception that men were better qualified to protect and defend. What they didn't know was that it took a lot more than dumb muscle to prevent, predict, and secure. If an offender found opportunity for even an unsuccessful attempt, security had usually failed. It didn't matter how big or strong you were, a bullet killed indiscriminately.

She leafed through the stamped bundle of sheets she'd been given concerning the president's upcoming appearances. Tomorrow's Find Your Sport event on the South Lawn featured dozens of Olympic champions and was expected to draw twenty-five thousand people, most of them kids. Thomas would be stretched thin trying to appear at all the activities scheduled for the daylong extravaganza. Shield only hoped the president would be a bit more concerned about her safety than her privacy.

❖

Southwest of Baltimore, Maryland
Next morning, February 27

Elizabeth Thomas picked absentmindedly at the tray of food that Beard, as she'd come to think of him, had delivered for her supper. Both of the men who tended to her always wore ski masks when in her presence, but one obviously had facial hair beneath and the other didn't, so that was how she distinguished Beard from Cleanshaven.

Many others were likely guarding her. Whoever had managed to pull off such a well-orchestrated kidnapping—killing all of her Secret Service detail in the process, without hurting her—would certainly take extensive measures to ensure their important captive couldn't escape or be easily rescued. A security camera in the corner of the windowless room kept constant tabs on her except when she was in the adjoining bathroom.

She had spent many long hours trying to surmise who was behind the plot. Only one of her minders—Cleanshaven—spoke to her, and he had a trace of an accent, though she couldn't be sure what it was. East Bloc, maybe Slovak or Russian. He was always extremely polite and respectful, but he answered with as few words as possible, and only then to benign queries. If she asked for something to drink, he'd reply, "What would you like?" but would ignore completely any questions related to where she was, who was holding her, how long she would be here, or what they wanted. He'd simply shaken his head when offered money to help her escape and shrugged when she asked why they'd taken her wedding ring.

The food they provided her, like her accommodations, was high quality. This morning's eggs Benedict had been accompanied by a fruit medley, fresh-squeezed orange juice, and cappuccino. Most likely it came from restaurants, or else they had a top-notch chef in their employ. Somehow they seemed to already know a lot of her favorite foods, though Cleanshaven had told her not to hesitate to ask for anything in particular she might want. Despite the excellent menu, she rarely ate much, too distraught and preoccupied by her confinement.

Aside from that, she was probably one of the best-treated prisoners in history, but she couldn't care less about the fancy food, comfy bed, and wide assortment of *New York Times* bestsellers they provided her to occupy her time. She wanted to know what the hell was going on in the outside world. Was the vice president continuing business as usual, or had everything come to a virtual standstill with her kidnapping? Had her captors made their demands? Did they leave any clues to help authorities find her?

Though uncertain exactly how much time had elapsed—they had knocked her out after getting her out of the elevator and she'd woken up here—she surmised from the meals they'd given her that she'd been missing for at least three days or so. She was growing more pessimistic with each passing minute. Her kidnapper's demands must be unreasonable ones for it to be taking so long to free or find her. Like many previous presidents, she held to the dictum that America didn't negotiate with terrorists and had said so to the world in her inaugural address.

If her vice president agreed, and if the nation's top law-enforcement officials were unable to discover her whereabouts, what would happen to her?

The White House

Ryden looked out her bedroom window at the preparations taking place on the South Lawn. So far, her public appearances had been contained to small venues. Today, she'd have to perform in front of some twenty-five thousand people, who all wanted to get a good look at the president to shake her hand or have their picture taken with her. Ratman had told her that Elizabeth Thomas's family would be there, too.

She felt nauseous at the thought of having to see them. Surely a family member couldn't be fooled, definitely not one as close to Thomas as her sister. She'd been nervous enough just telephoning Nancy after the assassination attempt to assure her she was all right. Nancy had wanted to chat and hear a full report of what had happened, but Ryden was able to cut the discussion short with excuses that too much of importance was demanding her immediate attention. She'd promised to call back another time for a lengthier visit but had yet to follow up.

What if Nancy or her other family realized she wasn't Elizabeth? Ryden had visions of someone pointing at her and screaming, like they did in *Invasion of the Body Snatchers*. Would she have time to run and escape, or would she be shot down on the spot? The lawyer had said that if she told anyone or tried to insinuate something publicly or otherwise, she'd be terminated…but what if she was discovered or suspected against her will? Would they still shoot her down?

She had no doubt they would. She suspected they'd make it look like a public attack on the president, though they'd have to replace her body at the morgue with that of the real president because certainly an autopsy would be done, as with JFK. She would leave this world as silently and unwanted as she'd entered it, and perhaps she'd be sealing Elizabeth Thomas's fate as well—if she was even still alive. Her only hope in the event she was exposed was to run—find a way to get out and keep running, but this new guard dog Kennedy, her primary, would make it even more difficult.

She looked at herself in the mirror. Maybe she was just being paranoid. With the surgeries and other improvements, even she couldn't tell the difference between them now. Ryden Wagner had disappeared somewhere under Elizabeth Thomas, and the only inconsistency was well hidden under her clothes: a birthmark on her lower back that they couldn't laser away like they had other moles and freckles, but fortunately a difference only Thomas's deceased husband could have caught.

Ryden jumped when she heard a knock. "Yes?"

"Madam President, it's Kennedy. I'd like to review your schedule for today."

Damn, this woman wouldn't leave her alone. "Just a minute, please." Ryden threw a robe over her nightgown, hurriedly put in her contacts, and opened the door. "Come in."

Shield forced herself not to stare at the president's disheveled hair and face still devoid of makeup. She'd always considered Thomas a striking, proud-looking woman, but only now did she realize how attractive she really was. Without the in-house stylist's coiffure and perfect cosmetics, she was even more Harper's type—a natural beauty.

The president sat at her vanity table and looked at her through the mirror as she ran a brush through her hair. When Shield didn't immediately elaborate on why she was there, Thomas got up and faced her. "Well?"

Shield looked down at her folder but remained at the door. "Today…the Find Your Sport event."

Thomas walked to the window. "Oh, that's today?" She looked outside. "And I've been wondering all morning what a beach-volleyball court and temporary soccer field are doing out on the lawn."

Turning back to Shield, she said wryly, "I see why you come highly recommended."

Oh boy, this is not going to be easy. Thomas clearly did not relish having her as her bodyguard.

"I was about to say, should you want to depart the festivities for any reason, please refrain from doing so on your own. Thousands of people will be here today, and although every single one of them will have been scanned and checked, we can never be too safe."

"Is that all?"

"Yes."

"Then we're done."

Shield started to leave but hesitated at the door. "Madam President..." She turned to look at her. "My abilities to guard you are not compromised because of my gender."

"That's wonderful," Thomas replied flippantly as she removed her robe and tossed it on the bed.

Shield quickly averted her eyes but not before she got a good look at Thomas's rather sheer, cream-colored nightgown, trimmed in lace, which allowed a far-too-revealing view of the slender figure beneath. This woman was not only frustrating but also distracting as hell. "Is your dislike personal?" Joe had told her back in Greece that the president was distant, but he hadn't said she treated him with cold indifference, and the expression on the woman's face in Greece was anything but cold.

"Men are less chatty. Are you usually this talkative with your subjects?"

"No, Madam President." For someone who advocated gender equal rights, Thomas was doing a miserable job at setting an example. "If you have any doubts, however, I'm sure my boss can have me replaced." Shield wanted to tell her to go to hell. She'd worked too long and too hard and had put her life on the line more than a few times to protect self-proclaimed important people to have to put up with this ungrateful woman.

"This boss of yours," Thomas said, her voice edged with contempt, "who would he replace you with? A mute, perhaps?"

"I..." Shield was getting very close to not giving a damn about whether this woman lived or died, but she did care about what Pierce would say if she walked. She'd given an oath to do her job to the best of her abilities. She forced a smile. "Have a good morning, Madam President," she finally said, and left.

She went back to her own room and had to force herself not to slam the door. *Great. Another snobbish bitch.* Although she'd studied the White House and its environs through maps on her way to Washington, she had been up most of the night while a guard from the Uniformed Division stood outside the president's door. She wanted to familiarize herself with the grounds and all possible exits, as well as everything planned for the next day. As a result, she hadn't gotten more than two hours' sleep, and that, combined with Thomas's attitude, was really making her cranky. Shield just wanted to get on the first plane to Tuscany and never leave Italy again.

She paced, listening for sounds from the other room indicating the president was nearing departure, and an hour later, her phone rang.

Thomas was short and to the point. "I'm ready."

CHAPTER NINE

Inspired by Team USA's #1 showing at the 2012 London Olympic Games, Elizabeth Thomas had made Find Your Sport the theme for her version of the Democratic initiative to solve childhood obesity within a generation, following in the footsteps of the Obama Let's Move campaign. A host of Dream Team medal-winning athletes would be on hand to participate in interactive sessions with the kids, designed to help them discover sports and activities that would motivate them to lead more active lives. Ryden hoped that having Michael Phelps, Gabby Douglas, and Missy Franklin here, in addition to many other favorites, would take some of the attention off her.

The thousands of children and parents who'd been invited all had to pass through even more extensive screening than usual because of the assassination attempt. In the last administration, the First Lady had spearheaded the day's fitness festivities, but since Thomas's husband had recently passed away, it was up to Ryden to make up for the absence of a First Spouse. That meant she would have to rotate among all the activities to mingle with the visitors. Her schedule had been cleared of everything else for the rest of the day.

She stood behind the closed door that would take her out to the crowd, with just Harper Kennedy in the room with her. Considering that scores of media representatives and Thomas's family would attend, it would certainly be her biggest challenge to date. Ryden took deep breaths to steady her rapid breathing, but that didn't help calm her nerves. *You're going to do fine*, she kept telling herself. *Just remember your training. No one will...*

She suddenly felt a little light-headed, but even as that fact registered in a slight blur of focus, she felt a sturdy mass against her back and a steadying arm around her waist.

"Are you all right, Madam President?"

"I...I think so." Ryden blinked hard. "What happened?"

"You almost passed out."

Ryden remained against Kennedy's body, still too shaky to move. "I didn't touch my breakfast," she lied. "Not very wise."

"Maybe you should sit down." Kennedy helped her to an armchair. "Get the president a glass of orange juice," she said into the communications device in her sleeve.

Very soon, a sweet middle-aged woman named Betty, one of several domestics who attended the chief executive, came through the door with a full glass. "Is Madam President not well?" she asked.

"A dizzy spell, that's all." Ryden's head was clearer now, but her hands still shook.

Ratman barged into the room. "What's going on?"

"The president is unwell," Betty replied.

"I don't remember asking you," he said sharply. "Please, return to your duties."

"Of course." Betty hurriedly left.

"What's wrong?" he asked Ryden.

"I got dizzy. It's nothing serious."

"Good. It would be…disappointing to stand all these people up." He shot her a warning glance.

If her hands were shaking before, they were almost out of control now. She had to do something before Ratman and his watchdog considered her incompetent. "I'm much better now." She got up and Kennedy rushed to her side. "I'm fine, Ms. Kennedy. No need to fuss over me."

Ryden went to the door, took another deep breath, and walked out to meet the thousands waiting outside. As soon as she emerged and stepped toward the microphone, the noisy crowd quieted. Except for some of the children, all eyes were on her.

Shield stayed very close to the president while remaining out of her way as Thomas kicked off the first two events, lacing up sneakers for a brief run with Allyson Felix, then shedding her footwear entirely for a little beach volleyball with Misty May-Treanor and Kerri Walsh. In keeping with the theme and informal dress code for the day, Thomas had opted for designer activewear, but Shield didn't want to blend in. In her dark suit and sunglasses, she wanted to make it clear to anyone watching that Elizabeth Thomas was being well guarded.

The president had transformed herself into her smiling public persona the instant she greeted the crowd, leaving any trace of worry or nervousness at the door. Shield could understand the dizziness having been due to low blood sugar, though she seemed fine now. However, the chief executive's rattled nerves really puzzled her. Thomas was a veteran at national politics and this event was far less demanding than her other duties, yet her hands had been shaking so badly, Shield thought they might come loose.

And the shaking had intensified when Kenneth Moore walked in. And although he seemed genuinely concerned about Thomas's well-being, something about his attitude and close scrutiny of the president didn't make sense. Even now, he constantly stood a few feet away from Thomas and at all times was within earshot. Was this extreme behavior toward her because of the attempt on her life? That, combined with the loss of her husband, could be why he was so watchful of her. Shield knew presidents usually got close to their private advisors and vice versa, so maybe he was being overly protective because of her probable fragile state.

As if on cue, Moore approached Thomas and whispered something in her ear. The president smiled and waved across the lawn to a woman Shield recognized as Thomas's sister, Nancy Payton. Nancy waved back enthusiastically and, with her husband, son, daughter, and family dog—a German shepherd mix—made her way toward Thomas.

Shield followed the president as she headed to meet them. She stood a few feet away as Nancy wrapped her arms around Thomas and kissed her on the cheek. The rest of the family took turns doing the same, and the young children jumped up and down, excited to try out some of the activities.

"How you doing, Peanut?" Nancy asked, her expression one of sisterly concern. "I can't stop thinking about the attack."

Thomas seemed to be considering how to answer when the little boy grabbed her hand.

"Did Michael Phelps bring his medals? I want to see them," he begged.

Thomas smiled and put her hand on her nephew's shoulder. "Yes, he did. And I bet he'll even let you hold them."

"Hey, you never said hi to Toby," the little girl said excitedly.

Thomas looked down at the dog and bent over. "Hey there, buddy." The dog sniffed the air. "What, no hello for me?" Thomas took a step closer, and the dog growled, then barked a warning.

Shield intervened immediately by putting herself between the president and the dog.

"Toby only barks when strangers try to pet him," the boy said. "He's never barked at you before, Auntie."

"Maybe he's just nervous from all the activity," Nancy said. "Why don't you take him for a walk, guys, and let him get familiar with the surroundings?"

Thomas kept smiling. "Poor thing," she said, her eyes still on the dog. "Go have fun, Toby."

The dog turned around at his name and started to growl again. The boy pulled him back. "Bad dog." He headed away with the animal, his sister close behind, toward a cordoned-off area nearby to watch Kayla Harrison in a judo demonstration.

"I don't know what got into him. He's gaga about you," Nancy said.

Moore stepped in. "Like you said, just too much going on for him. We might have to lock him up."

Thomas turned to her special advisor. "That won't be necessary. He's harmless."

"That may be so, but that scene got people's attention," Moore insisted.

"I said, that won't be necessary."

Shield noticed the subtle shaking of Thomas's hands just before she clasped them behind her back. Thomas turned to Nancy and her husband and smiled. "Come on, guys, let me show you around."

Shield stayed alert behind them as the president walked the couple through the tourist route, showing them the grounds and where all the activities of the day were scheduled, but she couldn't stop thinking about what had happened with the dog. She'd been around canines ever since she moved to Italy and had never witnessed anything like that before. Her own dogs were her friends, as well as her property guards. They would get aggressive only when on guard and nervous only if a stranger approached—never a friend or someone they'd met before.

Shield stared at the president, who was walking a few steps ahead. Thomas's sister and brother-in-law were completely engaged in the tour and the little facts Thomas was telling them, mostly nonspecific information readily available on the Internet. Maybe she wasn't allowed to share anything less generic, even if it was to family.

Moore generally walked beside Thomas, looking very alert. But when the president and her family stopped to chat in the still-dormant Rose Garden, he waited off to one side, near Shield.

"There's plenty of security," Shield told him. "She's in good hands."

"I'm sure she is. What happened at the fund-raiser was organized.

Whoever was behind it knew what they were doing."

"A terrorist's cunning or expertise doesn't exclusively reflect someone else's incompetence. Very often, their ability to succeed hinges on having knowledgeable individuals to help them."

"What do you mean?" he asked.

"I mean, I hope the ongoing investigation leads to some satisfying answers."

"Such as?"

"Per fas et nefas," she replied.

Moore translated from the Latin. "In good and bad things."

She nodded. "In other words, by any means necessary."

"So?"

"The organization I work for trains us to believe the cause justifies the means."

Moore looked at her. "And?"

"I suspect whoever helped the attackers is an insider, who believes in someone else's reasons or has his or her own for doing so."

Moore cleared his throat. "That's a heavy accusation."

"Are you surprised?"

Moore hesitated before he answered. "I guess not, but it's a damn disturbing theory."

"I don't think it's a theory," Shield said. "That's why I don't intend to let her out of my sight."

Near Colorado Springs, Colorado

Jack unfolded the stub and dialed Yuri's Dratshev's number from a phone booth. She had stopped using disposable cells since her last job and didn't intend to get one now just to hear out the mob boss.

The Russian picked up. *"Da."*

"It's Jack."

"Good. You got my message yesterday." He sounded almost relieved.

"I got it last week."

"No, that was another job, for other reason."

"I haven't looked for another message since," she said.

"I tried to reach you again."

Anyone who'd used her in the past was rarely persistent. If Jack didn't get back to them within a couple of days, they'd assume she was unavailable either because she had another job or because she was dead or arrested. Dratshev, on the other hand, would keep trying to contact her until the cleaners was out of stubs. He'd always had a lot of respect for her ability to do any kind of work without complications.

"Two jobs in one week? Business is either going really well or really bad."

"Business is business. Sometimes I win, sometimes I lose." Dratshev wasn't his usual self. Annoying and crude as the guy was, he was always in a good mood.

"I bet some new laws have thrown a wrench in your plans."

Dratshev was silent. "I don't plan to buy a ranch," he finally said.

Jack almost laughed. "I mean, someone is making problems for the metal business." That was the term Dratshev used when referring to the weapons trade.

"Ah. *Da*, that *suka*." Dratshev hesitated before adding, "Fuck her. She will change her mind if she wants money to invest in her America. I have other merchandise until then." The mob boss wasn't getting to the point and didn't seem eager to talk about what was on his mind.

"Okay. Well, anyway," Jack said, "I'm calling to let you know you have to stop asking for me."

"Why, we are friends, no?"

"No. But that aside, I'm retired."

"You mean—"

"I mean I don't work anymore."

"But for me you make exception."

"Not for you or anyone."

Dratshev sighed. "Just one more?" He sounded desperate, and the words *big money* hadn't even come up.

"What's up?"

"A friend wants to meet you."

"Why?"

"I don't know. She wants to talk to you, not me."

"She?" It was rare to have a woman in this business.

"Da."

"How does she know me?"

"I don't know, but she knows I know you," Dratshev said.

"Who is it?"

"Someone with big money and…big power."

So, someone else was the one with big money this time. "An associate of yours?"

"*Da*. We have business in common."

"Tell her no."

"I can't. She doesn't like that word."

"Tell her I'm dead."

"She knows you are alive."

"Who the hell is she?" Jack was getting irritated.

"Her name is TQ. They call her the Broker."

"I don't know any TQ." Jack's heart was pumping so hard she could see her shirt move. "But what the hell, one last job for big money can't harm. Give me her number."

"No number," Dratshev replied. "She calls me."

Just then, Cassady came out of the department store and waved at Jack when she saw her in the booth.

"Listen, tell your associate I'll talk to her," Jack told Dratshev. "I'll call you back tomorrow."

"Jack, this woman, she—"

"She what?"

"I have never met her, but she is very scary."

"Thanks for the heads-up," Jack said hastily, and hung up.

Cassady had just reached her when she stepped out of the booth.

"Who was that, hon?" Cassady asked.

"Someone left me a message at the cleaners. I wanted to see what it was about."

Cass frowned. "Are you kidding me? We agreed you'd never contact these people again."

"I know this guy. He's the one who hired me for Owens."

"Dratshev."

"I wanted to tell him I'm retired and no longer available."

"Christ, Jack, you promised." Cassady shook her head in disbelief as her posture went rigid. "No contact."

"Relax, babe. I told you, it's no big deal. Do you really think there's a chance in hell I'll get involved in all that again?"

"I just don't see why it was important for you to contact the Russian scumbag."

"Because, he'd just keep trying to find me." Jack put her arm around Cass's shoulders and squeezed. "Forget it, baby. It's all taken care of." She kissed Cass on the mouth. "So, what did you buy for the concert?"

CHAPTER TEN

The White House

Ryden's long day hosting the Find Your Sport event had jangled her nerves until she was ready to scream. Ratman, too, had seemed nervous the whole time, particularly during the period in which she'd entertained Thomas's sister and family. Her schedule had called for an after-event private visit with them over dinner, but Ratman had abruptly canceled it, announcing that an urgent matter had come up that demanded the president's immediate attention. As it turned out, there was no such crisis. Moore obviously just wanted the family to leave, fearing Ryden would slip up or have too much of their attention once away from the festivities.

So far, it was the one single decision he'd made that she agreed with. Nothing had drained her more since the beginning of this charade than having to be around the Paytons. She had studied the family's history, but no amount of studying could prepare her for the idiosyncrasies of close relatives, particularly siblings. What were Thomas's giveaways— the nuances of behavior and speech that only those she let her guard down with would recognize? And how could they possibly prepare her to respond to memories shared only between the two sisters?

Ryden had noticed Nancy's gaze on her more than a few times, and it had thrown her completely off her game when Nancy had referred to her as Peanut. She'd never had siblings, but she'd been in foster homes enough to know that sisters and brothers often gave each other nicknames. It had been obvious that Nancy had expected her to react accordingly, probably by calling her by her own nickname. Instead, Ryden had smiled and pretended to be distracted by her nephew's enthusiasm about the festivities.

Finally alone in her bedroom, with Ratman nowhere in sight and his guard dog Kennedy ensconced in her own room, she had begun to relax a little. She lay on the bed, breathing deeply, until she felt calm enough to let her mind wander away from today's events and into the realm of unpleasant possibilities of what they'd do to her if she couldn't pull this off. Would she have agreed to all of this had she known what they would require? She'd asked herself this very question too many times to count and had always come up with the same answer. Her fate would have been sealed had she declined. At least this way, she had a chance to stay alive.

She got up and walked to the window, too restless to sleep. What if she found a way to escape? Didn't they have tunnels under the White House that led to some obscure exit? She'd seen that in a movie somewhere. But those were probably guarded, too. Everything in this place was guarded. How about if she managed to slip away from Kennedy somehow during the next big conference somewhere and disappeared? No, that wouldn't do either; the whole world would be out looking for Elizabeth Thomas.

And calling the police was not an option. Who could she point to, and who would believe her instead of Ratman? Even after she proved she wasn't the real president, Ratman would deny ever having known otherwise. She'd still take the fall for killing the Laudens, not to mention facing new charges for being involved in whatever conspiracy and crimes against the president. She couldn't stop from dwelling on one disaster scenario after the other.

She paced the room, feeling claustrophobic. She sat down on the bed again, but the sensation of feeling trapped only intensified. She couldn't breathe. *God, I need some air. I need to get out of here.* She threw on her robe and opened the door. When she saw the way was clear, she ran down the corridor to the Yellow Oval Room, which gave her access to the massive Truman Balcony.

She felt as though someone had a death grip on her throat. She threw open the balcony doors and leaned over the rail, gasping for air, unmindful of the chill. She tried to calm herself by thinking of pleasant things—new candle designs and past vacations she'd taken—but soon her mind was on Ratman again and what he would do to her if she failed.

Shield came out of the shower, wrapped herself in the huge towel— complete with an embroidered presidential seal—and stepped into the bedroom. She'd hoped the hot water would relax her after the long, exhausting day with Thomas, but for a reason she couldn't grasp, she felt wired. In actuality, she'd felt so from the moment she stepped into the White House. The pressure of sitting the U.S. president, especially one who had been recently attacked, would explain that, but deep inside, she sensed it was more, though she didn't know why. Her instincts were never wrong, however; she suspected it would be only a matter of time before her restlessness was justified.

She was changing into her pajamas when she heard Thomas's phone ring. It kept ringing for what seemed forever. The president was clearly either in no mood to pick up—which was highly improbable considering her position—or she was unable to answer, a possibility if she was in the bathroom. Had Thomas stepped out for whatever reason, she knew to inform her bodyguard.

Shield retired to her bed fifteen minutes later, still not tired but knowing she should make the effort because the president's day started at six a.m. and she needed to be alert. It was already well after midnight. As she reached for the bedside light, the phone in the next room rang again. When no one picked it up, she grabbed her Glock from the drawer of her nightstand and went to the door that adjoined their rooms. Rapping sharply, she called out, "Madam President?" No one answered.

She turned the knob and walked into an empty room. When she checked the bathroom and found it empty as well, she bolted out of the room and into the corridor, where she stood still for a moment in the hope of catching movement or sound. Neither happened, but she did detect a small draft on her bare feet.

She ran down the hall and stopped in front of the door to the Yellow Oval Room, used primarily as a private meeting space or sitting room. The door, usually closed, was now slightly ajar. She knocked but didn't wait for a reply. Proceeding quickly inside, she found the doors to the Truman Balcony wide open, the curtains in a frenzied dance because of the breeze.

"Madam President," she said as she pushed the curtains aside to find Elizabeth Thomas leaning over the railing, grasping the rail. "Are you all right?"

When Thomas didn't reply, Shield went to stand beside her, the cold metal sending a shock through her body.

"I'm…fine." The president sounded out of breath, like she'd just run a marathon, and she was clearly using the rail for much-needed support.

Normally, Shield would have lectured her about taking off on her own, but right now Thomas looked like she could barely stand. Something was very wrong. "Should I call the doctor?"

Thomas spun around and looked at her like she'd said something crazy. The exterior security lights on the White House were bright enough for Shield to see that the president was unusually pale. "You can't call a doctor!" Thomas said, a little too loudly.

"With all due respect," Shield said, "you don't look well, and you almost passed out this morning."

"I'll be fine," Thomas insisted. "I'm just tired and…stressed. Besides, I really don't need the added attention." She looked at Shield's bare feet. "You're the one who's going to need a doctor."

Might the president have been drinking? "The in-house doctor is very discreet," she said.

Thomas gave her a quizzical look. "What are you saying?"

"That he won't share your…medical information or condition, and I definitely don't intend to tell anyone, either."

Thomas threw her hands up. "What…kind of place…is this?" Her breathing became labored again, and she looked on the verge of panic.

"Excuse me?"

Thomas turned her back to Shield and hung over the railing, clearly trying to catch her breath. "Just go away," she rasped.

"I can't do that, Madam President." Shield tried to conceal the clatter of her teeth. She was freezing in her light pajamas and bare feet.

"I don't need an audience."

"There's no shame in having a panic attack, Madam President. At least let me help you to your room before you catch pneumonia." When Shield put her hand on the chief executive's shoulder, Thomas jumped.

"Don't touch me."

"I'm sorry. I just want to help you."

Thomas turned to Shield and stumbled against her before regaining her footing. "Thank you, but all of you have given me more damn help than I can handle, so no thanks." She pushed past Shield and took a few steps into the Yellow Oval Room but stopped when she saw Kenneth Moore standing in the doorway to the corridor.

"I have been trying to call you. What's going on?" Moore sounded like a father who'd caught his daughter up after curfew. Shield didn't like the way he looked or talked to Thomas and didn't know why the president put up with it.

"Nothing is going on. I'm fine."

"Kennedy?" He looked to Shield for an answer.

"I escorted the president to get some fresh air."

"In your pajamas?"

Kennedy looked at her frozen feet, now burning from the change in temperature. "I like the cold."

Moore checked his watch. "At one in the morning?" He glared at Thomas.

The president looked away and Shield could see her hands had started to tremble again.

Something told her that Moore was the last person Thomas wanted to see right now. She clearly wasn't as close to him as Shield had assumed.

"Madam President, are you ready to go back in?" Shield asked.

"Yes. It is rather chilly, isn't it?" Thomas walked quickly past Moore into the hallway.

"Is something wrong with the president?" he asked Shield as she started after her.

"As far as I can tell, she just needed to unwind."

"Did she say anything?"

"No, sir."

"Nothing at all?"

"Like what?" Shield pretended ignorance. She wasn't about to tell him about the president's panic attack.

Moore looked at Shield closely for a long time. "I worry about her," he finally said when Shield didn't flinch or look away. "She hasn't been the same since the assassination attempt."

"I'm sure she'll feel a lot better once we find out who's responsible," Shield replied. "Now, excuse me. I have to get back to the president."

Ryden was about to shut the door to her bedroom when Kennedy appeared on the other side of the threshold.

"How do you feel, Madam President?" the bodyguard asked.

"Better, thank you." Ryden's hands had started to shake again at seeing Moore, so she jammed them in the pockets of her robe.

"Can I ask the doctor for something to help calm you down?"

"That's not necessary." Ryden had expected Kennedy to tell

Ratman she was unwell and that she'd run off without warning, but the guard dog had protected her instead. She wasn't sure why, but she did appreciate that much. "Where is Mr. Moore?"

"Down the hall. I didn't see him leave the Yellow Room."

Ryden opened the door farther. "Come in, please." Kennedy stepped inside and Ryden shut the door. "What did he ask you?"

"If something was the matter with you."

"What did you answer?"

"I didn't tell him that you seemed…unwell."

"Thank you."

"I realize it's a very stressful period for you," Kennedy said, "but I assure you, I will do everything in my power to make sure nothing happens to you."

"Until I finish my term," Ryden replied, not bothering to hide the sarcasm in her tone.

"If necessary, then yes."

"Then do me a favor."

"Of course."

Ryden had gotten sick and tired of people referring to her as who and what she was not. Every time they did, she became more aware of the lies, deceptions, and danger she was in. Kennedy knew better, anyway, and there was no reason to keep the show running when they were alone. "It's bad enough I need a permanent babysitter, but since I do, stop calling me Madam President when there's no one else around."

"That would be against protocol," Kennedy said calmly.

"I realize. But it would make my life here a little easier."

"Very well then, Mrs. Thomas."

Ryden let the sound of that name sink in for a few seconds. "Call me Elizabeth." She figured at least that name could belong to anyone, and she wouldn't necessarily have to associate it with the president.

Kennedy stood dead still as she studied Ryden intently for several seconds, the same way she had when they were first introduced. The bodyguard nodded. "As you wish…Elizabeth."

That does sound a lot better, Ryden thought, and realized her hands had stopped shaking. "That will be all for tonight."

Kennedy turned to go. "Sleep well," she said, and closed the door behind her.

❖

Shield tried to sleep but ended up tossing and turning most of the night. Something was up in the White House, something aside from the fact she was convinced an insider had cooperated with Thomas's attackers. Shield had no proof of the latter, but most organized attempts on a high-profile individual, especially a president, often involved internal assistance.

Thomas and her sidekick Moore presented a whole new dimension to the definition of high-strung. Most probably, the attack played a big part, but that didn't explain Thomas's trembling and apologetic behavior whenever Moore was around, as if she feared him. Nor did it explain Moore's almost threatening demeanor toward the president. At times, he acted as though he owned Thomas, and he was never out of earshot whenever the president made an appearance, even when she was with her family.

Elizabeth Thomas herself was another kind of peculiar. She didn't seem happy about having around-the-clock protection and seemed to dislike Shield, but on the other hand had asked to be called by her first name. According to Joe, the president's ex-bodyguard, Thomas never so much as acknowledged her Secret Service agents, let alone ask them to call her by her first name.

What was going on? It was an irrational thought, but could Moore possibly *have* something on the president? What could Thomas have to fear from the aide who'd been with her for years? The two were clearly both involved in something, but what?

And why were they doing such a miserable job at keeping to protocol? Shield had guarded presidents before, both national and international, and so far, the relationship between president and advisor had ranged from basic courtesy to close friendship. Under no circumstances was the president submissive to an advisor, not unless...

Shield jumped up off the bed. Unless Thomas wasn't interested in protection because she didn't fear a repeat. And that would only be because there was no actual danger. The only threat she felt was from Moore. *Because he knows what happened or didn't happen the day of the attack.* Could it be that, for some reason, Thomas had helped stage a fake attack? If so, then for what gain?

The CIA was very capable of orchestrating anything, from an assassination attack, to suicide, to homicide. If any of her suspicions were true and the Agency had helped the president, then she was probably in danger as well. The CIA was one entity very few ever messed with.

She went into the bathroom and shut the door. At this point, she didn't put it past them to tap her room and every other room in the White House. Shield turned on the shower and pulled out her secured cell phone. "Shield 29041971."

"How can I help you?" the male voice replied.

"Put me through to Pierce."

He came on the line a short time later, sounding very alert, though by her watch it was after two a.m. in Colorado. "Go ahead."

"I have reasons to believe Lighthouse and her special advisor know something about the attack."

"Explain."

Shield told him about the president's behavior and Moore's attitude toward her.

"I see what you mean," Pierce said, "but what would they have to gain?"

"That's what I haven't figured out."

"I'll have Reno look into their records, but you realize everything is highly classified."

"I'm sure that's the case where Lighthouse is concerned, but if we can find anything on…Watchdog, we might be able to determine what they're involved in."

"Watchdog it is," Pierce said, agreeing to the communications name for Moore. "And he's definitely easier to trace."

"That's right."

"Roger that." After a brief pause, Pierce said, "You do realize the Agency has toes we don't necessarily want to step on."

"The same way we don't want them stepping on ours. What happens if it turns out they're involved?"

"We follow the unwritten protocol."

"We walk away."

"Correct."

"Let me know ASAP."

"Keep me updated," Pierce said. "And don't act on anything unless I okay it."

"I know how they play," Shield replied, referring to the CIA. "I'm not about to get myself *accidentally* killed."

CHAPTER ELEVEN

Aboard Air Force One on approach to Ottawa International Airport
Next evening, February 28

Ryden glanced out the window at the Canadian capital coming into view below. Once the White House stylist had put a few finishing touches on her hair and makeup, she'd asked for a few moments alone before they landed to prepare for tonight's dinner. Everyone had readily departed the private office area of the plane except Moore. Kennedy wanted to stay as well, but Ratman had insisted he needed to discuss confidential matters with the president, so she waited just outside the door.

Mimicking Elizabeth Thomas presented one daunting challenge after another. Ryden wanted the moment alone to calm her nerves, and Moore was anything but helpful in that regard. Yet she was almost glad he'd stayed, because she was worried as hell about her first public appearance out of the country, even if it lasted only a few hours, and could benefit from any last-minute advice. He'd spent hours briefing her that morning, but she still wasn't confident she could match Thomas's off-the-cuff eloquence at a formal state event.

The Canadian prime minister had invited her and a few key congressional leaders to a lavish reception and dinner to break the ice for future dealings with the new U.S. leadership. Nothing of real import would be discussed in detail, but the venue was perfect for the unexpected to happen. There was no way to brief her on every matter that might come up.

Ratman kept his voice low. "Are you clear on who is sitting next to you and what topics to broach and which to avoid?"

"Crystal. But what happens with any questions I'm not equipped to answer?" she asked.

"Throw them a generality, insinuating you're not willing to talk about the subject," he replied. "They're all very susceptible to that approach because they all practice it."

Ryden made it through the cocktail reception without encountering any missteps that might indicate she wasn't the real U.S. chief executive. It helped that she kept circulating among the crowd, keeping largely to inane pleasantries, with Ratman at her side to whisper in her ear if needed.

The state dinner that followed in the ballroom of Rideau Hall was more difficult because Moore was seated several tables away and she was trapped beside the prime minister, who wanted specifics, not small talk. The governor-general of Canada was on her other side, and he, too, didn't seem content with generalities.

"I was under the impression this was to be a get-acquainted dinner," she told the two men with a wry smile, "not an inquisition about my future plans." She hoped her joking but reproachful demeanor would forestall further questioning, but neither took the hint. They merely laughed and continued pressing her on this or that issue until she was counting the minutes until the evening ended. Her answers had been short and aligned with Thomas's agenda.

She was so nervous she had to stop to think at one point which fork to use, though she'd mastered the art of table etiquette with Tonya. And the intense scrutiny made her mistakenly glance at the wrong wrist when she started to check the time, though she thought she covered the blunder well.

Two hours into the event, she needed a break to breathe and calm her nerves, so she excused herself and headed toward the ladies' room.

Shield wasn't standing guard close enough to hear what was being said between the dignitaries at the state dinner, but she did have a clear view of everyone at the table. In addition to Thomas, a dozen key U.S. senators and members of Congress had made the trip, though the entire Canadian contingent—fifteen in all—seemed to be interested only in the new U.S. president. During the cocktail reception, each of the Canadian leaders had tried to extend their one-on-one time with Thomas, but Kenneth Moore, always at her side, kept her circulating through the crowd. Moore's perpetual alertness was even more apparent than usual tonight, especially when one of the hosting dignitaries appeared to be pressing Thomas with questions.

The president appeared to be calm, smiling now and then, but a bit less relaxed when the reception gave way to the formal dinner. Just like she had done when Shield had first seen her in Greece, Thomas would occasionally play with her wedding ring while she mulled the answer to a question. Shield guessed the president had lost a bit of weight, since the ring seemed loose on her finger.

Most of the Canadian bodyguards and U.S. Secret Service present were assigned to specific posts. As the president's primary, however, Shield was free to walk around as she saw fit, so now and then she would change position. She went from standing against the wall behind Thomas to another discreet location where she faced the president. Here, she had a very clear view of Thomas's gestures and reactions and, after a few minutes' observation, was now more concerned with those rather than any danger. Shield couldn't discount the possibility of another assassination attempt, or that she might be wrong concerning the previous attack, but the more time she spent around Thomas and Moore, the more convinced she was that they were involved in something nefarious.

Though she kept her attention primarily on her subject, Shield also remained attuned to everyone else in the room, alert to anything unusual. She noticed that one of the waitresses, a very cute young blonde, kept glancing in her direction. At first, Shield thought it was the girl's fascination with all the security, but when the woman smiled shyly at her, and her stare became more intense, as if trying to get her attention, Shield realized she was being flirted with. She ignored the girl but kept an eye on her in her peripheral vision, so she was surprised when Thomas pointedly looked from the waitress to her. Shield stared right back, unflinching, until the president looked away.

After an uneventful hour and a half had gone by, the president discreetly looked down at her bare left wrist. She let half a minute pass before she looked down at her right hand, where her watch was. *Strange*, Shield thought, but then again, so was everything about this mission.

Half an hour later, Thomas got up, and her massive Secret Service contingent followed. Shield approached the president and followed her out to the foyer while the other ten bodyguards cleared the way.

Thomas paused for a moment and looked around.

"Can I help?" Shield asked.

"No, I found what I was looking for," the president replied as she headed toward the ladies' room. "I won't be a minute."

Shield didn't say anything but followed her.

"That's really not necessary," Thomas said when she intercepted her at the door.

"I'm sure you're right." Shield tried not to sound sarcastic. "But it's my job." She checked the outer lounge/powder room and interior stalls while Thomas stood at the door. Although security had already checked everything far in advance and again during the evening's festivities, she secured the rooms once more and motioned for the president to enter.

Thomas took a seat in the lounge before one of the mirrors and opened her purse. "I'm certain you have better things to be doing than check bathrooms," she said before touching up her lipstick.

"You're right, I do." Shield stood a few feet behind her, studying the president's face in the mirror. "But like I said, it's my job."

"And yet, for someone so concerned about protecting me, you seem to find time to enjoy yourself in the process."

"Excuse me?"

Thomas looked at her in the mirror. "Please refrain from unprofessional behavior in my presence, and save it for the bars."

"Unpro…" Shield lowered her voice. "I don't understand."

"I said you could call me by my first name in private," the president said. "I didn't say you were free to pick up women on the job."

Where the hell had that come from? Shield was a professional at all times while working; she'd barely even glanced at the waitress. She was about to fire back with something caustic but stopped. The Secret Service contingent was just outside and she was wearing a communications device, so the other agents might already have heard the whole conversation. Shield had a name in her field and wasn't about to mar it because Thomas was looking for reasons to fire her.

None of this was making sense. One moment, the president wanted them on a first-name basis, and the next she was trying to pick a fight. Did Thomas have regrets about how open she'd been with Shield the other night? Was she afraid she might have insinuated something incriminating, or did she regret having shown how afraid she was of Moore?

Shield looked at the president and smiled. "My apologies, Madam President." She went back out into the foyer and shut the door behind her.

Ryden stared at the mirror. She looked as infuriated as she felt, more with herself than anyone. She had no idea where all that had come from, especially since her bodyguard hadn't done anything wrong. Though Kennedy might be Ratman's guard dog, so far she had been polite and discreet. She'd even lied for her to Moore.

Kennedy, however, unnerved and unsettled her; the way her bodyguard scrutinized her every move made her feel transparent. That scared her in a way even Ratman didn't. Kennedy's steel-blue stare seemed to see inside the real *her*—Ryden the florist and candle maker, the insecure, repressed, and distant orphan who'd come to fear affection, not the blackmailed and threatened look-alike liar she was now. That possibility frightened her more than the dangerous web of deception she was trapped in.

She had spent the last forty years surviving, not living. Too afraid to get close to anyone, she'd known foster kids couldn't afford the luxury of love or attachment, so she'd learned to make herself invisible in order to be accepted or at least tolerated. That way, one of the foster families would let her stay and include her in their life, and maybe someone, someday, would care enough to even love her. That day never came.

When she'd turned eighteen, she was free to be where and with whomever she chose. But freedom meant nothing because she'd become too afraid to fully live.

Ryden looked up at the mirror. She'd been so lost in thought she hadn't realized she'd been crying until she saw the smudged mascara. Maybe this time when she was freed from this new hell and received a new identity and fresh start, she'd find the strength to live.

She wiped her eyes and straightened her skirt and blazer before opening the door. Kennedy, standing just outside, turned to look at her, but Ryden stared straight ahead. She just didn't have the strength to face those soul-searching eyes. Without a further word to her bodyguard, she returned to the dinner.

Soon the evening finally came to a close, and the White House retinue returned to Air Force One. Ratman once again secluded himself alone with her in the office of the plane, leaving the bodyguard outside.

"You did well tonight, as far as I could tell," he said. "Any complications during dinner?"

"No," she said hastily. "My dinner companions kept pressing for more specifics about future trade and the European economic crisis, but I stuck to what you told me."

He withdrew a piece of paper from his pocket as he nodded approvingly. "I have a slight addition to your schedule tomorrow." Handing the typed sheet to her, he said, "I need you to make a phone call in the morning precisely at nine a.m. Your schedule is free then. I'll have a special cell phone for you to use, and I'll be listening in to feed you anything further you need to say."

Ryden glanced down and read the lines. At least one of the reasons for all the intrigue involved in putting her in the White House became suddenly clearer.

CHAPTER TWELVE

Arlington, Virginia
Next morning, March 1

Senate Majority Leader Andrew Schuster smiled as he peered out the window of his tri-level Tudor mansion, watching his son Matthew chat excitedly with two of his neighborhood friends. Matt was no doubt regaling them with descriptions of their visit to Disneyland to celebrate his eighth birthday, one that neither of his parents had thought he'd see.

Three months ago, Matt had been near death, but the liver transplant had transformed him into an active, healthy kid with a bright future. Andrew still had moments of regret that he'd had to arrange a black-market deal to get his son moved up the waiting list and procure a matching organ, but only because an innocent man's life had been cut short to make it happen. He still asked himself repeatedly, would he have taken the deal with the Broker if he'd known the young donor would be killed to make it happen?

At least the truth had never come to light, which would have crippled his rising political career. As the Senate majority leader, he was one of the most powerful men in Washington and well positioned to make his own run for the presidency in eight years—four, if Elizabeth Thomas decided not to run for reelection.

Andrew sincerely liked Thomas and personally agreed with most of her announced legislative agenda, especially her controversial plan to combat the illegal-arms trade. The president wanted to create a whole new department within the ATF—Bureau of Alcohol, Tobacco, Firearms, and Explosives—to deal exclusively with the problem. The plan would provide the new department not only with ample resources and funding to do the job but also with legislative muscle to strengthen penalties for those who continued to deal in black-market weapons. Despite major opposition from the National Rifle Association and other pro-gun groups, the Democrats had regained narrow control of both houses of Congress, so the proposed plan should sail through without major obstacles.

The jangling of his office telephone interrupted his musings. The private line was unlisted—only key political figures had the number. "This is Andrew."

"Good morning, Senator Schuster. It's the president." Elizabeth Thomas's familiar Maine-tinged accent was immediately recognizable. "I hope I'm not interrupting something important."

"Of course I am always at your disposal, Madam President," Andrew replied warmly. "How may I be of service?"

"You'll be getting a phone call at this number in one hour from a mutual friend, regarding an upcoming change in my proposed congressional agenda regarding the illegal-arms trade," Thomas said cryptically. "I will continue to push the plan publicly, but I want you to take a leadership role in opposing it. In other words, I need you to reverse your position and ensure that the deal is killed in the Senate."

Andrew wasn't certain he was hearing right. What possible reason could the president have for asking her key congressional ally to oppose one of her primary objectives? "But, Madam President, you know how strongly I endorse this bill. We've spent months garnering the necessary support in both Houses to pass this important legislation." Not to mention, he thought, that he'd be committing political suicide. The Democratic National Committee would be all over his ass to support the president, and without them he had no chance of gaining higher office. Everyone would think the gun lobbies had bribed him.

"I'm not at liberty to discuss my reasons for asking you to do this, Andrew," Thomas said. "I realize I'm asking you to take the fall, as it were, for the reversal of my decision. But I hope I can count on your discreet support."

Andrew wasn't certain how to respond, with his own political ambitions at stake. "With all due respect, Madam President, even if I do as you ask, I'm not certain I can single-handedly kill this plan if you continue to push it. We've gained too much momentum to stop it."

"I'm sure you're underestimating your influence, Senator. Start working on the reasons why you've had a change of heart regarding the bill. I'll be holding a press conference soon on this issue, and I want you well prepared to oppose me."

Without waiting for a reply, the president disconnected.

Andrew paced for the next hour, waiting for the follow-up phone call, hoping it would better explain what was up with Thomas. He'd kissed a lot of asses and called in a lot of favors to engender support for the illegal-arms plan, and he was getting angrier by the minute at Thomas's unreasonable request, especially in light of his fervent support of her from the beginning of her presidential bid.

He'd just about decided to tell Thomas that he wouldn't be her fall guy when the phone rang again. Glancing at the clock, he confirmed that exactly an hour had passed since the president had hung up on him.

"This is Andrew."

"Good morning, Mr. Schuster. This is the Broker."

A chill went through him. This wasn't possible. The organ dealer who'd helped his son was the "mutual friend" he shared with President Thomas? "I'm listening."

"I presume you were anticipating my call?" the icy voice inquired.

"Yes and no. I hardly expected you to be on the other end."

"A man in your position should be well familiar with the real movers and shakers in Washington," the Broker replied.

"It is the extent of your influence that's surprising."

"Well, now you know, which should be reason enough to follow through on what the president asked you to do. If you comply, your political career might still be salvageable. I'd hate to have to leak to the media the story of why your son is alive and well today and able to play with his friends. And I'm sure you want to keep it that way. I have this nasty habit of being an Indian giver."

The clear threat to Matt instantly deflated every objection he'd worked up to disregard Thomas's bizarre request. "You can rest assured," he told the Broker, "that I'm now fully on board with whatever the president needs me to do."

"Excellent. I knew you'd see it my way."

Southwestern Colorado

Reno knocked on the door to Montgomery Pierce's office and got an immediate "Enter." Pierce had called him the first thing this morning to ask what he'd come up with via the computer searches that had kept him up most of the night. Reno understood Pierce's impatience at getting good intel for Harper Kennedy, since Shield suspected the

Agency could be involved in the assassination attempt. The CIA was one agency that even the EOO kept clear of—Reno was under strict instructions to never even attempt to hack into their database without prior clearance from Pierce himself. So far, that had never happened.

"What have you got?" Pierce said without preamble. "Shield checked in a little while ago and is due to call back in a couple of hours."

"As expected, it's been difficult to find anything significant about the president that wasn't in the file you already gave her," Reno replied. "Can't get access to Lighthouse's phone records, computer, anything of that sort. The Castle's security is impenetrable."

"And Watchdog?" Pierce asked.

"Better luck there. The guy earns two hundred and eighty grand a year, or thereabouts—the White House has to report all staff salaries. And his past earnings on tax returns averaged a hundred and fifty grand a year while Thomas was in the Senate. Yet the guy lives in a four-thousand-square-foot home and drives a Mercedes. They also have a country place in Vermont, and he and his wife frequent some of D.C.'s finest restaurants once or twice a week, according to his credit-card bills. It can't be family money either. Both he and his wife come from middle-class backgrounds."

Pierce sat up straighter. "So he's on the take with somebody, and for a while. Where's the money coming from?"

"He's pretty clever, this guy," Reno replied. "Has the usual D.C. area bank accounts, but aside from his government paycheck, many of his deposits show as cash—under ten thousand dollars each time, so it doesn't have to be reported, but usually close to the limit. And it gets better. He has a fairly new Grand Cayman account that's worth something in the neighborhood of two mil. I'm still trying to trace the origin of the money. No luck so far."

Pierce let out a low whistle. "Phone records?"

"The guy's landline and cell records don't show anything unusual. Certainly no calls to the Agency, just routine stuff you'd expect. Nothing stands out in the way of frequent contacts with any one individual or government department. Let me clarify that slightly as saying his *registered* cell doesn't turn up anything odd."

"Explain."

"His credit-card record showed he purchased a couple of cheap, prepaid cells at a Walmart in Maryland two months ago. His registered one is a BlackBerry."

"He doesn't strike me as the Walmart type, but maybe he got them for his kids or something."

"Possibly as gifts," Reno said. "Though his one son is grown and has a good job, and his wife already has an iPhone5."

"Anything else?"

Reno shook his head. "Nothing significant. No criminal record, aside from a DUI a couple years ago that was hushed up."

"I'll put out some feelers with my contacts in Defense, the Bureau, and Homeland Security. See if they have anything additional," Pierce said. "When Shield calls back, I'll transfer her to you."

"Roger that. Hope she's wrong about Agency involvement," Reno said as he got up to leave.

"Calling in favors from the CIA should really be a last resort," Pierce replied. "We need to exclude every other possibility before we do that. But we need to do it in a hurry because Shield is at risk until we know, and we don't want to spin our wheels only to find out the Agency will just cover it up again."

CHAPTER THIRTEEN

The White House
That evening

As Ryden ate her dinner in the private second-floor dining room across from her bedroom, she wondered why Kennedy—who'd been with her all day—had now been replaced by a Secret Service agent named Jason. She sat alone at the long table, two waiters catering to her, while he read a magazine from a chair by the door.

Tonight's fare included Caesar salad, beef bourguignonne, potatoes Florentine, and fresh asparagus with a balsamic reduction. She always ate until she was stuffed and included dessert with lunch and dinner, because her fast metabolism, combined with the stress she was under, burned up the calories with alarming speed. She'd already lost five pounds since she'd been here.

Ryden had never eaten a bigger variety of delicious meals. Betty always asked her in generic terms if she would prefer this or that—chicken or fish, potatoes or rice—but when the waiter served at dinnertime and announced the menu it was like listening to a foreign language. She'd never been to expensive restaurants, and although her crash course in French and culinary cuisine helped decipher some of the dishes, she still had no idea what to expect.

The same applied to the different wines they would present her with and expect her to choose from. As far as Ryden was concerned, they all tasted good, and since she really couldn't tell the difference, she usually left it up to the White House sommelier.

She liked to take her meals here. The view of the grounds was compelling, and she could shed Thomas's high heels and designer suits for more comfortable slippers and loungewear without fear of being seen by anyone but her servers and guards. But something was missing tonight. She'd gotten used to Kennedy's presence during dinner. The bodyguard would either stand or sit by the window and occasionally look outside. Although they rarely said anything, Ryden found comfort in her calm presence and silence. It wasn't until Kennedy became her shadow that she realized how tired she had grown of eating alone in her small apartment or in diners.

As a child, she would have dinner with whatever foster family she was placed with, which was her least favorite time of the day. Either her foster parents would find it the most appropriate time to argue, or the other foster kids would massacre each other over who got the larger serving. The only other person she had ever shared a meal with was Magda, during work in the back. She had found Magda's constant need to gossip about their customers tiring and only seldom amusing.

Even though Ratman had probably hired Kennedy, the bodyguard was the only one of the two of them who, despite the truth, still treated Ryden with respect. For some unknown reason, she felt safe when Kennedy was around, though vulnerable.

Kennedy had stayed at her post all day, but Ryden had seen little of her because she'd spent most of her time in closed-door meetings. She was sure Kennedy's absence now, when they would have been alone, had to do with the horrible way she'd treated her at the dinner event last night. Had Kennedy been allowed to quit? And if so, wasn't someone obliged to inform her of that fact? She looked at the male agent and cleared her throat.

"Yes, Madam President?" He immediately set aside his magazine and stood.

"What happened to Kennedy?" she asked nonchalantly.

"She'll resume her duties later tonight, Madam President."

"I see." Ryden felt relieved. "So, she's taking a break from me?"

Jason smiled. "Not from you, Madam President."

"Whom else?" Ryden smiled back. Why couldn't she let it go?

"I think she needed some private time."

"Oh? Is she all right?"

"Nothing serious, I suppose, since she's still in the House."

Ryden scooped up the last of her dessert—tiramisu this evening—and chewed slowly. Was Kennedy avoiding her until she was off to bed so she didn't have to face her? And if so, was she even allowed to? Sure, Ryden had snapped at her, but that was no excuse to forgo her duties and…ignore her. "Do you know where she is?"

The guard had remained standing. "I'm sorry, I don't, Madam President. I can find out in just a moment."

Ryden finished her wine and got up. "Don't bother. I'm going to retire early tonight."

Jason followed her toward the bedroom. She had just reached the door when she saw Kennedy walk out of the Yellow Oval Room farther down the corridor still wearing her trademark dark pantsuit and starched white shirt.

Shield had requested a time out for personal reasons without further explanation. She'd used the time to call the EOO for any news and to plant a listening device in Thomas's bedroom, using the adjoining door from her room while the president was eating dinner across the hall. She hadn't mentioned the eavesdropping to Pierce, but no risk was involved. Since she was the president's primary and the one responsible for the routine, weekly sweep of the room for bugs, the Secret Service wouldn't find the device by chance. She might, however, be able to overhear a private conversation between Thomas and Moore.

She'd eaten dinner then and was headed to her bedroom to get her cell for another call to Pierce, when she spotted the president leaving the private dining room.

"Does this mean you're on duty again?" Thomas asked her.

Shield was used to the cold, formal attitude of her subjects and even found it interesting when it came to attractive women, but Thomas had pushed all the wrong buttons when she'd accused her of playing on the job. Shield knew she had to be a professional and swallow her pride when it came to difficult and downright rude individuals, but nothing vexed her more than unfairness. That, combined with the fact that the EOO hadn't been able to offer any news yet in response to her inquiry, had put her in a less than pleasant mood. "Yes, it does, Madam President."

"Good, because I would like a word with you."

"Of course, Madam President." Shield looked at the other agent and nodded. Jason headed toward the stairway while she started down the hall toward the president.

Thomas met her halfway and gestured toward the room Shield had just come out of. "I don't see why we can't talk in there. Do you mind?"

"Not at all." Shield let the president go first into the Yellow Oval Room and shut the door behind them.

Thomas scanned the room and her gaze fell on Shield's meal tray. "I didn't know you were allowed to take your dinner in here."

"The perks of not being your average Secret Service."

Thomas approached the small table by the open balcony doors where Shield had sat and looked down at the bottle of wine. "They let you drink on duty?"

"You may have noticed I haven't opened the bottle."

"Then why is it here?"

"Because I felt the need to look at it since I can't be at home," Shield explained.

"I don't understand. You want to look at the bottle?"

"It reminds me of home and the job I love. I make my own wine."

"As in moonshine?"

"As in, I have my own company. A vineyard back home in Tuscany. It's quite a successful label."

Thomas picked up the bottle. "Il Grigio Angelo," she read. "They serve this here, although I haven't tried it yet." She sounded surprised.

"Here. In Europe. In every good restaurant."

"So, if you live in Tuscany, how did you end up in Washington?" Was Thomas going to get to the point of her request to see her, or were they going to talk about Shield's bio?

"The organization I work for—"

"The EOO."

"Yes, has us stationed all over the world. I usually baby... *guard*," Shield corrected herself, "European political dignitaries, and occasionally American ones. It depends on where I'm needed."

"Are you as good as they say?" the president asked.

"I must be, or I wouldn't be here."

"How does the wine fit into your life?"

"It's what I do when I'm not on a job."

Thomas sat down at the table, on the armchair opposite the one Shield had been in. "How did you decide to start a vineyard?" She sounded sincerely interested.

Shield sat down, too. "I started out by helping the owner—a friend. Eventually, I inherited the vineyard, improved the wine, and marketed it worldwide."

"I doubt you need this job, then."

"I don't. I do it because part of me *wants* to—even though I hate being taken away from my home—and part of me *has* to."

"Has to?"

"It's a long story, but let's just say I'm contracted to work for my employer indefinitely. In other words, until I'm no longer fit for my work."

"It must be difficult to leave your loved ones."

"Not really. I don't have any."

"I don't just mean a girlfriend," Thomas said.

"Why would you assume I had a girlfriend?"

"I...I simply meant I saw the way the waitress was looking at you."

Shield was glad for the opening. "About that. I never play on the job, and I have a strong disliking for being accused of something I didn't do."

"My apologies," Thomas said. "I never meant to offend you. I was tired and looking for someone to blame. I should never have reacted the way I did. It was uncalled for and unprofessional."

"I won't argue that."

"It's why I wanted to see you. I wanted to say I was sorry." The president was looking at her with an expression of sincere regret, a response Shield found uncharacteristic in light of her previous bodyguard's experience, but welcome nonetheless. Elizabeth Thomas continued to confound and surprise her.

"I appreciate that."

"I'm glad." Thomas smiled. "But what I meant earlier is that I assumed you prefer the same sex."

"How presumptuous. Is it because of my job?"

"I don't have to be a homosexual to have a gaydar. Am I wrong?"

Shield snickered at Thomas's use of the word *gaydar* and the president smiled. "No, you're not wrong. Is that going to be a problem?"

"Not at all. What you do in your spare time is none of my business."

"I'm glad," Shield repeated, and smiled, too.

"How about your family?" the president asked next. "Don't you miss them?"

"I don't have one. I was adopted by the organization when I was six." Shield rarely volunteered such information, but with Thomas, it didn't matter. The president certainly had a briefing file somewhere about the EOO, if she cared to read it.

Thomas looked at her intently, then averted her gaze. "That must have been rough."

"I guess...at times, anyway. I've never spent too much time

dwelling on what could or should have been."

"You've never wondered what it would have been like to have a family?"

"Sure, but I can't say I've ever missed it," Shield replied. "It's hard to long for something you've never experienced."

Thomas stared out the window toward the Washington Monument in the distance for a long while, seemingly lost in thought. In Shield's experience, people often felt sorry for you when you told them you were adopted, but Thomas instead looked hurt. "So, I assume you've never felt the need to look for them," the president finally said.

"Never. All I know is I was born and adopted in Melbourne, Australia."

The president raised an eyebrow. "An Aussie?"

"In blood, yes, but an Italian at heart."

"How was it growing up in an organization?"

"It's funny how that varies from kid to kid. Some love it, make friends and enjoy the constant playing and schooling and find it a home, and others...don't."

"And how about you?"

"I was one of those who didn't. I've never liked noise, and boy, there was a lot of that."

"Yes." Thomas sounded wistful. "I mean, kids seem to love screaming. My sister's kids do, anyway."

"Not me, and I was never very social. Spent a lot time on my own and out of other people's way. Kids welcomed me when I sought them out, but they never went out of their way to track me down. I think they found me a bit odd. Most adopted kids crave acceptance. I just looked forward to getting out and on with my life. I wanted to find my place in the world, not a family."

"Did you?"

"I did," Shield replied. "When I found Italy."

Thomas sighed. "It must be wonderful to know where you belong."

"You sound like you don't, when you appear to have everything."

"Appear being the key word."

"It's definitely not easy being you."

Thomas shook her head almost imperceptibly and let out a small laugh devoid of humor. "You have no idea."

"I don't even want to imagine having to live your life."

"This life, the one before. Trust me, you don't want to imagine either."

Rich political families could definitely come with drawbacks. Cold, ambitious parents more interested in grooming successors than in loving their child. But no one could have forced Thomas to become president. You needed to want and fight for that position wholeheartedly in order to obtain it, especially if you were the first female to hold the highest office in the world. But she couldn't argue that it came with a lot of sacrifices and potential dirty work. "I guess no one is ever really prepared for what's expected in your position, no matter how much they groom you for it."

The president looked away. "You can say that again. Sometimes I wish I had made different choices, but..." Thomas massaged her temples. "Well, what choice did I really have?"

"What is it you want?" Shield asked.

"I should say I want my life back, but I don't. I...I just want to live. For once, I want to be free of everything, including myself...who I was before all this."

Shield didn't know how to respond, so she didn't. If she hated anything, it was superficial sentiments and conventional comfort speeches. She wasn't about to tell Thomas her life wasn't so bad, because it clearly was, and who was Shield to tell her otherwise? She also wasn't about to tell Thomas things could get better because Shield couldn't know that, either. If she was right and the president had gotten to the point of having to fake an attack and get five people killed in the process, chances were things could only get a lot worse.

Judging from her panic attacks and almost tangible fear, Thomas had clearly been persuaded to do something she didn't want. Her statements tonight seemed to confirm that supposition. Shield was almost positive the president had to be *convinced* to go along with whatever was happening, because one sentiment was missing from her demeanor: guilt. But who could have so much power over the president of the United States?

They sat in comfortable silence for a while. Shield picked up the bottle of Il Grigio Angelo. "Would you do me the honor of trying my wine?" she asked Thomas. "Since I'm sure you're an excellent critic, your opinion is important to me."

"I don't know that I'm an expert and by no means a connoisseur."

Shield found it hard to believe that the president hadn't had her share of good wine, coming from a prominent family and considering all the formal dinners she'd no doubt attended as a senator. She was probably just downplaying her privileged background and being careful not to give the impression of a chief executive who enjoyed alcohol. "But you enjoy a glass now and then?"

"Very much."

"Will you try some?"

"I'd love to."

Shield uncorked the bottle and poured for the president.

"How about you?" Thomas asked.

"I'm on duty."

"I won't tell, and I'm sure just one won't compromise your ability to protect me."

Shield smiled. "It won't. But aside from that, we only have one wineglass and I'd rather not ask for another. It would draw attention, and I don't want that."

"Very well." Thomas lifted the goblet. "Cheers, then." She took a sip.

Odd, Shield thought. The president, because of her position, had to have been trained in the basics of wine. Yet Thomas had skipped swirling, sniffing, and allowing the burgundy liquid to permeate her palate before she swallowed. Maybe wine wasn't her thing, after all. Shield was disappointed. She didn't know why, but she wanted Thomas to like it. "What do you think?"

"It's heavenly." Thomas leaned back in the armchair with the goblet. "Truly delicious."

"Do you generally enjoy wine?"

"I know this will sound very wrong, but I really don't know much about it."

Shield laughed. "I can tell."

Thomas looked chagrined. "Uh-oh. That bad, huh?"

"May I?" Shield looked at the glass.

Thomas handed it over and Shield held it up to the setting sun. "This is a merlot."

"Okay."

"Can you describe the color?"

"Red."

"Red wine is produced from grapes that are not only red, but purple and blue as well. The many different varietals of red wine give it names like dark red, light red, almost black, maroon, deep violet, and burgundy. If you look at it again, how would you describe it?"

Thomas looked from her to the wine. She stared at it for a while and pursed her lips. "Maroon, almost black."

"Very good." Shield lifted the wineglass and swirled it. "Aerating the wine like this introduces more air molecules into it, which can capture the aroma molecules and carry them up to the nose. More dominant aromatics that arise after swirling can overwhelm some subtle ones, so most professional tasters will sniff the wine briefly first before swirling. The closer the nose is to the wine, even right inside the glass, the greater the chances of capturing aromatics. A series of short, quick sniffs versus one long inhale will also maximize the likelihood of detecting aromatics. The human nose starts to fatigue after around six seconds, and so a pause may be necessary between sniffs." She stopped swirling and placed the goblet under Thomas's nose.

The president took successive brief sniffs.

Fast learner, Shield thought. "What do you smell?"

"Fruit, but not sweet. Earth, and…smoke?"

"Excellent. Inferior merlots can smell like vinegar."

"This definitely doesn't smell like vinegar."

"I know." Shield didn't want to sound arrogant, but she prided herself on the quality of her wine.

"How would you describe it?" Thomas asked.

"A full-bodied and complex ruby, with a soft sweetness and velvety aftertaste. Hints of wild cherry and blackberry, finessed with a slight cocoa tone and undercurrents reminiscent of the rich, smoky soil of Tuscany."

Thomas sighed. "That's beautiful. So…romantic."

"And now, finally, is the time to taste."

Thomas lifted the glass to her mouth, never taking her eyes off Shield's, as if waiting for her permission.

"Before you…" Shield stopped.

"Yes?"

They were staring at each other and Shield couldn't look away. The president looked more relaxed at that moment than Shield had ever seen her—softer, somehow, and more…*real*, not the figurehead politician, but a warm and inviting woman. Again, Shield was struck by how beautiful Thomas was when she was stripped of her perfect media-friendly hairdo and flawless makeup. She'd evidently showered after her workday before changing into the comfortable-looking long-sleeved blue T-shirt and designer sweatpants she now wore; her fresh-scrubbed face and slightly flyaway, short brown hair gave her an enticing approachability. But the vulnerability in Elizabeth Thomas's dark eyes really drew her in and made her forget momentarily what she'd been about to say.

Shield also couldn't remember when she'd decided it was proper to stare at Thomas's kissable mouth. What was she doing? This woman was the American president and was also apparently involved in some scheme.

"May I…" Thomas's hoarse voice brought her back.

"Yes…if you know how."

Thomas paused a long moment before replying in a soft voice, "Teach me."

Shield shivered involuntarily at the words. Damn it, this was insane. Was she actually flirting with Thomas? And more insanely, was the president actually flirting back? "Take a small sip and keep it on your tongue. Give it a chance to mix with your saliva. It decreases the acidity and enhances the flavor."

"How long?"

"You'll know."

Thomas slowly brought the glass to her lips and, her eyes still fixed on Shield's, took a small sip. The setting sun had created a green hue in the president's deep-brown eyes, and her lips shone from the maroon liquid. Thomas closed her eyes to swallow and let out a small groan.

Shield's whole body reacted to the sound, every muscle tensing involuntarily, and she had to stop herself from moaning as well.

"Your wine is…delicious." Thomas's voice was barely audible.

Unable to trust her own voice, Shield smiled and looked out the open doors to the balcony.

The situation was becoming more unprofessional by the second. Flirting on the job, and never mind with Thomas, was against her every taught and self-imposed code of ethics. Shield cleared her voice before she spoke.

"I…" they said simultaneously.

Shield gestured for Thomas to go first.

"I was going to say, I think it's time I turned in," the president said.

Shield immediately stood. "You have a busy day tomorrow."

"Indeed. What were you about to say?"

"There's something I've been meaning to ask."

"Oh?"

"Do you really not remember me?" Shield asked. "Or is there a reason you won't acknowledge having met me?"

"Remember you from…?"

"Greece. The summit. I know you saw me, because you looked right at me and nodded."

"The global-warming summit? I…I don't, I'm sorry."

Shield felt oddly disappointed she'd not made more of an impression. "It's okay. I was just curious."

The president got up and faced her. They were less than a foot apart. "Thank you for the wine and the lesson."

Shield took a step back and looked away. "It was my pleasure, I'm glad you enjoyed it."

Thomas headed out and Shield followed silently a pace behind. She opened the door for the president and Thomas stepped into the foyer.

As she opened the door to her bedroom, with her back turned, the president said, "Good night, Kennedy."

"Sleep well, Elizabeth."

Chapter Fourteen

Ryden dropped on her back on the bed and covered her face with a pillow. "Oh, my God. Oh, my God. What just happened? What did I just do?" She had little to no experience with flirting, but even *she* knew what had just taken place, and for the first time in her life, she had flirted back.

Not that guys had ever swamped her with flowers, romantic dinners, and heated insinuations, but her limited practice had been one-sided and uninteresting. In her forty years she'd had three relationships, although that term was overrated when trying to characterize what they'd really been. Not one had lasted longer than a few months, and all had involved infrequent, uneventful, physical obligations. The men were nice enough but had done nothing for her libido. Hell, the only reason she knew about the existence of the G-spot was because she'd accidentally read about it when she clicked on an evidently dubious website called Fun With Candles.

Ryden might have carried on with the men for the sake of having someone in her life, but the prospect of having to endure the occasional sex was unbearable. They weren't rough or indifferent to her needs; they would try everything short of performing circus acts to satisfy her but never could. And in the end, they'd all call her frigid and leave, blaming her for making them feel incompetent.

Seven years ago, she'd concluded that her loveless childhood had made her incapable of feeling what she was supposed to feel and had stopped dating altogether. She had no desire to put herself through that kind of disaster again.

But if she was indeed frigid, why was her body aching? How did Kennedy, a woman, make her feel more desire and desired than she had ever imagined possible? No man had ever looked at her the way Kennedy had, and no one had ever made her feel the need to scream *I want you.* There was no doubt Kennedy had flirted with her, was there?

"I'm going through a stress-induced mid-life crisis," she muttered to herself. "Give me a break. That's obscene. That's impossible, not to mention crazy. What's wrong with me?"

Maybe, she mused, the attraction came from the fact that Kennedy had been adopted, was an orphan like she was, a kindred spirit. *But since when does empathy produce bodily fluids?* Ryden looked in the direction of her crotch. "God. I'm a total mess."

And Ratman would have a stroke if he found out. She'd almost laugh if she wasn't scared shitless of him. "There's the silver lining everyone talks about."

She got up and paced the room. Could Kennedy be playing around just to have something extra to blackmail her with? "No, that can't be." Kennedy had seemed sincere and almost uncomfortable with herself during their flirtatious banter.

Although the evening was chilly, Ryden felt like she was on fire. She opened the window and hung her head out. "What's happening to me?" she asked the stars. Once she'd cooled off a little, she shut the window and turned to stare at the door. It had never looked more appealing. "Who am I kidding? I don't have the guts to run."

The ringing phone interrupted her monologue.

"Yes?"

"You sound breathless." Ratman.

"So?"

"Is something wrong?"

Not if you consider me wanting to run the hell away from this place normal. "No," she replied instead.

"I was told you were in the Yellow Room with Kennedy."

"That's right."

"What were you doing?" he asked.

Oh, you know me. I love to wine taste with attractive women and wish to hell they'd kiss me. "Nothing much. I had a glass of wine."

"And Kennedy?"

"She doesn't drink on duty."

"I meant," he snapped with irritation, "did she say anything?"

"Like what?" What was up with the interrogation? "Kennedy talked about wine." *And I hope to hell she doesn't say otherwise.* "Why are you asking about Kennedy?" Did the Rat hear something? Had Kennedy just spoken to him?

"Just want to make sure she's taking good care of you."

You have no idea how good. "She's very professional. Doesn't talk much and is quite boring."

The answer apparently satisfied him because he changed topics. "Have you checked your schedule for this week?"

"I'm prepared for tomorrow. I'll read the rest of this week's schedule tonight." Ryden glanced over at the folder, which she'd tossed on the bed earlier. She'd apparently lain on it when she came in and hadn't even noticed; it was crumpled and folded at the edges.

"Good."

The only thing good, *creep*, she thought, *is that the phones are tapped, because it means you refrain from saying, "So far, so good. Keep it that way and you'll live."*

"Well then, get some rest for tomorrow."

Fat chance since my body feels more wired than a guitar. "I will."

"Good night, Elizabeth."

I hope you slip in the shower and break your neck. And FYI, Elizabeth only sounds good when Kennedy says it. "Good night," she replied, and hung up.

Kennedy even makes Elizabeth *sound sexy.* "Yup, time for a shower," Ryden told herself as she headed toward the bathroom, still tingling from the interaction with Kennedy. "A bucket of ice and tranquilizers wouldn't hurt, either."

Houston, Texas

TQ watched the maid pour her nightcap—bourbon, neat—and set it on her desk atop a coaster. She smiled. "The eye patch becomes you. You finally look interesting."

The young woman bowed. "Thank you, madam."

The phone rang and TQ sighed when she saw the number on caller ID. "Get out," she told the maid before she answered the phone. "And?"

"She asks a lot of questions," Yuri Dratshev replied.

"I'm sure."

"My men say nothing."

"Your family's life depends on it, after all. Is that everything?"

"She is asking for a TV. She wants to hear the news."

"Good. It's time we gave her one." She reached for her bourbon and took a sip. Disciplining the maid had ensured no further problems.

The amount in the glass was precisely to her specifications, and the glass had been placed exactly where she wanted on her desk.

"But she will find out," Dratshev said.

"Yes, Russian genius."

"You want her to."

"The president has to be prepared, for when the time comes."

"When the time comes?"

"Were you listening at all while I outlined this operation? I honestly don't know how someone who needs to be reminded to blink can be so successful."

"I pay people to remind me."

"Don't get cocky. I can have your family wiped out before someone has the chance to remind you."

After a long silence on the other end, Dratshev came back on the line, his voice much more subdued. "I also talked with Jack."

TQ sat up and leaned forward, resting her elbows on the desk. "Yes?"

"She will see you."

"You told her who I am?"

Dratshev hesitated. *"Da."*

"I don't recall asking you to do that."

"You did not say I should not," he hurriedly explained. "I told her you want to talk. That's all."

"What did she say?"

"She never says a lot. She said she does not know you and to give her your number."

"So she wants my number," TQ said, amused.

"Do you have a job for Jack?" he asked.

"You could say that."

"She asks for big money, but she is good. She is the one who brought me Owens's head. You know—the serial killer."

TQ had read about the Headhunter being caught and killed in Vietnam a couple of years back. "They said the feds found him."

"No," Dratshev replied. "His ugly head is buried in my garden. She asked for three million, I gave her half in front."

"Up front."

"She never accepted the rest after she personally delivered his head."

"I wonder why."

Dratshev laughed. "Maybe because she liked killing him. She's a very good killer and she can find anyone. You will be happy with her work."

"Tell her to call me at 713-555-2457."

"Good."

"And get the president a television."

"*Da.*"

TQ hung up and leaned back in her chair. *So you're that good, are you, Jack? Let's see how long it'll take to make you scream out my name for mercy.*

Now she just needed a way to force Jack to come to her, and Dratshev might have given her some ammunition. The death of Walter Owens had been all over the news, and she recalled something about the leader of a Vietnamese skin-trade organization being captured in the same assault that had brought him down. Perhaps he could shed some light on Jack and her involvement.

TQ had good contacts all over Asia, particularly in prisons, because that's where she procured many of her black-market human organs. She telephoned her primary contact in Saigon and asked him to personally visit the skin-trade chief. If the man could provide her with Jack's Achilles's heel, she had the means to make his confinement much more comfortable than it probably was.

Southwest of Baltimore, Maryland
Next morning, March 2

Elizabeth Thomas restlessly paced the perimeter of her comfortable but claustrophobic confinement, wishing like hell she knew what was going on in the outside world. Without a watch or window, she had to rely on the number of breakfasts served to measure how long she'd been here, and she knew more than a week had passed now since they'd abducted her in the elevator.

Cleanshaven had come to take away her breakfast tray some time ago, so it was probably mid-morning. Apparently they had decided to ignore, yet again, her pleas for a television or radio so she could keep up with what was going on and pass the long hours with something other than the books they'd given her, none of which could hold her interest.

Was the Secret Service having any luck tracking her down? Did they believe her dead? Had her kidnappers made ransom demands?

And how and what was the vice president doing in her absence? She'd selected her running mate largely because, as a popular Southern governor, he could deliver the block of votes needed to win the election. He also, fortunately, supported much of her agenda, but not all of it. He'd been frank in opposing her health-care plan and energy-alternative initiative when they'd both been campaigning for the Democratic nomination. Would he use this opportunity to forestall some of her key directives?

She paused in her pacing and tensed when she heard the sound of the key in the lock. From her reckoning, it was much too early for lunch, the next time she would usually see one of her guards.

Cleanshaven stuck his masked face through the doorway and motioned for her to move to the farthest corner of the room.

She complied. "What's happening?"

A few seconds later, Beard carried in a flat-screen television and set it up on a table opposite the bed. Cleanshaven plugged a cable from the wall into the back, while Beard handed her the remote.

"Thank you," she said as she flicked the set on, eager to find out what was happening with the investigation into her kidnapping.

Without a channel guide, she had to flip past several sitcoms and soap operas before hitting any sort of news broadcast. A local TV channel was showing a live broadcast of a police chase. The video, taken by a news helicopter, tracked a stolen truck speeding along a highway, with several cruisers in pursuit. Though the report contained no relevant information about her abduction, she stayed tuned long enough to hear the station's ID: WBAL. She was being held somewhere in, or near, Baltimore. Shocked that she was being held captive so near D.C., she viewed the development nonetheless as good news. Surely that would make it easier for authorities to find her.

She surfed some more channels and stopped when she hit CNN. They were in the middle of a sports wrap-up, showing highlights of last night's NBA games. After a couple of minutes of clips, the sports anchor threw back to the news desk, where the anchor team teased some of the stories that would be reported at the top of the hour following the commercial: the latest on a massive, late-season snowstorm that had buried the Rockies, the search for a missing murder suspect in Philadelphia, and details about the Argentine president's upcoming visit to the White House.

Thomas sat on the bed, puzzled, as a series of advertisements for laundry detergent, dog food, and diapers played out on the screen. Not only had she heard no mention of her abduction and the investigation to find her, but she also couldn't imagine why the Argentine visit would be proceeding as scheduled.

Surely, she thought, she'd just missed some earlier update on the kidnapping. She got her answer ten minutes later, after sitting through the reports about the snowstorm and murder suspect.

"Argentine President Juan Carlos landed this morning at Andrews Air Force Base," the anchor reported as video of Carlos emerging from his plane and being greeted by an American welcoming committee was shown on the screen. "His three-day visit to the nation's capital will include a speech this afternoon before the U.S. House of Representatives and an evening reception at the Argentine embassy attended by key congressional and military leaders. President Carlos is seeking support for his initiative to hold joint military maneuvers with U.S. Forces this fall, among other issues. Tomorrow, he'll be welcomed by an official state dinner, and the next day he will meet privately with President Thomas in a closed-door session at the White House."

Thomas stared at the monitor, thoroughly confused.

The anchor came back on. "President Thomas will be spending the morning meeting with the joint chiefs of staff to get their reactions to the proposal," he said. Video showing Elizabeth Thomas—at least she could have sworn it was her—started playing on the screen. "Yesterday, Thomas delighted a group of Australian and French tourists taking the White House tour with a surprise appearance as their guide led them through the Red Room. This video was provided by one of the Aussies, who said Thomas stayed for ten minutes to chat with the group, sign autographs, and pose for pictures."

The sound on the clip was turned up as the video zoomed in on Thomas's face. "I hope you all enjoy your visit," the president told the group. "I'm afraid I need to get back to work."

"In her press conference following the attempt on her life," the anchor said as he came back on screen, "President Thomas vowed to carry on with business as usual, and this surprise appearance, along with the Argentine president's visit, are clearly intended to reinforce that message. There have been no developments, meanwhile, in the investigation to determine who was behind the well-orchestrated attack that killed her five Secret Service agents, buried earlier this week, and no group or individual has to date claimed responsibility."

She was too stunned by what she was seeing to even register whatever story came next.

It wasn't her on the screen. But whoever had taken over for her was a perfect double in every way. Even the voice was the same.

Her heartbeat accelerated. An imposter was running the country, apparently very convincingly, too.

And no one was looking for her. They didn't even know she was missing.

The realization was chilling. Who was behind this? Why was all this happening? And what the hell did her captors plan to do with her?

Houston, Texas

TQ snatched up the phone impatiently when the caller ID informed her that her contact in Vietnam was calling back, hopefully with something she could use to lure Jack into meeting her on her own terms. "Yes?"

"The man you asked me to see was very happy to take your deal," the contact reported. "He was anxious to get a private cell with better food and his own guard who will see to his needs."

"Only if he had something worthwhile," TQ snapped. "And?"

"He said that this Jack was not alone when they came to his home, first posing as a skin-trade dealer and later to take Walter Owens. She had her girlfriend with her, a woman named Lauren Hargrave. Owens kidnapped this Lauren woman when she went snooping around his hideout, and it made Jack very, very angry. Before he died, Owens asked Jack if she would ever feel worthy of Lauren, and she said no."

"Go on," TQ said.

"It was Lauren who cut off Owens's head, and the two of them together gunned down all of this man's associates, so she was not the naïve mistress she pretended to be," the contact replied. "The man is blind, so he could not tell me what either woman looked like, but he said his associate described Lauren as blond, young, and very beautiful, and Jack has a scar on her face."

"Give him what he asks for," TQ replied, and hung up.

So Jack did have a weakness—a woman, though Lauren Hargrave might not be her real name if the two of them were posing as skin traders, which they obviously were not.

She sat bolt upright. A young blond woman had also been involved in the whole affair that had killed her brother and resulted in the death of Andor Rózsa in France. She hadn't paid much attention to the woman because she'd been too focused on trying to find Jack.

Typing a few keystrokes on her computer brought up news stories and images from the event. The unidentified blonde had been held captive by Rózsa and was taken to a hospital by helicopter after her rescue on Rózsa's boat. The media reports said the feds were claiming credit, but TQ knew that Jack and a friend named Brett had been responsible both for saving the woman and for her brother Dario's death.

She sent the news reports and a few stills she found of the blonde, all of her being loaded into the helicopter, to one of her contacts in France and told him to bribe whatever hospital officials necessary to get all he could on the mysterious kidnap victim.

Three hours later, he sent back an e-mail reply.

> *Her name is Cassady Monroe. She is twenty-eight years old, five feet seven inches tall, and weighed one hundred sixteen pounds when she was rescued. Her hospital records do not list a home address or phone number. The night nurse who tended her said a woman named Jack stayed at her bedside. Jack was tall, five-nine or so, with dark hair and a scar from her cheek to her lip. The two women talked frequently about going home to Colorado. They also talked about Cassady Monroe's work as a violinist. Apparently she was going to miss a concert she was supposed to perform in.*

A simple Internet search for *Cassady Monroe violinist* got TQ one step closer to finding the woman who dared challenge her.

CHAPTER FIFTEEN

The White House

Shield sat in her usual chair by the window as the president had her breakfast in the private dining room. If she was confused about Thomas before, she was completely baffled after last night. Any doubts she might have had about whether Thomas had been flirting with her were erased by what she heard after the president retired to her room.

The bug Shield planted while Thomas ate dinner had picked up the president's monologue and thoughts about her. But none of this made sense. Every news and tabloid report throughout her political career and presidential campaign had portrayed Thomas as a very happily married woman, one who was now mourning the loss of her beloved husband. The intel she'd gotten from Pierce even seemed to confirm that.

Could it be the marriage was a sham, covered up to make her more palatable to the conservative, pro-family electorate? It had happened before—similar rumors existed about the Clintons, among others.

Clearly a lot was going on, and as much as Shield wanted to take a peek at the truth behind the curtain, part of her hoped she wouldn't find anything. Yet whoever was on the phone with Thomas last night, and Shield was convinced it was Moore, had sure taken a lot of interest in what Shield had to say to the president. What was Moore afraid of?

Shield had spent the night reviewing her conversation and evening with Thomas. She was no stranger to sexual attraction and fulfillment of physical needs, but she couldn't remember ever having had a more erotically charged encounter, and definitely not with a straight woman. Matters had only gotten worse when she found out the feelings had been mutual. She'd spent the late-night hours dwelling on her unprofessional behavior and the early-morning ones wondering what would have happened if she'd kissed Thomas.

Sleep had been elusive; she hadn't gotten more than a couple of hours. Thomas's words, *Oh, my God. What did I just do?* kept ringing through her head, and although she felt the same way, she couldn't help getting flustered over the fact that this beautiful, yet cold and powerful woman, had cracked.

Thomas, nevertheless, was different this morning. She had barely nodded her good morning and was now sitting with her back turned to Shield while she had her breakfast and watched the news. It was all for the best, Shield thought. It was how it should be.

Still, as she watched the president eat, shoulders tense and with no one to talk to, Shield couldn't help but feel for her loneliness. Thomas had selected a demanding and accountable life for sure, but having no one to share the weight of her choices and give her strength only made the burden heavier.

Thomas alternated her attention between the various news channels broadcasting from three flat screens mounted on the wall in front of her. She currently had the sound up on MSNBC, which was replaying stock footage of the president as it announced there had been no new leads in the investigation into the assassination attempt. The video included older shots of her giving speeches during her presidential campaign and ended with the press conference she'd held announcing she was all right and would continue business as usual. Shield noticed that the more recent footage showed Thomas looking almost younger and a bit thinner. People lost weight all the time because of loss of a spouse, or stress, but that still didn't explain her fresher, more appealing appearance now.

Shield turned her attention back to the president when she saw her fumble with the remote, muting MSNBC and turning up the volume on CNN, which was broadcasting a report on a fugitive wanted for the murder of a divorced couple. The suspect was a forty-year-old florist. Thomas listened closely, almost frozen, except for the slight tremble of her hand. She dropped the remote when the picture of the wanted woman came on the screen.

Definitely not what you expected a murderer to look like, Shield thought. The suspect was more the cute bookworm type, with her long brown hair and warm green eyes behind thick myopic glasses.

"Authorities in Philadelphia are asking the public for help in finding Ryden Wagner, indicted by a grand jury yesterday in the stabbing deaths of Tim and Rhonda Lauden. The divorced couple was found murdered nearly three months ago, in the home they once shared on the northeast side," the anchor reported as photos of the couple replaced the mug shot of the suspect. "Detectives who went to

Wagner's apartment to take her into custody say she'd not been seen there since she was questioned following the deaths. She'd also not reported for work at the flower shop where she'd been employed."

The next video on the screen showed a diminutive, older woman with olive skin and dark hair, in front of an establishment called The Bloom Room. "I'm sure Ryden didn't do this," the woman said, as a title identifying her as MAGDA PAGONI, SHOP OWNER appeared beneath her face. "It has to be a misunderstanding. I've known her for years, and she wouldn't hurt a fly. She probably left town because she's scared, that's all. She's innocent. I just know it."

A photo of two young boys on bicycles appeared on the monitor as the anchor said, "The Laudens left behind two sons, who are being taken care of by their maternal grandparents." Then the mug shot of the suspect came back on. "Ryden Wagner is forty years old and has green eyes and light-brown, shoulder-length hair. She is five feet five inches tall, weighs approximately a hundred and twenty, and wears thick glasses. Her car, an older Subaru Outback, was found parked outside her apartment. If you see the suspect, you are asked to call Philadelphia homicide detectives at the number on your screen."

Ryden opened her mouth, gasping for air. She had forgotten to breathe when her old-self mug shot appeared on the news. How would she ever forget that horrible picture of her, with WANTED FOR MURDER written under it? And the picture of those poor orphaned kids, and the footage of Magda in the shop, who kept repeating Ryden was innocent.

And my God, Kennedy, behind her all this time, silently watching; she'd heard it all. Ryden didn't dare turn to look at her. She didn't know how she could ever face her after this.

If Kennedy *was* in on this fiasco with Ratman, how much had they told her about Ryden and her previous life? Was she aware of how they'd set her up to blackmail her to cooperate? And did she know what Ryden looked like before the surgeries and other alterations?

Ryden could see the resemblance between her old self and new. Sure, they'd tweaked a few of her features: cheekbones, chin, nose. But the changes seemed minimal. And most of the other alterations—the stylish haircut and coloring, the Lasik to get rid of her glasses, the dental work, contacts, the classy makeup and flattering clothes, all were changes she could have made on her own but never had any interest in.

Maybe she should have taken more notice of her appearance in the past. In the photo on the news, she appeared older than she really was, haggard and unkempt. Only now did she fully realize how much she'd let herself go. If Kennedy had met her before all the changes, she probably wouldn't have noticed her even if she'd slapped Kennedy on the ass. *Why am I even thinking about another woman? Is this latent lesbianism?*

If it was, it couldn't be happening at a more unsuitable time with a more inappropriate person. She was trying to gather the strength to get up and go to the Oval Office but didn't know how to face Kennedy. *Think of an icebreaker.*

Ryden made a point of looking out the window. "So, how about the weather? Pretty mild for March," she said, not daring to turn around.

Kennedy cleared her throat. "Quite."

Way to go on picking a topic, Ryden. What kind of exchange could she expect from that? A breakdown of this week's forecast, accompanied by a statistical pie chart? "Anyway, I have to deal with some matters, so..." She actually had a lot to do to prepare for tomorrow's state dinner, her first as host.

In addition to memorizing the speech Ratman had written for her welcoming the Argentine president, she had to familiarize herself with the many protocols that surrounded the event. One of her first meetings this morning was to finalize preparations with the key White House staff who were involved in organizing the massive undertaking: the chief of protocol, executive chef and executive pastry chef, social secretary, chief floral designer, chief usher, and chief calligrapher, among others. Tonya had already briefed her to a large degree on what to expect at such functions, and Ratman would be present today to help her with any last-minute decisions, so she didn't expect any snags that might tip off any of them that she was doing this for the first time.

"So...?" Kennedy repeated.

Ryden finally turned around. "I just mean, I..." *God, think of something.* A knock interrupted the process of sticking her flat-heeled shoe in her mouth.

"Come in," she said, and both of them turned toward the door. Ryden felt almost giddy for the disruption.

Ratman came in and handed Ryden an envelope. "It just arrived." He looked from her to the envelope, as if asking her to see what it contained.

She tore the envelope open, and he stood over her as she read. Her hands shook and she had to steady her elbows on the table. "It's from

Juan Carlos."

"What does he want?" Ratman asked.

"The president is asking for my permission to dance with him at the state dinner tomorrow," Ryden replied.

"You can always decline, Madam President, but I advise against it. We have certain common interests."

"I haven't danced in years. You know my husband wasn't much for it." Tonya hadn't included dancing in her training. Higher priorities dominated, and it wasn't expected that she'd have to, since Thomas was newly widowed and rarely if ever had danced in public.

"It'll just be a waltz."

"But I...I don't know how to," Ryden mumbled.

Moore hesitated before saying, "You have a day to learn."

"Or I can tell him I'm mourning my husband and find dancing premature."

Ratman looked at her sternly. "We have common interests, Madam President, and we need his...cooperation."

Ryden sighed. "How am I supposed to learn in a day?"

"We'll find you a teacher."

Ryden gasped at the thought of going through such a thing. The idea alone was excruciating. Not just because she'd never danced in her life, but the touching...she hated the touching. She couldn't stand anyone so close to her, invading her personal space. "I can't." Ryden stood her ground. "I don't want someone touching me, even if it's a teacher. I'm not ready for that."

"Just one dance, Madam President. It's important." When Ratman loomed over her, her hands began to shake again.

"With all due respect, Madam President," Kennedy said from behind them.

Both Ryden and Ratman turned to look at her.

"Yes?" Ryden replied.

Kennedy took a step forward. "I can teach you the basics, if you will allow me."

"You know how to?" Ratman asked.

"I wouldn't offer otherwise."

Ratman turned to Ryden expectantly. "Kennedy can teach you."

"What can I possibly learn in a few hours?"

"Anything is better than not at all." Ratman glared down at her.

Oh, peachy. She could barely stand to look at Kennedy this morning. How in the world was she going to dance with her? "But...

she's a woman."

Kennedy turned to her and said stoically, "I can teach you, Madam President, even if…I'm not a man." The words were polite but the tone icy.

"We need this," Ratman said.

She got up and walked past Kennedy without looking at her. "Fine. I'll be ready in an hour." *Because that's how long it's going to take me to mentally prepare myself for humiliation.*

It wasn't that she was a slow learner or lacked grace. She found physical closeness difficult, and for some reason she didn't want to give Kennedy that impression.

Near Colorado Springs, Colorado

Jack stuck her cell into her back pocket and went into the kitchen to make herself a sandwich. She was restless and had no appetite, but she should get something in her stomach since she hadn't eaten much in the last twenty-four hours. Cassady was in Boston and still not answering; the conductor required all the musicians to turn off their cells during rehearsals. She'd already sent a half dozen texts and left a voice mail for Cass to call her the minute she was free again. If she wasn't careful, the constant barrage of *I love you and I miss you like crazy. Is everything okay?* messages might soon annoy Cass.

She retrieved the disposable prepaid cell she'd bought the day before and dialed the number Yuri had given her.

"So, how's your brother?" Jack said as soon as the line picked up.

Without skipping a beat, TQ replied, "Dead."

She snapped her fingers. "Oh, that's right. I keep forgetting I killed him."

"You called. How wonderful."

"Yeah, well, once in a while someone amazing comes along…and here I am."

"Indeed."

"So, how do you see this playing out?"

"You're going to come to me," TQ replied confidently.

"How clairvoyant of you," Jack said. "What else do you see in your crystal ball?"

"Options."

"I can either bury or burn you. I'm open to both."

"The options, arrogant friend, are for you."

"Interesting. Do enlighten me."

"You are either going to come to me out of your own free will, or I am going to force you."

"Chilling scenario," Jack said as she slathered some mayo on a piece of bread. "You should sell the movie rights."

"I see the financial possibilities in that." TQ laughed. "But I'm holding out for a conclusion."

"I hate to keep you in anticipation, so here's how many fucks I give: I'm holding up a finger. Guess which one."

"Although I'm enjoying the banter, this conversation is becoming more counterproductive by the retort, and I'm a very busy woman. I suggest we bring it to a close fairly soon."

"Good, because I've gotten more excitement out of a Cracker Jack box, and I've got things to do myself," Jack replied. "That BLT ain't gonna eat itself."

"Very well." TQ paused. "You either come to me, or I can come and get you."

"I'm more than willing to meet you in person," Jack said.

"And what would you do once we met?"

"Pretty much the same as you, and something tells me that doesn't include dinner and drinks."

"You're wrong, Jack. I don't want to hurt you. I merely want your cooperation."

"Explain."

"I want you to work for me," TQ said.

"Say what?"

"You come highly recommended."

"Have you been taking expired drugs?"

"I've experienced firsthand how…capable you are."

"It doesn't take a lot of skill to execute point-blank," she said.

"But it takes a lot of nerve to kill someone like my brother."

"Not really, him being a cripple and all."

TQ chuckled. "It's not polite to mock the physically challenged."

Jack took a bite of her sandwich. "It is when they're organ-stealing murderers. In other words, deranged assholes. Pretty much like you."

"My brother was a talentless little man who depended on me for a reason—to wheel his sorry existence out of bed. I, on the other hand, Jack, am a savior. I give to people what doctors and belief cannot. I give them life."

"I think I just heard harps play and angels sing. You do realize you kill people every time you save a life."

"Some deserve to live more than others."

"The ones who can afford you," Jack said.

"Those who put a loved one above the costs."

"Let's just agree you're—"

"God?" TQ sounded serious.

Jack laughed so hard she thought she might lose her lunch. "You... are...hysterical," she said between spurts of laughter.

"You know what else is hilarious, Jack?"

Jack poured a glass of milk to wash down the sandwich. "Let me have a swig of milk before I choke." She lifted the glass to her mouth.

It was TQ's turn to laugh. "I hear a talented violinist is rehearsing for this weekend's performance of Albinoni's 'Adagio in G minor.' And I happen to know you're not with her, since her every move is being monitored."

Jack slowly placed her glass back on the counter. "This is between you and me." She reached in her back pocket for her regular cell phone.

"Oh, and don't bother warning Ms. Monroe. You see, a certain gentleman is seated in the dark auditorium as we speak. Should she happen to reach for her cell, he is instructed to execute her on the spot."

"Don't hurt her."

"The only one who can harm her is you. It's your call, Jackie. Had you agreed to come to me of your own will, you would have saved yourself the agony of option number two."

"Where?"

"Someone will pick you up at the old Bingham's warehouse in Denver."

How the hell did she know they were in Colorado? "I can be there in two hours."

"Oh, and Jack? Please come alone. My men are going to follow Ms. Monroe until you are safe and sound in my company. One wrong move or phone call and I will finish what Rózsa couldn't."

Jack's heart rate accelerated. "That's ridiculous. Anyone could call her, her work—"

"Then the sooner you get here, the less chance of that happening while she's being watched," TQ said calmly.

"Make it an hour and a half, bitch." Jack hung up.

CHAPTER SIXTEEN

The White House

Shield wasn't sure what had prompted her to make the offer, but Thomas's reply had made her immediately regret it. She couldn't figure the president out, and that was frustrating. One moment, Thomas was in control: witty, charming, and respectful of Shield. The next, she was afraid, humorless, distant, and rude. The president clearly had regrets about their flirtatious exchange, which was understandable. It was also probably why she had to point out that Shield was a woman and thereby incapable of teaching her to dance. But did Thomas have to keep her back turned to her all morning or act so appalled at being touched?

Shield knocked on her bedroom door an hour later, dreading the alone time with the president.

Thomas opened the door and stepped out. She'd changed from the casual attire she always wore at breakfast to a tailored gray silk blouse and charcoal skirt. "I'm ready." She'd taken a few steps down the hallway before Shield noticed her shoes.

"Madam President."

Thomas stopped. "Yes?" she replied without turning around.

"Your footwear."

"What about it?" she asked, still with her back turned.

"Not suitable for a dance lesson."

Thomas looked down at her low-heeled black pumps. "They're comfortable."

"But inappropriate. You'll have to learn to dance in heels, because I presume that's what you'll be wearing tomorrow night for the dinner."

The president turned and walked past Shield back toward her room. "I'll make the adjustment." When she reemerged a short time later, she was wearing three-inch lavender heels, and the added lift brought her up roughly to Shield's height.

Thomas swept past without a glance and headed down the Grand

Staircase to the East Room, the largest room in the White House, where the entertainment portion of the state dinner would be held. A small stage had already been set up on one side for the orchestra, and folding chairs were stacked against one wall. The rest of the room was bare; the grand piano had been taken out, and the Aubusson-style carpet had been removed from one end to expose the polished oak parquet floor for dancing. Either the president or Moore had evidently called ahead, because a White House aide was standing by with a portable music player and speakers.

"Good morning, Madam President," he said as soon as they entered. "I've gotten the music list from the orchestra and have a couple of their waltz selections for you to choose from."

"Thank you," Thomas replied. "That will be all for now. I'll call you if we need you."

As he departed, Shield disconnected her communications device. She went to the president and faced her. "First, let's go over the hold. You place your left hand on my right shoulder, with your elbow bent."

Thomas placed her hand on Shield's upper arm.

"Higher, please." Shield took her hand and moved it to her shoulder. "Very good. Now…" Shield extended her left arm. "Put your right hand in mine, in a loose grip, and I'll put my right hand around your waist, like this."

Thomas stiffened as soon as Shield touched her.

"I know I'm not a man." Shield couldn't help herself, remembering the president's previous comments. "But please try to relax."

Thomas avoided eye contact when she replied. "I didn't mean…"

"You try to maintain this hold, and this distance, throughout the dance," Shield said, standing about a foot away. "On the first beat, I step forward with my left foot, and you step back with your right."

The president moved forward instead, which resulted in a chest-to-chest collision. "I'm sorry." Thomas looked uncomfortable.

"No need. It takes getting used to." Shield hurriedly put the correct distance between them. "On the next beat, I step forward and to the right with my right foot, making a kind of L, and you mirror what I'm doing with your left foot, stepping back. Your partner, presuming he's good at this, will be subtly leading you with his hands."

She demonstrated, tightening her hold slightly on the president. For someone who busied herself with paperwork, phone calls, and meetings, Thomas's hands felt rougher than Shield expected. "Next, shift your weight to your left foot, while you keep your right foot stationary. On the third beat, you slide your right foot over to your left and stand with your feet together."

Thomas still appeared tense as she looked down at her feet as if willing them to move. Shield placed her foot between both of Thomas's and nudged her right foot to the left. Thomas looked at her bewildered.

"You can do this," Shield said, and Thomas charily moved her foot. "Very good."

"On the fourth beat, step forward with your left foot, while I step back with my right foot. Great. Now, on the fifth beat, I step back and to the left with my left foot, tracing a backward L and shifting my weight to my left foot, while you mirror me with your right foot, stepping forward."

Thomas followed her lead.

"On the last beat, slide your left foot toward your right, until your feet are together. That's the pattern. Now we repeat from step one, and as you dance each pattern, your partner will move you across the floor, turning your orientation slowly to the right by slight variations in the placement of your feet. This is where you really pay attention to how he'll be leading you with his hand on your waist and with pressure against your palm. Shall we try a few patterns without the music first?"

"You're the teacher."

They took it from the top, and although still rigid in her movements, Thomas at least remembered the steps. After a half dozen patterns, Shield released her hold, and Thomas immediately pulled back a few steps like she couldn't wait to let go.

"I think we're ready for the music," Shield said sternly. She hadn't expected Thomas to launch into a tight embrace, but she didn't know why she had to act so scared, almost relieved, Shield had let go. She walked over to the CD player. "I'm sorry I'm making you uncomfortable, but can you hold on long enough to try it with music a few more times?"

Ryden tore her gaze away from those penetrating eyes. Kennedy looked frustrated. She understood the sentiment, since she knew she wasn't a natural at this, but did the bodyguard have to be that obvious? "I think I can manage."

She'd never felt at ease when anyone invaded her personal space, but being close to Kennedy was unbearable for reasons she couldn't understand. Her touch was firm but gentle, her scent intoxicating, and her shoulders slender yet strong. Kennedy moved with the smooth grace of a feline predator, something Ryden had never witnessed before. In complete contrast to the men she had gotten close to, who were rough, hurried, and anxious to grab her ass and make her feel disturbingly like an object, Kennedy made her feel uncomfortably like the woman she always dreamed she could be.

"Very well." Kennedy pressed the Start button and came to stand before her. She put one arm around Ryden's waist and held the other up, waiting for Ryden to place hers. "Madam President?"

Ryden tentatively placed her hands.

"Do you remember the moves?" Kennedy's eyes searched hers.

"I…think so."

"Follow me and you'll do fine," Kennedy said, and moved into her.

They danced for ten minutes with Ryden counting steps to herself. She avoided eye contact because the few times she had dared a glance at Kennedy's profile, she lost her footing.

"You're doing great," Kennedy said when Ryden followed her spin. She hadn't realized when she'd stopped counting and simply allowed Kennedy to lead her smoothly across the floor.

Ryden smiled. "This isn't so bad." She felt weightless.

"I'm glad you think so." Despite her encouragement, Kennedy remained serious and distant.

"You protect me, teach me about wine and, now, how to waltz. I'm a genuine handful."

"Just doing my job."

"Not exactly. I'm sure your responsibilities don't include making up for my ineptness."

"I do what's necessary."

"I wonder what's next, then." The words spilled out of her before Ryden realized what she was saying.

"That would depend on you, Madam President." Kennedy gazed so intently at her Ryden had to look away.

"The girls in Tuscany must be all over you."

"I guess."

"Yet you say you don't have anyone special."

"I used to."

"What happened?"

"A woman named Carmen. I stopped dating after her."

"You loved her a lot."

"Let's just say she spoiled me for any other."

"I see," Ryden said curtly. "I'm sorry to hear that."

"Why?"

"You're successful, intelligent, and...attractive."

Kennedy arched one eyebrow and swirled her before she replied. "I'm also not interested."

"Something is holding you back."

Kennedy abruptly slowed them, almost to a halt. "That something is a dislike for settling."

"You're not ready to settle down?" Ryden asked.

"I'm not prepared to settle for an imitation of what I want," Kennedy replied, and picked up the pace again.

"What do you want?"

"Someone who doesn't bore me with petty issues, melodramas, and inane exchanges...and someone who doesn't need me for what I can buy them."

Ryden realized for the first time how lucrative Kennedy's business must be and that plenty of women would want to take advantage of that. Though she'd noticed that Kennedy was always meticulously well groomed, only now did she note the smooth, expensive fabric beneath the hand that rested on Kennedy's shoulder. The navy suit had been tailor-made to fit her. The white shirt beneath was no ordinary off-the-rack, either, but made of quality materials and required cufflinks. Kennedy's were gold, square-shaped, and with some kind of design carved in them that Ryden couldn't discern from the glimpses she got as they danced. Kennedy was understatedly elegant, not enough to draw any attention to herself, though clearly the woman didn't need this job.

But they did have something in common. Kennedy, too, didn't like pointless conversations and small talk. Did she think their conversation tedious? Was that why she was being so quiet and distant? Ryden, disappointed by the prospect, began counting her steps again, turning her head away to concentrate on the wall behind Kennedy.

She jumped when she felt Kennedy's breath close to her ear.

"What do you want?" Kennedy asked.

Ryden turned her head slightly, to find Kennedy's face very close to hers. She was wearing a V-necked blouse, and Kennedy was staring at her exposed neck.

"I mean," Kennedy murmured in a low voice, "aside from stopping the illegal-arms trade, more jobs, equal job rights for both sexes, and world peace?"

"I...I, uh..." Ryden couldn't stop staring at Kennedy's mouth. "Don't know."

Kennedy's soulful blue eyes sought hers, and Ryden lost herself in them; she let herself be swept across the floor in widening patterns while they remained looking at each other. Ryden didn't know if her feet were touching the ground or how much time was passing. She didn't care if the world fell apart, because she felt like a princess in the arms of her knight.

Ryden also didn't know when or how, but they had closed the distance between them until she could feel Kennedy's hips and breasts against her own. They moved as one.

"Who are you?" Kennedy suddenly asked.

It took a few seconds for the question to register. "You know who I am." Ryden's voice sounded breathless, even to her own ears.

"I mean, aside from the obvious."

Was this a serious question or a trick one? Kennedy knew very well who Ryden was.

"Who is the woman behind the façade and what does she want?" Kennedy asked.

"I'm not sure I understand."

"Would it clear it up if I said, what we did yesterday, what we're doing now, is highly unprofessional on my behalf and vastly unconventional on yours."

"I know."

"What's going on, Elizabeth?"

"I..." Ryden stopped dancing and let go. She walked to the CD player and turned it off. "I don't know, but..."

"But?"

"It has to stop."

Kennedy stared down at her feet. "I know." She looked disappointed, or maybe embarrassed. Ryden couldn't tell which, but maybe, like her, Kennedy felt both.

Exasperated, she ran her hand through her hair. "You can't even begin to imagine what...what..."

"Of course I can," Kennedy replied quietly. "And I would never say anything."

A knock on the door interrupted them.

"Come in," Ryden said.

The aide who'd left them the CD player entered and stopped just inside the door. "Madam President, Advisor Moore asked me to remind you of your appointment with him in thirty minutes."

"Tell him I'm aware," Ryden lied, and headed toward him. In reality she'd forgotten about it completely. She was happy she could remember her name at this point.

"Of course," the aide replied, and moved to the side as Ryden passed him by.

Kennedy followed her to her bedroom and Ryden stopped outside the door. Unable to face Kennedy, she remained with her back turned. "I was going to say, you can't even begin to imagine what you're doing to me," she said before she disappeared into her room.

CHAPTER SEVENTEEN

Denver, Colorado

Jack had been warned about TQ and the influence she had on higher-ups, but it boggled her mind that the bitch had been able to find out about Cassady—certainly no easy feat. Too afraid to call Cass, the only other option that crossed her mind was Montgomery Pierce. She hated to admit it, but the EOO probably had the kind of power needed to deal with someone like the Broker. Jack reached for her phone a few times during her drive to Denver but couldn't make herself contact him.

It wasn't so much pride that stopped her, but fear. She had no control over what Pierce and the rest would do, and she refused to take any chances with the woman she loved. Cass had already been through too much, and Jack was damned if she would let that bitch hurt her.

No, this was Jack's war. Pierce had warned her that the Broker wouldn't forget, and from the short discussion with TQ, Jack knew she wasn't the type of woman to forgive, either. She had fueled this war by killing Dario, and she was going to make sure no one else paid the price.

Jack parked her black 1967 Mustang in front of the warehouse. That way, it was exposed and clear for anyone to see; now was not the time for heroics or taking stupid risks. She knew TQ meant it when she said she'd terminate Cass if she tried anything or wasn't on time, because it was exactly what Jack would do. She grabbed her Glock from the passenger seat and got out.

The place was massive and long abandoned. The warehouses on either side were, too. TQ had done her homework. There was no point in looking for another entrance. The bitch would have enough eyes and capable manpower to sure as hell have this place completely secured. They could likely take her out at any moment.

The sun was about to set when Jack knocked twice on the metal door, then went inside, Glock exposed to show she meant business but not concealed so as to get herself killed. They'd expect her to be carrying, so there was no point in denying or hiding it.

Jack cautiously entered the dim warehouse. She detected no sound from within or sign of movement, and she couldn't see clearly where she was going, but she was sure she'd find out soon enough where the bitch wanted her.

She took a few more steps through the dark entryway and reached an open door. The fading daylight through the filthy windows inside allowed her to make out one chair in the center of the otherwise empty room, a pair of handcuffs resting on the seat.

Jack looked around before she picked up the cuffs and sat. She didn't expect TQ to show up in person. As far as anyone knew, the woman was a ghost. No one in law enforcement and no one Jack knew in the underworld had ever met or seen her, and who knew if that was even her fucking name.

Jack was curious where TQ's men would take her. She didn't know what the woman had planned for her, but immediate death clearly wasn't it. She had mentioned working for her. Jack figured if she got close enough to the Broker to discuss a deal, she'd find a way to either kill or bargain herself out of it. She just hoped the miserable bitch would keep her word and leave Cass alone.

She placed the Glock gingerly on the ground in front of her, kicked it a few feet away, and handcuffed herself to the chair like they expected her to. "Let's get on with the show."

Moments later, a small man or woman—Jack couldn't tell which in the fading light because he/she was wearing black clothes and a black plastic mask—approached from the front. Without saying a word, the stranger stopped before her and lifted one gloved hand to expose a syringe.

"I guess it's good night, motherfucker," Jack said.

The White House
Next evening, March 3

Ryden stood in front of the full-length mirror in her bedroom, unable to believe it was really *her* staring back in bewilderment. Never had she been this beautiful—the stunning dress and hair, the jewelry, the shoes. She looked like a princess. What would Kennedy think of her tonight, especially in light of her not-so-spontaneous admission?

Ryden knew she would regret saying what she had, but at that moment, the closeness, the feel of Kennedy had overpowered her, and she was helpless to deny or dismiss the attraction. Yes, Kennedy was a woman, but Ryden hadn't cared and still didn't.

If Kennedy wanted to, she could get her in serious trouble, but Ryden somehow knew she wouldn't. For some inexplicable reason, she trusted Kennedy. Or at least she wanted to, just as much as she wanted to kiss her.

She touched her lips; it had been years since she'd used them for that purpose. "What if I forgot how to kiss?" she said to her image. "What if I never knew how?" She shrugged. "What does it matter? It's not like it's ever going to happen."

The knock at the door meant it was time to exit her dream world and enter the nightmare with Ratman at its center. It was time for their meeting.

She opened the door for him and then immediately went and sat at her vanity table.

"Are you adequately prepared for this evening?" Ratman asked as he entered. He stopped in the middle of the room.

Ryden picked up the guest list and scanned it for the hundredth time. Anything to look busy and get him away from her as quickly as possible. "Ready as I'll ever be." She'd created her own memory game for matching faces with names and titles.

"Most of these people are new to you, so you need to be absolutely clear on who's who."

"Unless someone has recently had a major face job, I can handle it." *Now get your ugly self out of my room.*

"Kennedy tells me your dance lesson went very well."

"Did she?" Ryden asked, unable to keep the enthusiasm from her voice.

"Yes. She said you were ready to teach Carlos a thing or two."

Ryden's cheeks warmed. "I don't know about that, but I'm glad she thinks I did well." She smiled.

"You seem to enjoy her company."

"I guess."

"Strange," Ratman said. "Not too long ago you described her as a boring mute."

"I never said I didn't like her. Maybe I prefer boring mutes."

"Did you know she's a dyke?"

"It came up," Ryden said nonchalantly. "How is that relevant?"

"We don't want people thinking your new best bud is queer."

"I'm a Democrat and supportive of same-sex marriage, remember?"

"You, Madam President…" his tone oozed sarcasm as he took a few steps closer, "are whatever I say you are." She looked up at him in the mirror and he smiled, exposing his little rat teeth.

"How much does she know?"

"Kennedy?"

Ryden nodded.

"Has she said anything to you?" Suddenly his smirk was gone and his tone worried.

"Why are you so concerned about what Kennedy has to say?"

"Because she suspects inside help and involvement concerning the attack."

"You mean…" So Kennedy had no idea. Ryden didn't know if she should be happy or upset. Of course she was thrilled to learn that Kennedy wasn't Moore's lackey and in on the conspiracy. But if Kennedy *had* known she was a fake, at least her attraction to Ryden would have been sincere—directed at the blackmailed frumpy florist. But this…this meant the bodyguard was attracted to Elizabeth Thomas, the Harvard-educated, eloquent president of the United States. Everything she was not. "You mean she doesn't know?"

"And for you and your buddy's sake," he warned, "it had better stay that way."

Ryden nodded but her mind was a million galaxies away.

"So, you're all ready for tonight?" Ratman asked cheerily.

"Everything is under control."

"I must admit, I never expected you to be this competent. Your learning and memorizing abilities would put many a scholar to shame."

"A matter of life or death can do that to you," she replied dryly.

He laughed. "Then again, she wouldn't have settled for anything or anyone less than ideal."

Ratman was talking about the woman behind this whole orchestration, the one responsible for ruining her life. Ryden had never met her in person but had had the displeasure of listening to that cold, menacing voice on the speaker during her training, when she would call for updates or, more often than not, with threats to her life if she failed. What she wouldn't give for a baseball bat and a few undisturbed minutes with that arctic bitch.

"She's a regular talent spotter," Ryden said. "She should consider *American Idol*."

He walked to her side and lifted her face to him by her chin. "Watch how you speak of her."

Ryden nodded and he let go.

She wasn't going to give him the pleasure this time of seeing how much he unnerved her, so she turned to the vanity table for something to busy her hands with before they started to shake. She picked up the hairbrush and busily pulled the loose hair from it.

"You've become a remarkably beautiful woman." He stood behind her and started to massage her shoulders.

Ryden tried to get up, but he held her down firmly. Then when he was sure she wouldn't move, he slid his hands downward to the front of her décolleté, stopping just above her breasts. She suppressed the urge to bolt. She *really* wanted to get up and stab him in the eye with the brush handle, but instead she sat very still as she watched his moist hands through the mirror reach even lower. It was like she was having an out-of-body experience; she refused to believe this beast was touching her.

"Maybe, we can…" Ratman sounded hoarse. "We can work out an arrangement for the duration of your stay." He bent over and licked her neck. "What do you say, Madam President?"

"Please." Ryden looked at him in the mirror. "Please, stop before I lose control."

"Oh? And do what, beautiful?" He kissed her shoulder.

Ryden started taking shallow breaths as her insides churned. Her stomach couldn't take any more of this—the disgusting saliva and breath on her neck and his hands on her. Her eyes started to tear up from the sudden need to empty her stomach. "I'm…I'm going to be sick," she managed to say.

Ratman must have seen it in her face because he pulled back immediately, allowing her to run to the bathroom.

"Disgusting," Ryden heard him say before she shut the door. "Get yourself cleaned up and ready," he called out. "The guests arrive in an hour."

Southwestern Colorado

Montgomery Pierce frowned down at the tuna salad and fruit plate

Joanne Grant had just delivered for his dinner. He would kill for a cheeseburger and fries—it had been months since he'd had them—but she'd insisted on overseeing his meals until his blood pressure returned to normal limits. Sighing, he picked at the salad. Small price to pay, he told himself, to finally have love in his life and someone to come home to. In recent months, he'd toyed with proposing marriage, though they'd have to keep it secret or the whole no-fraternization rule among ops would have to go.

His phone buzzed. "Yes?"

"Shield's on line one."

He hit the button. "Pierce."

"I have confirmed that some kind of conspiracy is going on in the White House," Shield said. "Watchdog is certainly a part of it, but the real figurehead calling the shots is a woman—and it isn't Lighthouse. Lighthouse is somehow being coerced into participating in this and she's afraid."

"Explain."

She relayed the relevant parts of the bugged conversation she'd just overheard between Thomas and Moore, and asked whether Reno had been able to come up with anything new on the president's special advisor.

"Nothing yet. Whoever made the big payments to Watchdog's Grand Cayman account has taken extraordinary steps to avoid being traced. Reno has tracked the money through four dummy corporations on three different continents so far," Monty replied. "It's time to send someone in to bug Watchdog's home."

"Agreed," Shield said. "Though I don't expect we'll hear anything from that. He seems to spend most all his time in the House, watching Lighthouse very closely. He's at her side at every opportunity, often whispering in her ear. Not enough to really draw undue attention to himself, but definitely a lot more than his previous counterparts."

"We'll let you know if we turn up anything else. So far there's no sign of Agency involvement. But from what you say, Watchdog is concerned about you, so stay sharp and let us know if you need backup."

"Roger that."

After Shield disconnected, Monty stared down at his dinner for a few seconds before pushing it aside, his appetite gone. Even if the CIA wasn't involved, the confirmation that someone outside the White House was powerful enough to exert such control over the president was daunting news. What was the objective? And how many were in on it?

He feared for the country and for Shield. She was a top agent, but she was alone in there, among who knew how many conspirators.

Outside Houston, Texas

Jack woke up in the same cuffed-to-a-chair position, only this time in a cold, white, fluorescent-lit room, and she'd been stripped down to just her underwear and T-shirt.

She surveyed her surroundings. No windows, and apparently only one way in and out—through a steel door. Two cameras were mounted high on opposite sides of the ceiling. The temperature was moderate, but if she had to sit still much longer she'd start to feel cold. Her head was a bit fuzzy and her mouth dry.

"So, now what?" she said to the camera facing her. When no one answered, Jack continued. "I hope you kept your word about Cassady."

"And what if we didn't?" replied a low male voice. It was slightly distorted—coming through a speaker she couldn't see.

"I kept my part of the deal."

"Madam is very pleased you did."

"She kept her word, right?"

"You'll have to ask her."

"Answer me, goddamn it."

"I did."

Jack wriggled in her seat and realized for the first time that her ankles were cuffed to the chair and the chair was bolted to the floor. "Where is she?"

"Ms. Monroe?"

"No, you fuck. I mean TQ."

"She has prior obligations this evening."

"What…what the fuck? She had me brought to this isolation cell and she isn't even here?" She struggled against her handcuffs, but they held fast.

"That's correct."

"Where the hell is she?"

"I can't answer that."

"What the fuck can you answer?"

"I can tell you that madam will be with you at her first convenience."

"What am I supposed to do till her convenience?"

"Wait."

"Like this?" Jack looked down at herself. "What if I need to use the toilet?"

"Your chair is equipped with a pan."

Jack moved her ass and felt a hole beneath her. "This is insane."

"Then I suggest you practice control or deal with the consequences."

"You gotta be fucking kidding," Jack yelled. She waited for a reply and, when it didn't come, feared the man had left. "Food. How about food?"

"You can do without for a fairly long time."

"Not without water, sadistic fuck."

"We will supply you with water when we see fit," the voice replied.

The lights were so bright they hurt her eyes. "Can you dim the damn lights?"

"No."

Jack knew constant intense lighting was a popular method of torture; she had undergone that treatment in Israel. It had taken her years to put those weeks of torture and pain that had changed her forever behind her, and now, here she was, more than a decade later, reliving the same introduction to hell. This was just the beginning of what most probably was yet to come, and honestly, she didn't know if she would survive it. This time she had Cassady in her life, but she wasn't sure even her love for Cass would be enough to fight her way out of this.

She closed her eyes and let her head drop to her chest. "I can't do this again," she mumbled.

CHAPTER EIGHTEEN

The White House
That evening

Kennedy left the wall behind Thomas and started toward the president the moment she got up from the dinner table and announced to her black-tie guests that it was time to adjourn to the East Room for entertainment provided by the White House Marine Orchestra.

In addition to the president of Argentina and his much-younger wife, the one hundred and thirty or so invited guests included diplomats, members of Congress, cabinet members, and a scattering of A-list Hollywood celebrities—all of whom had been lucrative fund-raisers for the Democratic Party. But Kennedy focused on Elizabeth Thomas, and not just because that was her job. She couldn't take her eyes off the president for long, even if she'd wanted to.

The president was stunning tonight in her floor-length Vera Wang gown. The pale-lavender dress was made of a material that shimmered slightly when it caught the light, and the cut, exposing just one of Thomas's smooth, pale shoulders, was stylishly sexy yet maintained the right amount of decorum for the occasion. And for once, the White House stylist had given her a hairdo and makeup job that Shield approved of—the more natural coiffure and subtle cosmetics enhanced, rather than harshened, Thomas's innate beauty.

Thomas's smile, however, was forced. Not surprising, given the exchange she'd heard earlier between the president and Moore, and not to mention the stress of hosting such an important and protocol-ripe event. Most observers probably would not note any problem, but Shield had seen Thomas's true, spontaneous smile and could spot the difference. None of the smiles tonight had been reflected in the president's eyes.

Some guests took seats in the East Room and others remained standing while the orchestra opened with a medley of Latin tunes, including "Down Argentina Way." The guest of honor, seated in the first row between Thomas and his wife, smiled and clapped approvingly.

Then it was time for the prearranged waltz between the two presidents. Thomas had chosen "Fascination," one of the tunes they'd practiced with. Shield suspected the selection had revolved more around the length of the options—this was the shortest one—than the president's personal preference, given Thomas's remarks the day before.

When the conductor gave a slight nod in Juan Carlos's direction, the Argentine president stood, bowed to Thomas, and offered his hand. She took it, rose from her chair, and allowed herself to be led to the middle of the dance floor amidst a smattering of applause. Once they were in position, the orchestra began to play.

Shield felt an unfamiliar pang of envy watching them glide across the floor, Carlos's hand on Thomas's waist, too tight for her liking. Thomas was doing a splendid job, though she appeared less relaxed than she had the day before once she'd allowed herself to surrender to being led. That forced smile was fixed on her face throughout the entire dance.

Though Shield stood against the wall with other bodyguards, in the darkened perimeter, Thomas was apparently well aware of her position. More than once, Thomas looked directly at her, albeit briefly, as she was spun around the floor.

Though it was rarely difficult for her while on the job to maintain the stoic, somber presence characteristic of bodyguards, she couldn't keep from nodding encouragingly at Thomas during a couple of the longer glances her way.

Moore mingled with the crowd and he, too, would occasionally look Thomas's way and smile. Shield realized her fists were clenched; how she wanted to punch that grin off his face, make him suffer for what he'd tried to do earlier. She was happy she'd only had audio and no video to the president's bedroom, because she wasn't sure she'd have been able to refrain from barging in and wiping the floor with him. No one would have been able to blame her either, because she would have been doing her job protecting Thomas.

What had he gotten Thomas involved in? And how long had he been harboring sexual feelings for the president? Was it before or after her husband's death? At this point, Shield didn't put the man's demise past the creep's abilities. They had announced that Thomas's husband had suffered a sudden heart attack, but prompting one was child's play for anyone who knew how.

The music finally stopped, and Shield exhaled when Carlos let go and the two presidents parted. Thomas smiled and nodded politely, to all appearances the picture-perfect, graceful leader of the country, but Shield could tell she felt uncomfortable. Her hands trembled slightly when she touched her neck, her eyes were too intense—dark and troubled—and she looked like she was suffocating. Shield wanted to sweep in and take her away to her home in Tuscany, show her what it was like to breathe again.

When Moore approached Thomas and led her toward one of the guests—an older woman—Shield repositioned herself closer to the president.

Ryden had kept counting the whole time she danced. Not because she needed to, but because it helped her cope with the Argentine president's tight grip on her waist and Ratman's beady eyes. When that ceased to work, she stole glances at Kennedy and tried to imagine she was dancing with her. Every time Kennedy smiled at her, she'd briefly close her eyes to retain the image of that beautiful smile.

"Where to now?" she whispered to Ratman as he led her off the floor and through the crowd.

"Someone wants to say hello."

"I've met everyone on the list."

"This one arrived late."

"Who?"

Ratman stopped in front of a beautiful, middle-aged woman. Her white hair was pulled back tightly, and her dress looked very expensive and classically chic. She was of average height, but that was about the only average thing about her. Ryden had never seen a more elegantly ominous presence. Neither had she seen eyes so black, like they lacked a soul.

"Madam President," Moore said, "I'd like you to meet Theodora Rothschild."

According to Ryden's briefing notes, Rothschild was one of the few guests the real president hadn't already met in person. "Of course. Owner of the Rothschild Auction Houses. How wonderful to meet you in person." Ryden extended her hand.

The woman took it and a chill ran through Ryden, as though her core body temperature had dropped from the cold hand. "The pleasure is all mine."

Ryden gasped aloud. That icy voice was one she would never forget. "I...I know—"

"Stay in character, Madam President," Rothschild warned her.

Ryden looked away. "Of course."

"I came to see whether you're indeed doing the wonderful job Moore is telling me you are."

Ryden couldn't bring herself to look at those terrifyingly dead eyes. "I hope everything is to your satisfaction."

"Very. Keep up the great work. A new...life is just around the corner."

"I look forward to that." Ryden tried to keep her voice steady.

Rothschild laughed coquettishly when the Speaker of the House passed by. "No need to keep you longer. You have guests to entertain, and I have a visitor of my own to see to." Rothschild extended her hand and Ryden had to muster all her courage to take it. "Smile and say something trivial," the bitch ordered.

Ryden plastered on a forced smile. "Have a nice—"

"Yes, yes. Run along now." The cold creature shooed her away with her eyes.

Ryden needed to compose herself before she could resume her duties as hostess. Even finding Tim and his ex-wife dead and the prospect of a lethal injection hadn't frightened her more than this lifeless being.

She was grateful that at least this affair was in the White House, so she could escape to her room for a few minutes. She headed up the grand stairs to the second floor. Shaken, she turned when she heard steps behind her.

"It's only me." Kennedy looked concerned. "Are you all right?"

"I don't know." She crossed her arms. "Yes."

"Can I help?"

"I need a few minutes to collect myself."

She continued down the hall and heard Kennedy say from behind her, "Beacon is fine and in my sights."

She opened the door to her room and was about to close it when Kennedy gently pushed the door to stop her. "If there's anything at all I can do or get you—"

"I need to use the ladies' room, that's all."

Kennedy reached for her transmitter and turned it off. "Then why are you shaking?"

She hid her hands behind her back. "I'm tired."

"You look like you're about to have a nervous breakdown."

She looked down the hall. Two Uniformed Division guards had followed them and taken up positions nearby. "We're drawing unnecessary attention."

"Moore is in the East Room." Kennedy said it like she wanted her to know it was safe to talk.

"Still, I…"

"Do you want me to come in?"

She opened the door farther and stood to the side.

"What's going on?" Kennedy asked as soon as Ryden shut the door.

"Like I said, I'm tired."

"With all due respect, you may be able to fool the rest, but not me. You haven't been…well, since I arrived here." Kennedy took a few steps toward her. "What's going on behind the scenes may be none of my business, but your safety and well-being are."

"I really don't know what you're talking about."

"You're scared, Elizabeth."

"No, I'm…"

"And my guess is Moore has a lot to do with it."

Was it that obvious, or was Kennedy on to something? Ratman had told her Kennedy suspected something. Was she trying to get her to talk? Although she trusted Kennedy and wanted to tell her everything at this moment, somehow Moore would discover any wrong move, and she'd have to face not only him but that dreadfully cold woman. Even though Moore had been the one to continually threaten her, that lifeless, treacherous being was the real danger. Theodora Rothschild would be ruthless about terminating her and whoever else revealed their scheme without a second thought. "Kenneth Moore is a fine man. He cared a lot for my husband and stood beside me after his death." She looked Kennedy straight in the eye. "He's been very supportive."

"I've seen the way he looks at you," Kennedy replied. "It's not support he's offering."

What had Kennedy seen? Ratman had shown nothing but a professional interest in her, and if it weren't for what had happened earlier, even she would've never guessed. "I resent that."

Kennedy raised her hands in surrender. "If whatever you two have going on suits you, then I'll back off."

"Then back off." She was desperate for the conversation to stop.

"Elizabeth, you're lying."

Why was Kennedy pressing? She couldn't handle any more drama right now. "What if it does suit me?" She clenched her fists. "It's none of your concern."

"I don't believe you, and it is my business if you're in danger."

"Are you jealous?"

"Of what?"

"Moore."

Kennedy narrowed her eyes. "Why would I be?"

"Don't think I haven't noticed the way you look at me."

Kennedy took a few steps nearer and stopped a foot away from her.

She would have normally backed away at such an intrusion into her personal space, but she couldn't and she didn't want to.

"And how is that?" Kennedy asked.

She couldn't pull her gaze away from Kennedy. "Like...like..."

"The way you're looking at me right now?"

It would be so easy to kiss her, Ryden thought. "I like you, Kennedy, but that's it." She looked away. "I'm not gay and—"

"And you're the president," Kennedy said. "And I'm your primary guard, and it would be highly unprofessional to..." She went silent and turned toward the door.

"To what?" Ryden asked.

"Nothing. I'm out of line. This whole conversation is out of line." Kennedy gazed at her. "Just remember that should you need someone to talk to, I'm here."

Kennedy had obviously said something because she saw her lips move, but Ryden had blocked it out. "It would be unprofessional to what?" Now Ryden pressed the issue.

Kennedy walked up to her and put her arm around her waist. Their lips were an inch apart and she was dizzy with excitement and expectation.

As her breathing quickened and her heart raced, she repeated, "To what?" in a whisper. She dropped her gaze from Kennedy's eyes to her mouth.

When Kennedy brought her head closer, Ryden forgot to breathe. "To kiss you," Kennedy said against her lips and then pulled away.

Ryden stared at her, dazed.

"I was right." Kennedy let go of her. "You don't want Moore any more than you want whatever he's gotten you involved in." She walked to the door.

"And this is how you make a point?" Ryden yelled.

"I can't protect you if you won't let me, Elizabeth."

"I can have you fired."

"But you won't."

"Because you'll tell the world I wanted to kiss you?" She was furious. "Is my life a game to you, like it is with everyone else?"

"I don't play games. That would be your friend Moore, and I could care less about announcing anything to the world. All I care about is doing my job and you…are my job."

"If you don't play games, then what were you trying to prove a second ago?"

"What I already suspected."

"That I'm attracted to you?" Ryden asked.

"That you're afraid, lonely, and that something very wrong is going on." Kennedy walked through the door and closed it behind her.

Kenneth Moore led Theodora Rothschild away from the East Room and into the Red Room so they wouldn't be overheard. The event was winding down and nearly all the media had already departed, so there was little chance of someone photographing TQ. But she was ultra-sensitive to that possibility, and Moore also wanted to minimize his being seen with her.

"She is the perfect political decoy," TQ said as soon as he'd shut the door. "I struck gold with this one, and it took me only four tries."

"I saw the missing-person pictures of the others on the news. Well, two of them anyway. The blonde wasn't reported locally." He went to the bar and poured them two cognacs as Rothschild took a seat on the couch. "Good luck finding and identifying scattered ashes."

"I warned them," she replied. "I told them there was no space for mistakes or imperfections. Well…except the one who died during surgery."

"No one could have foreseen her intolerance to anesthesia." He handed her one of the snifters and sat beside her. "Her heart seemed fine."

"But it wasn't. What a disappointment."

Kenneth lifted his cognac in a toast. "Just as well. None of them were half as convincing as the florist."

"No telling what rock talent might be hidden under, dear friend,"

TQ replied. "A florist, an uneducated orphan, is more convincing than anyone could have imagined."

They both laughed at that, but Kenneth stopped abruptly when he remembered the loose end they had to consider. "We need to have that press conference ASAP." He put his glass down.

"Of course."

"I mean really soon."

TQ's expression grew serious as well. "Is something the matter?"

"Her bodyguard, Harper Kennedy—some private-contractor dyke the Secret Service assigned to her after the attack—she's snooping around. She suspects internal involvement, and I don't like the way she looks at me."

"Why haven't I heard of her before?"

"She hasn't been a real threat, but our florist has taken a liking to her."

"Who does this Kennedy work for?" she asked.

"The Elite Operatives Organization."

"I've heard of them."

"I've asked around. It wasn't easy to find out much. Only the highest levels of government know about their existence. It would appear they are very capable, and their agents are adopted and trained at a very young age. They require a handsome payment, but they get the job done whatever the cost or risk to themselves."

"I'm aware. That's why I considered them in the past."

"It would be wise to steer clear of Kennedy," he said.

TQ smiled. "Since when do you get paid to think?"

"I just mean—"

"If I have to deal with Kennedy or the EOO, I will."

"I know." Kenneth took a sip. "Senator Schuster has had enough time to come up with his arguments against the president's illegal-arms plan."

"More than enough. Have the double call him tomorrow and tell him she'll hold her press conference in three days. She'll announce she's putting the plan on indefinite hold because his opposition has killed its chances in Congress. He'll hold his own press conference immediately after to explain his reasons."

"Will do."

"We should be able to deliver Thomas back to America shortly after," TQ said.

"And the florist can join her unsuccessful predecessors."

"And so will her bodyguard."

"Kennedy? Why?" He didn't like the idea of crossing the EOO and inviting even closer scrutiny of himself.

"Think, Kenneth." TQ sighed. "How am I supposed to let the one person who's spent so much time with the florist, and is suspicious of her and you, continue to guard the real president?"

"But…"

"But what?" TQ leaned forward. "Do you have a problem with that, Kenneth?"

"This organization means business. They're dangerous."

"Business is my life. Also, nothing is more dangerous than power, and I have power."

CHAPTER NINETEEN

The White House

When the president reemerged from her bedroom after ten minutes alone inside, Shield followed her back to the East Room. Whereas Thomas would previously look in her direction now and then, she now avoided any eye contact.

As soon as she was at the party again, the president seemed to scan the room. For what, Shield wasn't sure, but Kenneth Moore and the older, attractive woman Thomas had been introduced to just prior to her leaving were now absent. Though Shield hadn't been close enough to hear their conversation, she'd seen the surprised, almost shocked expression on Thomas's face. She made a mental note to inquire about the woman later.

Some of the guests were waiting to thank the president and bid her farewell, so Thomas made her way to them. She was poised, as she usually was, but Shield noticed that her eyes were void of emotion, almost cold.

Shield had never meant to play with her and hadn't; what she *had* done, however, was get herself into an impossible predicament.

Thomas clearly wasn't interested in Moore, and was even afraid of him, but Thomas's words had touched her to the core. Although the president was straight and used to be married, Shield couldn't bear the thought of any man touching her. She was upset even now just picturing it. So when Thomas had said Moore's advances were welcome, Shield felt the need to prove her wrong.

She'd wanted to prove that whatever was going on between her and Thomas, no matter how simple, temporary, or superficial, was still more real than what Thomas could feel for another, let alone that despicable little man she was protecting.

The memory of those few seconds, so close to the president, flooded her consciousness. Those full lips…those warm and vulnerable dark eyes…the intoxicating scent of Thomas, all combined into the most intimate, sensual sensation she had ever experienced, even if it was an impossible if not catastrophic scenario. Why did this have to happen? Her life was fine as it was—her wine, home, and Monica, all picked and combined like her grapes to create the flavor that suited her. Thomas, conversely, was a complicated vine she couldn't fuse with herself or her life.

The president shook hands with the last of her guests just as Moore returned. He whispered something to Thomas, smiled when Thomas nodded, and left again.

A few moments later, the president turned to leave as well, and Shield followed her to the Oval Office. Thomas practically shut the door in her face, and Shield was about to call in a replacement so she could take a break when Moore showed up.

"I take it Madam President is inside," he said.

"That's correct."

"We are not to be disturbed."

"Understood."

"About that theory of yours, how's it panning out?"

"Theory, sir?"

"The insider-collaboration-to-kill-the-president premise." He smiled. "Your conspiracy theory?" he added in a belittling tone.

"I never said whoever is involved was trying to kill the president," Shield said, matter-of-factly. "Just like I never said it was a theory."

"Oh?"

"If the assailants wanted to kill the president that day, they would have."

"So, it was a warning? To show us what they're capable of?"

"I think it was a perfectly choreographed theatrical attack."

"Interesting." He crossed his arms and looked down as if considering the possibility. After several seconds, he touched her shoulder. "The only thing your theory lacks is motive." He squeezed her shoulder as if encouraging a child. "Keep at it, though. I find our little talks amusing." He laughed and let go of her. "Now, if you'll excuse me."

Shield grabbed him by the elbow before she could stop herself. "I don't know why or exactly how you're involved, but I do know that Thomas—like Bush and so many others—has been reduced to a puppet president."

"That's ridiculous."

"How close were you to her husband Jeffrey?" she asked.

"Quite."

"So he must have seen the way you look at his wife."

"You're out of line, Kennedy."

"I know," she said, close to his face. "And I frankly don't give a shit."

"I can have you fired."

"You know you can't touch me."

"I can talk to your employer."

"Why don't you?" It was her turn to smile. Shield opened the door to the Oval Office. "I'm sure he'd love that."

"You'd be wise to stick to what you were hired for." He walked past her. "I'll let you know if the president needs to...use the bathroom." Moore grinned and shut the door.

Outside Houston, Texas
Later that night

Jack kept her eyes closed because of the blinding light. There wasn't anything to see, anyway. She'd studied every inch of the room as best as she was able and had discovered no opportunity for escape or reprieve from her confinement. Every now and then, she would move her hands and feet to try to keep the circulation going. So far, she'd managed to avoid soiling herself, but her bladder ached for release.

"How nice to be able to put a face to the voice."

Jack recognized TQ's voice over the intercom. She wasn't sure how much time had elapsed, but it wasn't more than a few hours, which was less than she expected. Staring up at the mounted camera, she replied, "Likewise." She looked down at herself. "I intended to come dressed for the occasion, but something tells me you prefer your women stripped and bound."

"I do so appreciate vulnerability."

"And anonymity."

"What's in a face, after all?" TQ asked.

"You seemed pretty anxious to see mine."

"But you're so much more than a face, Jack."

"That's right. I'm your brother's executioner." Jack smirked.

"That you are."

"Nothing you do to me will bring that disease back."

"Nor do I want him back," the cold, disembodied voice replied. "My affairs are significantly less intricate without him to worry about. Life is much less complicated without attachments. Take Ms. Monroe, for example. You wouldn't be here if it wasn't for your sense of obligation toward another."

The mere thought of anyone touching her blond angel, especially after all she'd already been through, sent a wave of despondency through Jack. "You promised to leave Cass alone."

"And I have. I always keep my promises."

"What do you want?"

"I've debated that question since…well, since you executed Dario in my ear," TQ said.

"He was so fond of being a spectator," Jack said, recalling the man's propensity for orchestrating hookups between call girls and their escorts from behind a two-way mirror. "I thought it was time to make him the star."

"Very creative of you."

"I'm flattered you think so." Jack shrugged.

"Hmm. Kill you or hire you? That's the question."

"The only line that matters is the bottom one, so get to it."

"For someone in a very…compromised position, you seem to think you can call the shots."

"This is your show to run," Jack said. "I just want to know what the hell you want from me. If you wanted to kill me, you could have done that without the boring prelude."

"Maybe I want to take my time. Ever considered that?"

"Been there, done that, and kept the scars."

"I've noticed. Tell me how it happened."

"Why would I?"

"Because I can keep a certain loved one alive."

"Is this how it's going to be? You're going to threaten me with Cass every time you want something?"

"You leave me no choice, since you hold little value for your own life. I'm going to ask you one last time, Jack. What happened to you?"

"I was tortured in Israel by this guy Amzi, who was supplying guns and explosives to some Palestinian radicals. I managed to escape before he killed me."

"What were you doing in Israel?"

"I had taken a job for a rival weapons dealer," Jack lied. She was protecting the EOO and wasn't sure why. Maybe because Cass worked for them. "And in the process fell for a woman. Turns out she was a spy. She pretended it was mutual to get information and then handed me over to Amzi."

"You seem to have this nasty habit of getting involved with the wrong women and sacrificing everything for them."

"If you're implying Cass is one of them, then you're wrong."

"What do you think she'll do when she finds out you're missing?"

"Look for me."

"With what resources, Jack? She's a violinist."

"I didn't say she'd find me."

"True."

"Do you want her to look for you?"

"No."

"Oh?" TQ sounded surprised.

"I want her to stay the hell away from you."

"Do you really think she could get anywhere near me, or even suspect that I'm behind this?"

"No." Jack lied again.

"Why not?"

"I haven't been honest with her. She doesn't know what I've done or who I've worked for."

"Not even after you teamed up with special forces to save her from Rózsa?"

The bitch had done her homework. "I told her someone owed me a favor and let me tag along."

"The FBI owed you?"

"An old school buddy works for the bureau."

"How convenient."

"Exploit whoever, whenever, right?"

"My kinda gal. How did they torture you in Israel?"

Jack had spent years trying to forget what had happened to her, and this psychotic bitch wanted to take her back. "They hurt me."

"How?"

"They used me as a punching bag. Whipped and starved me." Jack left out the rape, the thing that had hurt and degraded her the most.

"How did you escape?"

"After a long while, when they thought I was too weak to stand up, I managed to strangle one of the guards with the chains they bound me with and ran."

"Brave, resilient woman."

"I guess."

After a long pause TQ continued. "I don't want to hurt or torture you, Jack."

"Then tell me what the hell you want."

"I want you to work for me."

"Doing what?"

"Whatever I ask."

"Like?"

"What you are infamous for," TQ replied.

"Poker?"

"I want you to take care of some of my business."

"Be more specific."

"Sometimes I need to make certain individuals see things my way."

"You want me to hurt people."

"Hurt, execute, whatever is necessary."

"I don't do that anymore," Jack said.

"Because your girlfriend asked you not to?"

"Because I don't want to."

"Once a paid assassin, always a paid assassin, Jack. You can't refute your nature."

"What if I decline?"

"What if I have Ms. Monroe shot during the concert?"

"No. You can't touch Cass."

"Then you can't decline."

The bitch left her no choice. "I'll do it."

"I need proof."

"So do I. I want to hear Cass is okay."

"Fair enough," TQ replied. "I'll talk to you soon."

"I want to meet you in person."

"We'll get to that but not just yet."

The static disappeared. TQ was gone.

The White House

Thomas's meeting with Moore lasted an hour. Both came out with blank, distant expressions, and neither looked at Shield. When Shield followed the president to her room, she shut the door in her face without so much as a good night. Thomas was clearly upset with her, and she couldn't fault her.

When Jason, her Secret Service replacement, arrived to take the night watch outside the president's door, Shield left for her bedroom.

Although she was exhausted, she couldn't stop thinking about Moore and his hold on Thomas. After tossing and turning for a couple of hours, she reached for her iPhone and Googled *Jeffrey Thomas Elizabeth died.* She had no proof, but her gut told her Moore was somehow involved in his death.

News reports said Thomas's husband had been playing a round of golf at the Bath Country Club near the couple's home in Maine when his heart failed during the game. His wife Elizabeth, who was campaigning in Vermont at the time, rushed to Mid Coast Hospital in Brunswick, accompanied by her special advisor, Kenneth Moore, a close family friend. But Jeffrey Thomas was pronounced DOA before she arrived. He had stopped breathing in the ambulance and could not be revived.

Reporters covering the story from the hospital said the presidential candidate was too distraught to make any official comment about her husband's sudden death. The only video of her was several seconds shot by a local TV station, of Thomas and Moore getting out of a car in front of the hospital and going inside. Thomas's face was a study of sadness and pain, as though she already had been informed of her husband's passing. Moore's countenance was somber.

One news story, shot several hours later outside the couple's home, said that Elizabeth Thomas had released a statement saying she hoped the media would respect her need for privacy during this difficult time. Kenneth Moore, shown on camera outside the two-story brick residence, said that he was deeply upset by Jeffrey's death. "He had been a heart patient for years," Moore told the reporter, "but you're never prepared for the tragedy of a friend's death."

The news reports went on to say that Jeffrey Thomas, an attorney, was fifty-six at the time of his death, thirteen years older than his politician wife. The couple had been married for twenty-two years and had no children. Shield could find no reference to whether an autopsy had been performed.

By the time she got through finding everything she could on the Internet, it was three a.m. in D.C., one a.m. in Colorado. She could have waited for morning, but she dialed the EOO's number and asked for Reno.

"All of you are responsible for the black circles under my eyes," he said immediately.

"Sorry about the late hour, Reno."

"Yeah, that's what you all say."

"What happened to that sunny personality of yours?"

"I was told it bothers some," he replied grumpily.

"Who?"

"Jack Harding and Chase."

"You mean Phantom."

"She doesn't like that name."

"What's the deal with her, anyway?" Shield had been away on assignment when the rogue former agent had returned to the EOO headquarters a few months earlier. She'd teamed up with agent Chase to track down Andor Rózsa, the madman who had kidnapped her partner Cassady Monroe, aka operative Lynx. "Strange that Pierce let her get away with going AWOL."

"No one really knows why, but there's talk," he whispered.

"Ah, yes. The ever-growing grapevine."

"That's funny." He chuckled. "You owning a—"

"Yeah, yeah. I get it." She cut him off before he finished pointing out the obvious.

"Now, you see? It's that exact attitude that's changed me."

"It shouldn't matter what people say. Just keep being your sunny self. We have enough cynics among us as it is."

"You think?" he asked sarcastically.

"At least your positive outlook makes you original, compared to most of us."

"True."

"So, here's what I need: Jeffrey Thomas's autopsy reports."

"Give me a few."

Shield stared at her bottle of wine on the dresser as Reno clicked away. But instead of traveling back to Tuscany, her thoughts took her to Thomas. Was she already asleep? How long would she give Shield the silent treatment? She was just trying to keep Thomas safe and… "What the hell, Reno, did you just swallow a bird?" she asked when slurping sounds and a loud gulp interrupted her thoughts.

"It's cola. Need the caffeine. And yes, I've been told that, too, bothers people."

"Let me guess."

"Yeah. Same duo."

"Now officially a trio."

"But it makes me original, right?"

"Wrong."

"So, anyway…turns out no autopsy was done on Thomas. He was a longtime heart patient and they didn't find it necessary to perform one."

"I see."

"Anything you want to share?" he asked.

"Like I've said, I don't trust Moore."

"You think he was involved in Jeffrey Thomas's death?"

"Tell Pierce I'm taking some time off tomorrow," she said. "The president doesn't have anything scheduled but meetings within the House. She should be fine for a few hours with the regular guards."

"What are you up to, and can I help?" Reno sounded eager, like he always did when a conspiracy was involved.

"I'm going to visit a certain country club. I'll let you know if I need your expertise."

"Cool."

"Thanks, Reno."

"*Finally* a thank you," he shouted. "Is it so hard for some to acknowledge I'm a human being and not an android?"

"Good night," Shield said. *Poor guy's cracked. He really needs a vacation before he breaks and even the company shrink won't be able to glue him back together.*

CHAPTER TWENTY

Outside Houston, Texas
Next morning, March 4

Jack's bladder hurt so much she bent over in pain. She'd be damned if she'd give TQ the satisfaction, but she didn't know how much longer she'd be able to master her bodily functions. She was cold, her head hurt from the bright light, and although she was parched, any liquid intake would only worsen her situation.

"Hello, Jack." TQ's voice filled the room.

"What time is it?"

"If I wanted you to know, I would have greeted you accordingly."

"I'm gonna say it's morning."

"Maybe," TQ said teasingly. "Then again, maybe not. So, how is life in a box treating you?"

"Nice and quiet in here, and I love what you've done with it." Jack looked around.

"Thank you."

"You said you were going to let me hear Cass was all right."

It was quiet for a while, then TQ's voice came back. "I keep my promises."

The door opened and the same small-framed person she'd seen in the warehouse came in and approached her. She could tell now it was a man. He placed an iPad in front of her and pressed Play. The camera was zoomed on Cass during rehearsals, and the date stamp on the video was, from what Jack calculated, that morning. She would have doubted the date, knowing it could be manufactured, but the conductor spoke and announced that opening night was tomorrow. Jack sighed in relief.

The little man turned off the iPad and left without a word.

"Like I said, I keep my promises," the bitch's disembodied voice said.

"You mean you like to know you have something to blackmail

me with."

"That, too. How is your vision, Jack?"

"A bit blurry." In reality, the lights, in combination with her migraine, had almost rendered her blind. Shutting her eyes didn't help because the light penetrated her lids.

"Your eyes seem quite red—irritated, if you will. Most would be practically blind by now."

"I'm special that way."

"Pride is a dangerous quality."

Jack shrugged. "I'm all about danger," she said flippantly. If that crazy bitch was convinced she was still a killer, she'd do her best to keep her believing that. She'd let her think she was the Queen of England if that meant keeping Cass safe and getting her blind ass out of here.

"I like your perseverance, Jack. It shows character. The kind most don't have, or fake."

"Well, I have it, and sure as hell don't need to fake it."

"Are you sure?"

"Do you doubt me?"

"You haven't soiled yourself, and you must be in dire need of water by now," TQ said, "yet you haven't given in to either need."

"Can't do much about water."

"You can ask."

"I was told to wait until it was brought to me."

"You could have asked, anyway."

"I don't beg."

"Not even if that meant saving Ms. Monroe's life?"

"Then I'd beg," Jack replied.

"So you see—"

"I wonder what it's like to be so lonely, so alone, you have nothing and no one you love enough to beg for their safety. And no one in the whole wide world who loves or cares about you to do the same. Can you imagine how sad and empty life must…" Jack paused. "Oh. Oops, I'm sorry. I just described your life."

"No need to apologize. My life is exactly the way I want it. Yours, on the other hand…"

"Mine, on the other hand, is the life of a paid killer. Don't think for a moment I've deluded myself into thinking I'm worthy of anyone's love or a normal life. I go through the moves and hope Cass doesn't see me for what I really am."

"No redemption in love, Jack?"

"Hardly," Jack lied.

"Why not?" TQ almost purred.

"Because for the right price, I'd still take whoever out."

"But you said you don't do that anymore."

"It's easy to make proclamations when there are no temptations."

"Are you claiming you've still got it?" the ice bitch asked. "That you're capable of killing?"

Jack lifted her half-opened eyes to the camera. "Yeah."

"I'm glad to hear that." TQ stopped talking, and Jack was too exhausted to pursue any further conversation.

She had dozed off when she heard a clamor of scuffling just outside. The door opened, and two men dragged someone in. Jack blinked several times to clear her eyesight. The man in their custody struggled to break free but was pinned facedown on the floor next to her.

"What's going on?" she asked.

"A little gift to feed your appetite," TQ's voice answered over the loudspeaker.

Jack looked back at the man on the floor and did her best to focus her vision. He was naked except for his boxers, balding and middle-aged, with thick glasses and a familiar tattoo on his thigh. Leaning forward as far as her restraints would allow, Jack squinted to be sure she was seeing right and made out the image of a baby rattle and the initials BJC.

TQ's two henchmen let go of the guy. One of them uncuffed her from the chair, and then both left the room.

The bald guy rolled over onto his back and then sat up, obviously too terrified to move any further. He trembled as he looked around the room.

Jack pushed off the arms of the chair and got up, but her legs were too numb to hold her weight so she sat back down and stomped them to restore circulation. "What's he doing here?" she asked as a painful tingling returned to her limbs.

"Go to the door and slide the meal slot."

"I'm not hungry."

"Then I hope you find my offering irresistible."

Jack got up. Her legs were a lot better, but she had a hard time getting to the door; her eyes were mere slits because everything was so damn blinding white. She eventually managed to find and slide the little panel, and she stuck her hand in. The feel of steel surprised her.

"What are you up to?" Jack asked, and pulled the gun in: a SIG Sauer from the feel of it.

"I want you to kill that man."

"No! Please, I haven't done anything," the man pleaded as his shaking intensified. "She's crazy. Please, don't—"

Jack turned to him. "Shut the fuck up." She looked back at the camera. "What's that going to prove?"

"That you still have a taste for it."

"I don't kill for free. What's in it for me?"

"Better accommodations," TQ replied, "and a meeting with me to talk about your future."

Jack lifted the SIG Sauer and the man struggled to his feet, begging for his life. Her eyes still on the camera, Jack fired one shot, and he dropped to the floor and lay still.

Applause came over the loudspeaker. "Brava." Then the room filled with TQ's cold laughter. "For someone with compromised vision, you sure got him where it counts."

"I always execute between the eyes."

"And blindfolded?"

"On instinct."

"How lovely."

Jack looked in the direction of the man. The wall behind him was a blurry red. She walked up to him and fired one more time in the same spot.

"I'm sure he was dead the first time."

"This one was for kicks." Jack wanted to spit at his sorry ass but refrained.

"We're going to get along swimmingly."

"Now get me the fuck out of here," she said, desperate to use the bathroom. "I don't want to be around when he starts to stink."

Bath, Maine

Once she'd signed off with Reno, Shield notified the Secret Service she was taking some time off, booked a flight, then caught a two-hour nap. She was dressed and en route to Dulles Airport to catch her plane by six, before the president even woke up. After a two-hour flight and fifteen-minute ride in her rental car, she arrived at the sprawling Bath Country Club, a public course busy with early morning golfers despite temperatures in the low twenties.

She noted the security camera mounted over the main entrance and others in the lobby. At the main sign-in desk, she asked to speak to the manager, and within a couple of minutes, an athletic-looking guy in his late thirties, wearing khakis and a V-neck sweater embroidered with the club logo, came out of a back office and asked how he could be of help.

Shield introduced herself and flashed him her White House credentials. She told him she was there to check out the area for a possible future visit from the president.

"We are delighted President Thomas would consider visiting us," he said. "What happened with her husband here was most unfortunate."

"Yes, it was. I'm sure you did everything in your power to accommodate the situation."

"Of course."

She glanced up at the lobby camera. "Do you have security cameras everywhere?"

"Of course," he said again. "The entrance, bar, restaurant, here, and several on the course itself."

"Good. Do you mind if I take a look at the feeds in your monitor room?"

"Not at all. Follow me, Ms. Kennedy."

Shield was taken to a small office dominated by three rows of monitors mounted to the wall and spare CCTV cameras and related equipment stacked on a shelf. A young man was seated behind a desk, his glance darting from one monitor to the next.

"I doubt the president will want to golf," Shield said. "Perhaps a bit too premature still."

"I understand," the manager replied.

Shield looked closely at the monitors displaying images from the course. "Where exactly did Mr. Thomas collapse?"

"Right here." He pointed to one of the monitors.

"Do you keep digital records?"

"Usually only for a few weeks, but in Mr. Thomas's case, we kept it."

"Why?"

"I don't mean to sound insensitive, but it's not usual to have a first man die…I mean collapse, at our club."

"You kept it for memorabilia reasons?"

He looked chagrined. "We also didn't know if the FBI would want to take a look at it."

"Did they?"

"No."

"It was a straightforward situation," she said. "Mr. Thomas was a heart patient, after all."

"Indeed."

"Did you notice anything out of the ordinary that day?"

"Such as?" He looked at her suspiciously.

"In light of the attack on President Thomas, we want to make sure everything runs smoothly. I have to know if we need to eliminate anything or anyone as a possible threat." Her response didn't really answer his question, but when it came to Thomas's security after the attack, everyone jumped to attention.

"Of course. I understand." The manager cleared his throat. "Such a wonderful woman. She used to come here with her husband before her election. It's horrible when things like this happen." He looked skeptical.

"So, nothing out of the ordinary?"

"Like I told the FBI." He touched his nose. "Mr. Thomas arrived around noon, had coffee and lunch with his three friends, and an hour or so later, all of them left for the course."

"And the restaurant is monitored, you said."

"Of course. These cameras, right here." He pointed to a quartet of monitors in the right corner. The club dining room had twenty or so tables, a third of them currently filled with golfers having breakfast or coffee.

"And I assume you kept the footage of those as well?"

He looked away, embarrassed. "Indeed." Did the guy ever use any other words except *indeed* and *of course*?

"I would like copies from that day of every area he visited."

The man lifted his eyebrow.

"I, too, am guilty of morbid curiosity." Shield tried to sound a bit embarrassed at the admission. The man smiled and Shield continued. "But I want them primarily to study the area."

"Of course. I understand."

"Do you mind if I take a look at the footage while you make copies?"

"Well…I—"

"For practical purposes," she said. "If I have any questions, I can ask while I'm here."

He seemed to consider it a few moments. "Please, follow me."

The manager took Shield to his office and sat her at his desk. He retrieved a DVD from the bookcase behind her and inserted it into the drive in his computer, then pulled up a chair for himself. "This is a comprehensive copy you can have."

The footage was pretty boring for the first forty minutes, with Jeffrey Thomas at the restaurant drinking coffee with his friends and seemingly enjoying himself. He took a pill and had lunch. Shield was about to press Forward when she caught a slight change in Thomas's expression. He went from smiling and talking to silent and withdrawn, his eyes and mouth tight with worry or pain; Shield couldn't be sure which. "Didn't you notice his discomfort when you viewed the footage?"

"I did."

Shield backed up the copy and hit Pause. "It's clear he took his pill before he ate."

The manager moved in closer to look. Shield let the footage continue and noticed Thomas grimace after he took a good sip of coffee. He said something to his friends and took another, smaller sip. This time his expression was less sour, and he continued to drink from the mug throughout lunch.

"Do you have a list of people on duty that day?" she asked.

"Yes, but why?"

Shield backed the tape up all the way to the beginning, before Thomas and his friends placed their orders. She paused it when the waiter came into view. "Who's the waiter?"

The manager peered at the still image. "I don't recognize him offhand. I'll have to ask." He picked up the phone and called his personnel staffer. "I need the names of all the waiters present on the twelfth of October, working the morning shift."

Shield kept her eyes on the young man on the monitor while she waited.

The manager jotted down some names and hung up. "All but one of the three people working that morning are full-timers and have been with us anywhere from a year to five years."

"And the one?"

"A temp from an agency. He came in to replace his girlfriend, who'd called in sick."

"Do you have his name?"

"Dennis Weitman."

"How about an address or number?"

He picked up the phone and called personnel again. "Lives in Bath and gave us a cell-phone number." He wrote it down.

Shield pulled out her cell and dialed Weitman's number. She got a recording telling her the number was no longer in use. "Is the girlfriend working today?"

He shook his head. "She left to take another job not long after this happened." After another call to personnel, he wrote down the woman's name, number, and address. "Her place isn't far. Just down the road a couple miles."

She pocketed the information. "What agency sent Weitman?"

"We use Rapid. Here's that number."

Shield Bluetoothed the restaurant footage onto her phone before she ejected the DVD. "Thank you for your help. I'll let you know if I need anything else."

"What does all this mean?" the manager asked. "This Weitman temp, was he involved in something?"

"I can't know that."

"This could be catastrophic for the country club. We make good work of hiring capable personnel."

"Please, don't jump to conclusions and don't spread stories. I have no proof this young man, unbeknownst or otherwise, was involved in anything."

"Of course. Any stories or rumors would be disastrous for our reputation."

"Thank you again," she said. "I'll show myself out."

CHAPTER TWENTY-ONE

Shield got back in her rental and called EOO headquarters on her cell. She forwarded the footage to Reno's e-mail while she waited for him to come on the line.

"I need current info on a Dennis Weitman," she told him. "Lived in Bath, Maine, and worked for the Rapid Temporary Agency last October. He's the waiter in the footage I've just sent to your e-mail."

"Hang on, let me take a look," Reno replied before taking a noisy slurp of whatever liquid he was consuming. "That's the president's husband in the bottom of the screen, right?"

"Yeah. Work your magic and see what you can get off this. Jeffrey Thomas had some obvious discomfort in the video, and this waiter who served him is in the wind."

"You got it."

"I'm en route to see his girlfriend," she told him as she started the car and pulled away from the curb. "I'll call you back after I'm done there."

The address the country-club manager gave her was that of a low-rent apartment complex desperately in need of attention. The exterior paint was peeling and cracked, the parking lot was full of potholes, and the lawn was riddled with yellow spots and dog feces.

Inside the entryway was a wall of mailboxes and a massive speakerphone system that allowed residents to buzz visitors in through the locked interior door. Shield hit the button next to a plate that read, J. GINGRAS, 2D. "Julie Gingras?"

"Yeah," a woman's voice replied.

"I'm with the Secret Service. I'd like to ask you some questions."

"What about?"

"Your work at the Bath Country Club."

"I don't work there anymore."

"Please open up."

"Whatever, I'm busy."

"We can do this the hard way if you refuse to cooperate."

A few seconds later, Gingras buzzed her in. Her apartment was on the second floor, and the young woman stood waiting at the top of the stairs. "Show me your ID," she said as Shield neared.

Shield flashed her White House credentials as she walked around the girl to the open door of 2D. "Let's do this inside."

The girl walked in first and Shield shut the door behind them.

Julie Gingras's long blond hair covered most of her face, the same way dark stains covered most of her worn T-shirt. Without a word, she curled up on the couch and stared at some infomercial on TV. The small apartment, with its kitchenette, looked like a department store had exploded in there. Clothes and shoes covered almost every surface, and dirty plates were piled up on the sink and coffee table.

The furnishings and clothes were all feminine, however, with no indication that Weitman or any other man was also living there.

"So?" Julie said distractedly.

Shield walked over to the television and turned it off.

"Hey." The girl complained with a frown. "I was gonna buy that Miracle Mop."

"Nothing short of a fire hose can clean this place up."

"Whatever."

"I have some questions regarding your sick leave on the twelfth of October."

"That was like eons ago. So?"

"I understand your boyfriend took your shift that day."

"I had the flu. So?"

"I'd like to talk to him."

"Why, what'd he do?"

"I'm not sure yet," Shield replied, standing over the girl. "That's why I want to see him."

"Good luck with that." Gingras stared at the blank TV screen.

"Where is he?"

The girl shrugged. "Dunno."

"What time does he get back?"

"Like, never. We broke up in November when I caught him screwing my best friend, like on our bed."

"Do you know where I can find him?"

"The scumbag moved back to Boston."

"Do you have an address?" Talking to the girl was like pulling teeth.

"Ipswich Street, 'cross from Fenway Park."

"Number?"

"152, I think."

"Thanks."

"Whatever. Tell him I said I hope he rots in hell."

Shield had barely shut the door when the blare from the TV started up again.

"Got anything yet on Weitman?" Shield asked Reno as she headed toward the highway.

"He has a pretty extensive rap sheet for a twenty-six-year-old," Reno replied. "Stole a car in his teens, lots of petty drug busts, then served a couple of years for breaking and entering. Nothing in the last year or so, however, and can't find a current on him. No driver's license, and he hasn't filed taxes in the last couple of years. If it helps, most of his history—school, arrests and such—was in Boston."

"I'm headed there now. His girlfriend gave me an address. Send me his mug shot, and call me back if you get anything I can use."

Dorchester, Massachusetts

Dennis Weitman cursed aloud when the phone bleated again, jarring him from his near-coma slumber. He hadn't gotten home until six that morning and had promptly passed out on the couch after a night of pill popping and sex. He fumbled for the receiver, trying not to tip off the couch. "What?"

"Listen, stupid. Someone was just here asking about you. Not that I owe you any favors, loser, but I thought you might wanna know."

"Who is this?" Dennis scratched his balls, half-awake.

"It's Julie, you fool."

"Hey, Jules. What's up, babe?"

"Don't babe me, and are you even listening? Some Secret Service woman named...something Kennedy is looking for you."

"Why?"

"Something about you taking my shift at the golf club in October."

Dennis sat up. "What exactly did she say?"

"Nothing. She just wanted to know where to find you."

"What did you tell her?"

"I gave her an address near Fenway. Some girl's I went to school with."

"Good. What did you tell her about that day?"

"I didn't tell her you made me call in sick, if that's what you mean."

"Good. Good."

"Why is she looking for you?"

"Don't know, babe. Listen, I gotta go."

"Hey, wait. I—"

Dennis hung up the landline and made a call from his unregistered cell. "Hey, it's Weitman."

"I hope you have a good reason for calling this number."

"Some Secret Service chick named Kennedy is looking for me, asking about the golf club."

"Who has she contacted?"

"My ex. The one I took the shift for."

"What did Ms. Gingras tell her?"

Dennis frowned, surprised they even knew his ex's name. "Julie gave the woman a fake address to get rid of her."

"I see."

"Listen, I don't want any trouble with no Secret Service."

"Don't panic, Mr. Weitman. We'll take care of it."

"Damn right you will. Last thing I need is cops crawling up my ass."

"We'll make sure that doesn't happen. Keep a low profile until we find out what this is about."

"You know what this is about. Someone knows or someone talked. Either way, I just got paid to do a job. None of this is my shit to deal with."

"Thank you for notifying us. You have nothing to worry about. We'll get back to you when we know something."

"Damn right you will." Dennis hung up. "Motherfucker." He kicked the coffee table and got up to shower.

A quick call to the airport confirmed there were no direct flights between Portland and Boston, so Shield decided to drive the hundred or so miles and arrived at Fenway about one in the afternoon. It didn't take her long to determine the address that Gingras had given her was fake. Number 152 was a broken-down tenement, long unoccupied, that was due to be torn down to make way for a new parking lot. None of the area merchants recognized Dennis Weitman's mug shot.

Frustrated, she called Reno back. "The address I had is bogus. Got any leads where he might be?"

"Weitman has no family to speak of," Reno replied. "No one visited him in prison. But Harry Brinker—his cellmate when he was in the MCI-Norfolk facility—lives just outside Boston, and Weitman was registered at that address when he was released a year ago."

"Mail it to me, and a mug shot of Brinker."

"Coming your way."

"Talk to you later." Shield hung up.

She entered the address into her GPS and turned the car south. Thirty minutes later, she stood at the door of a tiny prefab house surrounded by a wire fence, in a slummy area of Dorchester. The house was tired and worn, and a large, balding beige patch served as lawn.

Shield went up three steps to the small porch. As soon as she knocked, she heard movement from inside. "Mr. Brinker, please open up."

"Who's there?"

"Agent Kennedy. I'm with the Secret Service."

Several seconds passed before an overweight man in his mid-thirties opened the door but left it on the chain. He wore soiled sweats, and a cigarette dangled from between his brown-stained fingers.

Shield held up her ID. "I was hoping you could help me find Dennis Weitman."

"Dunno him."

"Your ex-cellmate. He registered your home as his address after his release."

"Oh, that Weitman. Yeah, he was here for a week, maybe. That was over a year ago."

"Do you know where he went after that?"

"Nah, we didn't stay in touch." He was blinking so fast Shield was surprised he could see her.

"Do you mind if I come in?"

"What for?" Brinker asked. "He's not here."

"I'd like to check that for myself."

"Do you have a warrant?"

"No, but I can get one. All I want is to make sure he's not in there."

The big guy took a quick look behind him and turned back to

her. "I don't think so. If you want to come in, I'm gonna have to see a warrant."

These were the times Shield regretted working under her own name instead of a cover. Under other circumstances, the door would be hanging on its hinges and the fat guy would be sweating on the couch with her gun in his face. Shield took a deep breath. "Look, I'm not here to make any trouble for you. I just need to talk to Dennis."

"What about?"

"I want to ask him some questions about a past employer."

Brinker looked away briefly again. Shield was sure he was checking with Weitman about whether to let her in.

"I'd help, lady, but I don't kow where he is."

"Very well then, you don't leave me a choice. I'll be back in an hour." Shield returned to her rental sedan, certain that it wouldn't take long for Weitman to come running out, looking for a place to hide. She drove away and parked around the corner where her car would be concealed but positioned so she had a view of the front porch through the shrubbery.

The door opened five minutes later and Brinker emerged to scan the area. His mouth moved; he said something aloud and then Weitman came out, small duffel bag and car keys in hand. He hurried to an older Plymouth and took off. Shield waited a few seconds to follow him.

Weitman pulled onto the freeway and headed north at the speed limit, with Shield pacing him several cars behind. As they followed the signs toward Salem, rapidly eating up miles, she realized that the car directly behind the Plymouth—a silver Ford sedan—wasn't following the natural flow of traffic, but was altering its speed to keep its position. Someone else was also following Weitman.

Shield called Reno and asked him to trace the plates on the Ford. He reported back that it had been reported stolen an hour earlier.

Weitman exited the freeway and turned into a deserted parking lot behind an after-hours strip joint. The silver sedan kept pace until he did, then continued down the road past the club.

Shield grabbed her gun from the dash as she stepped on the gas and stopped right behind the Plymouth, trapping Weitman between her car and the wall of the building. She jumped out and pointed the gun at him. "Secret Service. Show me your hands."

"I'm unarmed," he shouted, and put his hands on his head.

"Get out of the car."

"Why?"

"Because I said so."

"I have nothing to say."

Shield opened the door for him and grabbed him by the collar.

"Chill," he said, "I'm coming out."

"Keep your hands where they are."

"I didn't do anything." He slid out of the driver's seat with his hands still on his head.

"I want to talk about Thomas."

He leaned against the car. "I don't know any Tho—"

Weitman's eyes went blank as blood oozed from a small hole that suddenly appeared above his left eyebrow. Almost simultaneously, Shield heard the muffled discharge of a weapon. As Weitman dropped to his knees in front of her, Shield immediately ducked and fired over the car in the direction where the gunshot had come from. No more shots came her way, but she heard a car take off in the distance.

Weitman lay limp on his side in front of the open door of the Plymouth, his eyes wide open and a growing puddle of blood under his head. So, the ex-girlfriend hadn't been angry enough with him to not warn him. Too bad Weitman had to alarm whoever had hired him.

Shield wasn't exactly heartbroken by his demise, but she did regret not getting the chance to make him talk. She dialed 911 from the pay phone outside the club and told the operator a man was down and gave them the address. She wasn't about to get involved or offer any information that would wake any sleeping dogs to her suspicions concerning Jeffrey Thomas's death. So far, she had little to no proof, and any media and fed attention would lead to a wild goose chase that would only alarm those behind Thomas's death and hamper her search.

Whoever killed Weitman hadn't stuck around to kill her as well. Either they hadn't been ordered to or they didn't want to stir up trouble by killing White House security—something that would certainly trigger an extensive investigation. Shield pulled out of the parking lot and took off in the direction she'd heard the car speed away. She was sure it was the silver sedan that had been following Weitman.

She drove around for an hour before deciding to give up. Whoever had shot Weitman had probably ditched the stolen car.

"Weitman's dead," she told Reno as she headed slowly toward Logan Airport, still watching out for the Ford.

"You okay?" He sounded concerned.

"I'm fine. They dropped him right in front of me just as he was getting out of the car."

"Before or after he gave you a name?"

"Before."

"Did you see who shot him?"

"They snipered him. I'm sure it was the guy from the stolen car. I tried to find him, but no luck."

"Crap. What do we do now?"

"You're going to book me on the next flight out of Logan. I have to get back to Washington."

"The president awaits."

"Yeah." She heard Reno typing away at his computer in the background.

"How is she to be around?"

"She's hard to read. High-strung most of the time."

"She's pretty attractive for a president," he said.

"She's even better in person."

"Is she any fun?"

"She can be when she's not nervous or irritated with me," Shield replied.

"Why you?"

"It's complicated." She thought back to the night she almost kissed Thomas.

"What did you do?"

"My job."

"I guess she doesn't like being babysat."

"Frankly I don't know what she likes," she said distractedly. "She's…not what I expected."

"What does that mean?"

"She's very sensitive and almost innocent, in a way a woman her age shouldn't be. Like she doesn't fit the role."

"She sounds too good to be a president."

Shield sighed. "She is. She's unpretentiously charming, almost disarming."

"We are talking about the U.S. president, right?"

"Hey, I'll catch you later."

"Shield?"

"Yeah?" She was still scanning the streets for the silver sedan.

"Are you all right?"

"You mean conspiracy and Jeffrey Thomas's assassin getting killed in front of me, aside?"

"That, too, but are you all right with Thomas?"

"Sure."

"Sounds to me like you like her. A lot."

"Later, Reno. Text me the ticket info." Shield hung up.

CHAPTER TWENTY-TWO

The White House

Ryden had managed to get through her closed-door session with the Argentine president, and several important meetings that followed, to Ratman's satisfaction. But she still had three more to go before she was done for the day, and she wondered how she'd manage. She felt pushed to the very limit of her patience. After running a brush through her hair, she glanced at her schedule and wearily pushed herself up from the vanity. The next item on her agenda, a briefing from Homeland Security in the Roosevelt Room, would likely involve an elaborate multimedia presentation of some sort.

She found the backup Secret Service agent outside her door in the same position she'd left him, like he hadn't dared to move. "When is Kennedy expected to return, Jason?" she asked.

He cleared his throat. "She didn't say, Madam President."

"Of course not. I mean, why bother? It's not like she has a job to do."

"I…I'm…I don't…"

"Tell Kennedy I want to see her."

"Of course, Madam President."

She was wired so tight, her responses had become abrupt even to Ratman, but at this point, his menacing stare didn't affect her. Every time she'd exited one meeting to go to another today, she'd expected to find Kennedy waiting for her outside the door. Instead, she would find her backup agent, who'd jump to attention at the sight of her. His expression was usually a mixture of frustration and fear she might ask him about Kennedy.

The twenty minutes alone in her room, her first real break, had done little to soothe her frayed nerves. Ratman had been at her side the entire endless day, beginning with her meeting with Juan Carlos and continuing through appointments with the joint chiefs of staff and several cabinet members. He had made sure she followed her script and gave them all the correct answers, and in between each appointment, he'd grill her to make sure she'd done her homework about whatever was coming next.

Around nine p.m., after her last meeting, she announced to that miserable excuse of a human that she was retiring for the night.

"I'll walk you to your room." Ratman's tone was smooth, almost flirtatious, as he followed just behind her toward the stairway to the second floor.

"Thank you, but that's not necessary."

"I know," he replied with a smile.

"Whatever," she said under her breath as she headed up the steps. She couldn't be bothered to argue with him. She was too tired and too irritated for a confrontation. "I need to be alone. It's been a long, draining day, and frankly, I'm in no mood for threats or advances or whatever else you have in mind."

His smile instantly disappeared, and he grabbed her arm as they reached the upper corridor. To all appearances, it was a benign gesture for her to slow down, but his pointy little fingers dug hard and deep into her flesh. "Don't push it," he whispered. "Just because they can hear and see us doesn't mean you can talk to me like that, florist."

Ryden stopped and smiled. Her bodyguard was a good distance out of earshot. "You know, you used to scare me, but…" She shrugged. "I got over it."

"Did you, now?"

"The way I see it, you need me. And *will* need me until I get the job done. So get your ratty little fingers off me and leave me the hell alone until it's absolutely necessary to burden me with your foul existence."

"Ah, she has a backbone." He released her and clapped three times but remained serious. "One I can snap in two."

"You could, but you won't, because you need me."

He leaned in. "What happens when I don't?"

"Is that a threat?" She raised an eyebrow. "Because, according to our agreement, you can't touch me once I'm done with this charade."

"You're right," he replied. "*I* can't."

"Good. Now act your role and fuck off, because the president told you to."

Ratman turned on his heel and walked down the stairs.

Ryden went to her bedroom and locked the door, then leaned her back against it and released a long breath. She didn't know where or how she'd bought the balls to talk to that despicable man the way she did, but right now and all day, for that matter, she'd felt too irritated to care about what anyone thought. She was annoyed, and tired, and... where the hell was Kennedy?

She practically ripped her clothes off with disgust. She didn't want any part of her present life permeating her skin, reminding her how weak she was for letting herself get involved and manipulated into playing the role of a strong, powerful, elegant woman. A woman who had nothing in common with the type of woman *she* was.

Ryden took her time in the shower and, still refusing to wear anything that was Thomas's, sat on the bed with nothing on beyond her underwear. Her conversation with Ratman had given her the strength, and enhanced her need, to be the woman she'd always wanted to run away from and change—a simple person who craved simple pleasures and didn't have to answer to anyone. So what if Kennedy would never desire someone as plain as Ryden the florist? She was a good, decent, hardworking woman, and as long as *she* was proud of herself and the difficulties she'd overcome, then screw Kennedy and every other Kennedy for wishing her to be someone else. Someone refined, with immaculate table manners and knowledge of expensive wines, and... "I could use a glass of wine right about now."

She eyed the adjoining door to Kennedy's room. "You think you can play with people. Does that make you feel special?" Ryden got up. "Special, my ass. You wouldn't know a good, decent woman if she slapped you on the ass. How dare you try to kiss me and then...how dare you manipulate me, too?"

Ryden got up and knocked on the door. She waited, biting her lip and prepared to give Kennedy a piece of her mind. But when no answer came, she did something completely out of character. She tried the door to see if it was unlocked.

It was. Of course it was. Kennedy had to be able to reach her immediately at any hint of danger.

Ryden knocked one more time, her hand on the knob, before she entered Kennedy's room. It was too dark to see anything, so she made her way toward the light switch, hoping it was where her own was. "Crap it all to hell," she shouted when she stubbed her toe on something. Limping, she found the switch.

Except for a few items on the dresser, the room was seemingly devoid of anything personal except for the musky, alluring scent that was Kennedy. Ryden opened the closet and found three black suits and two blue ones, an array of shirts, three belts, and a few pairs of black shoes. Every item appeared well sewn and the fabrics and leather expensive. "Looks like the wine business is doing well."

Part of her wanted to feel guilty for what she was doing, but the other half couldn't and didn't want to resist. She didn't know why she was in Kennedy's room, and although she'd feel completely embarrassed if Kennedy walked in and found her there, practically naked, Ryden almost wished she would. *I wonder what her pillow smells like.* "Okay, now you're just being scary."

And why the hell did it matter what it smelled like, anyway? Kennedy was just another manipulative idiot. Ryden spotted a bottle of wine on the bedside table and picked it up. "Il Grigio Angelo." But not the one she'd tried that day with Kennedy. This one had a gold label that said SPECIAL COLLECTION. Kennedy must have gotten it from the White House's wine cellar. "If it's fit for a president, then it's fit for a florist. Besides," she said, raising the bottle toward Kennedy's neat rack of suits, "you shouldn't be drinking on the job anyway."

Ryden took the bottle back to her own room. "I deserve a night off." She dialed Betty for a corkscrew.

By the time Shield returned to the White House, it was eleven o'clock. According to Jason, everything had gone smoothly except for Thomas's foul mood at the fact that she'd taken the day off. "She said she wanted to see you when you got back."

"How long ago did she retire?"

"Two hours."

"Okay. Thanks."

Shield decided to stop in her room to drop off her bag before she saw Thomas, but as soon as she flipped on the light, she realized someone had been in there. The closet door was half an inch ajar, and her private-collection wine was missing. She was about to run out of the room in search of answers when a knock from the adjoining door stopped her.

"So you're finally back," the president said loudly through the door and then laughed. "Did you have a nice time with that someone you had to see?" Thomas sounded different, somehow.

"Elizabeth, are you all right?"

The knob turned, and a moment later, the president stood looking at her curiously from the other side, dressed only in a pale-blue nightgown that ended mid-thigh. It was made of silk, with spaghetti straps and a lace-trimmed bodice. She had Shield's bottle of wine in one hand and a half-full goblet in the other. "Care for a glass?" Thomas asked.

"What are you doing?" Shield asked quietly, trying to control her anger.

"You've been holding out on the good stuff."

"All my wine is good, but that's beside the point."

"Hmm." Thomas lifted the bottle and eyed it. "This one here says Special Collection. You can't tell me it's not better."

"You were in my room."

"You're sharp."

"You have no right."

"And *you* shouldn't be drinking on the job," the president said, and chuckled to herself.

"I didn't…don't. It was a keepsake I like to have with me whenever possible." Shield's heart sank when she realized the bottle was more than half-empty. "It was a special bottle. The only one of its kind."

"Settle down." Thomas waved the bottle in the air. "I'll get you another one."

"You can't."

"I'm the president. I can do anything." Thomas laughed.

"Why were you in my room?"

"Like I said, I'm the president. I can do anything."

President or not, Shield was close to losing what little patience she had left. No one invaded her personal space or touched her things. The loss of her beloved bottle was particularly upsetting. "Look, Madam President," Shield said, not bothering to hide the sarcasm from her voice. "I don't know what you're going through, but you have no right to be in my room unless you need me because of an emergency."

"Maybe it *was* an emergency," Thomas replied, "but then again, you wouldn't know because you weren't here."

"If that's the case, you had a guard with you all day."

"And if they were competent to begin with, they wouldn't have hired you." Thomas hiccupped. "Am I right, or am I right?"

"What was the emergency?" Kennedy crossed her arms over her chest, not believing a word of it. Had anything happened, she would have been informed immediately.

"I wanted to talk to you." Thomas entered Shield's room on unsteady feet and leaned against the dresser.

Kennedy followed her with her gaze and turned to face her. "So I heard. I was about to come to you when you knocked on my door. What do you want to see me about?"

"I um...I..."

"You're drunk, Madam President."

"I'm tipsy, and stop calling me that. Call me Elizabeth like I asked you to. Or better yet, call me Lizzy."

"I can't do that. Maybe you need to sit down." Shield walked over to Thomas and slowly took the bottle and then the glass from her hands. She placed them on the dresser and put an arm around Thomas's waist.

"This feels nice. Maybe we should go for a walk. It's a lovely evening," Thomas said as Shield led her to the armchair.

"I don't think you should be going anywhere." Shield helped her sit.

"Party killer."

"How much have you had to drink?"

"A glass...or three."

"You really are a lightweight." Shield took a seat on the armchair across from her.

"So, how was your day, Kennedy?"

"I had to fly to Maine for business."

"To see someone."

"Yes."

"Who's in Maine?"

"Your late husband's golf club."

"My who?" Thomas looked confused.

"Mr. Thomas."

The president blinked several times. "Oh, yeah. Him."

Shield was certain Moore was involved in the death of Thomas's husband Jeffrey. But Thomas herself, under the influence of alcohol and unconstrained by lucid emotions and responses, seemed to be showing absolutely no emotion for her late husband. Maybe this wasn't such a bad situation after all. It seemed a perfect opportunity to get more information from the president about what was going on. "How was your relationship with Mr. Thomas?"

"Just fine."

"Did you love him?"

"Sure, he was my husband," she said flippantly.

"And Moore?"

Thomas grimaced like she'd just licked a lemon. "What about

him? I sure as hell don't love him."

At least she finally admits to disliking that bastard. "Did he and your late husband get along?"

The president shrugged. "I don't know. I guess."

Shield wasn't about to remind Thomas of her previous statement, avowing how much Moore cared for her and her husband. "You must have been pretty scared during the attack."

"That was something, all right." Thomas's voice and demeanor were devoid of any grief or melancholy. Anyone in her position would at least show discomfort at the mere mention of such a dramatic memory.

"What happened in there?"

"I can't talk about that." Thomas looked away. "But hey…I get to live."

"It might help you cope if you share," Shield said. "You need to talk to someone, Elizabeth. You can't do it all on your own."

"I can't talk to anyone, especially not you."

"Why not? You can trust me."

"Funny you say that." Thomas smiled. "Because I do, more so than anyone else I know. Which is also funny, since I hardly know you."

"You know me well enough to understand I want to keep you safe. I'd never harm you, Elizabeth."

"I also know you like to manipulate and humiliate."

"I…"

"You acted like you wanted to kiss me."

"I did that to make a point, not to hurt you."

"Same thing," the president said quietly. "And you did…hurt me."

"Elizabeth, did your husband know you…like women?"

"No."

"And Moore?"

"How could they? I'm not gay."

"You do realize I'm a woman, right?"

"Of course, but I'm not gay, and I've never wanted to kiss a woman before."

"Do you think it's a shock reaction to your attack?"

"Who knows what it is?" Thomas raised her hands, exasperated. "All I know is that you made me feel stupid for feeling attractive."

"I'm sorry. It wasn't my intention."

Shield wasn't getting the answers to the questions she wanted, and Thomas seemed to be sobering up pretty fast.

"Am I not your type?" the president asked.

"You're a very attractive woman."

Thomas blushed and probably didn't even know it. She looked so soft and vulnerable at that moment, her cheeks flushed, that Shield found it hard not to stare. "But?"

"You're the president, and I'm security."

"What if I wasn't?"

"Then I wouldn't be here," Shield answered diplomatically.

Thomas looked almost defeated. "Because I would be some plain Jane and not the president."

Shield didn't know how to respond to that. Truth was, she would have wanted to kiss Thomas no matter who she was, and it had taken all her restraint to walk away from that beautiful mouth. Having her just out of arm's reach now, dressed so provocatively, was a true test of her professionalism.

"What's your story, Kennedy? Why aren't you capable of wanting someone who's not all that powerful…like a plain florist, for example? Why does it take someone like a friggin' president to get your rocks off?"

A florist? Where did that come from? "I never said that."

"Oh, please. I bet you're just as demanding for quality in your women as you are for your wines." Thomas got up. "A simple house brand can be pretty damn good, too."

Shield stood as well. "That's very true."

"Then maybe you should get off that high horse of yours and try it."

"You don't know me well enough to assume you know anything about me." Shield was getting irritated with Thomas's accusations.

"Then why don't you tell me what it is about powerful women that does it for you?"

"That depends on your definition." Shield struggled to keep her voice low. "If by power you mean I need a president or whoever with a title to get turned on, then you're very mistaken."

"What's your definition?" Thomas asked.

"I like women who know what they want and fight for it. I like survivors—someone who's not afraid of falling because they know they can get back up."

The president stood a foot away, her head tilted to the side, staring at her. "What else?"

"Someone I can count on to stick with me when I fail, show me they love me, want me, and not just wait by the sidelines for me to comfort them for my failures because for some obscene reason their pain is way more important than mine." Shield exhaled a long breath. "In other words, I don't want powerful women. I want one strong one." She raised her hands. "Okay? Satisfied?"

Without warning, Thomas closed the distance between them and placed her hands on Shield's shoulders. On her tiptoes, she gave Shield a soft, almost shy kiss on the lips, then turned around and walked to the adjoining door.

Shield, in disbelief, remained rooted where she was.

"I'm not powerful," Thomas said without turning around. "But you have no idea just how strong I am or how much I have to fight to survive." Then she was gone.

Shield didn't realize she'd licked her lips until the aftertaste hit her senses—wine, with a hint of Thomas's own sweet flavor.

The situation between them was getting more absurd by the day.

How could Thomas feel such distress concerning Shield's opinion of her and show absolutely zero sentiment about her husband's death or the attack?

Shield had witnessed plenty of people in post-death and danger shock and denial, but no matter how strong they acted, she could always see the truth in their eyes. That was where grief could not be hidden or denied. Thomas, however, was so far removed from any emotion she hadn't even asked why Shield had gone to her husband's golf club. Come to think of it, Thomas had never shown any distress in regard to anyone, other than Moore.

Then again, she also didn't seem emotionally inept. On the contrary, the president was a passionate woman, capable of deep sadness. Shield couldn't remember a moment when Thomas hadn't had to force a smile, except for the times they were alone.

A dirty political game was going on, but one of the players didn't fit the profile.

CHAPTER TWENTY-THREE

Houston, Texas

Jack sat in a comfortable leather armchair that faced away from the massive windows dominating one wall of the spacious apartment. It wasn't like she could have admired the view, anyway. Retractable, locking window screens blocked any possibility she might be able to recognize where she was, but the amenities of her surroundings were a world away from those of her last captive environment.

The owner had an impressive bankroll and an appreciation for unparalleled excellence in all things. The floor looked like it was Italian marble, the rugs priceless Arabian antiquities, the furniture handcrafted of leather and expensive woods.

The most impressive features were the art and artifacts all around, which looked like originals as far as she could tell. Oil paintings in elaborate frames adorned the walls, and custom glass display cases held a variety of masks, tapestries, coins, and other ancient relics. More glass cases, custom designed with their own ornate stands, had been built to display the heavier and larger objects, which included sculptures, a full suit of armor, and what looked like pieces of an ancient Greek column and Egyptian obelisk.

The opulent apartment was tomb quiet and obsessively immaculate, like no one lived there, as though it had been hermetically sealed away from the likely urban landscape outside.

When they'd come to get her from the white room, they'd finally let Jack use the bathroom and had given her water and a couple of ibuprofen. They'd also returned her clothes and watch, but not her Glock and cell phone. Then they'd blindfolded her and placed her in an elevator that immediately started to ascend when the door shut. After she'd been transferred into a vehicle, they'd injected her with something to knock her out, and she'd awakened here, in the chair, without restraints.

She leaned her head back and shut her eyes, grateful for the dim lighting. Her headache hadn't completely disappeared, but the painkillers they'd given her were the biggest gift she'd ever received.

Though Jack heard the door open and shut again, she kept her eyes closed. "Evening." No one answered, but she still didn't move. "What, no greeting?"

"Proper manners command you look at someone when you greet them." The now-familiar icy voice rebuked her.

"They also dictate you don't kill."

"I have never personally killed anyone."

"'Personally' being the key word." Jack rubbed her eyes. "Anyway, I was talking about me. Funny how you didn't seem to have a problem with my *savoir-vivre* when you asked me to off that guy."

"And how instinctively and easily you did it."

Jack lifted her head and opened her eyes. Her captor, dressed in an elegant cerulean-blue business suit, faced her from ten feet away. "I'm flattered you think so."

TQ was and was not what Jack had anticipated. She hadn't expected the cold bitch to be a very attractive middle-aged woman. What she had expected were the cold, almost dead eyes and demonic smile. Jack smiled back. "So, who did I kill?" she asked as though she didn't know.

"Someone who owed me."

"Money?"

"Don't be silly. Why guarantee any kind of financial loss, or otherwise, by killing someone who owes me? It's wiser to keep them alive and suffering one way or another, until they pay or deliver."

"He disappointed you."

"And that, Jack, is inexcusable."

"How?"

"He molested a donor."

"Involuntary donor."

"I don't believe in discrimination."

"Why would you care if the donor was molested? I mean, an organ is an organ."

"An organ is a profitable organ when the donor isn't dead longer than two hours."

"What took him so long?"

"The donor died during the molestation."

"You mean because of it." Jack regretted not having shot that piece of shit a third time. She'd recognized the tattoo on his thigh—BJC: a club of pedophiles that kidnapped or bought young kids for sex and then disposed of them. She'd first seen the insignia years earlier, when some Czech hired her to go after the guy who'd killed his brother in a private nightclub. The killer bore a BJC tattoo, and her search for him put her into the filthiest, most disgusting possible company of men. If she thought she'd have had even one chance in a million to survive, she would have killed them all.

TQ waved her comment away. "Either way, my employee didn't have the dignity to stop and prioritize, so he continued with whatever he was doing until it was too late." In other words, he continued to rape the victim after they were dead.

"I see," Jack said.

"Do you know who I am, Jack?"

"A megalomaniac gone awry." Jack looked around the room. "And this museum you call home proves it."

TQ's content expression evaporated. "That's a crude way to phrase your perception of me."

"Call 'em like I see 'em."

"I rarely if ever let anyone in my home, so show respect."

"To what do I owe the honor of being the chosen one?"

"You intrigue me."

"I overwhelm you." Jack smiled. "And you hope this vulgar display of wealth will exhibit your power and put me in my place. Show me how inferior I am." She laughed. "Yup. Me-ga-lo-ma-ni-ac."

"We're going to have to work on your manners."

"Speaking of which," Jack replied, "are you going to offer me a beverage?"

"You're absolutely right. What would you like?"

"Do you have whiskey in house?"

TQ clapped, and Jack heard a sound from behind her. She jumped up, in an efficiency of movement, and grabbed the person behind her by the throat before they could react.

"Nice." TQ clapped.

As soon as Jack realized she was holding a young Asian woman with an eye patch, she let go. "I'm sorry," she told the terrified girl.

The woman rubbed her throat and nodded.

"Tell her what you want," TQ said.

"Johnnie Black," Jack replied, and the girl disappeared into another room. "I hadn't seen her."

"I keep her next to the bookcase in the corner," TQ explained, like she was talking about one of the antiquities on display.

"You must trust her a lot if she can be present during your conversations."

TQ shrugged. "It's not like she can run to anyone with information."

"You keep her imprisoned."

"For you, a prison. For her, a home. It was either this or a lifetime in a Chinese penitentiary."

"And we all know what that means." Many Chinese prisoners were executed for their organs.

"Indeed. So I kept two alive for myself and saved their lives in the process."

"A true philanthropist."

"I know," TQ replied with a serious expression.

This woman was more disturbed than Jack even dared imagine.

The Asian girl came back with Jack's drink in a heavy crystal glass and placed it on a coaster on the table in front of her.

"Thank you."

The girl nodded.

"You don't have to thank her," TQ said, annoyed. "She's doing her job."

"Thank you," Jack said again, and the young woman smiled.

"Remember what I did to your eye?" TQ glared at the girl. "You have only one left."

The young woman quickly bowed her head, clearly horrified, and took her place next to the bookcase.

TQ kept staring at her with pure hate.

Jack cleared her throat. "So, why am I here?" she asked, to pull TQ's attention away from the girl.

TQ turned her head slowly in Jack's direction. "I've told you. I want you to work for me."

"Do what?"

"Like I said, whatever I ask you to."

"Steal organs?"

"You need medical expertise for that, and as talented as you are, I doubt you have the knowledge. For now, I want you to prove you can be an asset."

"Explain." Jack took a sip of whiskey.

"I need someone eradicated and I want you to do it."

"If I refuse, then…?"

"Then I also refuse to let your beautiful girlfriend live."

"Fair enough." Jack tried to sound cool and businesslike.

TQ smiled a reptilian smile. "I'm always fair."

"Who do you want me to off?"

"Two people. Ryden Wagner and Harper Kennedy. They have to be dealt with simultaneously."

"Who are they?" In the past when Jack took jobs like this, she specifically refrained from asking anything about her targets because it made her job and objectifying easier. But that was then. She wasn't about to go back to being a ruthless killer. If there was such a thing as a hell, Jack was certain she'd already bought a one-way ticket to it, but she wasn't about to disappoint Cass and herself by returning to that life. She'd had to justify killing someone less than an hour ago by telling herself the guy deserved it.

"I don't accept questions concerning my orders," TQ replied, "but this warrants an exception."

"Because?"

"One of your targets, Harper Kennedy, works for a privately contracted organization called the EOO. They have very capable and highly trained operatives. You will need all your skills to destroy that one."

"The EOO," Jack repeated, to make certain she'd heard right.

"You've heard of them."

"Yeah, but all I know is what you've already mentioned." Jack had never met this Harper Kennedy, but the name fit because of the distinctive surname. "I don't know if I want to get involved with killing one of their people."

"You can't handle it?"

"I can handle a contractor," Jack said. "I don't want to deal with the wrath of the organization."

"No one does. You'll have to make sure they never find out who did it. Should they link you or me to Kennedy's death, I will spare them the trouble of killing you."

"Goes without saying." Jack took another sip of whiskey. "Business is business, and any business must be protected."

"Wise beyond your humble means."

"Why is this Kennedy a problem for you?"

"She's been hired to protect Wagner, who belongs to me."

"Protect her from who?"

"Me," TQ replied cryptically, "but Kennedy doesn't know that."

"Is Wagner a deserter? Is that why you want her dead?"

"Wagner is a means to end. She was hired for one specific purpose, and once her job is done, she is ineffectual."

"I still don't see why Kennedy is a problem."

"I've invested a lot in Wagner, and it's paid off," TQ said. "She is doing a marvelous job. But she is getting increasingly emotionally unstable and too close to Kennedy—her security guard—who is already suspicious about certain affairs of mine."

If an EOO op was hired to babysit someone, that individual was either a major threat who warranted constant surveillance or a VIP who needed constant protection. This Wagner was probably in the first category. She couldn't imagine why any op would choose or accept to become a bodyguard. Personally, she couldn't see throwing herself in front of a bullet to protect anyone besides Cass. "When?"

"Not long anymore. A few days."

"What happens after this hit?" Jack asked.

"You wait until I need you again."

"And in the meantime?"

"I've made arrangements for you."

"How long do you want to keep me here?"

"Until I trust you to come to me when I call. And yes, of course you could entertain the idea of notifying Ms. Monroe or running away while out on this job. But you won't be alone or have a cell phone. And should you upset me for any reason, I will—"

"Yeah, I get it." Jack didn't want to hear another threat on Cass's life.

"Good. Now, I need to get my beauty sleep, and you need to leave me to it." TQ clapped her hands and the Asian woman came to stand in front of her. "Take her to the men waiting outside."

Southwestern Colorado

Montgomery Pierce sat in his well-used, comfortable armchair and looked out at the mountains, some of the highest peaks still dotted with snow. The secluded two-story brick home he'd purchased when he became chief administrator was just down the road from the EOO campus. At sixty-three, he was more content with life than he had ever been, and if it weren't for the doctor's orders to avoid exertion, stress, and most of the foods he loved, things would be damn near perfect. The woman he'd loved since his twenties was finally at his side, the organization was blooming both with profit and new talent, and Jaclyn was alive and happy with a wonderful woman.

Although his relationship with her was based on frustration, mostly on Jaclyn's side, Monty was happy enough to share any moments he could with her. Joanne insisted they have a good talk, and although he was tempted after Jaclyn found her mother in France, he frankly wouldn't know where to start or how to end a truthful conversation without another blowup between them. Some things were better left unsaid, he insisted, especially since Jaclyn had very little tolerance and understanding for anything that had to do with him.

The phone rang once, jarring him from his reverie.

"Monty, it's Cassady." Joanne came out of the bedroom and handed him the phone. "She sounds worried."

Ops never called his private number unless it was a dire situation. "Cassady?"

"Sorry to bother you at home, but I'm worried about Jack."

Monty sat up straight. "Is she all right?"

"I don't know. I'm in Boston preparing for the concert, and Jack hasn't called me once in three days."

"Maybe—"

"Monty, three days. She normally calls me several times a day. She didn't even want me to go to Boston alone. I had to convince her to stay home." Cassady spoke unusually fast, and Monty could hear the anxiety in her voice. She'd been through a lot of stress in recent months, but Cassady Monroe was a top operative and not one to raise an alarm without good reason.

"I see."

"The performance is tomorrow, and if she doesn't show up then, either, I don't know what I'm going to do. I don't know how I'm supposed to sit there and perform if—"

"Cassady, I know you're worried, but try not to jump to conclusions." Only when Joanne touched his hand did he realize how hard he was squeezing the armrest.

"I don't know what to do," Cassady repeated. "I'm coming back tonight. Screw the concert."

"There's probably a good explanation. Stay where you are and I'll look into it." He turned to Joanne. "Get David."

"What are you going to do?" Cassady asked.

"Check your place." Monty glanced at his watch. Cassady's house near Colorado Springs was about three hours by car.

"She'd answer the phone if she were home."

"Maybe—"

"Oh, my God. You don't think she fell in the shower or something. Or… She's dangerous in the kitchen, you know." Cassady was rambling now. "Maybe she blew the place up, but…no, that can't be. They would've called me if the house had gone up in flames."

"Get a hold of yourself. Why didn't you call me sooner?"

"Really, Monty, do you think I didn't want to? Jack would have killed me if I told you I was worried about her, let alone ask you to check on her."

"Why didn't you ask a friend?"

"She doesn't have any, except for Landis. I tried her, but she's away on a job."

Monty covered the receiver. "Why is David taking so long?" he asked Joanne.

"He'll be here any moment, honey."

"Part of me hopes she's passed out on the floor," he said into the phone to lighten Cassady's worry. "Who knows what she'll do if she sees me there."

"Deal with it," Cassady replied seriously. "She'd be a lot less messed up if you were honest with her."

"Honest with her?"

"You know what I mean."

"I don't."

Cassady sighed. "Stubbornness, like denial, is hereditary, after all. It doesn't take a genius to connect the dots, you know. She may look like her mother, but the rest is all you."

Just then, David Arthur walked into the living room. Cassady's statements had shocked and appalled Monty so completely, he hadn't heard the doorbell. "You haven't told her," he said, gripping the phone tightly.

"I haven't told anyone," Cassady replied. "It's not my place, and I'm not about to make your life easier by being the one to tell her."

"How would the truth make a difference?"

"Jack has more trust issues and disregard for her well-being than the rest of us put together."

"Why?"

"Maybe because on some instinctual and very deep subconscious level, she knows. And I gotta tell ya, the realization that the man you're supposed to trust blindly turned an indifferent eye to the fact that you were practically beaten and raped to death is a pretty damn hard fact to forgive."

"I'm not…wasn't…indifferent to what happened," he said. "I was devastated but couldn't show it. I didn't know how to. If I could—"

"Don't tell me, tell her. Because if something happens to Jack because of how she is, who she's become because of you," Cassady paused for emphasis, her voice like ice, "I am going to personally kill you."

"Do not threaten me, young lady, and do not forget who I am."

Cassady was apparently too worked up for his rebuke to affect her. "Where the hell is Arthur coming from, Siberia?"

"He just walked in. We're leaving now."

"Call me ASAP."

"Of course."

"And, Monty?"

"Yes?"

"Grow a pair," Cassady said, and hung up.

"What was that about?" Joanne asked, clearly having guessed the gist of the conversation.

"You heard. Cassady knows."

"And Jaclyn?"

Monty shook his head. "Maybe Cassady is right. Maybe I—"

"Yes, you do, Monty, but first things first."

"What's going on?" Arthur asked.

"Jaclyn's missing." Monty got his Glock and shoulder holster from the bedroom and put them on. "We're checking their house."

"Let's go," Arthur said immediately.

"Joanne, call whoever we have in the New York area and send them to Jaclyn's address." Monty gave her a quick kiss good-bye.

She nodded as she handed him his car keys and coat. "Your cell and lock-pick kit are in the pocket. Call me as soon as you know something."

Monty made the normally three-hour drive to Colorado Springs in two hours and fifteen minutes. He told Arthur about his conversation with Cassady, and Arthur listened without interruption.

"She's right, Monty. You need to tell Jack."

"I do. It's the least I can do."

"It's also the most. We all know what it's like to grow up without a family," Arthur said as they neared Cassady's street. "The same way we all know what it's like to want and need one. Jack has Cass now, but take it from an old bastard like me. Jack needs a family more than any op we've ever had."

"But I was there all along."

"You weren't there, you were around. You never made her feel anything other than necessary for the organization—an operative."

Monty gripped the wheel tighter as the two-story adobe-style home came into view. David was right. "She never knew how necessary she was to me."

"You're the lucky one, Monty. You had what the rest of us only dreamed of—a family—and you never acknowledged her."

"I screwed up."

"Sure did."

"How do you think she'll take it?"

"How would you, if your father was under your nose the whole time and never told you?"

"I should probably wear a vest."

"Yeah, good idea," Arthur replied seriously.

He thought about what Cassady had said. "Time I grew a pair."

They pulled into the driveway and Arthur put his hand on Monty's arm. "Life is getting shorter by the second, and we're getting too old to wait for right moments. At our age, buddy, every moment is the right one."

They went to the front door, and Arthur knocked loudly several times. When no one answered, Monty pulled out his lock pick and opened the door.

"We've made these kids too arrogant to realize an alarm system is not useless," Arthur said when they entered the house a second later.

Monty turned on the lights next to the door. "Jaclyn, it's Pierce," he called out.

"And Arthur. Probably wise to warn her," he said to Monty, "before she puts a hole in your head."

"Jaclyn?" Monty called out again. "Cassady is worried about you." When no one answered, he looked around the room. "They have an alarm, after all," he said, gesturing to the small control panel on the wall and the two motion detectors.

They looked at each other and drew their automatics. Arthur signaled to Monty that he was going upstairs.

Glock in hand, Monty headed for the kitchen. He found a half-eaten sandwich and a carton of milk on the counter. The carton was half-full. "Doesn't look good," he mumbled.

"Monty?" Arthur said from behind him.

"Yeah?" He turned around.

Arthur held up a piece of paper, torn from a yellow notepad. "I found this in the bedroom, on the pillow."

"What does it say?"

Arthur looked down at the note. "It says: *I have to do this. I'm sorry, baby. I can't bear the thought of anyone ever hurting you again. Know that I will always love you. Jack.*"

Chapter Twenty-four

The White House
Next morning, March 5

Ryden awakened with a massive headache that refused to subside even after plenty of coffee and a shower. She'd had three glasses of wine before Kennedy showed up and had asked Betty for another after she'd returned to her room. She was too aggravated and wound up to sleep after her encounter with Kennedy to go to bed.

She'd never been the one to initiate a kiss or any physical contact with another person, but Kennedy had made her feel helpless to do otherwise. So she had reacted on pure instinct, not caring about the fact that it was unprofessional, inappropriate, and unlike her. She didn't know what she expected to feel after kissing a woman, but she certainly hadn't counted on spontaneous arousal. It was a simple kiss, but Kennedy's soft mouth, her breath, and her tight shoulders had made for a remarkable aphrodisiac. If such a quick brush of lips had undone her, she shivered at the thought of what a slow, long, and thorough kiss might reduce her to.

Kennedy, however, had shown no emotion at all at the encounter—hadn't responded one way or another—and Ryden felt frustrated and embarrassed for disregarding that lack of response. She had reacted like the numerous desperate drunks she'd encountered and despised, and completely ignored Kennedy's trepidations and obvious disinterest.

Unsteady on her feet, she sat at her vanity to prepare herself to face the day. "Snap out of it," she said to her reflection as she ran a brush through her hair. "You have a million things to worry about, and here you are throwing yourself at a woman and adding problems to the pile." She needed to concentrate on getting out of here and the new life ahead, and forget Kennedy and this obscene infatuation that would lead absolutely nowhere, anyway. But why was the thought of never seeing Kennedy again disturbing and... "God, how am I going to face her today?"

The ringing phone interrupted her musings. "Yes?"

"I want to meet in an hour," Ratman said. "We have to prepare your speech on the illegal-weapons issue."

"The press conference isn't due for another week."

"We had to push it up."

"Why?"

"Does it matter?"

"I...no." And it really didn't. She was curious about the change in plans but didn't care either way. The weapons legislation was one of the primary items on Ratman's agenda for her, so as far as she was concerned, accelerating the announcement just meant she was another step closer to freedom and further away from this complicated existence. She hung up the phone and headed to the massive closet.

"Focus on the prize," Ryden said aloud as she plucked a coral-colored blazer-and-skirt ensemble from the rack of designer suits. "Nothing else matters."

Shield received an early, terse call from the president, notifying her of a change in the day's agenda. Thomas was skipping breakfast and would be starting her day with an unscheduled meeting with Kenneth Moore in a half hour.

When the president emerged from her bedroom right on schedule, Shield, waiting outside in the hall, tried not to look at Thomas's mouth. "Good morning."

"About last night...I'm not a big drinker."

"I gathered." Shield smiled.

"No offense, the wine was exceptional," Thomas rubbed her right temple with two fingers, "but I woke up with a horrible headache."

"Like you said, you're not a drinker." Shield stood with her hands clasped behind her back. For someone with a headache, Thomas looked beautiful, almost radiant. She'd done her hair and makeup herself, and chosen an ensemble that was tailored to subtly accentuate her slim hips and high, round breasts. "If it's any consolation, you seem...rested."

Thomas looked away. "I don't know what possessed me to enter your room and take your wine."

"You needed to unwind. No harm done."

"Anyway," Thomas said with an air of flippancy, "I can't remember very much about last night, so if I said or did anything to offend you, please forgive me and forget I was there. I can assure you, it wasn't personal and it won't happen again."

"I'm not thrilled about having my room raided, but that aside, you didn't say or do anything unpleasant." She unwittingly focused her gaze on Thomas's lush, full lips, glossy with a coral lipstick that complemented the color of her suit.

"Good to know." Thomas sounded relieved. "I've witnessed inebriated people make complete fools of themselves."

Did the president really not remember their conversation, or kissing her? "That may be true, but alcohol also enhances any preexisting mood."

"Either way…" Thomas waved her hand dismissively. "It's all a crazy blur. So again, forgive me if I did anything to offend you."

Shield knew she should leave last night alone and feel glad for Thomas's memory loss, but she couldn't and didn't. Instead, she took a step closer to the president, and as she did, she unplugged the communications device in her sleeve so they wouldn't be overheard. "There was nothing offensive about your kiss."

Thomas blushed and looked away. "Why are you doing this?"

"Because I know you remember."

"Then you also know I'm trying to deny any recollection."

"So you remember."

"I don't understand you." Thomas sounded angry. "You vehemently point out every reason in the world why we need to keep it professional, and then you turn around and seek confirmation of my attraction to you. Are you after validation, a need for acceptance, or some sadomasochistic satisfaction?"

Shield stared at her, unable to answer. Thomas was right, and she didn't honestly know *what* she was after or why she felt the need to bring up that kiss. She'd always been professional at work and, after Carmen, distant in her private life and relations. As a rule, she didn't care who remembered her and wasn't out to make a lasting impression, but for some reason Thomas's opinion mattered.

She'd struggled all night with how Thomas's frustration had led to her uncharacteristic confession of what she needed in a woman, and she'd also thought about that spontaneous, sweet kiss, absent any motivation other than unpolluted want. Shield needed confirmation of the purity she'd felt in that kiss. "I'm not sure," she mumbled, more to herself than Thomas.

"Get over it. I've been under a lot of stress, I'm tired, and I miss my recently deceased husband. You just happened to be on the receiving end of misplaced emotions, a temporary distraction." Thomas turned on her heel and headed toward the stairs.

Shield wanted to tackle her, pin her down and say something, anything to hurt her back.

She quietly caught up and said, "So, who's playing with whom?"

"You're a big girl," the president said. "Deal with it."

"I can deal with it just fine."

"I'm glad."

"Question is, how are you dealing with the political game you're participating in?"

Thomas stopped halfway down the steps and turned around. "What game?"

"I know Moore is up to something," she whispered, mindful of the pair of guards positioned at the bottom of the staircase. "It's only a matter of time before I find out what, but what I don't understand is your involvement and his power over you."

"I've slighted you and you are obviously being irrational," Thomas replied in the same low tone.

"Am I? Is it a coincidence your hands shake whenever he's around?"

Thomas looked at her with a mixture of fear and disbelief.

"You're terrified of him."

"I'm not." Thomas stood her ground.

"What did he make you do?"

"Even if you were right, why would I tell you anything?"

"Because if Moore can kill once, he can kill twice."

"Kill?" Thomas glanced nervously toward the other bodyguards. "Killed who?" For the first time during this conversation, the president looked sincerely worried.

Before Shield could answer, Kenneth Moore came into view at the bottom of the staircase.

"There you are." Moore smiled up at them. "Is there a problem?"

"No, sir," Shield replied as the two women descended to meet him. "We were just talking about our mutual passion for tennis. Madam President agreed to teach me a few tricks tomorrow."

"I see." Moore looked apprehensive. "How interesting."

"Hardly," Shield said. "It's common knowledge Madam President is a strong player."

"*Madam President* is," Moore agreed cryptically.

Thomas laughed nervously and clasped her hands together to hide the slight shaking. "Oh, I don't know about that. It's been months, and I'm sure I'm not up to par."

"Time for our meeting, Madam President." Moore took the president's arm and led her away toward the Oval Office. "We have a lot to talk about."

Southwestern Colorado

As soon as Pierce called her with the news of what they'd found at her house, Cassady Monroe booked a ticket on the first plane out of Boston, which left at five a.m. There were no direct flights, so by the time she picked up her car in long-term parking and reached the EOO headquarters, it was almost one in the afternoon. She found Pierce in his office with Grant and Arthur. "Let me see the note," she said without preamble.

"Your concert is tonight," Pierce reminded her.

Cass extended her hand. "The note."

Pierce gave it to her and Cass read it three times before she looked up at them.

"It's not a suicide note," Arthur said.

"And I'm sure she didn't walk out on you." Grant put a hand on Cass's shoulder.

"Then what the hell is going on?"

"When we got there, the alarm hadn't been activated," Pierce said.

"Jack always turns it on. She's afraid of me walking in on a burglar. The fact that I can take him down or sense someone is there doesn't seem to impress her."

"We also found a half-eaten sandwich and milk on the counter," Arthur said.

"She'd never do that." Cass didn't know if she should feel relieved or more worried. It was becoming clear Jack hadn't just left or done something to hurt herself, so that meant… "She left to protect me from something."

"Some*one*," Pierce said.

"Who?"

"Do you know if she had any contact with past…clients?"

"Yuri Dratshev was in touch a week or so ago. He said he had a job for her."

"You said she stopped taking hits," Arthur said.

"She has." Cassady didn't bother to hide her irritation. "Jack said Dratshev wouldn't stop trying to reach her, so she planned to call him to tell him she'd retired."

"I want to meet with Dratshev," Pierce said to Arthur.

"With what excuse? Arthur asked.

"I'll think of something."

"You don't think he did something to Jaclyn?" Grant asked.

"I doubt it," Cassady replied. "As far as I know, he has a lot of respect for her, especially after the Owens case."

Pierce got up. "Maybe, just maybe, Jaclyn decided—"

"I know where you're going," Cass glared at him, her temper rising, "and no…Jack promised she'd never go back to that life."

Pierce raised his hand to calm her. "Cassady, listen to me. Maybe she was threatened to do so."

"What would Dratshev threaten her with? He doesn't know where to find her. He doesn't even have her real name. He doesn't know anything."

"Maybe he managed to find her, somehow. It's possible he took Jaclyn at gunpoint, which would explain the sandwich."

"Why would he come with it now, nearly two years later?"

"Could be something good came up, and he desperately wants Jaclyn for the job," Arthur said.

"And is using something," Pierce added, "evidence, or whatever, against her if she doesn't accept his offer."

"Do you think he's threatening her with me?" Cass asked.

"Why would you think that?" Pierce replied.

"Yes, I think he is." Grant looked at Cassady. "Jack wrote that she had to do this because she couldn't bear the thought of anyone ever hurting you again. I think Jack decided to go to him to protect you."

"Then why the undertone of finality?" Cassady looked down at the piece of paper. "'Know that I will always love you,'" she read. "Jack knows I'd forgive her. I'd understand her having to take a job to save her own or my life. I'd do the same."

"I don't know what to tell you, Cassady," Grant said.

Pierce turned to Arthur. "Does the Russian still live in Manhattan Beach?"

"I'll have Reno check," Arthur replied.

"Have me booked on the first flight out tomorrow," Pierce said. "I want to see him ASAP."

Arthur started to leave, but Cassady put a hand out to stop him. "Make that two tickets."

Pierce frowned. "We don't know what he's holding against her. It may be you, or it may not. It's not wise to expose the company or your relationship to Jaclyn and give him ammo."

"How would I be exposing the company?"

"He knows who I am," Pierce replied. "Yuri and I have met."

Houston, Texas

TQ smiled as she looked out the window of her office at the downtown skyline. Everything was falling nicely into place. Her guest, confined to another of her apartments in the same building, was cooperative, the double was performing even better than she'd hoped for, and the culmination of her plan to cripple the illegal-weapons agenda was only hours away. She couldn't wait to be able to return her attention fully to growing her business and, with it, her power. Now all that remained was to tie up all the loose ends. She called Kenneth Moore to make sure everything was on track for the big announcement.

"We are going public with it tomorrow," Moore said.

"As scheduled then. I'll call the Russian imbecile to have his people get Thomas ready."

"Oh, and the florist and her gal pal need to be taken care of as soon as the switch takes place," Moore said.

"Of course. You sound worried. Do you want to share something?"

"I think Wagner talked to the bodyguard."

"What makes you think that?"

"I caught them talking, and when I asked what it was about, Kennedy said the president had promised to play tennis with her."

TQ straightened in her chair. She knew the double's capabilities well; she'd studied every facet of the woman's past and had herself decided what should be included in her training. "What did Wagner have to say about that?"

"She looked uncomfortable," Moore replied. "I doubt Wagner offered to play anything against the guard."

"Of course not, you idiot. She's never held a racket in her life."

"How sure are we about that?"

KIM BALDWIN & XENIA ALEXIOU

"Sure enough to know Kennedy made it up on the spot."

"We're going to upset some very dangerous people by killing one of theirs," Moore said.

"They'll never find out who did it."

"You seem to have a lot of faith in the unpredictable Russian."

"It's not Dratshev I'm placing my chips on. I know he's capable of using the florist as a bargaining tool, either with me or with the police."

"Exactly."

"That's why I've chosen someone with too much at stake to disappoint us."

"How do you know he has the nuts to do it, let alone do it right? Threatening someone's life or their family doesn't mean they won't screw up."

"First of all, it's a she," TQ replied. "Secondly, she's one of the best in the business, and last but not least, her Achilles's heel is worth more than anybody's money can buy."

"And you own that heel."

"Obviously."

"Well, good." He sounded relieved. "Because frankly, I'm ready to have this over with. I haven't slept in six months, my wife won't stop complaining about my lack of libido, and I'm losing my hair."

TQ sighed. Moore was an essential ingredient to her plan's success, but he was proving to be too high-maintenance. "Aside from irrelevant, it's also an I-don't-give-a-damn tidbit of information. Make sure Wagner does her homework and stop whining. It's very unbecoming."

She disconnected and dialed again. Yuri Dratshev already knew the time and location for the switch back; she needed only to tell him that things could proceed as scheduled.

Yuri Dratshev picked up immediately. *"Da?"*

"Your guest is ready to go home," she said.

"I will take care of it."

"You are not to touch the florist," she reminded him, "or her friend. My people will deal with them."

"What friend?" he asked.

"It doesn't concern you. Once your delivery is made, your job is done."

She'd barely hung up the phone when it rang again. The caller ID told her it was the guy she'd put in charge of watching Cassady

Monroe. "Yes?"

"We lost Monroe."

She put the call on speakerphone. "Tell me I heard wrong."

He cleared his throat. "I don't know how it happened."

"I pay you enough to make sure you know how everything happens."

"She must have left late last night or very early this morning."

"Where were you?"

"The hotel across the street."

"Sleeping."

"I stayed on watch until two."

"I don't pay you to fucking sleep." TQ slammed her hand on the desk.

"We were taking turns. The lights in her room were still on when Mike took over."

"So Mike should have seen her leave."

There was a prolonged pause on the other end. "He didn't."

"Pray tell."

"He fell asleep."

"Where is he?"

"Next to me."

"I don't like disappointments."

"I know, ma'am."

She couldn't abide incompetence. Everyone who worked for her was aware of the penalty for failing to deliver. "Then you know what you have to do."

"Yes, ma'am."

"Once you're done with him, I want you to spend all eighty-six thousand, four hundred seconds of every day looking for her."

"Yes, ma'am."

CHAPTER TWENTY-FIVE

The White House

Ryden spent an hour that morning and nearly two more that night with Ratman, preparing for the big announcement on the illegal-weapons plan that she would deliver the next day. Rehearsing her scripted statement took no time at all—she had Thomas's accent and mannerisms well in hand by now. But she would face some tough grilling from the White House Press Corps, and Ratman wanted to be sure she was well versed on how to respond to any question that might come up.

Since there was a protocol for White House briefings—a clear pecking order regarding who in the press pool got called upon, and when—she also had to memorize the names and faces of the key reporters who would be present.

Only after they'd covered every eventuality thoroughly did Ratman agree to call it a night. As they emerged from the Oval Office, Kennedy, standing outside, turned and looked at Ratman in pure distaste.

Part of Ryden was glad Kennedy felt the same way as she about the miserable excuse for a human, but Kennedy was oblivious to the fact that she was pressing her luck.

Ratman had made it very clear that he would not hesitate to kill Kennedy if Ryden ever confided in her or turned to her for help. And Ryden certainly believed he and that cold bitch Rothschild were capable of cold-blooded murder. She had witnessed firsthand how they had set her up by orchestrating the murder of an innocent couple, plus they'd taken out five Secret Service agents. Kennedy either had no idea just how dangerous Rothschild and her people were, or she was just plain crazy in thinking she could uncover and stop this political game.

Ryden had expected Ratman to say something about the tennis game she'd promised Kennedy, and the fact that he didn't disconcerted her. He knew she couldn't play, let alone to the president's standards, so he must have known either she or Kennedy was lying. Why hadn't he said something? Where were the usual threats? He wasn't one to ignore or let any comment go unnoticed.

She had to get Kennedy off her back and away from interfering with Moore before it was too late for both of them.

"We need to talk," she said to Kennedy in a low voice when they reached her bedroom. Jason, the night shift bodyguard, was positioned farther down the hall at the top of the stairs.

"That's why I came up with a game of tennis."

"We can't be seen together."

Kennedy looked confused. "It's my job to be with you at all times."

"I mean we can't be seen talking anymore."

Kennedy opened the door for her and stood aside. "Let me know if you need anything, Madam President," she said, loud enough for the other guard to overhear.

Ryden nodded and went inside.

Seconds later, a knock came from the adjoining door. Ryden threw off her suit jacket before she opened it, and when she did, she put her finger on her mouth. Kennedy started over the threshold, but Ryden pushed her back into her own room and followed, shutting the door behind them.

"What happened?" Kennedy asked after she'd unclipped her communications device and set it on her dresser.

"My room could be bugged."

"It's not."

"How do you know?"

"Because it's my job to check."

"Either way, I don't trust anyone."

Kennedy settled into one of the armchairs near the window. "What happened in there?"

"No questions, Kennedy. I will be the one asking." Ryden remained where she was, too restless to sit.

"Very well."

"What did you mean by, 'if he killed once, he can kill twice'?"

"Did that get your attention because it shocked you or because I know about it?"

Ryden clasped her hands together behind her back to keep them from shaking. "I said, no questions."

"I don't know what Moore wants," Kennedy said, meeting her eyes, "but I do know he wants it bad enough to have killed your husband."

Ryden didn't believe she'd heard right. "My…what are you talking about?"

"Mr. Thomas was killed at the country club. Some waiter served him poisoned coffee to made it look like a heart attack. They played on the fact that your husband had heart problems to avoid an autopsy."

"Oh, my…" They'd certainly proved they were capable of doing virtually anything to get what they wanted, from killing the Laudens to set her up to kidnapping the president of the United States and killing five Secret Service agents. But knowing they had the power to murder Thomas's husband and get away with it, completely undetected, was a whole different kind of scary. "How do you know Moore was behind it?"

"I don't have proof yet, but my instincts are never wrong."

"And why are you trusting me with this information?" Ryden asked. "How do you know I wasn't involved?"

"Maybe you were. I don't know. All I know is that you're terrified of him and there's got to be a good reason." Kennedy was spot-on, on both accounts, but if Ryden admitted it, they were both as good as dead.

"First of all, my husband died of natural causes. Secondly, I'm not afraid of Moore. My only issue with him is that he's pushing me to act like the president this country elected at a time when I feel my world has fallen apart. My husband's death has taken a heavy toll, evident from the fact that I even tried to kiss you. I'm tired, confused, and lonely. Frankly, I don't know where I find the energy to get up in the morning."

"And Moore is pushing you to perform?" Kennedy eyed her suspiciously. "Nothing but a friend with your best interest in mind."

"Indeed. I've told you all this before. So I'm asking you to stop making up stories, looking for what isn't there, and sticking your nose in government issues."

"What you told me about Moore the other day doesn't fit your story. When I asked you about him, you practically gagged, and I'm sure it wasn't the wine."

Ryden sighed for effect. "He tires me and at times aggravates me because he pushes too hard. That's all I meant."

Kennedy stood up. "You're lying."

"Excuse me?" she replied, sounding appropriately offended.

"You have the power to fire his ass, but for some reason you insist on protecting him."

"Fire him?" Ryden practically shouted at the absurdity of the idea.

"The man tried to molest you, and all you did was walk away. Why is that, Elizabeth?"

How could Kennedy possibly know that? Ratman was nothing but decent in public. "Have you gone insane? He's never touched me."

"Really. Because it sure sounded like it when he came to your room the night before last."

"What—"

"As you know, I'm responsible for checking your room for listening devices, which means I can place them at will because no one else checks." Kennedy looked down at her, her arms folded across her chest. "I heard what he tried to do, and I also heard your disgusted reaction to it. He talks to you like he owns you."

Ryden's face burned and her hands tingled. *Breathe,* she told herself. "I can have you fired right now."

Kennedy approached her and stopped a foot away. "Why, Elizabeth? Why are you afraid of him?"

"How dare you spy on me."

"I was…*am* concerned about your safety. I was sent here to protect you."

"But you were not sent to look for an unfounded conspiracy," she said. "All I see is a nosy guard throwing false accusations. If there was any truth to your obscene theories, we'd be up to our noses in officials. Is your employer even aware of all this?"

"I'm not at liberty to discuss my employer."

"But you are at liberty to destroy my life with false accusations."

"The elevator attack was a setup and you know it."

"Oh, look. Another crazy theory."

Kennedy looked dangerously angry. "Is it? Is it? If they wanted you dead, you'd be just that."

"I was saved by good men who gave their lives for me."

"Doesn't it bother you at all that these *good men* died for no reason?" Kennedy shouted. "They gave their lives to protect someone who was never intended as a target, anyway."

Where was Kennedy getting all this? It was bad enough she had to live with the deaths of innocent men for the rest of her life, but to have Kennedy rub it in her face was unbearable.

Kennedy continued. "What do they have on you? What are you

involved in that can make you justify what happened to those men?"

"Nothing," Ryden insisted.

"Then that's very sad, because I wanted to believe you didn't have a choice. That your life, or someone you cared about, was at risk."

"Stop it," Ryden yelled back. "You don't know anything. I haven't done anything."

But Kennedy apparently wouldn't let go. She took another step closer, until they were only a couple of feet apart. "You are responsible for the deaths of five innocent men, and I want to know why."

"I would never hurt anyone."

"I believe that," Kennedy said. "That's why I was hoping for your cooperation. I don't have some death wish. If I had the slightest suspicion you were voluntarily involved, I would have kept my mouth shut. But I believe you were coerced—threatened somehow. Let me help you before more people, including yourself, get hurt."

The exchange was becoming more heated by the second, and Ryden struggled to come up with a way to get Kennedy to stop this interrogation. "You needn't concern yourself with my well-being."

"It's my job."

"Then do your job and stop looking for ghosts. Just let it go."

Kennedy's expression softened. "I can't," she replied.

"Why?"

"Because I know you're in trouble and I want to help you. There's got to be a way to get you out of whatever mess you're in."

"I'm not in any mess, and I sure as hell don't play the damsel-in-distress role very well, so I have no need for a knight in shining armor to rescue me. If I were in any trouble at all, I'd find a way to deal with it the way I always have."

"Why can't you accept my help?"

"Why do you care?"

"Because…" Kennedy looked flustered. "Because, I just do."

Ryden wanted desperately to run to her and tell her everything. For the first time, she felt an urgency to talk, and Kennedy was so close to the truth. But neither of them stood a chance against these people. "There's nothing to help me with."

"Stop lying," Kennedy said, clearly frustrated. She shook Ryden by the shoulders. "Who are you protecting?"

Myself was the ugly, honest answer. "Get the hell out of here," Ryden shouted.

"You're in my room," Kennedy hollered back.

Ryden pushed her away and walked to the door. "Leave. Do us both a favor, and leave."

Manhattan Beach, New York

The GPS on Montgomery Pierce's rental car accurately pointed him to Yuri Dratshev's red-brick mansion in an upscale neighborhood, though he could have picked out the Russian mob boss's home on sight. The exterior was a mishmash of garish excesses—a gold cupola topped the structure, six gold Roman columns flanked the front door, and the lawn was full of statues, mostly Italian nudes. Security was also well evident. A forbidding metal fence surrounded the estate, and cameras covered every angle of possible intrusion.

Monty pulled into the driveway and announced himself over the intercom. Half a minute later, the gate opened and he drove in to find a guard with a machine gun waiting to admit him at the front door.

The goon led him to Dratshev's study, where more kitschy accoutrements awaited: red velvet curtains and animal-skin rugs, mounted trophy heads and a cherry desk inlaid with a massive, colorful, Orthodox mosaic of the Virgin Mary.

He was taking off his coat as Dratshev appeared in the doorway.

"How have you been?" the Russian asked. So many years had passed since they had seen each other that Monty scarcely recognized him. He'd gone completely bald or was shaving his head now, and his neatly trimmed mustache and trademark narrow beard, which ran along his jawline to the bottom of his ears, were more gray than black. Even his demeanor was different. He'd always been the picture of arrogant braggadocio, but today he looked worried. Although he smiled when he shook Monty's hand, his dark eyes spoke another truth.

"Not relevant, nor do I think you care. I'm here about Jack." Normally, Monty only referred to her as Jaclyn, but it was no business of Dratshev's to know Jack's birth name.

"Jack who?"

Monty suppressed a cringe. "The one you occasionally hire for hits."

"Have a seat." Dratshev gestured toward the corner that held a couch, coffee table, and two armchairs, as he shut the door. "Vodka?"

"I don't drink." Monty threw his coat over the back of one of the armchairs and took a seat.

"That's not what I remember." Dratshev laughed. "I remember you and me putting a whole bottle away, just the two of us." He poured himself a glass from a bottle on his desk and took the armchair across from Monty.

"I don't drink anymore."

"Pity. Life is clearer through the thick bottom of a tumbler."

"I have glasses for that now." Monty patted his breast pocket.

"Age, she is a heartless bitch."

Monty tapped his fingers on the armrest when Dratshev went quiet. He stared at the Russian, waiting for the man's reaction to his visit and inquiry about Jaclyn.

"So." Dratshev finally spoke and leaned forward. "I don't work for you anymore."

"That's correct."

"So, why do you come to me looking for help?"

"Because I can."

"I don't owe you any answers."

"Just because you're not my CI anymore doesn't mean I can't destroy you."

"You said you would release me after I gave you that fucking crazy arms dealer in Israel," Dratshev said. "I delivered."

Monty had pulled any and all strings ten years ago to track down the Israeli bastard who had taken and hurt Jaclyn, and when he found him, he personally buried him alive. "Because you wanted him out of the way. He was taking your clients."

"But I gave him to you when you said it was personal."

"And then you gave me another one, and then another one, and then—"

"So, who cares?" Dratshev's tone was matter-of-fact, but he took a long swig of his drink.

"I let you live twenty years ago in exchange for intel and cartels."

"We smoked, had vodka together," Dratshev said. "I bring you girls. We became friends."

"We were associates."

"And now you are a middle-aged, boring fuck."

"Maybe, but I can take you down."

"Bullshit."

"I can call all those dealers you helped me put away. I'm curious as to how fast they can get to you from behind bars. My guess is between two to three hours."

Dratshev's eyes widened so much he looked like a cartoon. "That's not our deal."

"So?" Monty shrugged. "Who cares?" he repeated with Dratshev's flippancy.

The Russian seemed to consider his alternatives for several seconds before he spoke again. "Why do you want Jack?"

"That's none of your business."

"Do you know her?"

"None of your business."

Dratshev stared down at the vodka in his hand. "I don't know where she is."

"You're lying."

Dratshev took another long swig. "I tried to find her for a job."

"What job?" Monty asked.

"I don't know. A business associate asked me to find her."

"And?"

"I left a message. Jack called me back. I gave her the number of my associate, told her it was big money. Jack always works for big money. I didn't hear from her again." He seemed to be telling the truth.

"Let's start with you giving me the contact number you gave Jack."

"It's no good now, for sure. Only for Jack," the Russian replied.

"Who's your associate?"

Dratshev shook his head. "I can't talk about that."

"You mean you won't."

"No. I mean I can't." The Russian sounded nervous. "Listen, I don't know if you ever met Jack. I don't know if you want to kill her or make hits for you, but I like her. I don't want her to get hurt."

"You like her," Monty repeated dubiously.

"*Da.*" Dratshev met his eyes. "She is a cold executioner, but there is something good in her heart."

"I think she's in trouble," Monty said.

"Maybe. She is not exactly a libra." Dratshev snorted. "But why do you care?"

"A what?"

"You know, woman who works with books."

"Librarian."

"That's what I said."

Monty willed himself not to roll his eyes. "Did she take the job for your associate?"

"I don't know."

"Find out."

"If she did, you don't want to get involved." That meant a lot coming from the Russian, since he was aware of what Monty was capable of and what power he had. Monty had told him years ago that he worked for the Agency.

"That's for me to determine," Monty replied.

"If Jack is with her, you can't do anything about it," Dratshev said. "She will have to stay there, probably forever."

"So your associate is a woman."

He looked away and didn't answer.

"Arms dealers, drugs, prostitution, organs, terrorism. I've handled them all," Monty said. "Which one is it?"

Dratshev looked at him and simply nodded.

"I see." The woman he was referring to apparently liked to dabble in a bit of everything.

"What would Jack have to do for her?"

"What she does best, I think. Find and kill." Dratshev laughed. "Why do you care? It was her decision to take the job. Find someone else." He took a big gulp of vodka and gargled with it.

Monty slammed his hand on his armrest. "I don't think it was her decision."

Dratshev choked on the liquid and broke out in a horrendous cough.

"Who is she?" Monty yelled. "Who is Jack working for?"

"I can't tell you."

"Are you afraid of her?"

"Also."

"Also, what? Do you work for her?"

"With her, for her." He shrugged. "It's hard to tell."

"Arms?"

Dratshev glanced quickly left, then right, almost unconsciously. "This is a big deal, Pierce. No one can know."

"Big money?"

"Big stakes. What I did this time can put me away for the next ten lives."

"That's your business. I'm not here about that." Monty sat back and crossed his arms over his chest. "Remember how you and I used to work together? You would give me a name and I'd make sure no one ever found out. I got what I wanted, and you got to stay on top and keep the buyers to yourself. If this person is involved in the arms trade, which is your main financial source and occupation, you get to keep her clients."

Dratshev coughed again, placed his tumbler on the coffee table, and leaned forward. "I can't do it. The *suka* will find out I told you. I know she will. And when she does, my whole family will go down the shitter, liter…literary…"

"Literally," Monty finished for him.

"She will cut us up in pieces and flush us down the shitter."

"I got that."

Monty had seen the Russian hesitant, scared, and uncooperative before, but he'd never seen him petrified at the mere thought of giving a name. Who had that kind of power over a kingpin like Dratshev? He wasn't the brightest light on the tree, but he was good at what he did, and everyone feared him in the arms business. Dratshev didn't need more than a simple dirty look to put a bullet in someone's head.

Maybe this woman—who wasn't exclusively in the same line of work—had the upper hand in some other business. But how many women headed multiple, dubious enterprises? Monty tapped his fingers again on the armrest, a nervous habit. He could only come up with two names: one had been imprisoned last year on racketeering charges, and the other…

He stopped tapping. "I'm going to mention a name." Monty wanted more than anything, more than any other time in his life, to be wrong.

Dratshev nodded once.

"Is the woman Jack is working for called TQ…the Broker?"

Dratshev stared at him intently, the prominent vein in his forehead throbbing to the beat of his heart. Suddenly, without a word, he got up and left the room.

Monty's hand went numb. He sat back and stared at Dratshev's empty chair for a long time. "I told you she'd come after you, Jaclyn." He rubbed his face. With unsteady hands, he grabbed Dratshev's expensive notepad and pen off the coffee table and wrote: *Your cat is safe. Come home. 19 8 1 4 5.* He folded the paper, wrote *For Jack* on it, and left it on Dratshev's desk, hoping the mob boss would pass it on if possible. "Please, be alive. I'll find you, if it's the last thing I do."

Chapter Twenty-six

The White House
Next day, March 6

Shield entered the White House Press Room and surveyed the throng of reporters assembled for the impromptu press conference. Many were speculating on the reason for the gathering, and she herself was curious about what event might have transpired to prompt this last-minute addition to Thomas's schedule. Something was brewing—the president had taken breakfast in her bedroom that morning and seemed even more preoccupied than usual during their silent journey from the residential quarters to the main floor.

They hadn't talked at all since yesterday, when Thomas had told her to leave, and Shield honestly didn't know what to make of her plea. Was she being asked to leave because Thomas was angry with her and didn't want her prying in White House business? Or was it a warning? She had a feeling it was the latter.

But if the president was trying to warn her off, then why was Thomas so adamant about keeping dangerous secrets? And why was she so upset with Shield wanting to protect her?

Under other circumstances, when confronted with an attitude or lack of cooperation from some overinflated diva, Shield would have asked for a replacement. She had done it once before. But she couldn't let go of Thomas. Something about this enigmatic president made Shield want to protect her out of personal concern, not duty. If only Thomas would let her.

White House aides admitted a few stragglers into the room and then closed the doors, indicating the press conference was about to begin.

Ryden's nerves escalated as she stood outside the Press Room and heard the clamor from reporters inside. She was already on edge because this was to be her first full press conference. She'd managed to avoid having to answer questions during her only other appearance in this room—when she'd delivered the brief "I'm all right" statement scripted by Kenneth Moore after the assassination attempt. This time, she would have to face questions from the global press. Ratman had prepared her the best he could, with answers to every anticipated query, but unforeseen questions always popped up during these rare opportunities with the president that could catch even the real chief executive off guard.

Her makeup artist gave her a final once-over, then stepped back and nodded.

"Are you ready, Madam President?" the White House press secretary asked. He was a distinguished former journalist known for his coverage of conflicts in the Middle East.

Ryden nodded. "Go ahead, George."

He went into the room ahead of her and told the assembled press to take their seats. Once the din had quieted, he announced, "Ladies and gentlemen, the president of the United States will be reading from a prepared statement and will then take your questions."

Her cue. Ryden took a deep breath and straightened her posture as an aide opened the door for her. Flashes from cameras went off as she stepped to the podium. Surveying the room in a quick glance, she saw countless video cameras set up in the back of the crowded room, televising the event live around the world.

She deliberately avoided looking at Kennedy, who stood off to one side, her back against the wall.

"Good morning, everyone," she began. The statement was typed out for her on the podium, but she had it memorized. "I'm here today with an announcement regarding one of the major cornerstones of my political agenda—my plan to curtail and eventually eliminate the illegal-arms trade in the United States. It had been my hope that a concerted approach involving funding, legislation, manpower, and cabinet-level oversight would reduce this insidious threat within our borders and impact the black-market selling of guns abroad as well."

As Ratman had instructed, she maintained a serious and resigned expression as she continued. "One of the plan's key backers until now—Senate Majority Leader Andrew Schuster—recently met with me to discuss his concerns about the plan as drafted and to announce that he was withdrawing his support. Without his leadership on this issue, it stands no chance of gaining the required congressional votes for approval."

Shocked murmurs circulated through the crowed, and more flashes went off.

"Therefore, I am here today to announce that I am abandoning the plan as drafted. While it remains a goal of my administration to reduce the illegal-arms trade—which deals in billions of dollars in black-market weapons annually and is responsible for the deaths of thousands of innocent people—I must be content to participate in the efforts spearheaded by global organizations on this issue, such as the United Nations." She paused for a few seconds. "I'm ready to take your questions."

Nearly every reporter in the room raised their hand. Ryden had the protocol of who to favor first well memorized. Wire services came first, then the broadcast networks, national newspapers, newsmagazines, video, and, lastly, regional newspapers. How many actually were called upon was entirely up to her. She pointed to the reporter for UPI—United Press International. "Yes, Alex?"

"What were Senator Schuster's reasons for the abrupt about-face in his position?"

Ratman had guessed that would be among the first questions.

"I'll leave that to the senator to explain. As many of you know, he's holding his own press conference on the Hill in an hour," she replied. "I will tell you that our exchange was cordial, that I respect his position although I don't agree with it, and that this in no way will affect our future working relationship on other issues of national importance. Senator Schuster has been, and will continue to be, a respected leading voice in the Democratic Party."

She then pointed to the Associated Press reporter. "Next. Barry?"

The rest of the questions were all ones that had been anticipated, so she was able to deliver quick, eloquent responses without ever appearing flustered. No reporter delved into unrelated matters, because the content of her announcement had been so unexpected and of such great importance. After ten minutes, in keeping with Ratman's instructions, she begged off further inquiries with a polite, "I'm sorry, ladies and gentlemen, but that's all I have time for today," and hastily made her exit.

Shield stayed on the president's heels when she abruptly departed the briefing room, as surprised and mystified by the announcement as the media seemed to be. Thomas had been adamant and passionate about her feelings on the illegal-weapons issue and guns in general, a view that Shield shared and respected.

She knew the president's arms agenda was highly controversial, but as a professional, Shield was well aware that too many people took the ownership of weapons lightly. They figured it was normal to point one in someone's face and shoot and call it their constitutional right. Like Thomas, she believed that only the police and military—not thugs, yahoos, and civilians with a few rounds at the shooting range—should own guns. Never mind those small-penis idiots who considered shooting animals a sport.

They escaped the noisy chaos of the Press Room, and Shield followed Thomas across the hall into the deserted Cabinet Room, where the president paused and let out a deep breath.

"I didn't see that coming," Shield said. "I was frankly pleased with where you stood on weapons."

"Yes, well, Schuster pulled back." Thomas started to continue toward the Oval Office.

"Why?"

The president stopped but didn't turn around. "You sound like a reporter and I'm done answering questions. Also, I don't remember asking for your opinion on the subject, so please refrain from offering one. See me to my office and I'll let you know when I will need your services again."

Shield's job was going to become very unpleasant, to say the least, if the president insisted on dismissing and ignoring her. "Elizabeth."

Thomas turned to look at her. "Was I not clear?"

"Crystal, but..."

Thomas approached her. "You're skating on thin ice as it is, Kennedy. Remember who you are. Contrary to what you may believe, I can have you fired any time I please."

"Then why haven't you?" she asked. "It would appear I've given you plenty of reasons, and it's become abundantly clear you can't stand me."

"Because I don't have the time to busy myself with trivial topics," the president replied. "But stop pushing it, because if pressed, I can make the time."

"With all due respect, that's a lie. Although I'm sure my organization will arrange a replacement if asked to, I'm still here only because you know I'm on your side. And I am the only person in this prison that gives a damn about what happens to you."

"You only care because you think there's some plot to destroy the world and you're looking to prove yourself right. Both of us know you give about as much of a damn about me as the *National Enquirer*."

"You're wrong. I never said you're out to destroy the world, and I also have no interest in proving anything."

"Bullshit," Thomas said calmly and with a hint of a smile. "Either way, you have absolutely no proof of that. Now, you can either waste your time with useless and tiring conversation or do what you were hired for and stop harassing me before I have you arrested for defamation."

Shield crossed her arms. "What's changed, Elizabeth?" she asked slowly and with deliberate sarcasm, reminding Thomas how she'd insisted Shield drop the formality. "A few days ago, you wanted to jump me. Am I too close to the truth for comfort? Or am I supposed to believe you're over the distraction and confusion that is me?"

"The second, believe it or not," Thomas replied casually. "Everybody uses everybody."

"That's damn clear."

"Good. Now, if you don't mind, I need to get back to work." Thomas headed toward the door that led to her secretary's office.

Shield followed, as always two steps behind, but in reality a world apart.

Southwest of Baltimore, Maryland

Elizabeth Thomas stared at the screen, unable to believe what she was hearing, although the reporter was confirming everything her double had just announced from the White House Press Briefing Room. Her illegal-arms agenda was dead. That certainly answered at least part of the question about why all this had happened. Now she knew why they'd told her at lunch that it would be in her best interest to keep tuned to one of the 24-hour news networks today. They wanted her to see this.

One of the things that most surprised her, however, was that the reversal on the bill had come not from the imposter president, but from Senate Majority Leader Andrew Schuster. She'd considered him not only a reliable party stalwart, but a personal friend as well, someone who'd been with her in the battle against illegal weapons from the beginning. What could have compelled him to change his mind? Was it possible he had a double, too, who was doing the bidding of whoever was behind this?

The news report switched live to Schuster on the steps of the

Capitol, giving his own press conference. She turned up the volume. The man certainly looked and sounded like Schuster, but then again, she could scarcely distinguish her own double from herself.

"After due consideration," the senator was saying, "I've decided to withdraw my support for the president's plan to pump millions of dollars into a new initiative to curtail the illegal-weapons trade. At this vulnerable stage in America's economic recovery, we should focus our resources and attention on more immediate and grave concerns closer to home, like efforts to create more jobs and maintain our country's competitiveness in the global marketplace."

Thomas muted the volume when she heard noises from outside her room. She was rarely disturbed between meals, and dinner wasn't due for hours.

The door opened and a man came in, someone she didn't recognize. She could tell without even looking now whether it was Beard or Cleanshaven delivering her meals, based solely on their smell and the sound of their breathing. Cleanshaven always had a lingering scent of sweat about him, and Beard had the raspy exhalations of a heavy smoker. This new arrival wore a mask to hide his identity, as the other men did, but in every other respect he didn't resemble them at all. He was dressed in a tailored navy suit, and his starched shirt and expensive shoes and watch confirmed that he had money. He was not a hired thug or guard like the others, but evidently a man of some importance.

"Good afternoon, Madam President. I hope you have been treated well."

"And I hope you're here to provide me with some answers," she replied, standing to look him squarely in the eye.

"I am, indeed." He gestured for her to return to her chair in front of the television. "Please, have a seat. And hear me out completely before you ask any questions."

"All right." She went back to the big armchair, and he took its twin, a few feet away.

"I represent the person who had you brought here." He glanced at the muted television as he undid the button of his suit jacket. "I presume you saw the announcement a short time ago at the White House?"

"How can...whoever sent you...possibly think they're going to get away with all this? What's next in your sights—the alternative-energy initiative? Health-care agenda?"

He held up one hand condescendingly. "Please save your questions and just offer a yes or no, please."

"Yes. I saw it," she replied in a clipped tone.

"My client's objective has been met today, with the official abandonment of the illegal-weapons plan," he said. "So we will be returning you to the Oval Office very soon, probably tomorrow."

Elizabeth couldn't believe she'd heard correctly. "You're… returning me? You're going to just set me free…like that?"

"We never intended to harm you, Madam President. Only to ensure that this arms plan of yours never happens. Now…" He leaned forward and looked at her seriously. He had blue-green eyes, and she could see a smattering of crow's feet beside them that disappeared under his mask. He had to be in his fifties, at least. "If you do as instructed, you will soon be back in the White House and able to pursue everything else you wish to accomplish."

"What does 'do as instructed' mean?"

"We must ensure you never resurrect this arms agenda," he said. "And, of course, you'll never let on to anyone—ever—that it hasn't been you all along calling the shots. If you're even contemplating that, I'd advise you to think hard about it. First, no one would believe you. Our double has successfully fooled everyone…your cabinet, your vice president, even your family. And you can be sure that nothing will be left behind that would in any way confirm what you know. No fingerprints, stray hairs for DNA, or anything like that. We run a very clean operation, with no loose ends, as you witnessed yourself in the switch. You'd only damage what remaining credibility you have at this point if you say anything. Everyone would see you as a fragile, hysterical woman who couldn't handle the stressful demands of the job. You'd go right from the White House to the crazy house."

Before she could respond, he added in a threatening tone, "And of course, much more is at stake than your reputation if you do anything to alert authorities to what's happened. The repercussions would be swift and severe, and keep in mind the target won't necessarily be you next time, but those closest to you—like your sister and her family. Or your father. Oh, sure, you could assign them bodyguards or try to keep them in protective custody somewhere for a while. But you must know by now we have very highly placed resources and the ability to penetrate whatever security necessary to achieve our objectives. Nancy has two children, I believe?"

Elizabeth pictured the faces of her niece and nephew. While she might be willing to put her own credibility and life at stake to expose the conspiracy, she could never do anything to jeopardize them. If she had to choose between her arms bill and her family, the decision was easy. She would have to keep quiet; they'd proven what they were capable of. "I understand what's expected of me."

"Excellent. Your guards will be in very soon with some newspapers from the past several days and computer printouts so you can catch up on what's been happening in the outside world while you've been our guest. We want you to be able to pick up your duties without alerting anyone that something's amiss. You'll also be provided with what we need you to wear to make the switch back."

He got to his feet. "Questions?"

"How do you plan to reinstall me in the White House without anyone knowing?" she asked.

"You'll find that out in due time," he said, and went to the door. "Be patient, Madam President. This whole ordeal will be over in a day or two at most."

Southwestern Colorado

"You're not going anywhere, Cassady," Monty said, getting up from his desk. "Running off half-cocked when you have no idea where to start looking won't help. You know her best. We need you here." As soon as he'd finished briefing her on what he'd learned from Dratshev, Cassady headed for the door.

Anticipating just that reaction, Arthur now stood between her and her objective. "Come on, Monroe. Listen to him."

Cassady turned back and glared at him. "You have two minutes to convince me yours is the better option. You said the feds have been trying to find TQ for years."

"They haven't devoted the resources we will," Monty replied. "And we have a much greater incentive."

"If organ trafficking and the weapons trade aren't enough incentive for the feds, then what is? Wouldn't they have stopped her by now if they could?"

"Feds go after what they're told to. Too many powerful people are in no hurry to stop the likes of TQ because they either profit from her, collaborate with her, or fear exposure."

"And what's your grand plan?"

He turned to Joanne, standing beside him. "Honey, alert Reno to get Landis here ASAP." Landis Coolidge, aka Agent Chase, was the

EOO's best tracker. Monty knew her presence would reassure Cassady, since it had been Landis who'd helped Jaclyn find and rescue her from Andor Rózsa. Unfortunately, it would take some time to get her here, since she was on assignment in the South Pacific.

"We'll give Chase anything she needs, and I'm calling in every favor I'm owed," Monty told Cassady. "Contacting everyone I can who might have dealt with TQ or know more about her than we do. And Reno is going over her brother's records again. If we need to, I'll have him crack the Agency's computers. If anyone has a lead on her, they would." He would first try his contacts in the CIA, but he wasn't optimistic they'd be forthcoming.

"What happened to Dario's estate?" Cassady asked. "Who claimed his body and buried him? There's a place to start."

Monty shook his head. "Dead end. I explored that possibility right after he died, because TQ threatened Jaclyn. Federal authorities froze all of Dario's assets, and the funeral arrangements, such as they were, were made via phone by an attorney. There was no wake, and Dario was cremated."

"What happened to the remains?"

"Messengered to the attorney's office in New York. Reno searched the firm's records and found no mention of Dario or TQ."

Cassady's posture deflated. "We have to find her, Monty."

"We will, Cassady. I promise you, we'll keep looking until we find her. I'm not going to lose her again."

CHAPTER TWENTY-SEVEN

The White House
Next evening, March 7

Ryden picked at her dinner. The White House chef had prepared another tantalizing feast—tonight's menu included filet mignon, twice-baked potatoes, and an array of grilled vegetables, normally her favorite. But she'd barely managed a few forkfuls though she'd skipped dinner the night before and breakfast that morning. Her appetite had disappeared since she'd basically told Kennedy to go to hell.

The sentiment couldn't have been further from the feelings she had wanted to express, but she knew one wrong word would mean curtains for both of them.

Up until a few days ago, all that mattered to her was getting through this ordeal alive so she could start her life anew, but Kennedy had somehow managed to warp her priorities. Ryden was doing her best to keep her distance and discourage Kennedy from looking too deep into the abyss of deceptions, but it hurt to push away the only person who seemed to sincerely care for her. She had been groomed to be selfish—for an orphan, it was necessary for survival—so people like Kennedy hadn't existed in her reality.

But somehow Kennedy had managed to convince her that some people really did give a damn, and not because they could profit in some way. Ryden knew Kennedy was being honest concerning her motivation to uncover what was going on, that she sincerely cared about Ryden's safety on a personal level.

Why did it take a fake life to find an honest person? And why couldn't she bring herself to tell Kennedy the truth?

Not that it would matter. Even if she could have the unrealistic luxury of including Kennedy in her life after she was set free, she wouldn't have the guts to look Kennedy in the face after all that had transpired. She was too insecure about her background and bland personality, and she felt too guilty about what she'd done to even fathom embracing the acceptance and attraction of a woman like Kennedy, a rich woman who happened to have morals and self-sacrifice embedded in her genes.

No, she had nothing to offer a woman of such a high caliber, which made telling Kennedy the truth as unappealing as kissing Ratman. She would have to leave Kennedy and every thought of her here in the White House. Here, she was at least the kind of woman Kennedy could appreciate: a strong, capable leader who had achieved greatness but somewhere along the way, beyond her control, had become trapped in a deceitful game.

She could feel Kennedy's eyes on her back as she played with her food. Ratman had told her it would be unprofessional to skip another meal, so here she was, pushing it around, hoping the mess she'd made on her plate would fool the help.

Soon, she wouldn't have any more reasons to act or force herself to do anything. Judging from the calls she'd had to make to Senate Majority Leader Andrew Schuster, the illegal-arms bill was likely the main reason she'd been blackmailed to double the president. Now that she'd made the official announcement abandoning the plan, her work here seemed to be done.

Did Theodora Rothschild have further use for her? And if not, would she keep the promise she'd made to set her up with a new life somewhere, with further alterations to her features and money enough to start over? Rothschild, Ratman, and whoever else was in on this conspiracy had already proved themselves capable of anything and not ones to leave loose ends behind.

And what would they do to Kennedy, who would go from protecting her to guarding the real Elizabeth Thomas? Ratman and that hideous Rothschild woman had said the real president would never discuss her abduction and replacement once she was back in office, because aside from destroying her credibility she'd also endanger her family. But even if that panned out—even if Thomas played along—Kennedy would certainly be able to spot the difference now, and Ratman wouldn't allow anything to endanger his master plan.

After their discussion the day before she wanted desperately to get Kennedy out of here, so she'd talked to Ratman yesterday about replacing her bodyguard. She had told him Kennedy was asking too many questions she couldn't or wouldn't answer, and it was making her increasingly nervous and on edge. But Ratman, to her surprise, hadn't been impressed or worried; he'd shrugged off her concerns by saying, "Not my call." Maybe it wasn't his decision, but his indifference was worrying, to say the least.

Too anxious to continue the ruse of eating, she looked at the waiter who stood nearby, ready to attend to her every whim. "Why don't you join the rest in the kitchen?" She smiled. "I hardly have an appetite tonight, and I won't need anything else."

"But—"

"I would appreciate some alone time."

"Are you sure, Madam President?"

"I insist."

The man gave a slight bow and left the private dining room.

Ryden took a deep breath and hoped she'd live to regret what she was about to do. She set her fork down. "Would you please join me at the table?"

A few moments of silence elapsed before Kennedy replied from behind her. "I assume you're talking to me."

"Yes."

Without any audible movement Kennedy appeared at the table. Ryden could feel those beautiful blue eyes on her. "Have a seat," she said, unable to look at her.

Kennedy pulled out the chair next to her and sat on her right.

"I want you to leave," Ryden said.

Without a word Kennedy, got up.

"I want you to leave the White House."

"You finally made the time to have me fired?" Kennedy asked coldly.

"Tell your superior you want a reassignment."

"I won't, because I don't. If it's any consolation, I promise not to talk to you anymore unless completely necessary, Madam President."

"Please drop the Madam President bit."

"I prefer we didn't."

"Fine, whatever," she said. "But I insist you get out of here."

Kennedy sat back down. "That sounds ominous."

She shrugged. How was she going to make Kennedy realize she was in danger without telling her the truth? "Maybe it is."

"I wish you would stop playing with me."

"I'm not. I simply can't say more."

"I got that," Kennedy said. "That's been obvious since my first day here."

Ryden forced herself to look at her. "Please, don't fight me and don't ask me why. Just do as I say."

"I'm sorry. It doesn't work that way."

She placed her hand on Kennedy's. "Listen to me." She squeezed Kennedy's hand. "You are in danger."

"Why?" Kennedy looked surprised but didn't pull her hand away.

"If I could discuss that, I would have already told you. But I can't, so please don't make me lie more than I already have. Just trust me when I tell you there's a lot going on, things you could never begin to imagine. It's not safe here, Kennedy, and your curiosity has rubbed some individuals the wrong way."

"Moore and who else?"

Ryden looked away. "Who they are doesn't matter."

"It does to me."

"You can't stop them."

"I'm not alone. I have a very powerful company behind me."

"More powerful than the government?"

"Just tell me if the CIA is involved."

"Does it matter?"

"Yes."

"The CIA—to my knowledge, anyway—has nothing to do with it."

"Will you tell me what your part in all this is?"

Ryden shook her head. "I can't."

"Can you at least tell me if you were threatened?"

"I was."

"What would happen if these people and their game were exposed?"

Ryden tried to hide the shudder that went through her at the prospect, but the goose bumps on her arms betrayed her.

Kennedy must have noticed them, too. "I see," she said quietly. "I'm going to make some phone calls—"

"No!" Ryden practically screamed and grasped Kennedy's hand. "If they so much as suspect I had this conversation with you, they'll… they'll…"

"They won't," Kennedy said. "I'd never jeopardize you."

How could Kennedy still be so sincerely interested in her well-being, after being told they were in dire danger?

"Please, Kennedy. Just leave."

"I can't." Kennedy's piercing blue eyes locked with hers.

"I know it's your job to protect me, but I'm safer without you here."

"Are you?"

"They can tell I...I like you. They'll use that and then..."

"What exactly do they know?"

"That I like to spend time with you, talk with you."

"What else?" Kennedy looked troubled.

"Oh, they don't know about...that."

"Which *that* are you referring to?"

"No one knows I broke into your room, got tipsy on your wine, and...whatever."

Kennedy smiled. "You kissed me."

Her face flamed in embarrassment. "I'm sorry about that, I—"

"Was confused, troubled, and lonely. Yes, you've made that clear. But I haven't heard you say you regret it."

"I..." Her breath caught. "No."

"Good, because the only thing I'm sorry about is that you weren't sober at the time."

What Ryden wouldn't give to be in another place and time right now.

"Is that why you've been pushing me away?" Kennedy asked.

"I don't want you involved or hurt. I couldn't bear that." She looked down at their hands and realized she was absentmindedly caressing Kennedy's palm. She started to pull her hand away but Kennedy stopped her.

"I don't know what's going on in this place, or how they managed to involve you, but I can see you're somehow the victim."

I'm the biggest con and liar you've ever met. Lying to the country was painful enough, but deceiving this woman was agonizing.

"I'm staying here with you, Elizabeth."

Why wouldn't Kennedy listen? She was beyond frustrated—with Kennedy's stubbornness, with the mess she was in, and most of all, right now, with the fact that in the midst of all this chaos all she wanted to do was steal another kiss. "Kennedy, why can't you just listen—"

"I'm staying. And not because you're the president and it's my duty." She lifted Ryden's hand and raised it to her lips. "But because you're you."

CHAPTER TWENTY-EIGHT

Southwestern Colorado
Early next morning, March 8, one a.m.

Montgomery Pierce drummed his fingers on the conference table and studied Cassady's face as she poured herself coffee and took a seat to his left. The dark circles under her eyes matched Reno's, sitting to his right; none of them had slept since Jaclyn went missing. But despite the late hour, they were all alert and expectant because the front-gate guard had just phoned to announce Agent Chase's arrival. Monty hoped their best tracker could come up with a lead, because so far they'd had no luck whatsoever finding out anything about TQ. He'd called every contact he could think of and come up empty. Reno had been working around the clock as well but so far could find no record of anyone with that moniker or initials, at least none that matched.

"I've been working for the company for twenty years, give or take," Landis Coolidge said as she entered the conference room. "But you've never pulled me off a job before." She nodded at Reno as she removed her blazer and draped it over the chair next to Cassady's. "Hey, Cass, how's life?"

"They clearly haven't told you," Cassady replied, studying her face.

Chase looked at Cassady, then at him. "Tell me what?"

"Jaclyn is missing," Monty replied.

"What do you mean?"

"He means TQ is avenging her brother's death," Cassady answered.

Chase remained silent, staring past him, at the wall. Her jaw muscles twitched. Monty could see she was trying to hide her worry for Cassady's sake. "Do we know if she's alive?"

Monty looked at Cassady. "No, but I'm sure she is."

"Damn it." Chase retreated a couple of steps and leaned with her back against the wall. "Why can't that woman stay out of trouble?"

"Have a seat," Monty said. "I'll tell you what we know so far."

"I'm fine. Go ahead."

Monty told Chase everything they'd learned to date and that searching for TQ was proving an impossible task.

"No one knows who she is or what she looks like. We might as well be looking for a ghost," Cassady said when he'd finished.

"Ghosts don't exist. This bitch does, and we have to find her." Chase started pacing.

Monty had never seen Chase get upset; if she ever was, she never expressed it. But now she paced the room like a beast. "Maybe someone in China. The prisons. Can any of TQ's contacts there ID her?"

"No, I don't think so." Chase stopped beside the window. "We tried when we were looking for her brother."

"I don't see how this woman doesn't have records," Cassady said.

"What do we know about Dario's family?" Chase asked.

Reno looked down at his computer printouts. "Parents deceased. A female child, registered as stillborn, born ten years prior to Dario Imperi, but no other siblings. I couldn't find any record of another sister, which leads me to believe TQ wasn't really a sister or she paid someone to alter the records."

"What do we know about the stillborn?" Chase started pacing again.

"The family doctor signed the death certificate," Reno reported.

"Has anyone talked to the doctor?" Chase asked.

Reno shook his head. "Dead end. He died twelve years ago."

Chase paused behind Reno and peered over his shoulder at the printouts. "Do we know where the stillborn was buried?"

"Yeah," he replied. "Same cemetery in Wichita, Kansas, where the parents were interred."

"But…we don't know there's an actual body," Chase said.

"What do you mean?" Cassady asked.

Monty looked at Chase. "An exhumation."

"You think it's empty?" Cassady asked. "That the child never died?"

"Everything is possible." Monty smiled, happy to have anything at all to go on.

"Like I said, no one is a ghost." Chase started her restless pacing again. "I bet my PEZ collection that grave is empty."

"Why would the parents fake the death?" Cassady asked.

"Illegitimate child, couldn't afford a child, too soon for a child." Chase stopped and looked pointedly at Monty. "Or simply an inconvenient child. Pick one."

Cassady turned to glare at him as well. "Yeah, Monty. Pick one."

Monty wished both women would stop staring at him. Cassady was aware of who Jaclyn was to him, but did Chase know as well? And if so, did both of them think of him as despicably as he did of himself? As much as he had wanted to tell his daughter the truth, he'd never had a reason. He'd kept assuring himself all those years that Jaclyn was with him and that was all that mattered. But he'd never considered what mattered for Jaclyn. "There are reasons to give away or not want to acknowledge a child."

"If you say so." Cassady turned to Chase. "Which means the evil sister is alive and thriving."

"If TQ was given to another family, it was an off-the-record transaction," Chase said, "which would explain why we can't come up with anything, not even a social security number, under the Imperi name."

"How are we going to find out who took the child?" Cassady asked.

"We don't have the time to jump to conclusions, so first things first," Monty replied. He turned to Reno. "See if you can cross-reference—"

"I'm on it." Reno scooped up his printouts and headed back to his office.

"Skip the paperwork," Chase said. "Have someone in the area check it out now."

Monty reached for the phone and called Joanna. "Who do we have near Kansas?"

The White House
Two a.m.

Ryden was dreaming, deep in slumber, when the phone rang, but because she wasn't used to calls at this hour, the jangling startled her into heart-pounding full awareness in an instant.

She hadn't been able to sleep when she'd finally turned in close to midnight. Thoughts of Kennedy and everything she had told her kept replaying in her head. She wasn't certain that Kennedy realized the severity of the situation both of them were in. Though she was confident she wouldn't deliberately do anything to harm her, Ryden worried she might do something irrational to protect her and uncover whatever she thought was going on.

When she closed her eyes, all she could see was Kennedy. Her expressive blue eyes, determined chin, enticing mouth. That soft whisper of Kennedy's lips on her wrist; how could anything feel that soft? And how could a simple smile be so sexy? How had she never noticed women before, and especially women like Kennedy? Maybe because woman like this EOO guard usually didn't enter her world unless they were lost or looking for directions.

She glanced at the clock as she snatched up the phone before it could ring a second time. Two a.m. She'd slept less than an hour. "Yes?"

"It's time. I'll be at your door in ten minutes," Ratman said, and hung up.

Her heart boomed double time in her panic as she fumbled for the bedside lamp. When it blinked on, she let her eyes adjust and looked around the room, taking deep breaths. It was time to go home, wherever that might be. And it was time to start a new life—one that didn't include Kennedy.

Almost as if in a dream, she went to the closet to begin the departure procedure they had drilled her on. She grabbed the jeans, long-sleeve T-shirt, hoodie, and sneakers they had supplied her with—items that had nothing to do with the president's wardrobe—and quickly changed into them. She had nothing else to prepare or take; what she now wore was all she owned.

"I don't get to say good-bye," she mumbled, as she zipped up the hoodie. She walked over to the adjoining door and placed her hand on it. "Good-bye, Harper," she said, using Kennedy's first name for the first time.

The knock she had been waiting for since she entered the White House came promptly. She unlocked the door and Ratman walked in, while Jason, her backup Secret Service agent, waited just outside.

"I'm ready," she said immediately, wanting to avoid a private encounter with Ratman.

"Why so glum?" He smiled.

"Can we just…go?"

"Of course. Your father is in critical condition, after all." Ratman turned to Jason. "Get Kennedy and join us downstairs."

She could scarcely conceal her shock. "Are they both coming with us?"

"Of course," Ratman replied. "They're your guards, after all."

"But they—"

Ratman pulled her out into the hall and shut the door. "We have to move. The cleaners have an hour to remove all traces of you."

She walked behind him on unsteady legs. *Kennedy's going to be there. Escorting me.* The knowledge of what would happen next made her sick to her stomach.

Shield opened her door and found Jason standing outside. She'd thrown a White House robe over her navy pajamas.

"I was about to knock," he said.

"What's going on?" She pretended she hadn't heard the conversation from the other room. Moore had come to get Thomas; something apparently was wrong with her father.

"Beacon's father had a stroke and is en route to Suburban Hospital in Bethesda," he replied. "She's being taken out via the tunnels to keep things quiet. We have to move."

"Who's we?"

"You and I and Advisor Moore."

"I have to notify the Secret Service to get a detail and vehicles dispatched to whatever exit we're using. Why wasn't I told about this?"

"Moore called me. Don't know why." Jason rocked up on his heels impatiently. "Look, she has to move ASAP. Why don't you get ready while I arrange that?"

"Where's Beacon?" she asked.

"On her way to the tunnels. They're waiting for us."

"Call SS. Tell them to haul ass." She left the door open to ensure he made the proper arrangements as she dressed—casually, in jeans, button-down shirt, and jacket, so she wouldn't draw attention in the hospital. Poor Elizabeth, she thought. The last disaster she needed on top of everything else was a sick or dead father. First a murdered husband, and now this. The woman couldn't catch a break.

Shield could hear Jason out in the hall, informing the Secret Service about Beacon and making arrangements for three decoy cars to follow the presidential vehicle.

"Covered," he yelled when he hung up.

"Good. Let's go." Shield placed her Glock in its holster at her belt.

They were soon in the underbelly of the White House, heading down a long hallway. The president and Moore, engrossed in a whispered conversation, waited at the tunnel door at the end. Thomas was casually dressed for a change. She'd probably grabbed a comfortable outfit in case she needed to stay in the hospital with her father.

Suddenly, as they neared, Thomas rubbed her face and then kicked the wall. Shield had never seen her this upset. "We're good to go, Madam President," she said when she reached them. "We'll get you to the hospital as fast as possible."

Thomas nodded once and looked away. Moore put his arm around her shoulders. "He'll pull through. I know he will," he said comfortingly.

Shield unlocked the door to the tunnel. "Security is waiting at the exit."

"Good," Moore replied. "Let me know his condition," he told Thomas as he released her, "and if there's anything I can do for your family."

So Moore wasn't joining them for a change. She couldn't be happier that it was strictly family; Thomas could do with some time away from the idiot. Shield entered the tunnel first, with Thomas right behind her. Jason covered them from the back.

The concrete-and-steel tunnel was well lit, but tomb quiet and barren except for a trio of golf carts parked off to one side. Massive steel doors, all closed, lined both sides for the first few hundred feet. From her briefing and tour when she'd become primary, Shield knew this section of tunnel under the East Wing was the rarely used side—full of storage rooms and bunkers, primarily—all survival-scenario stuff. The stretch under the West Wing was busy virtually twenty-four hours a day now as they worked to finish the adjacent new Deep Underground Command Center.

Shield headed toward one of the golf carts and got behind the wheel. Jason sat beside the president in the rear seat, and they sped toward the exit. Shield remembered from her briefing that this tunnel came out in a wooded field five miles northwest of the capital.

"Few more minutes and you'll be on your way," Shield said over her shoulder when the exit door came into view a short time later.

"I guess."

What a strange answer. Shield parked the cart some yards from the exit and they got out. She led the way, with Thomas behind her and Jason covering the rear. "I'll be with you for the duration of your stay at the hospital."

"I...I figured," Thomas replied shakily. "You don't have to, though. I'm sure Jason is enough for now. Why don't you go back to bed and join me in the morning? I'm sure I'll be staying there way into tomorrow."

Another strange thing to say. What was going on? Thomas knew she couldn't go back, even if she wanted to. She was the primary.

"Looks like we'll have to skip our planned tennis match for tomorrow," the president said.

Shield stopped cold. No game was scheduled for tomorrow. She pulled her Glock and pivoted to face Thomas. They were two feet from the exit. "Jason, we're turning around."

Jason, still behind the president, yanked out his Sauer P229 pistol as he smoothly pulled Thomas into a headlock. He kept his face low, shielded by the president's. "One move and she's dead." He pointed the gun under Thomas's chin. "Now!" he yelled.

"What the—"

Before she could finish, the exit opened from the other side and three men in black ski masks rushed in, all with guns aimed at her and Thomas.

"Put your weapon down," one of them said, and pressed the end of his automatic against Shield's temple.

That son of a bitch Moore was behind this, or the tunnel would be swarming with security. He had to have made sure all the cameras were deactivated. How many in the White House were involved?

Shield hesitated. She was taught to never surrender her weapon. She turned slowly to Thomas, who stood stone still, fear evident in her eyes.

"Harper, put it down," the president said.

"Look, bitch, I can take you out now. Same to me," the guy beside her said in a thick accent. *Probably Russian*, she thought.

"Please. These people are crazy," Thomas pleaded. "Trust me."

"Trust you?" Shield said. "You know them?"

Thomas nodded.

"Bitch, somebody's about to get their blood mopped," another of the masked intruders said, and cocked his gun against Thomas's head. He had the same accent as the other. "Our cleaners can take care of it when they're done."

"Cleaners...done with what?" Shield asked calmly, puzzled with this surreal conversation.

"Do it," Thomas screamed.

Shield discharged the magazine. The clatter of it on the floor made Thomas jump.

"Let's go, *suka*." The guy beside Shield kicked the magazine to his associate and grabbed her by the arm. "Clear," he shouted.

Seconds later, two more men in masks appeared at the dark entrance, with what appeared to be a woman between them. When they stepped into the light of the tunnel, Shield gasped.

She looked from the woman, to Thomas, and back again. "What the hell—"

The new arrival was a bit heavier, but that was the only visible physical difference. She was dressed in a pantsuit identical to the one shown all over the media the day of the assassination attempt. The double looked at Thomas with disgust. "Tell your people they did an admirable job recreating me." She stepped closer, and the two men holding her moved with her, until the two women stood almost nose to nose. "But as is the case with all imitations, the interior is always inferior."

The woman Shield had been guarding started to respond, but the newcomer wasn't finished. "I want my wedding ring back."

"I left it by your bed," the look-alike in the jeans and T-shirt replied. "I'm so sorry. They didn't give me a choice."

"There's always a choice, even if it's death."

The double stared at her feet, her expression one of shame and embarrassment.

"I can't stand to look at her," the newcomer said. "Take her the hell away."

Jason escorted the new arrival—obviously the *real* Elizabeth Thomas—back toward the golf cart, while the masked men shoved Shield and the look-alike roughly out the exit and into the night.

CHAPTER TWENTY-NINE

Washington, D.C.

Jack was blindfolded during her transfer to the private plane that transported them to their final destination, so it wasn't until the aircraft descended some hours later that she was finally able to orient herself to where the hell she was. Looking out the Gulfstream's window, she spotted the Washington Monument in the distance, the pale obelisk starkly illuminated against the night sky by spotlights.

Bill, the tall, thickly built goon that TQ had appointed as her escort, led her to a white panel van when they landed and got behind the wheel. They headed out of the city, traveling northeast toward Baltimore. Freeway traffic was so sparse at that early hour Jack realized immediately they were being followed. Because Bill had to know it too, and was unconcerned, that could only mean that the dark sedan tailing them held associates—two of them, from their silhouettes. TQ was obviously being careful to make sure everything went off without a hitch.

Jack had been warned she'd have someone with her for the job itself, but the fact that more of TQ's people were along in another car threw a wrench in her plan. TQ wanted her to off some civilian and an EOO op, or else Cass would be killed on the spot. Jack's priority was Cass, but to kill another op even though she no longer worked for the organization was beyond even her morals. She'd come close once before, when she'd been working for a dirty politician.

Jack had fired before she recognized an EOO op—Agent Domino—holding a knife to the senator's throat. Fortunately, Domino's quick reflexes had saved her; she'd pulled the politician in front of her as a shield, and Jack had killed him instead, while the op escaped out the window.

Despite the outcome, Jack had felt guilty for a long time. Maybe she didn't like Montgomery Pierce, but she had no issues with the ops, who were just as much a victim of his ego as she was.

Tonight, she had intended to kill her driver and ask Kennedy to injure her. She planned to make it look like the EOO op had overpowered them both and escaped with Wagner. That way, she could return to TQ beat up, maybe even shot, and tell her she had tried but the op managed to steal Bill's gun. But explaining away three of TQ's guys would be a hard sell, even if she managed to shoot them all. Since Cass's safety was her top priority, she had only one option. She'd have to play along.

Bill pulled off the highway long before they reached Baltimore and drove deserted back roads for another few minutes before stopping in front of an isolated two-story home. The other car stayed on their bumper and parked behind them. "Why did we stop?" Jack asked.

"To pick someone up," he replied.

The two guys in the car behind got out and walked over. One approached Bill's window and waited for it to lower. "The Russian just called. They'll be ready to move in two." He ducked his head to look over at Jack. "He said he wants to talk to you."

"What Russian?"

"His name's Dratshev."

"What the hell is he doing here?"

"None of your business," Bill said.

"You know him?" the guy standing outside asked.

"We've met," Jack replied. "But what does he want now?" she mumbled to herself.

"Maybe he wants to screw you." The guy laughed. "How the fuck should I know?"

Jack smoothly pulled a Walther P99 semiautomatic pistol from Bill's shoulder holster and pointed it at the other one at the window. All three men, including the guy next to her, who apparently had a backup gun, drew their own weapons.

"Then why, bottom-feeding mutant, don't you ask the fucking Russian what he wants?" Jack dropped the gun on the driver's lap. "Just playin'."

Bill smiled and nodded appreciatively. "You are one crazy mother—"

"Looks like the Russian's here." Jack saw the big guy come out of the house and head toward them. She rolled down her window and, in Russian, asked how he was.

Dratshev smiled. "Not too fucked up," he replied. "Long time no see."

"Yup."

"You work for TQ now."

"Thanks for captioning my nightmare."

"For catching a nightmare?" the Russian asked with a confused expression.

"Never mind. So, what brings you to TQ's party?" Jack asked.

"Business."

"You mean it's not her fluffy disposition?" Jack feigned shock. "Which business?"

"My favorite toys."

"Gotta love any toy that profits a few million annually." Jack was referring to the illegal-weapons trade.

Dratshev changed the topic. "If you work for TQ, you work for me."

"That what you came to tell me?"

"*Da*. This deal means big money, so don't fuck up."

"Never. Your financial welfare means the world to me," Jack said sarcastically. "And I'm sure my buddy Bill here feels the same." She rolled her eyes in the direction of the driver.

"Good. So, good luck." Dratshev extended his hand.

Jack looked over at him, hovering outside her window, and extended her own hand.

The Russian shook it roughly. "Be wise." He winked.

Jack felt something in her palm. Paper. Whatever it was, Dratshev had his reasons for keeping it between them.

"Can't promise." Jack fisted the note and pulled her hand in.

Another unmarked white van, like the one they were in, emerged from behind the house and came down the driveway.

"We're ready to go." Bill started their vehicle and followed the van as it turned onto the street and headed back toward the highway. The dark sedan with TQ's men got in line behind the vans. "You used to work for him?"

"Yeah." Jack stuck her hand in her pocket to hide the paper Dratshev had given her. She'd have to wait for a private moment to see what it was.

"Hits, or what?"

"What is this, career day?"

They followed the other van for an hour as it skirted the nation's capital. Finally, it parked at the edge of a wooded area in the countryside, and four men in masks got out. A fifth emerged from the back, with a woman in a pantsuit whose head was covered.

"Who's that?" Jack asked.

"A woman," Bill replied.

"Killer observational skills."

"She's none of your business."

Bill kept his focus on the group as they headed into the woods, which gave Jack the opportunity to pull Dratshev's note out. She unfolded it, but it was too damn dark in the van for any amount of squinting to make it legible. It would have to wait until later.

"Why can't the Russians off the two women?" she asked, like she didn't know the answer. She wanted to find out what this idiot had been told, anything to find a way out of having to kill Kennedy. This Wagner she was supposed to kill, on the other hand, should have thought twice before joining TQ's clan.

"Because TQ wants you to do it."

"Doesn't make sense."

"She's testing you, genius," Bill said.

"I see. What else?"

"She doesn't want these two chicks to come back to bite her."

"Because she doesn't trust Dratshev will do it," Jack said.

Bill nodded. "I don't know why she trusts him at all."

"How's he involved in this deal?"

"Like he said. Business."

"Doesn't look like a business transaction to me," she said. "Looks more like an exchange."

"It is."

"The hooded woman for the other two."

Bill nodded.

"What's the deal?"

"None of your business."

"Where are we taking them?"

"There's an abandoned building an hour away, in Alexandria."

"Leave the bodies there?"

"Nope. Boss lady likes to play with fire." He laughed. "She wants them shot, then burned to a crisp. No evidence, no mess."

Jack's plans seemed to be headed a bit closer to hell with every minute that passed. Either way, she had to gain time, see if she could improvise a new way out.

"Here they come," Bill said.

Jack glanced at the side mirror. Dratshev's men were coming back out of the woods, this time with two women, neither of whose faces was covered.

Bill retrieved his gun. "Get out. It's go time."

Jack stood beside the van's open rear doors while the two women approached. Although it was dark, it was easy enough to make out who was who. Wagner walked with her head stooped, her demeanor submissive and defeated. The op—Kennedy—was alert and on guard, though she seemed more concerned with the woman she was with than the men with guns surrounding them.

Shield tried to focus on finding a way out of their predicament, but she had trouble shaking off the disturbing revelation in the tunnel. The woman she'd thought was Thomas walked just ahead of her, two men on either side. She was guarded by two as well, and the fifth masked gunman was directly behind her. The Russians were well armed—two had AK-47s—and all were so precise and coordinated in their actions she suspected they had a military background.

After a short hike through the woods, they emerged into a clearing where two vans and a dark sedan sat waiting. Two people got out of one of the vans—a man and a woman, both dressed in black—and opened the back doors as they approached. The Russians poked them forward with their automatics.

The imposter president, who had kept her head bowed the whole time, stepped into the vehicle first.

She started to follow, but the woman who stood by the door stopped her with a hand on Shield's back.

"Wait for my signal, Kennedy," she whispered, before she pushed Shield forward into the van.

Shield, in a crouch, spun around, but the doors slammed shut, leaving them wrapped in darkness.

Why would the woman ask her to wait for a signal?

She could hear the rapid breathing of her companion a couple of feet away to her right. Shield sat beside her, her back against the driver's side wall, as the van started up and began to move. There was no use fumbling around in the dark to see whether there was anything in here that might be useful. The meticulous planning of this conspiracy was evident. These people left nothing to chance. "Are you all right?"

The woman's panicky inhalations began to calm. After a long silence, she replied. "Yes."

"Good. Now, who the hell are you?"

"I told you to leave. I warned you."

"Who are you?" Shield tried to contain her anger.

"My name's Ryden Wagner."

"Why does that sound familiar?"

"My name's been all over the news."

"Remind me why."

"The homicidal florist from Philadelphia."

Shield flashed back to the news reports. This, all of this, was absurd. "Is there anything else you want to add to your curriculum vitae?"

"I didn't kill anyone. They set me up."

"Who did?"

"Some rich woman."

"And Moore was in on it."

"I don't know what his involvement is, exactly," Wagner replied, "but he works for her. That's why he was all over me."

"Why the president?" Shield couldn't believe any of this. "I mean, this is ludicrous."

"Apparently Thomas's agenda against the illegal-weapons trade is inconvenient for this woman who's behind it all, and she wanted me to take Thomas's place to stop it."

"And you simply agreed?" Shield was so exasperated her accent suddenly sounded much more Italian than she allowed when on a job.

"I didn't have a choice," Wagner curtly replied. "They were going to give me the death penalty for something I didn't do."

"Let me guess. They promised you a get-out-of-jail-free card, money, a new life, and a pony."

Wagner didn't answer right away. "I needed to believe them. It was either join them and live or certain death."

She remembered how Wagner had stared at the news reports about herself. The image of her mug shot sprang to mind. The cute bookworm type with the thick glasses. "The florist in the news looked nothing like you."

"They had me…altered."

"But still—"

"It was a bad picture, okay?"

"How long had they been grooming you?" A florist would need plenty of preparation time to pass so effectively and convincingly as the chief executive.

"More than two months of operations and lessons in… everything."

Who the hell was the woman behind all this? And where did she find the financial and other resources to accomplish such a scheme? "I can't believe you agreed to this," Shield finally said. "And I can't believe you acted the part so well."

"Look, I'm going to talk to them when we get out, explain to them you—"

"Why didn't you tell me?"

"Don't you think I wanted to? Moore would have killed us both if he so much as suspected I'd said anything. For the longest time, he even had me believing you were put there to spy on me. I had no idea Jason was the one hired to do that. Moore kept telling me I was surrounded by people involved in the plan."

"You even fooled Thomas's family." That was a weak consolation for Shield's own failure to see through the guise.

"I almost blew it when the sister got personal, but Moore stepped in."

"I just can't believe you didn't tell me. I could have gotten us out of there. I could've exposed Moore and the rest. Instead you lied and lied and led me to believe you…" What was the point? This woman was clearly too involved and too much of a coward to understand a word she was saying. She sighed. "Forget it."

They sat in darkness and silence for a long while.

"Where are they taking us?" Wagner asked.

"What does it matter?" Shield replied.

"I'm sorry."

"Really? Because that makes it better."

"I'm not going to leave you with them," Wagner said. "I'll tell them you have nothing to do with this."

"With what, exactly?"

"The plan. That you were never part of anything, knew nothing about me or Thomas or who's involved or why they did this."

"Is it because you're that naïve or because you're from the great state of denial that you think these people give a damn?" Shield tried to control the anger that for some reason outweighed her worry. "If I didn't know what was going on before, I know now. And aside from that, Moore is aware I suspected something was up and that I'd realize something was wrong the minute the real president returned. I would have landed here anyway. They're not going to let me, or you, for that matter, go anywhere."

"But they—"

"Does this look like a ride to freedom?"

"But they promised me—"

"Do you think they're going to leave any evidence or witnesses to what they've managed to pull?"

"I…"

"We're talking about the U.S. president, not some boyfriend you lied to about his ability to give you amazing orgasms. You've deceived the nation. The whole damn world. They're not going to let us walk and risk you or me talking."

"That was the deal, and excuse me for not choosing a lethal injection."

"That was never the deal."

"You're not listening. They—"

"They're taking us to a nice remote place to kill us."

Wagner shifted loudly. "Listen to me—"

"Stop," Shield said. "Just…stop talking. I can't listen to you anymore."

CHAPTER THIRTY

Jack could hear occasional yelling from the back of the van, and she
was pretty sure it was Kennedy. The two women either didn't know
their captors could hear them or they didn't care. What was clear was
that Kennedy was pretty damn pissed, and for good reason. Although
Wagner had sealed her own fate and probably deserved what was coming
to her, Jack had to find a way to get the op out alive. It wouldn't be easy;
the sedan with TQ's two backup goons was still on their bumper.

She turned to the driver. "Did TQ tell you one of the women is a
contractor for a private organization?"

"So?"

"I've dealt with companies like that. They won't rest until they
find out what happened to her."

Bill shrugged. "So? What if they do? No one can touch that crazy
bitch."

"And by that, you mean TQ."

"Who else?"

"You don't like her?"

He shrugged again. "I like her enough to want her alive and kicking
so she can continue to pay me what she does. The woman pays well."

"But you know she's deranged."

"I have a cousin who thinks he's Napoleon. He used to run through
Central Park wrapped in nothing but the French flag." He paused,
eyebrows furrowed as if trying to remember something. "Oh, yeah. He
ate bugs, too. Anyway, he's in the psych ward now. Straitjacket, padded
walls, the works, and shit." He chuckled and turned to look at her.

"Okay," Jack replied.

Bill stopped laughing. "TQ puts him to shame," he said seriously.

"Look, I don't want trouble with the authorities. My record's a
mile long, and they'll use anything to lock me up for life. I can't afford
to have some money-hungry contractor looking for me. Why not let
this one walk?"

"Because I enjoy breathing. I've done three years in Attica and I can tell you, it's nothing compared to how the bitch handles treason. She'd never buy some broad got away from the four of us."

The van pulled into an industrial complex on the edge of Alexandria, Virginia. The streets were vacant, the buildings closed and shuttered. This wasn't looking at all good, and Jack was running out of ideas.

"You know, scar aside, you're one fine-looking woman," Bill said.

"Say what?"

"I'm just saying, maybe we could get together later and fuck." He glanced at her. "What do you say?"

"I say, I'd rather fuck my hand for all eternity."

Bill smiled, as though oblivious to Jack's answer. "Well, think about it." He nodded toward a warehouse just ahead. "We're here."

Jack peered out the window at the dark, abandoned building as they parked. Both got out, and once Bill had retrieved an assault rifle from behind his seat, he opened the back. The sedan that had been following parked as well, several yards behind, its headlights illuminating the scene.

"Let's go, ladies," he said.

Wagner got out first and looked around, her expression one of terror.

Once she got her first good look at Wagner, Jack understood a great deal more about the exchange she'd witnessed earlier. The woman was a dead ringer for the president. What had she been assigned to do for TQ? The possibilities were mind-boggling.

"Where are you taking us?" Wagner asked.

"No questions," Bill replied.

"I was promised money and freedom," Wagner insisted. "I did what you people asked me to. I kept my word. Now you had better keep yours."

"Or what?" He pointed his AK-47 at her.

Kennedy jumped out of the van and stood in front of Wagner. She placed her hand on the weapon's muzzle. "Relax. She's afraid, that's all."

Bill pulled the automatic away and pointed it at Kennedy. "Don't touch my shit."

Kennedy raised her hands. "No offense."

He poked the muzzle in Kennedy's stomach. "You don't seem too worried. I can change that."

Jack could tell he was getting irritated. Their orders were to off the two inside, but if Kennedy pushed, Jack didn't put it beyond the idiot to shoot. It wasn't like anyone would hear them out here. Just then, the two goons from the sedan came to stand next to them.

Kennedy stared Bill straight in the eye. "You look pretty stupid pointing your *shit* at two defenseless women."

The two guys from the sedan laughed, which irritated Bill even more.

"Who the fuck are you calling stupid, Kennedy?" He shifted the muzzle from Kennedy's stomach to her head. "If anyone looks stupid, it's a fucking private contractor with a gun pointed at her head."

Maybe the words rang too true to Kennedy, because her stance said she was about to pounce, which would be a disaster.

"Whoa, big guy." Jack went to stand next to him, grateful he was too distracted to notice her hand slip in and out of his pocket. She looked intently at Kennedy. "Same goes for you."

Bill lowered his weapon. "Fucking contractor."

"Understand?" Jack asked, her serious gaze still on the op.

Kennedy continued to look at Jack as if trying to follow her.

"My people use *whatever means necessary.*" Jack used the EOO motto.

"So do mine." Kennedy looked confused.

"I'm scared," Bill said, oblivious to what was taking place. "This way." He gestured with his assault rifle toward the dark building.

Kennedy looked at Jack one last time and moved forward with Wagner, one hand on her elbow.

"I want to talk to my lawyer," Wagner shouted. "We had a deal."

"Hold on, I'll get him on the phone for you." Bill laughed.

Wagner pleaded. "Kennedy had nothing to do with this."

"Don't know what her deal is, but I'd take her out for the fun of it," he replied.

Wagner stopped walking and turned around. "Let her go, she hasn't done—"

He slapped her so hard across the face that Wagner fell down. "You don't tell me what to do, bitch. Now shut the fuck up."

Kennedy helped her back on her feet. "You have very bad timing when it comes to telling the truth."

Wagner was bleeding from her lip and nose. "I kept my mouth shut to protect both of us."

"Keep walking," Bill said. They moved forward again as a small group, with the two guys from the sedan following all of them from behind.

Once in the building, Bill turned on a flashlight and led everyone down a short, dark stairwell to the basement. While he covered the two women, one of TQ's men from the sedan flipped a switch and a single dangling light bulb came to life, casting shadows in the cavernous room.

The beams above their heads were damp with moisture, and large dark stains marred the concrete floor, both contributing to the rank, stale air. A few broken pallets lay beside a small half-wall of concrete to Jack's left, and stacks of metal barrels were bunched in groups around the perimeter, but the center of the room was empty. The EMERGENCY EXIT sign above a heavy door at the far end of the room illuminated it.

The second man from the sedan walked over to the most foreboding feature of the room, the massive industrial furnace that dominated one wall. He turned on the burner and opened the heavy steel door. "Should be nice and toasty in a few minutes."

TQ's three henchmen had clearly all been here before; separately, or together, they had used this building for similar purposes. Their expressions and demeanor indicated this was just another day at the office for them.

Wagner looked terrified. "What's going on? Why are we here?"

One of TQ's men laughed and turned to Jack. "Tell her. It's your show, after all."

Jack looked at Kennedy. "It would appear my new boss likes to haze her newcomers."

Kennedy simply nodded once.

Wagner stepped forward. "What does that mean?"

"It means Silent Death here is new, and this is her first test," one of the men said. He looked at the furnace and back to Jack, then crossed his arms over his chest. "You're on." He smiled as if anxious to see her perform.

Bill took the pistol from his shoulder holster and handed it to Jack. He stood to her right, facing Wagner and Kennedy, while TQ's two other goons stood to her left.

Jack stared at Kennedy. "Showtime."

Bill patted her on the back. "Damn right, and no worries about the contractor. She's all words. Take her out, and you never have to worry about her or her people coming after you."

❖

Shield stared intently at the dark-haired woman with the scar, trying to anticipate her intentions as she checked the pistol her associate had given her. Was she reading her right? Was this mysterious stranger trying to help them? She seemed to be their only possible way out of this situation.

"This is crazy," Wagner said with a trembling voice from her right. "Kennedy hasn't done anything." She went to step in front of Shield, but Shield quickly pulled her back behind her as the woman raised the weapon and pointed it at them. They were only ten feet apart.

Shield could feel Wagner's trembling hand on her back, and her rapid breathing from behind filled her ears.

The woman aimed the gun not at her, but over her shoulder, at Wagner. Her gaze, though, was fixed on Shield. She had expressive eyes—and they conveyed a clear, pleading message to play along. When Shield stared unflinchingly back with understanding, the woman gave the slightest, subtlest nod.

"I told you, they don't care," Shield said over her shoulder to Wagner. "Look at them. It's obvious they don't have a mind of their own. They're too stupid to know right from wrong or to realize what my organization will do to them."

The woman facing them lowered her gun. "You know, before I met one of you fucked-up contractors I used to care about these threats." She stepped forward until she was only two feet away. "But now," she continued, as she lifted the gun to Shield's forehead, "not so much."

"Do it," one of the men said, and his friends laughed. "Maybe you can get them both with one shot."

"No!" Wagner screamed from behind her.

The woman's intense green eyes looked from the gun, to Shield, and back to the gun. "By any means necessary," she muttered, repeating the EOO motto.

That was enough for Shield. She grabbed the weapon. Although outnumbered, it was her only desperate chance.

She got off three quick shots, firing next to the woman's head, and got two of the men—one in the head and the other in the stomach. She missed the third one as he ran for cover behind a stack of barrels near the stairwell. "Let's go." She grabbed Wagner by the wrist.

The woman who'd helped them was bent over, covering her head. She was in obvious pain from the loud gun reports so close to her ear.

Shield put her free hand on the woman's back. "Can you hear me? We have to run."

"Leave me."

Shield released Wagner. "Don't move," she told her. Then she turned back to the woman and put an arm around her waist. "We never leave one of our own behind," Shield said, not knowing if she could hear or if she was indeed one of theirs.

But the woman tried to pull away. "Leave me," she said again.

Shield couldn't understand what was going on with her and didn't have time for riddles.

"Watch out!" Wagner yelled, and pushed her forward. A second or two later, a shot rang out from the direction of the stairwell, followed by a muffled *chink* as it tore a bit of concrete from the floor near them. Wagner screamed again.

Shield pulled Wagner behind her and fired back. Once. Twice.

Wagner poked her on the shoulder and pointed to the emergency exit.

"Use me to get out," the dark-haired woman whispered. "Threaten to kill me."

"I can't do that."

The woman punched Shield in the face. "Fucking do it."

Shield aimed at the overhead bulb and shot out the light. "Move and I'll shoot you in the head," she said loudly.

With the woman in a headlock and Wagner behind her, Shield kept the gun pointed in the direction of the stairwell as she shimmied the three of them over to the emergency exit.

Wagner pushed the door open and held it.

Shield turned her body to let the woman she had hold of through it first, but as they crossed the threshold, the woman struggled to get away.

"What is your problem?" Shield said as she tried to get the woman to stay put. "Why are you—" She heard the shot before she felt it.

CHAPTER THIRTY-ONE

"Kennedy!" Ryden screamed, and shut the door. There were thirty feet from the bottom of another stairwell, and the vague reddish glow from the exit sign provided her enough light to see Kennedy, motionless, facedown on the floor. "Oh, my God. Kennedy!" Ryden fell to her knees. "Can you hear me?" She wiped the hair from Kennedy's face. "Kennedy, please don't—"

The woman in black bent over and grabbed the gun from Kennedy's hand.

"Are you crazy?" She turned to the stranger with tears in her eyes. "She was trying to get us out and—"

"I told her to leave me."

The woman looked down at Kennedy's back, where a dark hole had appeared in her brown leather jacket. "Give her a moment. She's winded, that's all." She flipped Kennedy over, onto her back, then slapped her.

"Don't you touch her." Ryden pushed the stranger away. "What are you doing?"

"She's wearing a vest," the woman replied, and went to stand with her ear to the door.

No sooner had the words left her mouth than Kennedy's eyes fluttered open.

"Oh, thank God." She caressed Kennedy's face.

"Are you all right?" Kennedy asked her.

"You're the one who got hit." She couldn't believe Kennedy was worried about *her* well-being after being shot at.

"I'm fine. He got me on the vest."

"I told you," the woman said.

Ryden glared at the stranger, trying to contain her anger. "She could have died because of you."

"Last time I checked, it was because of you she almost died," the woman replied.

"Are you in pain?" Kennedy asked Ryden.

"Why would I—"

"You're bleeding." Kennedy touched her left arm, at the shoulder.

She looked down and discovered a growing splotch of red on the sleeve of her hoodie.

"Flesh wound," the woman said. "He got you the first time he fired in there."

"But I didn't...*don't* feel any—"

"Adrenaline." Kennedy slowly got to her feet. "You'll feel it later."

"You two need to leave...now." The woman turned to them. "Take the van." She dug in her pocket and threw a ring of keys at Kennedy. "There's a safe house twenty miles from here outside Burke. Mitcham Court, north side of the big park. Stay there and have your people come get you. Keep clear of public places and transport, and ditch the car as far away from the safe house as you can."

"Can't we go to the police?" Ryden asked.

"No. The bitch has her people everywhere. Keep low until your own show up."

"You're coming with us," Kennedy said.

"I can't."

"I'm not leaving you here."

"Yeah, you are." The woman handed the gun to Kennedy and waited at the bottom of the stairs.

Kennedy led the way up, with Ryden behind her and the other woman last, but she'd gone only a few steps when she paused and turned to look at the stranger. "Who are you?"

"It doesn't matter."

"What you said—by any means necessary. Why did you say it?"

"It doesn't matter," the woman repeated.

"Why did you help us?"

"I helped *you*," she said to Kennedy, then tilted her head toward Ryden. "Not TQ's bitch. If you want to help her, that's your issue."

"Who's TQ?" Kennedy asked, and looked at her like she had the answer.

She, however, had never heard of anyone by that name. "I don't know who she's talking about."

"The hell you don't," the woman replied. "It's the same crazy bitch who hired me to kill you both," she told Kennedy. "The same woman who hired your friend here to play president. Enough talking. You need to go." She pushed past them and stopped at the door one landing above. It had another illuminated EMERGENCY EXIT sign above it. "This looks like it comes out the back of the building. You'll have to make it to the van from there."

"Come with us," Kennedy insisted.

"He may be out there, and he can't know I let you go."

"Then come with us. You'll be safe. My people will make sure of that."

"Your people don't give a damn about me."

They all heard steps on the metal stairwell above them, and Ryden squeezed Kennedy's arm. "He's—"

Kennedy placed her finger on Ryden's mouth and gently pushed the door open. The woman was right—they found themselves in a narrow alley at the rear of the warehouse.

Once they were outside, with the door shut behind them, Kennedy said, "I'll shoot him as soon as he comes out."

"No," the woman replied. "I need him to tell the bitch I tried to stop you."

"I don't understand you."

"You don't have to. Punch me in the face. Make it look good."

"What?" Ryden asked.

"To make it look like I struggled to get the keys from her," Kennedy replied, before she punched the woman hard in the face.

The stranger fell against the brick wall. "Great," she mumbled, and spat blood. "Now, give me the gun."

"What?" Ryden asked again. She couldn't understand what the hell was going on.

Kennedy placed the weapon in her hand.

"Get ready to run," the woman said.

Ryden watched in disbelief as the stranger aimed the gun at her own thigh and pulled the trigger.

"Fuck! I'm shot!" she yelled, and collapsed to the ground as blood poured from the wound. "They're out back!"

"I owe you." Kennedy picked up the gun.

"And don't you fucking forget it." The woman gasped, in obvious pain, as she clutched at her thigh.

Kennedy grabbed Ryden by the hand and ran around the side of the warehouse for the van. Before they got in, Kennedy shot out two of the tires of the sedan.

❖

Washington, D.C.

Although the bullet had passed cleanly through the fleshy part of her thigh, Jack's leg hurt like a bitch during the bumpy drive. TQ had sent a car and two men to pick up Jack and Bill from the abandoned warehouse. They were driven into the heart of D.C. to a service entrance behind a big glass office complex, then led to an elevator that took them down to the underbelly of the building.

From one basement to another, but the two were radically different. This space was clean, modern, and well lit, dominated by large wooden shipping crates piled in several groupings. The markings on the side indicated some had come from the Middle East, while others had Russian Cyrillic labeling or Asian characters.

Jack was surprised and troubled to find TQ standing in the middle of the room. As far as she knew, the bitch rarely left her penthouse. If she was here, that meant things were very serious.

TQ was on the phone with her back turned to them. "I want you to comb every inch of Washington and toll booth out of Washington. I don't care how many men you need to do it, just give them pictures." She hung up and turned to look at them before she dialed another number. "Have you found the van yet?" she asked whoever was on the other end. "I see." She sounded disappointed. "I've ordered all airports to signal me should they show up, and I have men at the train stations," she said. "Call me as soon as you find anything."

TQ shut the cell phone and walked past Jack, without looking at her, to Bill. "How exactly did they get away?" She was the picture of serenity, which scared Jack more than tripping while holding liquid nitrogen.

Bill explained how he had run outside when Jack shouted that the two women were getting away. When he found her, wounded on the ground, Jack had told him the contractor had used her as a shield to get to the exit and then punched her unconscious in the stairwell. When Jack came to, she went after them and got shot as the two women were in the process of getting away with the van.

"How did they get the keys?" TQ asked calmly.

"They must've taken them while I was out cold," Jack explained. "I need to sit." She bit her lip in pain. She could feel blood slowly trickle down her leg. It had saturated her black jeans.

"When I say so." TQ looked at Bill. "Correct me if I'm wrong, but weren't you the one driving?"

His look of terror at being questioned by his boss was undeniable. "I…I…yeah, I drove."

"Then do explain how Jack ended up with the keys."

"I…I don't know." He looked at Jack. "They were in my jacket." Bill felt his pockets as if expecting to find them there.

"They fell out and I picked them up," Jack said blandly. She'd picked his pocket when he'd been busy pointing his gun at Kennedy's head outside the building.

"Does that happen a lot?" TQ asked him.

"Never."

"How unfortunate for you it happened tonight." TQ took a step closer, so they were face-to-face. "How very unfortunate," she repeated.

Bill had a good six inches on her, but his eyes were wide in fear and his face was slick with perspiration. He backed up against the wall. "Don't believe her. She picked my pocket."

"You saying I stuck my hand in your jacket and you never noticed?" Jack took a painful step forward. "I doubt you'd miss that, since moments before I found the keys on the ground you'd asked me to fuck you."

"You took them from me." He turned to TQ. "I know she did. She spent the whole drive there trying to convince me to let the contractor go, because she was afraid of them coming after her." He looked at Jack. "You could have dropped them both, but you hesitated. It was like you were waiting for that bitch to go for your gun."

"Don't be stupid. She took me by surprise."

TQ arched one eyebrow. "Why do I find that hard to believe?"

"Hey, I'm not superhuman." Jack looked down at the small puddle of blood at her feet.

"You're also not an amateur. I'm sure you didn't get your rep by making unintelligent moves." TQ paced the room. "You killed a man you knew nothing about—an innocent individual who could have been a fed or cop—in front of me, without so much as flinching. You did it while practically blind and then went back for one more shot." She crossed her arms." You want me to believe some woman managed to take your weapon, punch you, steal the keys, and shoot you, all in the process of escaping?"

"That's the gist of it." Jack shrugged. She had to play it down. Any show of fear or diffidence would trigger TQ's thinly veiled patience and anger at tonight's massive failure. "My apologies."

"I'll get them next time," Bill said.

"Next time." TQ mumbled, more to herself than either of them. "Of course, because this was some silly, inconsequential job that can be done any old time." She removed invisible lint from her stiff and white-as-herself shirt.

Jack knew the signs. TQ was about to throw a shit fit. The two of them were about to get very dirty.

"Yeah, no biggie," Bill said. Was he stupid, or did he have a death wish? Didn't he recognize sarcasm and lethal composure?

Without taking her eyes off her shirt, TQ sighed. "Remove him from my life."

One of the two guys who'd brought them here—a short, barrel-chested guy who'd been watching the goings-on from a position near the door—drew a pistol and shot the dumbass in the chest. Bill fell to his knees and then slumped forward and lay still.

The short goon then trained his gun on Jack and waited.

"What to do, what to do." TQ started to pace again.

Jack tried to remain calm, but TQ was unpredictable. These could be her last moments. The bitch had just tossed the coin of Jack's life in the air, and all she could do was wait for the deciding heads or tails.

Yet it wasn't her own existence she cared about. They said that your life passes before your eyes before you die, but all Jack could see was Cass's future—one where TQ killed Cass as well.

"Look." Jack shifted her weight and cringed as pain shot up her leg. "I know I screwed up, but I'm good at what I do. You can't judge me based on one failure." She stuffed her hands in her jeans. "I need my own team to perform. Let me put one together next time, a few people I can count on. Not clowns like him." She looked down at the lifeless body next to her. "The guy couldn't even manage to keep the car keys in his pocket."

"Why didn't you pull the trigger, Jack?"

"I have anger-management issues," she replied. "The contractor insulted and threatened me with her organization."

"Since when do you care about contractors?"

"Since they almost killed me during a job."

"Why is it you're not concerned about me executing you instead?" TQ asked.

"I know—"

"Do you think I need you enough to overlook your failures, Jack?"

"No."

"Then?"

"I know you want to keep me alive for as long as it takes to get over yourself, which could be never."

"Myself?" TQ sounded intrigued. "How interesting. Do explain."

"You didn't come after me because I killed your brother. I doubt you care enough about anyone to seek revenge on their behalf." She had to remind TQ why she'd wanted Jack in the first place; she had to put TQ's anger back into perspective if she wanted to keep Cass alive. "I'm just here because you can't cope with someone else deciding destiny or calling the shots. I put a glitch in your plans, in your perfectly choreographed life, when I killed your brother and rubbed it in your face. If anyone should have decided about his miserable life and reveled in the choice of his death, it should have been you."

TQ clapped slowly. "Brava. Not bad for a lowlife assassin."

"You're not that complicated. Pretty transparent, actually."

TQ laughed. "Am I, now?"

"Just another statistic, really."

"How precious. Kitchen psychology." She approached Jack.

"Probably a case of a messed-up childhood," Jack replied. "Parents didn't love you, think you were good enough. For some reason, gave more love or saw more potential in your paraplegic brother. Maybe they never wanted a daughter in the first place and treated you like an afterthought. But you proved them wrong. You got even by becoming powerful and rich. You showed them who really calls the shots when it comes to rejection and pain—"

"Shut up." TQ shouted, completely out of character.

"How am I doing so far?"

"I said, shut up," TQ repeated, quietly this time.

"The truth's a remorseless bitch, isn't she?"

"Undoubtedly." TQ traced the scar on Jack's cheek with her index finger. "Yet nothing, compared to me." She went to the door but turned back, her hand on the knob. "I can end your life with the wave of my hand."

"But you won't."

TQ smiled. "My game, my terms, remember? You get to live for as long as I deem necessary. Now, if you'll excuse me, I need to take care of your failure."

She addressed the short goon standing there and his friend Hulk on the opposite corner. "You two...I want you to demonstrate just how remorseless I am, until I say otherwise."

CHAPTER THIRTY-TWO

Burke, Virginia

Shield drove slowly past the safe house. The cracker-box home was dark, and the overgrown yard, if it could even be called a yard, told her it hadn't been used in a while.

The isolated safe house was near the northern edge of Lake Accotink Park, an enormous wooded area big enough to get lost in. She skirted the edge of the park for nearly three miles before she began looking seriously for a good dump site.

She'd hoped to hide the van among the trees, but every possible avenue she explored had problems or carried too much risk of immediate discovery. She spotted the solution in an enormous car dealership coming up on the right. Shield followed the signs to the service department around back and parked in a lot filled with older vehicles waiting to be repaired or picked up by their owners. "Let's go," she told Wagner as she slid the keys under the front mat. "Follow me closely, keep quiet, and don't draw attention to yourself."

After a two-block jog they were inside the tree line at the edge of the park. They'd made it there unobserved, fortunately, because the bloodstain on Wagner's light-blue hoodie was getting too large to ignore. Since it was still much too early for park visitors, Shield kept to the main path that led north through the woods, confident they wouldn't be seen. Still, she remained quiet, alert to any noise or sign of movement ahead or behind them. Though it was black as pitch out, they could move quickly because the pathway was wide and had been paved for bicycles. Wagner did a good job of keeping up, though she was breathing heavily.

The one-story safe house, set a good distance from any neighboring homes, was sadly neglected, with peeling paint, an iffy roof, and a driveway of cracked concrete and tall weeds. All the curtains were drawn, and every window was opaque with filth. From the look of it, it might have been years since anyone had last used the residence for any significant amount of time.

Shield hoped they'd at least find a working phone.

"Are you sure this is the place?" Wagner bent over, hands on her knees, trying to catch her breath. The sleeve where she'd been shot was saturated with blood.

"There's nothing else around."

"What's this house supposed to be?"

"A safe house is a place where ops or agents can find refuge until further notice or a place to hide witnesses."

Wagner straightened and stared at the sagging porch. "It looks… spooky."

"As long as we find a phone, I don't care what the house looks like." Shield tried the front door, the Walther at the ready. Locked. Wagner stayed close behind her as she made her way around to the back. The back exit was locked as well, but the wood was so warped there was a gap between the door and frame, enough to pop it open with the security keycard from her wallet. The Russian goons who'd overpowered them in the tunnel had taken only her Glock.

"Wait here," she told Wagner. She slipped inside and slid her hand along the wall until she found a light switch. She flipped it on, relieved when a dim bulb came to life, illuminating a small, sparsely furnished kitchen.

She turned on more lights and looked around, giving the half dozen rooms a thorough check in the space of a couple of minutes. Two small bedrooms, one bath, a living room, dining room, and kitchen. Although everything was dusty and worn, the place did indeed conform to the usual safe-house standards: it was isolated, with a good view of the surrounding area, and had multiple exits and basic, functional furniture. Little else, except for a few kitchenware items and minimal bedding and towels. The less clutter in a place like this, the better. It was easier to tell immediately if anyone had been there and changed anything, and it was tougher to conceal cameras or listening devices.

Many safe houses also had a place to hide things—weapons, documents, even people. Did this one? For the moment, her priority was the phone she spotted on the end table beside the couch. "You can come in," she called out to Wagner.

Wagner, hugging herself, came in from the kitchen and looked around. "At least we're safe for now," she said with evident dismay.

"Have the White House luxuries spoiled the florist?" Shield knew she was out of line, but she didn't care. Wagner had proved to be a liar working for a dangerous woman named TQ, a woman she'd turned a blind eye to knowing anything about, and Shield was fed up with her lies and games. She didn't even know why she'd helped Wagner escape.

"My name is Ryden," Wagner replied angrily. "And no, the White House and everything about it is a nightmare I hope to one day forget."

"Then get comfortable. I don't know how long we'll have to stay here."

"I thought they were coming to get us."

"That depends on what's going on at headquarters and whether they think it's safe."

"When are you going to call them?"

"As soon as I figure out what to tell them."

"What do you mean?"

Shield locked the door and took a seat on the couch. "I want you to tell me what the hell is going on—who this TQ is and how she involved you. And then I want to know how the hell you pulled this off."

"Look," Wagner replied, as she sat on an armchair to Shield's left, "I know you're angry and you have every reason to be, but I did what I had to, to stay alive."

"The only reason you're alive, that *both* of us are alive, is by the grace of a complete stranger. I don't understand why she helped us, but we owe her our lives." Shield tried to keep her voice steady and not let her bottled-up anger take over. "What *you* did—your lies and deceptions, kidnapping the president and getting innocent people killed in the process, and then trying to seduce me to throw me off track—is not why you're still alive."

"They promised me freedom," Wagner said coldly. "And I did not try to seduce you."

"Stop repeating that ridiculous mantra. Did you really think they'd let a nobody live to tell what happened? High-profile people have been permanently silenced for a lot less. Do you have any idea how ludicrous you sound?"

"What the hell was I supposed to do? Go to jail and wait for death? Do you think I went looking for them, for this whole absurd weirdness?" Wagner winced. "They framed me, killed my customer and his ex-wife with my stem cutter, and placed it back in my shop where the police found it covered in blood. I didn't stand a chance."

"Didn't you get a lawyer?"

"A fancy-looking one came to me while I was being held for questioning. Initially, I thought my colleague sent him. I'd asked her to find me a lawyer, a pro bono one. Some guy in an expensive suit showed up instead and got me out then took me to his equally expensive office, where he told me if I refused to work for his client they'd provide solid evidence against me. Witnesses who saw me being intimate with the victim on various occasions."

"Were you?"

"With Tim? No. Never. I hardly knew the man."

"Who hired this lawyer to represent you?"

"He never said, but as time went by and they started to operate and school me, this woman would call to check on my progress. She never said so, but I know she was the client the lawyer had referred to. She was behind it all."

"Was TQ her name?"

"She never mentioned a name," Wagner replied. "No one ever mentioned their name, except for the woman who trained me, taught me manners, how to talk, sound, walk, politics, how to hold a damn fork, and every other little thing."

"How do you know this woman who called was the brain behind this scheme?"

"Just the way she talked to me. Like it was up to her to decide whether my transformation was successful and I was ready to proceed with what they wanted from me. It wasn't until I was ready for the job that they revealed who I was to double."

"The president."

"I only realized after the swelling from the operations had gone down and they let me look at myself for the first time in the mirror."

"This woman—"

"It looks like she knows or owns a lot of people in high places, including Moore," Wagner went on. "That's why I was terrified to talk to you or even suggest what was going on. The woman gets personal invites to the White House. That should tell you how powerfully dangerous she is. Christ, I wouldn't be surprised if she owned the place."

"How do you know she gets invites?"

"Because that's where I finally put a face to the voice. I'd recognize that voice anywhere."

Shield sat forward. "You what?"

"She was invited to the state dinner for the Argentine president, and Moore introduced us. She came especially to check on me."

"I saw her." Shield remembered the older, attractive woman who'd arrived late.

"It was because of her I needed to get away and collect myself. You came to my room that night and we almost kissed..." Wagner went silent.

"The woman with the white hair."

"And you didn't have the pleasure of talking to her. She has the coldest voice and deadest eyes I've ever seen. My skin crawled when I touched her hand. It was like ice."

Shield got up. "Who is she?"

"According to the guest list I studied and Rat...*Moore*...her name is Theodora Rothschild."

Shield ran her hand through her hair as she stared at the floor. "I know that name, but from where?" she said to herself.

"Of the Rothschild Auction Houses."

"The auction...you must be kidding."

"Why?"

"She's a client of mine," Shield said. "Her secretary places orders directly to Tuscany."

"But she doesn't know you."

Shield was still in disbelief. Rothschild was a huge name in the auction business, and although probably a wealthy individual, the woman had the power to own politicians and organize crimes of this magnitude? "Why would she? I've never dealt directly with her, and for privacy and security reasons due to my job with the EOO, I kept my company under Pepo's name. The original owner."

"But I swear I don't know who this TQ is that that woman who saved us accused me of working for."

Shield was lost in thought. "Huh? Yeah, the name doesn't mean anything to me, either."

She reached over and picked up the phone. "But maybe my employer knows." Thankfully, she got a dial tone. "Shield, 29041971. Put me through to Pierce ASAP."

Southwestern Colorado

Montgomery Pierce sat in his favorite armchair while Joanne massaged his shoulders.

"I guess I shouldn't be surprised the grave was empty," he said.

The op they'd sent to Kansas to check on Dario's supposedly dead sister had confirmed Chase's suspicions. Chase hadn't sounded at all surprised when Monty called to tell her but had tried to reassure him they at least had something to go on. First thing tomorrow morning, she was going to Kansas herself to find anyone who knew the Imperis.

Reno had been assigned to find any adoption papers from the period that matched, but so far, his attempts had been fruitless. The baby had probably been sold, and no legal papers were ever drawn.

Monty sighed and looked up at Joanne. "We have to find someone who knew the parents. Someone must know—" The ringing of his telephone cut him off. He jumped up to answer it.

"You can't keep this up, Monty," Joanne said as he reached for it. "I'm worried, too, but you're going to give yourself a heart attack if your blood pressure hits the ceiling every time the phone rings."

"I'm fine. Stop coddling me." He put the receiver to his ear. "Any news?"

"I have Shield on the phone."

Monty took the receiver with him back to the armchair. "Put her through."

He listened while Shield explained what had happened and how she'd gotten away. Halfway during the whole bizarre story he put the speakerphone on for Joanne, who was going crazy with his exclamations.

"I'll be damned," he said. "A fake president."

"A very convincing one," Shield said. "Do you know Theodora Rothschild?"

"Who?" he asked.

"Of the Rothschild Auction Houses. She's the one who framed and hired Wagner, and unless someone finds her, she will not stop looking for us. We're the only ones who know who she is and what she's done, and she's looking at terrorist charges. You know what that means."

"Where are you now?" he asked.

"We're at this abandoned safe house a few miles from Washington."

"You don't mean the one in Burke?"

"That's the one," Shield confirmed.

"How did you know about it?" he asked. "It's exclusively EOO, but we haven't used it in a decade or more."

"It looks it. This woman who helped us escape told me where to find it."

"How did she know?"

"I have no clue."

Monty looked at Joanne to see whether she knew about an agent under cover in the area. She shook her head, as mystified as he was. "What's her name?" he asked Shield.

"She wouldn't say. I asked her to come with us, but she said she had to stay or they'd kill her. She said she was working for the same woman as Wagner, someone named TQ. But Wagner says she's never heard of a TQ. You know, for a while I thought our helper was one of ours in deep cover—she used the EOO mantra to signal me."

"By any means necessary?" Monty said distractedly.

"I offered to help her. Told her my people would protect her, but—"

"But what?"

"It was strange, but she said my people don't give a damn about her."

Joanne gasped. "What did she look like?"

"Dark hair, cut kinda short," Shield replied. "She had green eyes, and a scar from her cheek to the corner of her mouth."

"Oh, my God!" Joanne cried out.

"One of the men called her Silent Death."

"Jaclyn," Monty said aloud, stunned.

"As in Harding?" Shield sounded surprised.

"Jaclyn is alive," Monty mumbled, and leaned back, ignoring the question.

"She saved my life," Shield said.

"Where is she?" he asked.

"Probably long gone by now. Somewhere at a hospital, I would think."

Monty gripped the armrest. "What do you mean?"

"After she gave us the keys to the van, she shot herself in the leg to make it look like I did it when she tried to stop us."

"Are you sure this Wagner doesn't know TQ?"

"She's admitted to everything else," Shield replied.

"It sounds like TQ and Rothschild are somehow connected, work together," Joanne said. He nodded. "Rothschild should be easy enough to find."

"She's a customer of mine," Shield offered. "She buys crates of wine directly from Tuscany."

"I doubt she has it shipped to her home. People like Rothschild use in-between addresses," Monty said. "Stay where you are until further notice. This TQ bitch means business. If she has to crawl under rocks to find you, she will."

"Harding made that clear when she sent us to the safe house."

"I'll call when I have something."

"They took my cell," Shield said. "I don't know the number here."

"I do." Monty hung up.

"What do we do about Wagner and the president?" Joanne asked.

"Thomas was returned to office hours ago," he replied. "So far she hasn't said anything about her kidnapping."

"She probably won't talk if she wants to keep her credibility."

"And life," Monty added.

"We do nothing," Joanne concluded, "unless it becomes our business."

"My business right now is to find Jaclyn."

CHAPTER THIRTY-THREE

Burke, Virginia

Ryden glanced around the living room while Kennedy spoke in muted tones to her organization on the phone. She'd never seen a more bare-bones living space. No pictures on the walls, not a single piece of decoration, no books, not even a television—the couch faced a massive fireplace instead. At least, she mused, the place would be a little cozier once they touched a match to the stack of wood that had been left for whoever took refuge here.

Kennedy hung up the phone and turned to her. "Make yourself at home. I don't know how long we're going to be here."

"Anywhere is fine as long as I'm free from those people."

"I'm going to look for something to clean you up."

Ryden wasn't sure how to take that and suppressed the urge to do an odor check.

Kennedy must have seen her surprised look. "Your arm is bleeding." She walked to the bathroom.

"Oh. Yeah." Ryden noticed for the first time how thoroughly blood had saturated her sleeve. Although she knew she'd been grazed, she'd hardly been aware of it because so much was going on and the wound hadn't really hurt. But seeing all that blood had suddenly changed things. Now it hurt. A lot. "Why the hell did I have to look?" she muttered.

"What?" Kennedy stuck her head out of the other room.

"Your eye is swollen." That mysterious woman who'd helped them escape had taken a good swing at Kennedy.

Kennedy disappeared again as she went to check herself in the mirror. "So I see."

"This place clearly hasn't been used for years. I doubt you'll find anything, but I'll take any expired painkillers you can find."

"Ten years, to be exact." Kennedy returned from the bathroom with a big first-aid box in her hands.

"Thank you." Ryden extended her hand to take it from her.

"Have you cleaned a bullet wound before?"

"Can't say it's on my list of experiences."

"Then remove your shirt and let me have a look." Kennedy appeared and sounded irritated.

"You don't have to. I'll let you know if it's bad." She wasn't about to burden Kennedy with cleaning her up. She could barely face her after tonight's revelations, and besides, she didn't feel comfortable being seen half-naked.

Not that Kennedy would give a damn either way. Any attraction she might have felt toward Ryden during their time in the White House had disappeared within seconds of her finding out the ugly truth of who Ryden really was—nothing but a lying, selfish florist. Why couldn't Kennedy understand that she'd just tried to stay alive? Although, in retrospect, it *was* stupid to trust these people, her gullibility and will to live should somehow excuse her actions. If Kennedy wanted to believe she was a maniacal terrorist and manic liar, that was her right, but Ryden was getting fed up with having to defend herself.

"You clearly want nothing to do with me, so please give me the kit." She snatched it from Kennedy's hands. "I can take care of myself. I always have." She went to the bathroom and closed the door and looked at herself for the first time in the mirror. She had definitely seen better days: pale from tonight's angst, black circles under her eyes from days of not more than a few hours of sleep, and the pain were starting to show in the lines of her face. "You look like a zombie," she said to her reflection.

She unzipped the hoodie and managed to slip her arms out with minimal discomfort. Then, without thinking, she began to lift her arms to remove her long-sleeved T-shirt and screamed as pain tore through her arm and shoulder.

Kennedy stormed through the door in seconds, gun in hand. "Are you…?"

"It hurts." The white-hot burst of agony had subsided, but tears still streamed down her face. She tasted salt as she licked her lips.

Kennedy placed the weapon on the sink. The bathroom was barely big enough to fit them both. "Will you let me help you?"

"I can't lift my arm."

"We'll do it slowly."

"I can't. Just cut the shirt off."

"We can if you want to walk around half-naked for the duration of our stay here," Kennedy said, a trace of a smile at the corner of her mouth. "It's up to you."

"I don't think so."

Kennedy stood in front of her and took hold of her good arm. "Let's start with this one." She coaxed the arm free of the sleeve. "That wasn't too bad, right?"

"No."

"Ready for the head?" Kennedy's voice was gentle, little more than a whisper.

She nodded and Kennedy gingerly pulled up the shirt. She ducked her head to help and winced as new pain resonated through her shoulder.

"Coping?" Kennedy asked.

"You're good at this."

"I hope you continue to think so after we're done with the other arm."

"Give me a moment." Ryden backed up, nauseated from the pain, and held on to the sink. "I don't understand why it hurts so much all of a sudden."

"Because you're tired and the adrenaline high is gone."

"I guess." She looked down at her half-exposed body. Why had she chosen to wear such a sheer, lacy, black bra? It left nothing to the imagination. Kennedy, she noticed, was staring at her chest, too. Her cheeks burned. "I…I um…"

"You didn't seem shy about seducing me," Kennedy said.

"I didn't…"

"Oh, that's right. You were in character."

"It was never part of any plan to seduce you." Dealing with the pain in her shoulder was bad enough. She didn't need Kennedy aggravating her already fragile state. "I told you then and I'm telling you again, I have never been interested in women and wouldn't even know where to start seducing one."

"Which only amplifies my sentiment. You don't expect me to accept the fact that a forty-something straight woman playing the role of the president suddenly decided to experiment."

"It wasn't a choice, and I was definitely not conducting any kind of sexuality research."

"Whatever you say," Kennedy replied flippantly, and turned her face away.

Ryden's cheeks flushed like they always did when she got angry.

She let go of the sink for a moment, forgetting about her pain. "What do you find hard to comprehend? The fact that I wanted you to kiss me or that I actually did?"

"You were drunk."

"Tipsy. I knew damn well what I was doing, and I didn't do it because of any ulterior motivation." She closed the foot of distance between them. "What gain would I have from seducing you? You have nothing I want."

"Nothing?" Kennedy asked arrogantly. "Not even the comfort my money can buy, for a new life far away from the people who hired you? Away from a career in flower arrangements?"

Her belittling tone exacerbated Ryden's growing anger. She pushed Kennedy away. "How dare you accuse me of—"

"Using me for a better life?" For the first time Kennedy lost her cool demeanor. "Isn't that why you agreed to this plan? For money and a new beginning?"

"They framed me," Ryden shouted. The T-shirt dangling from her shoulder aggravated her even more so she pulled it off. "How many times do I have to tell you?"

Kennedy arched her brow. "And how convenient that a florist in a dead-end job, making what—twenty thousand a year?—finally gets some cash to pimp herself and her life."

Ryden almost gasped. Sure, the idea of a second chance at a new life had been exciting, but she had agreed before they ever told her the terms, and by that time it was too late to change her mind. Even then, she would have accepted the offer anyway if it meant surviving. "For your information, my life was just fine before they took everything away. I loved my job as a florist, my candle making, and my tiny home. And yes, the death penalty would've put a glitch in my humble but otherwise satisfying life, so I accepted. You have no right to belittle my life or blame me for what I did, when all I'm guilty of is choosing to live." She took a deep breath.

"All you needed was some adrenaline." Kennedy looked at her shoulder, then bent to pick up the bloodied shirt. After handing it to her, Kennedy took the first-aid kit and went back into the living room.

Ryden stomped after her, the pain in her shoulder mostly forgotten in her growing anger. "I suppose it's easy for you to stand there, acting all righteous, when you've never had to decide between life or death."

Kennedy took a seat on the couch. "I make that call every time I throw myself in front of a bullet to save someone's life."

"Because it's your job," Ryden yelled, standing in front of her, trying to cover her nakedness with the soiled shirt. "I doubt you do it because you value a stranger's life more than your own or because you have a death wish."

"I do it because…" Kennedy looked away. "Because I don't have a choice," she mumbled.

"And that's how I felt."

Kennedy looked at her with sadness. "I never had a choice. It was made for me."

"When your organization adopted you."

Kennedy nodded.

"I guess orphanages and foster homes do that to a person."

"Do what?"

"Make them feel they should accept anything, out of gratitude for being selected and given a chance. I should know."

"What do you mean?" Kennedy asked.

"For years I was sent from home to home, trying to please whoever with the hope of being allowed to stay. I guess I wasn't good enough, not pretty enough, or who knows what the hell. Point is, I spent my life trying to please others just to make them love or at least care."

Kennedy was silent for a long while. "Let me take a look at your shoulder," she finally said.

Southwestern Colorado

Monty was closing the blinds to the conference room when David Arthur joined them, soaked to the skin from the thunderstorm raging outside. Joanne was already seated at the big table.

"What's Reno got?" Arthur asked.

"We'll find out soon enough," Monty replied, "but I could tell from his tone he's found something significant." Reno had summoned them for this predawn briefing; he'd been working nonstop since Shield's call to find out more about Theodora Rothschild and how she was connected to TQ.

"I hate this waiting around," Joanne said. "Every minute that goes by, Jaclyn is—"

Reno rushed in, his laptop in one hand and computer printouts in the other. "We'll find her," he said with confidence, "now that TQ's no longer a ghost."

They all took seats at one end of the conference table.

"The headline is, TQ and Theodora Rothschild are one and the same," Reno said as he passed printouts to each of them.

Monty scanned his. On top was a color passport photo of an attractive, middle-aged woman with white hair and eyes devoid of warmth or emotion. Beneath it was a birth certificate.

"Rothschild is her married name," Reno said. "She was born Theodora Quinevere Lassiter on March 29, 1962, according to her birth certificate. That's the same day as the faked date of death registered for Dario's sibling. The city matches, too—Wichita, Kansas. Parents of record are a Howard and Ellen Lassiter. He's deceased, and she's in a nursing home with Alzheimer's, so no help there. I wasn't able to find any connection between the Lassiters and Imperis, but they lived only a few blocks away from each other, so they may have known each other through a common church or school or something."

Monty scanned the next printout as Reno's briefing continued.

"Theodora Lassiter married Philip Victor Nathaniel Rothschild, heir to the British banking branch of the noble family, in 1982. A year later, Philip founded the Rothschild Auction Houses in Houston, but he didn't get much of a chance to enjoy it. He was found dead in his bed by their maid six months later, while his wife was away on a spa vacation. They performed an autopsy since he was only forty, but the results were inconclusive."

Reno picked up the computer sheet. "Theodora—TQ—took over the auction houses, which last year reported a net income to the IRS of forty-two million dollars. She never remarried, keeps a very low profile, and is rarely photographed. Her home address is a penthouse in Houston, but she also has an office in D.C. The addresses of both are listed at the bottom of page four in your handout."

"Great work, Reno," Monty said.

"We need to throw a lot of manpower at both locations simultaneously," Arthur said. "And we have to do it fast. Should we call in the feds?"

Monty shook his head. "Too risky. We have to deal with this ourselves. She's proved she has allies in law enforcement and government all the way up to the White House. We don't know who to trust, and I won't jeopardize Jaclyn's welfare or chance TQ getting tipped off and being able to destroy any records she has about her holdings and criminal enterprises."

"Who's immediately available for Texas?" Arthur asked.

"Cameo, Blade, and Wasp are here," Joanne replied, referencing three other top members of their Elite Tactical Force who'd come back to the Colorado campus for a debriefing from their last mission. "Viper and Ranger are both in Austin and can get there in no time."

"Get our jet readied ASAP," Monty said to Reno as he jumped to his feet. "And have my car brought around front."

Joanne protested. "There's no need for you to go to Texas. We have five people on it."

"I know. That's why I'm going to Washington," he replied. "The others can charter a private jet. If Jaclyn is anywhere, it's near the capital. She's hurt and bleeding. TQ would never have her travel back to Texas in her current condition, if Jack was ever even there in the first place. I know the bitch is holding her at her D.C. office or somewhere in the vicinity. Reno, you'll guide me when I get there."

"Us," Arthur said. "I'll get my gear and change."

"I'm coming with you, too," Cassady said from the door, where she'd apparently heard enough to get the crux of the plan.

"Then get ready," Monty said.

"You leave in thirty," Reno informed them.

Joanne frowned. "Monty, you are in no condition to—"

"I have to do this, Joanne." Monty went to her and embraced her tightly. "I'm going to personally bring my daughter back."

CHAPTER THIRTY-FOUR

Burke, Virginia

Shield scooted to the edge of the couch and Wagner sat next to her, though with obvious reluctance. "How's the pain?"

Wagner looked down at herself. "I don't really remember removing my shirt, but it hurts less now."

"I know. All you needed was a rush."

Wagner stared at her, incredulous. "You mean that whole conversation...everything was to piss me off?"

"It worked," Shield replied.

"But you still meant every word."

"More or less." Shield moved to pull her shirt away. "May I?"

Wagner let the garment fall to her lap. "How bad?" She winced when she took a good look at the wound. "What a mess."

"It'll look better after I clean it up." She removed gauze bandages and iodine from the kit. "It won't be pleasant."

Wagner took a deep breath. "I'm ready."

She took her time cleaning the wound, being thorough but as gentle as possible. She knew from experience how painful flesh wounds could be and this one was pretty deep, but Wagner never flinched or complained. She sat stoically, staring at a spot on the floor, and occasionally gritted her teeth. One thing was for sure—this woman was a survivor.

She was surprised to learn that Wagner was an orphan, too, and had spent her life trying to satisfy and seek approval. Her remarks were spot-on concerning Shield's decisions or lack of them. She'd been raised by a company, not a family. A company that had put a roof over her head and given her much in the way of education, but never a home. Pierce and crew made a point of never getting too attached to the children. They raised soldiers, not their own offspring, after all. But the fact that the EOO had deemed her worthy enough for adoption made her feel indebted, and that's why she never declined a job or gave less than her best.

Who knew where she'd be today if the EOO hadn't taken her in? Plenty of kids never got adopted and ended up in disturbed foster homes, run by couples looking to make easy cash that they never spent on the child. Wagner was a prime example. She'd had to fight for herself since she was born and had probably done it regardless of consequences or dreadful odds. Shield couldn't help but respect Wagner's tenacity and determination to survive in a world that had rejected her. "If you're not gay, and you weren't trying to seduce me for gain or because Moore asked you to, why did you kiss me?"

Wagner visibly flinched for the first time. "That hurt."

She paused, tweezers poised above the wound. "Try not to move, okay?"

Wagner went back to staring at her spot on the carpet. "I don't know," she said after a long while. "I've never done anything like that before."

Shield smiled. "You mean kiss someone or kiss a woman?"

"Both."

The reply was such a surprise Shield stopped cleaning the wound and looked at her.

"I've let men kiss me, but I've never made the first move," Wagner said.

Shield picked up the gauze. She wasn't sure why, but the thought of any man kissing Wagner disturbed her.

"I've never felt the need to make the first move," Wagner said. "Or the second, for that matter."

"Shy?"

"Not at all. Just indifferent. I dated men—three in total—because it was something girls were supposed to do. I got fed up with friends… acquaintances and colleagues, really…calling me a nun, so I started to hang out at bars after work to meet guys."

"How did that work out?" Shield had no desire to hear the details of Wagner's love life. Quite the opposite, actually. But something wasn't right about her sexual choices. Wagner had looked at Kennedy in a way that only a woman with a deep appreciation for another woman would.

"It didn't. I didn't. I went through the motions during all three short-lived relationships."

"Didn't they notice?"

Wagner hesitated. "Eventually," she mumbled as Shield wrapped the gauze around her shoulder. "Anyway, I gave up on dates years ago. I don't care what people say anymore. I refuse to put myself through the pain and embarrassment of explanations and verbal abuse."

"What do you mean?"

"Explaining to men why I...forget it."

"Why what?"

Wagner turned red and looked away. "It's personal."

"I understand. I don't mean to pry. I was worried they physically hurt you."

"No, nothing like that. Sure, they'd get rough sometimes out of frustration, but it was the verbal aggression that was brutal."

Shield remembered the insults Carmen had spat at her only too well, but there had never been any physical abuse. Was Wagner, like so many women, trying to cover for these idiots by belittling the topic? "Rough?" she asked. "You shouldn't excuse any kind of *roughness*."

"You don't understand. They never hit or hurt me, it's just..." Wagner looked embarrassed. "They'd get rough in bed because it frustrated them no end that I couldn't climax. It made them feel incompetent, and they'd eventually storm out the door screaming about how frigid I am. One called me a corpse." Wagner blew out a long breath. "Anyway, that was then. As long as I stay clear of dates and sex, I never have to hear those words again."

"How does your arm feel?" Shield asked when she finished wrapping her shoulder.

Wagner looked down as if surprised to see it was over. "Tolerable, as long as I don't move it."

Shield got up and found a towel in the bathroom she could fashion into a sling. "This will help take the weight off your arm," she said as she helped Wagner into it. Then she grabbed a blanket from the back of the couch and wrapped it around Wagner's shoulders. "I'll wash these," she said, picking up the soiled clothes, "and get a fire started."

She could feel Wagner watch her as she tended to her tasks. Once the fire was blazing, she scrubbed the shirt and hoodie and laid them to dry across a chair set by the fireplace. "I'm afraid you'll have to wait until tomorrow for something to eat," she said as she rejoined Wagner on the couch. "I'll go into town early in the morning, but we should lie low for a day at least."

"What's going to happen to me after we leave here?"

"I don't know. What you did is—"

"I know." Wagner watched the flames with a resigned, defeated expression. "Looks like I'm going to jail, after all."

Shield wanted to say anything to comfort her, but the law was clear and unforgiving when it came to the president's safety. "There's always a chance Thomas doesn't talk."

"That's what they planned on. Her silence."

"We'll see."

"Your people will have me arrested even if Thomas doesn't."

"Only if they're asked to," Shield said. "We don't take jobs unless we're hired."

Wagner's eyes met hers. "I disgust you, don't I?"

"No. I guess most people in your position would have done what you did."

"I'm so sorry I got you involved," Wagner said quietly, and looked away again. "I never meant for any of this to happen, and I never knew they were going to kill innocent people. They told me very little about their plans except what involved me directly."

Shield nodded in understanding.

"I wanted to tell you so many times, but…"

"Yes, you said. You were afraid."

"I wanted to trust you."

"But you didn't. What bothers me are not your reasons for doing what you did but your lies. I could have gotten us both out."

"I didn't believe you could," Wagner said. "This woman is so dangerous. I'd never be able to live with it if something had happened to you because of me."

"It almost did anyway."

"I just hope you can one day forgive me."

"Why does it matter?"

Wagner shrugged. "I…just do."

"The worst thing about being lied to," Shield said, not bothering to hide the hurt in her voice, "is knowing you weren't worth the truth."

"You asked me why I kissed you."

Shield turned to look at her.

"I did it because it was the only way I could tell you how much I trusted you."

"Are you in the habit of kissing everyone you trust?"

"Probably not, although I wouldn't know. I've never trusted anyone."

Shield got up to poke the wood in the fireplace. Sometimes, she wished she could say those same words, but her blind faith had once almost destroyed her and everything she cared about. "You're lucky."

"I thought so, too." Wagner bit her lip. "Until you made me realize how lonely and alone I was. How lacking in happiness."

Shield was confused. "I did that?"

"You made me feel beautiful, special, and respected. You…" Wagner swiped at a lone tear running down her cheek. "You made me feel something new, and I finally understood what it was like to be wanted."

Shield went back to the couch. She wanted to be the one to wipe away that tear but couldn't. She didn't know how to let go of the imposter and embrace this other woman.

Wagner apparently could sense her ambivalence. "You can't even say my name," she said. "You've avoided using it since you found out I wasn't Thomas."

"I'm sorry. I just don't know how to deal with you."

"With a florist?"

"Yes…I mean, no." Shield rubbed her tired eyes. "It's not that you're a florist. If nothing else, it's a more honest occupation than politics. I don't know how to handle Ryden when she looks so much like Elizabeth."

"*I* can hardly deal with it," Wagner replied. "But I assure you, the resemblance is superficial."

"I'll say."

"Yes, okay." Wagner shifted farther away on the couch with a scowl. "I know I don't have her education, wealth, or power. I'm a nobody with a rap sheet, wanted for murder, and God forbid someone of your caliber would ever…" She got up. "Regardless of what you think of me," she said, cringing from the pain, "I'm pretty damn happy with myself. I'm a decent, hardworking individual who's never harmed a fly. If you can't understand that, then too bad."

Shield got up as well and stood in front of her. "Someone of my caliber would what? What do you think my caliber is?" She was tired of people measuring her worth by her money.

"You have a name, money, stature."

"So?"

"So, I'm not Carmen or Thomas. I can't measure up to them."

"Carmen was a lying, deceiving bitch who was with me for my money and vineyard," she explained, a bitter taste in her mouth from the memory. "I met her in her uncle's restaurant, where she worked as a waitress. She and her husband—who I knew nothing about, but was the master of their twisted game—tried to make me give up half my property."

"What? How?"

"She never said she was married. She said she'd always been straight but had fallen in love with me. I believed her and fell hard for her and her stories. We lived together for four years, and I loved her, trusted her, and never had any reasons to look further. The next year, she started talking about signing over half of my property, putting the vineyards in her name because we'd been together for five years and she felt she deserved half of everything as my partner for her support."

"And you did it."

"Almost. I came home one day and found her in my bed with some guy who turned out to be her husband. Both of them had been living on my money for years. Every cent I gave to Carmen—all the money she'd ever asked for, for trips while I was away for work, expensive clothes, you name it—she used to support her husband and build up a pretty good savings."

"What did you do?"

"I told them to keep the money, but if I ever saw them anywhere near my property I'd shoot them. Haven't seen them since. That was three years ago."

"So, aside from being an evil conspirator out to help a villain take over the world…you also think I want to use you for your money."

Shield looked away.

"Well, that's just great. If it makes you feel any better, I'll soon be going off to jail and will never see you again." Wagner walked over to the chair with her clothes and felt to see if the T-shirt was dry. "I need to get some sleep. My shoulder hurts and I'm exhausted, as I'm sure you are."

Ryden flipped the shirt to let the other side dry, then did the same with the hoodie. Then she stared into the fireplace, opening the blanket slightly to let the heat reach her skin. Although she felt safe with Kennedy there, she wished more than ever she could be alone. She could understand and accept Kennedy's anger when it had to do with lying about who she was and what she had been asked to do. But she refused to deal with the accusation of being a gold digger.

Money had never been important to her. She'd spent just about every extra dime she'd ever made on shelters and animals. Ryden figured they needed it more than she did, and half the time she wasted what money she did have on her. She either lost it somewhere between cushions or cab seats or forgot and left it in a pocket and the washing machine destroyed it. What mattered were her wax creations and privacy. "We should stay in here with the fire. You can have the couch. I'll sleep on the floor," Ryden said, without turning around.

"No." Kennedy's voice came from right behind her.

She was so startled, she whirled around and almost collided with Kennedy. "I don't mind the fl—" She inhaled sharply when she saw the look in Kennedy's eyes. Dangerous but not threatening. Hungry but not angry.

"No, I don't think you're after my money." Kennedy stood so close Ryden felt her breath with every word spoken.

"G…good, because I don't give a damn about how much you earn, Kennedy."

"Good. And my name, *Ryden*," Kennedy stressed her name provocatively, "is Harper." Her gaze never strayed from Ryden's eyes.

"I know." She couldn't stop looking at Kennedy's mouth.

"And no, I don't think you're evil or deliberately hurt anyone."

"When did you change your mind?"

"When you took that bullet for me." Kennedy ran one finger up Ryden's injured arm, caressing it lightly and slowly under the blanket. "That shot was meant for me. If you hadn't shoved me, it could've gotten me in the heart. You didn't know I had a vest on."

"I saw him aiming at you." She was surprised to be answering coherently. Kennedy's eyes and touch were mesmerizing and put her completely off balance.

"I'm grateful you did."

"So, are you okay with the couch?"

Kennedy ignored her question and surprised Ryden with one of her own. "What do you feel right now?"

Ryden swallowed hard. She was breathing even harder. "My stomach, it's fluttering."

"Mine, too." Kennedy licked her lips and Ryden's whole body reacted.

Contrary to anything she'd ever done, she let the blanket fall from her shoulders and placed her hand behind Kennedy's neck. She pulled her close and, with their mouths touching, said, "I want…" Then she kissed Kennedy softly on the lips and pulled back.

Beneath her hand, she felt Kennedy shiver. As she ran her fingers through Kennedy's hair, she was filled with an excitement and aggression she'd never known before.

Kennedy gently placed her arms around her waist and pulled her close. She felt dizzy with desire, the pain a distant memory.

"Tell me," Kennedy whispered.

"I want to kiss you so much I can't feel my shoulder."

Kennedy looked from her mouth to her eyes. "Show me, Ryden." She sounded breathless.

Ryden involuntarily moaned before she pulled Kennedy's mouth to hers. She kissed Kennedy slowly, licking and sweetly biting her lips, and when their tongues finally met, both moaned in unison. Ryden had never kissed anyone so thoroughly, so passionately, and had definitely never wanted so much to rip someone's clothes off to feel every inch of their beautiful body.

As though her hand had a will of its own, her fingers threaded through Kennedy's hair, stroked her neck, then caressed a lazy path down her back, where she felt Kennedy's muscles tighten at her touch. "This is crazy," she said in Kennedy's mouth, unable to let go of those lips. "I don't want to stop kissing you."

She felt Kennedy smile against her mouth. "I don't want you to."

She attacked Kennedy's mouth again and sucked her tongue. She moved her hand from Kennedy's back to her ass and Kennedy moaned.

"Yes." Kennedy encouraged her, her voice a hoarse whisper.

Ryden pulled their pelvises tighter together, massaging Kennedy's ass as they kissed.

"You're driving me crazy," Kennedy said. "If we don't stop, I'm going to—"

She didn't wait for the rest. She grabbed Kennedy's hand and brought it to her breast. "Touch me."

Kennedy cupped her breast and Ryden threw her head back, so overcome with ecstasy she saw stars behind her closed eyelids. In a heartbeat, Kennedy unclasped Ryden's bra and gently caressed her nipples. Men never touched her like this; their fumbling efforts were always abrupt and brief, and her breasts were often an afterthought, a short, unsatisfying prelude to what they really wanted. She was melting under Kennedy's hands. She almost screamed in pleasure when Kennedy pinched her nipples. "I need your mouth there," she managed, her heart pounding in her ears.

Kennedy kissed her fiercely once more before she bent to kiss her breasts.

She ran her hands through Kennedy's hair as Kennedy massaged and licked her nipples. The stimulation was so intense she was rapidly nearing climax. "Harder. Please, Harper." She lightly pulled on Kennedy's hair.

Kennedy sucked hard on her nipples.

"Oh, God. I'm…please, don't stop." This was another new moment for Ryden. She was about to come, and Kennedy had never even gone under her belt. Was that possible?

"Come for me." Kennedy sucked one nipple as she massaged the other.

"I want to." Ryden's legs trembled, her stomach tightened, then her whole body spasmed as a powerful orgasm shot through her. She would have dropped to the floor if Kennedy hadn't held her tight. Out of breath, she rested her head on Kennedy's shoulder. "I didn't know that was possible."

Kennedy laughed. "Are you all right?"

"Embarrassed, but yes. I've never come with anyone, let alone without…"

Kennedy squeezed her tight, mindful of her shoulder. "Don't ever feel embarrassed for who or how you are."

Ryden looked at her. "I don't want to, not anymore."

"How's your arm?"

"Okay, I think, but—"

Suddenly, Kennedy froze and placed her finger over Ryden's mouth. "Chopper." She pointed up.

"Helicopter?" Ryden whispered. "Your people?"

Kennedy grabbed the shirt and hoodie off the chair and thrust them toward her. "They would've called to say they were coming. Get dressed."

CHAPTER THIRTY-FIVE

Shield grabbed the Walther from the table and killed the lights. She wanted to berate herself for letting her guard down even for a moment, but she couldn't regret the past few minutes and the way Ryden made her feel. "There's a bucket in the kitchen. Fill it up and extinguish the fire," she told Ryden as she went to the window to try to locate the chopper. She saw a pair of searchlights from above, scanning the terrain southeast of the safe house.

"They can't possibly know where we are." Ryden awkwardly poured water over the fire, one-handed. It sizzled and sent out a cloud of steam as it died.

"We have to get out of here."

"Go where?"

"Jack wasn't kidding. This TQ will do anything to find us."

"Jack? Is that the woman who helped us?"

Shield nodded.

"How can they know we're in this cabin? There are plenty of other houses not too far from here."

"And I'm sure they have orders to search them all."

"This hasn't been used in years."

"And they've probably seen the smoke," Shield pointed out. "The pilot's already informed TQ's footmen of the location. It won't be long before they storm through the door or blast the place." She went to the back door and peered out through the small window. "Let's go." She gestured to Ryden.

She held Ryden's hand as they dodged the searchlights and made it across the open field that separated the safe house from the massive park.

"You okay?" Shield asked when they stopped for air well into the tree line.

"Yeah, don't worry about me. I've been through worse."

"Sure you have," Shield replied dubiously.

"Hey, I outran every foster-brother bully and their idiot friends. You think some guys in the sky can catch me?" Ryden cradled her arm, the discomfort evident in her voice.

"Gotta hand it to you, Wagner. You don't take anything lying down."

"Yeah, well." Ryden huffed. "It's the new me. I never appreciated myself or my life until I almost lost them both."

"We need to make it to the highway and find a phone."

"Your boss?"

They both looked in the direction of the house when they heard loud voices.

"No one here, but the fire is fresh," a man shouted.

Shield grabbed Ryden's hand again and they took off, heading south through the park. They'd run for quite a while before Ryden pulled her to a stop.

"I can't..." She paused, taking big gulps of air. "My arm is bleeding badly and I can hardly breathe."

"We have to keep going," Shield said. "They're behind us. It won't be much longer before we're at the highway."

"Why don't you—"

She could hear the fear in Ryden's voice. "The new you, remember?"

Ryden hesitated a few seconds. "You might have to carry me," she said, and took off ahead of Shield.

They reached the highway at the southern edge of the park just as the first sliver of dawn appeared on the horizon. Shield cautiously checked both directions before she pulled Ryden out of the brush. A familiar neon logo beckoned. "There's a gas station half a mile down the road."

They stayed close to the trees, and twenty minutes later, Shield entered the gas station first with her head low to check for cams. When she saw none, she went back out to get Ryden. The lone attendant, a teenaged boy, barely glanced their way. She told Ryden to wait in the back of the store, out of sight, while she went straight to the pay phone.

"I need Pierce," she told the facilitator on duty.

"He's on his way to Washington, but Grant will take it." He put her through.

"Why's Pierce going to Washington?" she asked Joanne as soon as she came on the line.

"Rothschild and TQ are the same person," Grant replied. "She has an address there, where he thinks TQ is holding Jaclyn. He's going there to find her."

"Alone?" Shield asked, surprised. "She'll kill him on the spot."

"Lynx and Arthur are with him."

"Still not enough. She has more soldiers than the U.S. military."

"He won't listen." Grant practically screamed her frustration. "Any news from your side?"

"We needed to abort the house. They found it."

"We have a working safe house in Washington, at 1650 Corcoran Street, but that means going back."

"We'll have to risk it. I need a place to leave Wagner."

"And yourself," Grant said. "Call me when you get there."

"Where's Pierce landing?"

"Andrews."

"I'll meet him there."

"Shield, you—"

"Pierce is going to need all the help he can get, and…" Shield thought back to the woman who'd saved her life. "I owe Jack a favor. I'll make sure Wagner is safe, but I'm going to TQ's with him." She hung up and walked over to the young pimple-faced clerk who was manically texting on his cell. "I need you to call us a cab."

"Lady, you're in the middle of nowhere."

"Now," she said ominously.

"Okay, chillax." He put the cell down and dialed for a cab on the landline. He mumbled the address and hung up. "Dude said it could take up to thirty."

"We'll wait outside."

Twenty minutes later, the cab arrived, and Shield went back into the gas station. The clerk sat smiling as he texted and never even looked up. She checked the slim pickings behind him hanging off the wall. "I want condoms."

The boy finally took his eyes off the phone and looked from her, to Ryden, waiting outside. "Rrrright," he slurred. "You sure?"

"The black ones at the top," Shield answered stoically.

He placed his cell under the counter and slowly turned around. "They're XXL."

"Sounds about right."

He turned to look at her one more time before he returned to the wall. While he was on his tiptoes reaching for the small box, Shield silently leaned over the counter and snatched his cell. She got it into her jacket pocket just as the boy turned to face her. Though she could have just asked for it politely with her gun, the risk of him pressing the predictably hidden-under-the-counter silent alarm was too big, and the last thing she needed was a police chase for armed robbery.

"Anything else?"

"Got lube?"

"What?"

Shield got out her wallet and placed a hundred-dollar bill in front of him. "Keep the change." She pocketed the condoms and walked quickly to the cab, where Ryden was waiting.

"I can't believe you took his phone," Ryden said as she watched Shield dial Monty's number.

"I tipped him."

Washington, D.C.

TQ paced in her D.C. office. She had wanted to stay and watch Jack being tortured to calm her nerves and restore her balanced state, but the dire situation called for her immediate attention. She didn't even have her maids to release her anger upon.

She had rarely been so distressed or so close to having her identity unveiled, and on that one past occasion she had paid good money to make sure that person never talked. She had left him feeling safely assured that he was free to go on with his now-rich life, and then, once he'd let down his guard, she'd eliminated him.

The op and Wagner, however, posed a whole different problem. Even if they accepted her money in return for silence, she'd have to find them before they caused irreparable damage. She wasn't worried about the authorities or even the president, but the meddling and ruthless media would tear her apart.

Her people had just informed her that the cabin they suspected the two runaways had found refuge in had recently been evacuated. The targets were on the run. But at least they were still within the greater Washington environs.

She jumped with anticipation when the phone rang. The caller ID placed the call from her Texas home. "What?"

"Madam, a Mr. Montgomery Pierce called, asking for Theodora Rothschild. He said you have something that belongs to him, and he's willing to negotiate your identity in return for it."

She gripped the cell phone till her knuckles hurt. Who was this Pierce, and had Kennedy already talked to someone? "What else?"

"Nothing, madam. He left a number to reach him at your earliest convenience."

"I don't have time for this shit," she muttered.

"Would you like me to tell him you're unavailable?"

"Did I ask you to?"

"No, madam. It was a suggestion."

"Do you know me to be in the habit of seeking proposals from anyone, let alone a secretary?"

"No, madam."

"Do it again and I'll stab you in the mouth. Give me his number." TQ jotted down the digits and hung up.

She treated herself to a shot of red wine before she made the call.

"Pierce." The man was older, his tone one of confident authority.

"Mr. Pierce, this is Theodora Rothschild. How can I help you?"

"Wise of you to call me back, TQ. I am on my way to D.C. as we speak."

She hadn't expected this stranger who was looking for Rothschild to call her by her other business name.

She could hear the distinctive noise of a jet in the background. "Business or pleasure?"

"It will be my pleasure to destroy you and your business, should we fail to reach an arrangement."

"No need for dramatic statements, Mr. Pierce. Many have offered me deals and I have yet to disappoint. I'm sure we can reach a satisfactory agreement." Another money-hungry idiot threatening to expose her. "I can get you whatever money can buy, and I value discretion. Whatever transpires between us will stay between us."

"I'm not interested in buying or discretion. Like I told your secretary, you have something that belongs to me."

"I'm willing to give it back, assuming it's still in my possession." TQ placed her wineglass on the desk. Pierce could potentially be a problem. This was not the time to deal with idiots complaining about stolen artifacts, but she had to contain her anger and play along before he did something rash. "Can you be more specific? It's very possible I acquired something without knowing it was stolen."

"All you need to know is that I am willing to look the other way concerning President Thomas, her substitute, and your identity, unless of course you refuse to return what you took."

The last time TQ's heart did a somersault like this was *never*. Who the hell was this man?

"The president?" She feigned surprise. "I may be guilty of many things, but I have to admit I have no idea what you're talking about. Are you sure you have the right person?" So what if Kennedy and the florist had talked? They couldn't prove anything.

"As sure as I am that Thomas will talk if I offer her and her family protection from you."

"You have the wrong person."

"Who do you think the authorities and the media will believe: Thomas, or a thieving auctioneer-slash-weapons and organ dealer? They will rip you apart before they lock you up for life."

"Unfounded and obscene accusations," TQ replied. "You have no proof."

"As a matter of fact, I do," he said calmly. "I will expose every illegal transaction you've ever made and those who did business with you, starting with Zhang Anshun, the Chinese Supreme Court Justice. I can assure you he will admit to everything to save his skin and delicate position."

How did he know about Zhang, her key expediter for black-market organs? She ran her hand across her forehead, shocked to discover an unfamiliar sheen of perspiration. No one had ever made her sweat. "Who exactly are you, Mr. Pierce?"

"Someone with more power than you."

Anger replaced her worry. No one had more power than she. She'd worked hard to make sure of that. "And yet I have something you want," she said smugly. "Perhaps you overestimate your supremacy."

"I have the power to destroy you, and I don't need a fake birth certificate in order to kill. So tell me again if I overestimate my supremacy."

How could he possibly know about her birth certificate? "I don't know who you are just yet, Mr. Pierce, but there is nothing I can't find out, including who or what you treasure."

"If you find out who I am, then perhaps you can enlighten me as well, since I officially don't exist. As for what I treasure, it's no mystery, since I'm on my way to get it. A heads-up: I don't deal well with disappointment."

It was like listening to herself. Who the hell was he? Had she angered and stolen from someone in the CIA? "Why don't you tell me what you want and give me time to locate it or buy it back? It will make our transaction much smoother and faster." She placed her hand on the landline, to make an immediate call to whichever warehouse had his fucking artifact. If she'd already sold it, she'd have to find a way to get it back, and that would take time.

"I'm sure you haven't sold it. If, on the other hand, it has been destroyed..." He paused such a long while TQ thought the line had gone dead. "You will meet an equal fate," he finally said.

"I don't destroy anything of value."

"Then I sincerely hope we have similar tastes. I will be at your Connecticut Avenue address within the hour."

"I look forward to our meeting." She kept her voice calm, but her heartbeat accelerated further with the knowledge that he knew about her D.C. office and would be here soon.

"I probably needn't mention this," he said, "but should anything happen that might delay my timely return home, I have given orders to release all the information I have on you."

"I meant to ask you earlier," she replied. "How did you know I was in Washington?"

"There is nothing I can't find out." The line went dead.

She immediately dialed the number of her high-level contact in the FBI. She had to know who she was dealing with, obviously a worthy adversary. Pierce had considerable money—evidenced by his private jet and whatever priceless artifact she'd taken of his—he had power enough to find her and destroy her, and he was smart enough to ensure her devastation should anything happen to him. Although she admired smart people, she would not allow anyone to checkmate her at any game. "I need information and I need it now," she told her contact.

"What can I do for you?" he replied at once.

"Tell me who Montgomery Pierce is."

"Give me a second."

TQ heard him clicking away at a computer.

"I have quite a few with that name. Can you give me more?"

"In his sixties, I think, possibly CIA."

"I can't access the CIA without—"

"Don't, can't, and won't are unacceptable. Now search, before I personally take your father's liver back," she yelled.

"Give me a moment."

"Make it a fast one."

"I found a Montgomery Pierce with a military record, born in

1950. Stationed in France for three years. He left the military in 1974 to become a lawyer in New York, and then…" He paused.

"Then, what?" TQ snapped.

"His career ended in 1988. After that, nothing."

"You mean he died?"

"No, I mean he disappeared," the contact said.

"No one disappears. He's not a ghost. Was he married? Children?" TQ hoped she could find something to at least scare Pierce.

"Neither."

"Parents? Siblings?"

"No siblings. Says here he was adopted."

"By?" TQ rolled her eyes. "It's like pulling teeth."

"Sorry, but it's just that his record is very vague. It doesn't say who adopted him or what happened to him."

This sounded like her man.

"Aren't you people supposed to have everyone's records?"

"Unless someone higher up deleted or classified them," he replied, "in which case access is denied."

"When are records deleted or marked classified?"

"If someone is an Agency NOC."

"A what?"

"A non-official cover for the Agen…CIA, or…"

"Or what?"

"Or if someone is considered very significant because of their covert work for the benefit and safety of the United Nations," he said, "and when they are essential links between the USA and other countries. Their identity is then considered high-level security."

"Who has access to that level?" TQ checked her watch. Time was running out.

"Interpol. And before you ask, even if I could access their records, information like this is not kept on an electronic database for security reasons. Cooperation with people like him is unofficial, and treated as such."

"Which means what?"

"They work to make companies like the FBI, CIA, KGB, MI6, and you name it look good. They go above and beyond any law and answer to no one. Nobody cares how they get the job done, as long as the said companies can claim the glory and reap the media benefits."

"Who pays them?"

"Whoever hired them."

"In other words, these people are contractors," TQ said.

"Very similar."

Maybe Kennedy had talked, after all. "Do you have the address of a company called the EOO?"

She heard him type again.

"Most money-grubbing private companies like Xe advertise everywhere and are easy to find. Others…" The line went quiet again.

"What?"

"Like the EOO are not. Says here the address is classified."

"Not even a state?" she asked.

"Not even a country."

"I need more."

"I'm sorry," he said nervously. "But I simply don't have access."

"Try harder."

After a long silence and a deep sigh, he replied, "I'll do my best. Just give me some time. I can't promise you any—"

"I'm going to be in a meeting shortly. Fax me whatever you find."

TQ hung up. "What are you up to, Pierce? And what did I take from you?" She was screwed if she couldn't deliver what this man wanted, and even then she wasn't sure he'd keep his word, or let her live, for that matter. "But I decide when I die, and today is not the day."

CHAPTER THIRTY-SIX

Washington, D.C.

Jack tried not to throw up as she crawled to the concrete wall of the basement and propped herself against it. Her leg was bleeding profusely again and she left a wide swath of blood on the floor. TQ's two assholes had made a sport of kicking her where she'd been shot, and then one sat back as the other began to punch her relentlessly in the stomach.

She coughed up blood, the steely taste making her even more nauseated. Since they hadn't hit her in the face, she was probably bleeding internally.

"Take a break," the guy sitting said to his friend. "Where's the fun if she passes out?"

"I guess," the other replied. "It's time for lunch, anyway."

Relieved she could catch her breath, Jack rested her head against the wall as soon as they left. She badly needed something to wipe the terrible taste out of her mouth, and her T-shirt was too filthy and drenched in blood. She stuck her hand in her pocket in search of a tissue or anything at all and pulled out the folded note Dratshev had given her.

With effort, she focused on the words. *Your cat is safe. Come home. 19 8 1 4 5.* In disbelief, she read the note again, then once more. It was Pierce's handwriting and code; he was telling her Cass was safe. But how? And how did this note end up with Yuri? Did Pierce know about TQ?

Jack didn't care how he had gotten the note to her. Cass was safe, and that was all that mattered. "Fuck." She let her head fall back again with a thump. If she'd read the note earlier, she'd be halfway back to Cass's arms by now, planning how to get rid of TQ once and for always.

She stuck the note in her mouth when she heard approaching steps and chewed.

"We're baaa-ack," the Hulk sang. "Ready for round three?"

Jack no longer had to worry about the door opening any moment and Cass being pushed through it. Her only fear when they'd started to punch and kick her had been that TQ would bring Cass in as punishment, to make Jack watch as they...

She couldn't even bring herself to think about it. At least now she knew Cass was safe. She didn't have to worry that her own death would eventually lead to Cass's as well.

TQ was going to make her suffer for everything she'd done to her and her brother. And then she'd sit back with a cold glass of wine and an even colder smile as she reveled in Jack's slow death. But Jack had been down that road before. She knew the drill, and she'd sworn she'd never let herself go through that kind of pain and humiliation again.

Cass was a strong woman, stronger than Jack ever was and ever would be. She'd suffer the consequences of Jack's death, but she'd be alive and free to live a better life, without the constant threat of Jack's past catching up to them.

The decision was made. She had to give up. Not because she had nothing to live for, but because she had everything to lose if she didn't. "I'm sorry, baby, but you're better off without me," she mumbled.

The two men stared at her. "What?" the smaller one asked.

She swallowed the note and smiled. "Hey, assholes, miss me?"

Burke, Virginia

Once in the cab, Shield dialed Pierce's cell.

"Who's this?" he asked sternly, not recognizing the number.

"29041971." Shield used only her code, not her name, which told Pierce she was on an unsecured GPS line. "Where are you?"

"Minutes before landing," he replied.

"I'm headed your way."

"I have a van waiting outside. Meet me there."

"Roger that." Shield hung up. "Take us to Andrews Air Force Base," she told the driver.

"Are they coming to get us?" Ryden asked, excitement in her voice.

"No. We're going to meet someone."

"And then?"

"Back to Washington."

"Are you serious?" Ryden looked shocked. "What are we going to do there?"

"I have to take care of something. You're going somewhere safe."

"Without you?"

"I have to help my employer get one of our own back. TQ is keeping her captive."

"You mean the woman who helped us?" Ryden asked.

"Yes."

"That's crazy. TQ...Rothschild...*whoever* is going to kill you."

"Trust me, I'll be fine," Shield said. "The four of us stand a fair chance."

"Chance? You said yourself she owns an army."

"And we own the know-how."

Ryden nodded vigorously. "I'm coming with you."

"No, you're not. We're professionals and—"

"I can help."

"How?" Shield smiled.

"I really don't want you to do this."

"It's my job. They're my people and I have to help them."

"How about me? I mean—"

Shield grabbed her hand. "I'll come get you from the Washington safe house when it's over, but you have to promise to stay put until I get back or someone from the EOO contacts you."

"Another safe house?"

"This one's in use and secure."

"I thought your people were supposed to come get us," Ryden said. "Take us back safely. When was that plan abandoned?"

"There's a lot going on."

"Which means you don't matter? I mean, forget *me*. They probably think I deserve whatever I get, but aren't they supposed to care for your safety?"

"I *offered* to help them," Shield said. "The plan was to stay with you and wait for pickup, but I can't sit back and do nothing."

"That's your problem," Ryden replied. "You think you need to please everyone."

"That may be true, but it's who I am." After a long silence, Shield turned to her. "I'll make sure you're safe, okay?"

"It's not me I'm worried about."

Ryden was nervous about coming face-to-face with the people

who knew about her deception. They could have her arrested. Would this nightmare never end?

When they got to Andrews, Harper paid the cab driver and led her toward a dark van. She spoke in low tones with the driver, a thirtyish tank of a man in a business suit, and then opened the back door for her. This van was very different from the stripped-down one TQ's people had used. It was a luxury model, designed to transport celebrities or high-level government officials, and was as well equipped as any limousine, with a minibar, tinted privacy windows, and a DVD player with surround sound. Instead of the typical front-facing seat arrangement, the back held two wide, plush bench seats facing each other, with enough room for four on each side.

As they sat side by side on one of the benches, Ryden noticed a long, large, black duffel beneath the seat opposite. She wondered what it contained but didn't dare ask.

They didn't have long to wait. A few minutes later, two men and a woman joined them.

The first in was a sixty-something man in a business suit tailored to minimize the paunch above his belt. He had thinning blond hair, a pasty complexion, and deep creases in his face that gave him a permanently dour expression. At first glance, he seemed not at all the type to be heading into the lion's den that was TQ, but when she looked a little closer, she could see he was a formidable presence. Despite the bit of thickening around his waist, he seemed otherwise very fit for a man his age—the muscles in his biceps stretched his suit coat ever so slightly— and his eyes held a strength and resolve few men could match.

He greeted them. "Shield. Ms. Wagner."

Ryden caught the curious way he addressed Harper, but now wasn't the time for explanations. Probably a nickname he'd given her, she guessed. Appropriate for a bodyguard.

An attractive young blond woman in her late twenties was next into the van. She was dressed all in black—boots, trousers, and a turtleneck sweater. Behind her, another man in a suit, this one also in his sixties, maybe younger. With his copper-colored crew cut, streaked with gray, chiseled features, and lean, muscular physique, he looked like a career soldier out of uniform.

The trio took the bench seat opposite and the van got under way.

"Both men are my employers," Harper said, avoiding their names. "Lynx is a colleague."

The man with the light hair, sitting in the middle, seemed

preoccupied, his focus entirely on either his watch or the road ahead. His face was tight with worry and impatience.

The other two practically gawked at Ryden.

"TQ must've spent a fortune on your transformation," Lynx said to her.

"I guess." Ryden looked away, her cheeks warming from the intense scrutiny. "I never cared to ask."

"Dead ringer," the guy with red hair said. "Even your voice is the same."

"We have to drop her off at the Washington safe house," Harper said.

"I don't know about that," he replied. "Not that TQ is likely to run, but I don't want to give her too much thinking time."

"Who knows what that sick mind will come up with," Lynx said.

Ryden would probably be better off in a safe house, but for some reason, she felt more secure staying close to Harper. "I don't want to cause more problems than I already have. If you think I can wait for you in the van, that's what I'll do."

"We need to get to Jaclyn ASAP." The light-haired man checked his watch again.

"What's the plan?" Harper asked.

"We threaten to destroy her, make public who she is, if she doesn't give us Jack." The blond woman—Lynx—who'd initially looked like a model on a photo shoot or something, transformed before Ryden's eyes as she spoke about the woman who'd helped them. Her tone of voice, steely determination, and rigid posture—she looked coiled tight and ready to pounce—were sure signs of her underlying strength and lethal capabilities. "If she has so much as touched a hair on my woman's head—"

"I will kill her with my own hands," the fair-haired man said.

So Lynx had a thing for the mystery woman, Ryden realized. And the man in the middle had some vested personal interest in her as well, apparently, judging from his vehement response.

"I wouldn't trust her." Ryden took a chance and spoke. "She's... she's the deadliest-looking predator I've ever seen, and that's including the Animal Planet channel."

"We know better than to trust her, Ms. Wagner," the light-haired man said seriously. He looked at Harper. "Shield, you'll get your orders when we reach our destination."

"I don't mean to put anyone down, and I'll be the first to admit

I owe Harding my life, but what's this really all about?" Harper asked him. "She faked her death years ago to join the other side and, from what I understand, wants nothing to do with us. Yet, you not only let her live when treason is punishable by death, but you also come running to save her."

Valid question, Ryden thought. Although this Jack woman had saved both their lives, something was definitely very dangerous about her.

"It's complicated," Lynx replied, while the fair-haired man stared at the wall behind them, absentmindedly tapping his fingers on the edge of the seat. The closer they got to their destination, the more his anxiety showed in his face and body language.

Harper sighed. "Either way, I'm here to get her back, and for the record, I like her."

The man in the middle—obviously the guy in charge—sure was acting strange, Ryden thought as she studied his face. He certainly didn't seem like the average employer worried about a subordinate. More like a guy in a hospital waiting room, fretting about the condition of a loved one.

"Mister…" Ryden looked at him until he turned to face her.

"Yes?" His eyes met hers.

"Jack is a very strong woman." Ryden hoped that would help him relax. Though she didn't know him, or what the connection was between him and the woman they were headed to rescue, she felt for the big man. His paternal behavior indicated he clearly cared about Jack.

He didn't reply, and they drove the rest of the way in silence, the tension so palpable Ryden could hardly breathe.

Traffic was still light in the heart of the capital when they reached their destination and the driver parked at the curb. He remained behind the wheel while the others got out, all but Harper, who hunched down in front of Ryden.

"You'll be fine here," Harper said. "Do what the driver says, and do not leave the van unless you're told to."

"I understand."

"I don't know what they want me to do, but I will be back for you."

"Just…be safe."

"Will do." Harper smiled and Ryden's heart melted. "Later, then." She touched Ryden's knee.

"Harper?"

"Ye—"

Ryden grabbed her face with both hands and kissed her softly on the lips. "Thank you."

"For?"

"Let's go, Shield," one of the men yelled from outside.

"Be careful." Ryden tried to sound strong.

CHAPTER THIRTY-SEVEN

TQ would be damned if she'd show weakness or worry. Pierce was formidable, certainly. She had never been put in a situation as tenuous as this, and she hated the unfamiliar loss of absolute control. But she'd come to terms with the realization that she'd have to get this man whatever he wanted to return to her life. And if, for any reason, she couldn't recover what he'd come for and reach a deal, she had a contingency plan in place.

She sat at her desk, surrounded by four guards—one at each corner of the room—and tapped her long fingernails on the polished surface as she waited. The men had instructions to shoot Pierce on the spot should he try to kill her. She could accept being unveiled to the world, but she would not accept anyone else's terms concerning her demise. If worse came to worst and she had to dispose of Pierce, she'd have to leave the country tonight. Although not ideal, it *was* a way out.

The phone rang and she took her time answering. Her game, her rules, because in the end, it was always her game.

"Madam, your guest has—"

"Let him in and send him up." She disconnected and turned to the guard nearest the entrance. "Frisk him at the door."

While she waited, she pulled a mirror from the desk drawer and applied bright-red lipstick, something she bothered with only on those rare occasions she met a client in person. Then she smoothed a hand over her hair, put the mirror away, and sat back in her huge leather chair. She chose the appropriate confident smile when she heard the knock. "Come in."

"Mr. Pierce," her assistant announced as she showed him in.

The guard she'd appointed walked up to Pierce, and like someone who knew the drill, he lifted his arms and patiently waited until her man checked him over.

Her visitor wore an expensive Armani suit the color of anthracite, with a silk tie, starched white shirt, and handmade Italian lace-ups. His thinning hair was cut close to his head, like you'd expect from an ex-military. For a man in his sixties, he was rather handsome in a rugged kind of way.

When her guard finished and nodded his approval, TQ languidly stood and extended her hand. "A pleasure."

Pierce walked the few steps to her and took her hand. Contrary to most, he was in no hurry to pull it away. He held her there and examined her eyes. "That's yet to be determined."

TQ tried to pull her hand away, but he held hers firmly in his grip a while longer before he let go.

"Please, have a seat." She gestured at the leather armchair opposite her desk.

Pierce sat and crossed his legs at the knee, his arms on the rests. To all appearances, very comfortable. Not at all like the demeanor she was used to eliciting from those she deigned to meet with.

"Tell me, Mr. Pierce…" She sounded confident, successfully concealing her discomfort at his silence and penetrating stare. "How can I help you?"

Without blinking, he answered, "I am not here for your help. I'm here to retrieve what's mine."

"I'm more than willing to accommodate you, and forgive me in advance for any trouble I may have caused. Business is business, and how some of my artifacts are acquired is not always up to me."

"Perhaps the artifacts aren't, although I doubt you have no involvement in theft. But how you obtain people is up to you. I'm here for a person, not some ridiculous object."

If Pierce was after someone she had used for organs, she was in deep trouble.

"As you already know, I trade in organs," she said. "Illegally, yes, but my clients are significant individuals, aware of how the trade works and where the organs come from." She tried to control her voice. "It's very possible, however, the person you are looking for voluntarily donated an—"

"Her name is Jack, and she hasn't voluntarily donated anything."

She was caught so off guard she couldn't entirely hide her surprise. "Jack?"

"The woman you blackmailed into working for you."

TQ stared at him a while longer before she smiled and, soon after, began to laugh. "Are you telling me all this is about Jack the…paid assassin?"

"That's the one," Pierce said seriously.

TQ laughed again. "May I ask what your interest in her may be? Why someone of your stature would be willing to bargain so much for someone so inconsequential?"

"No." His eyes narrowed dangerously. "You may not."

"I can't fathom any reason other than she's done something to upset you. You're after her for the same reason I was. To make her pay."

"It's none of your business, Ms. Rothschild. Time is money, so let's move along."

"Of course." She felt almost giddy. Not only was the trade-off laughably easy, but Jack was going to pay her dues with or without her. Of course, she'd much prefer to end the assassin's miserable life under her own terms and after a considerable amount of pain. "You can have her, although I will miss playing with my toy girl."

"Where is she?"

"In the basement." TQ laughed. "In storage, until I was done playing and she heals."

Pierce got up. "How bad?"

"She was managing, when I saw her last. Of course, that was hours ago, and well…I left her in the company of two very eager men." She smiled as she imagined the kind of shape Jack must be in by now. "You're free to leave her with me. I'm sure I can make her pay for both of us."

Pierce banged his hand on the desk. "Call your men and tell them to stop. I want to see her. *Now*."

She jumped, startled. What a strange reaction from someone who wanted Jack to suffer as much as she did. She called her guy in the basement. "How's my friend doing?"

"She passed out."

"Shame. Anyway, enough fun for tonight. Shane will be coming by to pick her up. Both of you are done for the night." She hung up.

"One of my men can take you," TQ snapped, and one of the four men stepped forward. "Escort Mr. Pierce to the lobby. Then fetch the woman."

She extended her hand to Pierce. "It turned out to be a pleasure after all."

Pierce didn't take it. Instead he leaned forward and towered over her. "If you ever touch or go looking for her again, I will personally strangle you." He pivoted and walked to the door where the guard was waiting.

TQ got up when she heard the fax machine come to life not long after he'd gone. Distracted by his reaction, she picked the two sheets off the tray and glanced at the first.

This is all I could find. It's old, but it's all I can do. The rest remains out of my league. TQ flipped to the next page, where a full-color picture of a man stared back at her. Under the photo was the caption Montgomery Pierce, Chief of Covert Operations.

It wasn't the same guy at all. Who the hell did she just talk to?

"Stop him!" she yelled to the three remaining men. If Jack thought she could pull tricks and have some friend help her escape, she was sorely mistaken. No one fooled her. No one.

Jack had somehow informed this nobody about her real identity and the switch with the president. Although she didn't appreciate an outsider walking around with this information, he was as inconsequential as Jack, and no one would believe him. Definitely not without proof. She had to hand it to Jack for coming up with the name and identity of Montgomery Pierce, and someone to pull it off with a very convincing performance.

"It's almost over," Shield said, peering out at TQ's glass-fronted office building across the street. She couldn't keep from glancing at the van, parked down the block with Ryden inside.

She and her two companions had positioned themselves in the hotel restaurant because its front windows provided an ideal visual. All of them wore earpieces hooked into David Arthur's listening device. None of them had touched their coffee.

So far, everything was proceeding without a hitch. Jack should be out of there in a few minutes. Arthur was in the elevator, headed down.

Pierce, on the booth seat opposite, cracked a smile at her comment and then returned his attention to what Arthur was doing.

Lynx, beside her, was absorbed as well in every nuance of sound coming through their earpieces; she looked tightly coiled and ready to spring.

Pierce had wanted to confront TQ in person, but he'd had to abort the plan after he, Arthur, and Lynx had boarded the EOO jet for Washington. Apparently, the tension was too much for him, and he'd started to have chest pains.

Shield had no idea Pierce had health problems, but then again, his pale, sweaty complexion had never been as obvious as tonight. Arthur insisted on taking his place and had made the phone call from the jet, so TQ would recognize the voice when they met in person. According to Lynx, who'd briefed her once they were out of Ryden's earshot, Arthur had also insisted he was better suited because he was capable of staying calm in the face of the woman who had taken Jack.

Shield could understand that now. All during Arthur's conversation with TQ, Pierce kept mumbling about how he wanted to go in and kill her. He'd become particularly upset and enraged when TQ mentioned her men had been torturing Jack for hours. Shield and Lynx had had to hold him down, and then Shield had to hold Lynx down when she'd insisted she go in instead and beat TQ to oblivion.

"What's this?" they heard Arthur say. "Let go of me."

"We will, pal," another man said, "as soon as we get to where your friend is."

Shield heard a struggle and then TQ's voice. "You thought you could fool me? Well, the joke's on you, whoever you are."

More struggling. "Do you recognize the man in this picture?" TQ asked.

When Arthur didn't answer, TQ continued. "Let me enlighten you. His name is Montgomery Pierce, and he looks nothing like you. So, my question is, who are you?"

"I don't know what you're talking about."

"Take him to the basement and finish both of them. I've simply lost my will to spend any more time on that conniving lowlife assassin."

"Let's go," Pierce said as Lynx took off out the exit.

"No." Shield got in front of him. "Stay here. We'll take care of it."

"Out of my way." Pierce pushed her aside, but he'd gone only a step or two before he stopped short and grasped his chest. His face was ashen.

"You're not well, Monty. Look, I'll let you know if we need backup, okay?"

Pierce nodded. "Go," he rasped.

By the time she got outside to the curb, Lynx was speeding toward her in the van. The guy who'd been behind the wheel was now escorting Wagner, one hand on her elbow, briskly toward the restaurant.

The van slammed to a stop two feet away. "Get in," Lynx shouted.

Shield jumped in and grabbed the two automatic assault rifles that Lynx had already retrieved from the duffel in the back. "Let's do it."

They buckled up, and Lynx floored it at the first gap in traffic a second or two later. The van shot across the roadway, up half a dozen wide marble steps, and straight through the big glass entrance of the building. The SRS bags popped immediately, but Lynx kept going, the sound of screeching tires, shattering glass, and the rev of the engine deafening. Finally, the van hit something solid and would go no farther. Shield gave one rifle to Lynx before they got out.

"Give me your location, Arthur," Shield said.

"Two floors down," came a crackled response.

"Hang in there. We're on our way."

No sooner had she said that than TQ's men started shooting. Shield couldn't tell how many, but the shots seemed to be coming from all directions. They dove for cover behind the massive marble reception counter and fired back. Shield got one man in the chest while Lynx got another in the neck.

She pointed to the emergency exit a few feet away. Lynx nodded, and both kept firing while they ran to the stairwell.

They made it through the heavy door and heard voices from below. Both waited at the landing until two men came into view and showered them with bullets.

"One more level to go," Shield said as they headed down.

"Door at the end of the hall," Arthur's voice came again.

"Is she alive?" Pierce asked in her ear, obviously to Arthur.

"She's…we need to get her out now," Arthur replied.

Lynx accelerated at this, taking the last few steps two at a time, and was about to bolt into the hall of the sub-basement when Shield grabbed her. "Easy." Shield carefully checked to see if anyone was in the hall. "Two guarding the door."

"We have to take them out *now*," Lynx whispered.

Both took a deep breath and stepped into the hall, shooting. They ran to the door, stepping over the two corpses, and when they found it locked, Lynx started firing at the lock while Shield checked the bodies for keys. She was sure no amount of gunfire would open the thick steel door, and so was Lynx, for that matter. But Shield knew Lynx had only one thing on her mind and a lot of anger.

Shield put her hand on Lynx's shoulder, signaling her to stop. "Arthur, is there a lock on the other side?"

"I'm looking, but nothing here. You haven't even put a dent in it," he replied. "Jack's lost a lot of blood."

"Keep her conscious," Lynx yelled, and pounded on the door.

"I'm trying," he said.

"Someone's coming," Shield whispered. Both turned to look down the hall, rifles at the ready. Shield tried the door to her left while Lynx the two on the right. "Damn," Shield said.

"Get ready." Lynx lifted her rifle in preparation.

"Shield, Lynx. Cease fire," came Pierce's voice through the mic.

"What's going on?" Lynx asked.

"I'm almost there," Pierce replied.

Shield, shocked, looked at Lynx, who was obviously just as surprised.

"Monty, it's dangerous," Lynx said.

The elevator door started to open and both of them took aim.

"Put your weapons down," they heard Monty say before they saw him.

When the doors opened completely, Shield saw that Pierce wasn't alone. Next to him stood TQ, who looked scared but forced a smile nevertheless when she saw Shield.

"What the—" Lynx said.

"Move faster. You're on a time limit," Pierce said to TQ as they walked down the hall.

TQ picked up the pace and stopped three feet away from the steel door. She looked up at the right corner, straight into the sensor, and nodded. The door made a loud unlocking sound and opened.

Lynx ran in first, with Pierce behind her.

"You screwed with the wrong people," Shield said to TQ as they both waited outside.

"How's the florist?" TQ looked smug.

"How's your face?" Shield asked.

TQ's eyes narrowed in confusion. "My what?"

Shield backhanded her across the face so hard TQ hit the wall.

Lynx came out, with Pierce behind her and Harding in his arms. Lynx put her gun to TQ's head.

"We had a deal." TQ looked to Pierce.

"You had a deal with him, not with me," Lynx said menacingly.

"As much as I want to see her dead," Pierce said, "I'd much rather see her suffer." He turned in the direction of a sudden ruckus behind them.

"Police! Drop your weapons," a male voice shouted as a small army of armed men came into view down the hall. With them were two paramedics, carrying a portable stretcher.

"Who called for an ambulance?" Shield asked.

"I did," Pierce replied.

The cops came at them with their guns drawn, and both Shield and Lynx dropped their weapons.

"She needs immediate care," Pierce said. "GSW to the leg and internal hemorrhaging."

"Put her down," one of the policemen ordered, apparently the guy in charge.

"She needs to go to a hospital," Pierce insisted. "*Now*. If I have to repeat myself, you're going to find yourself writing tickets for the rest of your life. As to who I am, call the Agency and ask about a Montgomery Pierce. Maybe you should mention TQ has been caught."

"Who?"

"We had a deal," TQ repeated, terror evident in her face.

From the cop's expression, it was clear neither name registered, but he let the paramedics through. "Someone stay with her," he said to his men as the EMTs pried Harding from Pierce's arms.

"I'm going with her." Lynx jumped forward as they strapped Harding to the stretcher.

"No one is going anywhere until we figure out what happened here," the head cop said.

"Then get on the goddamn phone," Pierce ordered him.

Harding was taken away while the police kept their guns trained on the rest, and the one in charge stepped away to make the call. He came back moments later. "Thank you, sir," he said to Pierce, and extended his hand. "My sincerest apologies for the inconvenience. You and your people are free to go."

"About time." TQ made to push through.

"Not you." Shield pushed her back.

"What is this about? I am the victim here. This is my place of business they broke into."

"Have Mrs. Rothschild arrested for terrorism against the American government," Pierce said, "to name just the first of many charges."

TQ was handcuffed and pushed down the hall while the cop read her her rights.

Back outside, Shield found Ryden anxiously seeking her out

amongst the cars and cops.

"Thank God, you're all right," Ryden said, running up to her.

"I'm fine." Shield smiled.

"I panicked. Didn't know what to think when all the cops and the ambulance showed up. I thought…I thought…"

"Shh." Shield held her by the shoulders to calm her. "It's over. TQ was arrested."

"Ms. Wagner." Pierce came up behind them. "I'd like you to go with Chief of Police James."

Ryden looked from Pierce to Shield. "I'm being arrested."

Pierce hadn't discussed this with Shield, but then again, he didn't have to. Shield knew it was inevitable and she couldn't do a thing to stop it. She wanted to stop time, turn it back and change everything, but she couldn't do a thing.

"I'm afraid so," Pierce said.

"Tell them the truth, Ryden. Tell them what they did to you." Shield tried to stay calm. "You're a big part of the proof against TQ and what she pulled, but you were an unwilling accomplice. Let them see that."

"I don't think they'll care. I'm a criminal to them," Ryden replied. "That's all that matters."

"What you are, Ms. Wagner, will depend on the president's testimony," Pierce said. "As you know, she hasn't made any charges as of yet."

"Which means what?"

"That your future depends on her," Shield said.

Pierce gestured for the chief of police, who had been waiting out of earshot, to join them. Chief James looked at Ryden and hesitated. He appeared uncomfortable, probably due to her resemblance to Thomas. Reluctantly, he removed the handcuffs from his belt.

"No cuffs." Pierce stopped him. "Her arrest stays quiet until you hear from the president."

"You got it," James replied. "This way, ma'am." He gestured to Ryden.

"Tell them everything," Shield repeated as Ryden took a step toward James.

"I'm sorry…about everything." Ryden stopped again and turned to Shield. "I hope you can one day forgive me."

CHAPTER THIRTY-EIGHT

As soon as the ambulance arrived at the hospital, Monty was escorted to an exam room and given nitroglycerine for his heart, while a trauma team worked on Jaclyn elsewhere in the ER before whisking her away for surgery.

"You need to take it easy," the doctor told him. "Your heart's in bad shape, as you already know, and—"

"Yes, yes. I realize all that. Have you heard anything about Ms. Harding?" Monty buttoned up his shirt, feeling much better after the pill.

"I'll see what I can find out."

He headed out into the waiting area. Shield and Arthur, who'd gotten his forehead stitched, stood when they saw him approach.

"Nothing on Jaclyn, yet," Arthur said. "How about you? How are you feeling?"

"I'm fine now. Where's Monroe?"

"As close as they'll allow her to the operating room."

"What happened?" Shield asked. "How did you get TQ to cooperate?"

"When I heard you…" he looked at Arthur, "say that Jaclyn wasn't doing well, I headed out of the restaurant to come find you. I'd made it as far as the door when I saw TQ being escorted out of the building by five of her men." He filled them in on what they'd missed.

Monty hurried across the street and intercepted TQ as she and her goons neared a black Mercedes parked close by. "Ms. Rothschild."

He knew TQ had seen his picture when she'd made Arthur, and the fact that she blanched proved him right.

"Mr. P…Pierce. I…"

"We had a deal."

"Who was the man I saw in my office?"

"I prefer to protect my identity, but you leave me no choice."

"I didn't know."

"You've made a very big mistake, TQ."

"Is that so? Because frankly, I doubt you have any power over me at all."

"If I may?" Monty carefully reached for the cell inside his suit pocket and punched in a number. When the call went through, he said, *"This is Montgomery Pierce from the EOO. I need to speak to Madam President. Tell her it involves her safety."* He put it on speakerphone while he waited.

"The president's office," a male voice said. *"How can I help you?"*

"I need to speak to the president directly," Monty replied.

"That's not possible, sir."

"Tell her I know what happened to her. She'll know what I mean."

TQ didn't try to stop him, but she fidgeted with her purse.

Seconds later, that distinctive Maine-accented voice came on the line. *"This is President Thomas. Who is this?"*

"Chief Administrator of the EOO. We have worked for you in the past."

"What can I do for you?" the president asked carefully.

"I know about your abduction and replacement."

A long pause. *"How?"*

"That's not important. I also know you are afraid to talk because they said no one would believe you and you will lose your credibility and put your family's safety at risk."

"How do you know all this?" she asked.

"Madam President, we have helped people in your situation before, and we can do it again. I will provide the proof the world needs and give you and your family twenty-four-hour protection until the people involved in your kidnapping are arrested."

"Even if that's true, how do I know you'll find these people? I can't hide myself or my family forever. I'm the president, Mr.—"

"Pierce. We already know who did it."

"What?" Thomas snapped. *"Why haven't they been arrested?"*

"I can make that happen in approximately..." Monty checked his watch. *"Eight hours."*

TQ grabbed the cell from his hand and disconnected.

"Time is wasting," Monty said. *"You have eight hours, Cinderella."*

"Bring them both here," TQ said to her men.

"No." Monty was afraid Jack was too weak to cooperate on the trip up, and moving her around would only enhance the blood loss. If she was barely conscious, she'd never survive being manhandled by these butchers. "I'm going to get them myself and you're coming with me."

"You don't need me."

"I want you where I can see you until I get what I came for. Tick tock."

TQ pushed the goon behind her aside and stomped back to the building.

"Oh, and by the way," Monty said when they got in the elevator, "should Jack not survive, I will destroy you anyway."

"All this fuss for a nobody assassin," TQ said benignly as she looked at her reflection in the shiny metal door.

"Also, should you ever come near her or anyone she cares about, I will personally rip that ugly head you keep admiring off that skinny body."

"You called Thomas?" Shield asked.

"No, I called Wagner," he replied. "Of course, I called the driver first, who played the role of secretary."

"When did you have time to prepare them?" Shield asked him.

"I didn't. They both knew what to do," Monty said. "It was pretty evident when I called asking for the president."

"She's good," Shield said, referring to Wagner.

"If I didn't know better, I'd be hard-pressed to buy that she wasn't the real president."

"What's going to happen to her?" Shield asked.

"That's not up to us, but I'm sure it won't be good."

"They framed her to cooperate, and she did help us find out who TQ is. That's got to mean something."

"I hope for her sake it does."

"What do you mean?" Shield looked puzzled.

"You'll see," Monty replied.

Jack woke in such a fog she had trouble focusing. She didn't know where she was or how she'd gotten there, but what she could hazily make out in her limited field of vision—white blankets and an IV stand—indicated a hospital room. "Am I dreaming, or what?" she mumbled.

"Baby?" The familiar, soothing voice came from close by. "Baby, can you hear me?"

"Cass?" Jack tried harder to clear her fuzzy vision but couldn't.

"Yes, it's me, honey."

Jack felt warm lips touch her own.

"You're going to be fine."

"What happened?"

"You've lost a lot of blood, some ribs are broken, and you have a concussion."

"I was in a building, in this basement." Jack tried to remember. "They kept punching and kicking."

"Shh. I know."

Jack felt wet drops on her hand. "Are you crying?"

"You're safe now," Cass said, her voice breaking.

"Don't cry." Jack never could stand to see Cass cry; it hurt her to the core.

"I'm happy, baby. That's all."

"I'm so sorry I got you involved. TQ wanted to hurt you for what I did to her brother."

"I know."

"She said she'd let you live if I surrendered. I didn't have a choice. She'd keep coming for you if I didn't." Jack tried to move, but her head felt like it would explode from the pain. She groaned.

"Try not to get excited," Cass said. "You don't have to explain."

"You're easy to track down because of—"

"The orchestra. I know."

"How did you locate me?"

"Monty did. He…he found out TQ had taken you and did everything to find you."

"Monty?" Jack repeated, confused. "Why does he care?"

"Because…he just does." Cass caressed her hand. "He saved your life."

"Why?"

"Maybe you should ask him when you're all better. He's outside right now and would really like to see you."

"No. Not like this. I don't want him to see me like this."

"You look better than when he found and carried you."

"Say what?"

"He wouldn't let anyone else touch you. The paramedics had to pry you away."

Jack was either too dizzy to understand Cass right, or she was in a coma dream. "Cass?"

"Yes, baby?"

"I want to go home. I don't like hospitals."

"Soon enough. Get some rest and I'll see what I can do." Cass let go of her hand.

"Don't go." Jack tried to sit up, but the effort sent a white-hot burst of pain through her head and midsection. "Fuck. Damn it, that hurt."

"Jack, please stop moving."

"Stay with me."

"I'm not going anywhere, baby. Ever. Now, get some rest."

The Oval Office

Elizabeth Thomas sat at her desk, watching as her secretary admitted John Kaplan, director of the Central Intelligence Agency, and Calvin Sneed, the secretary of Homeland Security, into the Oval Office. Her advisor, Kenneth Moore, stood beside her, actually unusually fidgety—no doubt because she'd uncharacteristically sidestepped his questions about the reason behind the impromptu meeting.

The CIA had called an hour before, to tell her that Theodora Rothschild had been arrested—the woman behind her abduction and the one responsible for creating a double to take her place. Elizabeth had refused to answer any questions or admit to anything over the phone; she wanted to address the issue in person immediately.

Kaplan waited until her secretary had departed before speaking. "Thank you for meeting us on such short notice," the CIA director said. "But you understand this is a sensitive matter."

"Indeed," she replied. "Thus the lack of media and the fact that I wanted only you three men present for this discussion."

"Let me get to the point, Madam President." He cleared his throat. "The chief of the EOO, Montgomery Pierce, has proof of your kidnapping and replacement in the White House from February twenty-fourth until last night. We are not sure what Mrs. Rothschild aimed to accomplish, but it is an act of terrorism against you and the country. We need to know why you haven't come forward with this information."

"What are they talking about?" Moore looked like he'd just heard pigs could fly. "Elizabe…Madam President, is this true?"

"Let me ask you this." She addressed Moore. "Did you notice any difference, any change in me—my looks or otherwise—during this period?"

"Of course not," he replied. "This is insane. What are they talking about?"

Elizabeth had wanted Moore there to prove a point to these men. Even her closest aide had apparently failed to pick up on the fact that anything was amiss—either while she was gone or since her return to the White House. He'd arrived for work early that morning, his usual cheery self, seemingly oblivious to anything different about her. His only comment had been about her looking rather tired; he'd also mentioned that her sister had called, anxious to spend some time with her because they hadn't seen each other since the Find Your Sport festivities. Clearly, the double had even fooled her sibling.

She stood and paced behind her desk. "It's true," she finally said to Moore. "I was kidnapped and replaced by a double."

Moore gasped. "No. How can that—"

"A very convincing one," Elizabeth added.

"No doubt about that," the CIA director said. "We have her in custody and are tempted to salute her every time we see her."

"But…but…" Moore looked aghast. "This is crazy. I would have known. I would have at least—"

"My own family didn't see the difference." Thomas ran her hand through her hair. "And after having met the double, I can see why."

"You met her?" Moore practically shouted. "How could all this take place under my nose? I spent plenty of time with you in the past weeks. I never had reason to suspect anything."

Elizabeth nodded. "Yet you were in the presence of a stranger."

Moore sat down, shaking his head in bewilderment. "How did this happen?"

"During the attack at the Jefferson Hotel. They exchanged us in the elevator."

"We even gave you around-the-clock protection after the assault," he mumbled.

"Harper Kennedy," the secretary of Homeland Security said. "From the Elite Operatives Organization. She's the one who uncovered the truth. She didn't know what, but she knew something was different about you."

"Whatever happened to Kennedy?" Moore asked. "I haven't seen her all day."

"It's funny how a complete stranger realized something was wrong," Elizabeth said.

Moore frowned. "I feel like such a failure."

"Because you are," Secretary Sneed said.

"Excuse me?" Moore replied, clearly offended.

"Kennedy named you as Rothschild's inside person. You were in on this plan from the beginning. Senator Schuster was also blackmailed to retract his compliance in the weapons law, because apparently Rothschild threatened to remove the black-market organ she sold him for his son."

Elizabeth felt faint. Moore was involved in this? Her longtime family friend and trusted confidant? "Is this true?" She looked at Moore, but he didn't answer and refused to meet her eyes.

"According to Kennedy," the secretary continued, "Moore is also responsible for the death of your husband, Madam President. He hired someone to poison him at the golf club, because the double, as convincing as she was, would have never fooled your husband."

Speechless, Elizabeth walked over to Moore, still seated in a chair by her desk.

He looked up at her. "I can explain, it's not all true—"

She slapped him hard across the face.

Kaplan cleared his throat. "What did they aim to accomplish, Madam President?"

Elizabeth glared at Moore. "Speak."

"Not until I see my lawyer."

She turned back to Kaplan. "I've been looking for any new amendments for hours. The only change in my plans has to do with the illegal-weapons agenda."

"Oh," Kaplan and Sneed said simultaneously.

"Is that the only change?" Kaplan asked.

"As far as I can see, yes."

"Pierce from the EOO mentioned that Rothschild was a weapons dealer, among other things."

"It's a multi-billion-dollar enterprise," Elizabeth said. "I knew it would rub many the wrong way, but I never thought they'd go this far."

"It's not the first time," the CIA director said. "We've—"

"I'd rather he wasn't present during any further conversation,"

Elizabeth cut in, glancing at Moore. "Please, get him out of my sight."

Kaplan made a phone call and no one spoke further until the president's secretary escorted a blue-suited agent into the room.

"Take him in," Kaplan told the agent, nodding toward the special advisor.

Moore stood. "I want to see my lawyer." No one reacted as he was led away.

"As I was saying," Kaplan continued once they were alone again, "we've covered many instances of attacks against presidents by extremists and terrorists, and we have even personally assisted in providing doubles."

"But it doesn't change the fact that you were abducted and your safety and position as president of this country compromised," the secretary of Homeland Security said. "Why haven't you pressed charges?"

"I don't intend to," Elizabeth replied.

"Madam President—" The secretary began to argue.

"Please." She gestured for him to stop. "Rothschild—or her people, to be more precise, who appear to be Russians—has threatened me with my family's life. She will keep that promise in or out of jail."

"We can give them around-the-clock protection for as long as you serve your term."

"And what happens when my term is over?"

"We will continue to—"

"But not as passionately, and let's face it, I cannot have my family under constant surveillance for the rest of their lives. My sister's kids deserve a normal life, and so do my sister and her husband."

"Fair enough, Madam President," the secretary said. "We will find subtle ways to monitor their safety."

"And the worst part," she ignored his remark, "is that I am the first female president of this country. How do you think my abduction will sit with the rest of the world? My decisions so far will all be discredited. Every media journalist will throw doubt on any change I've made and will make. Soon, people will refer to me as the double instead of the president."

"Not to mention everything they'll start looking into, to prove it's not the first time," Kaplan said. "Every conspiracy nut and individual like Assange will dig until they expose anything they can." His eyes narrowed. "And we do not want that."

"The nation elected me for a better America," Elizabeth said.

"They trust I can give them a better tomorrow." She stared at the large presidential seal embroidered into the Oval Office carpet. "And I will not let them down. I refuse to let anyone take away or befoul my reputation and ability to make decisions for the future of my country."

No one spoke for a long while. She was damned if she was going to let anyone deprive her of her dreams and everything she'd worked for. If the world found out about this, her reputation would be destroyed, her decisions doubted and ridiculed. It would only be a matter of time before she'd have to choose between stepping down or serving her country with infamy and disgrace. She was not about to become another Bush.

"What do you suggest, Madam President?" the HLS secretary asked.

"That we do nothing. Reveal none of this," the CIA director put in. "It wouldn't be the first time,"

"Indeed." Elizabeth agreed. "Everything said in this room stays here."

"We can't just let Rothschild off the hook," Secretary Sneed said. "And what about Moore and Wagner?"

"Wagner was blackmailed into compliance," Kaplan told her. "She was a florist with a squeaky-clean record until they framed her for first-degree murder. She was facing the death penalty when Rothschild's lawyer bailed her out and made the offer. They trained her for months, but she didn't know what they were up to until after all the surgeries had taken place."

"But she complied, nevertheless," Elizabeth said.

"Correct," Kaplan said. "But she has been very cooperative and a key to unraveling this mess. Moore continued to threaten her with her life every day, until she was taken together with Kennedy last night to be killed."

"Did she really think Rothschild was going to let her live?" Elizabeth asked.

"She shamefully admits to wanting to believe her in order to save her own life."

"Very unfortunate for her, but we can't risk word of this getting out…"

"No, we can't," Kaplan said. "I'll take care of Rothschild, Moore, and Wagner."

"Did Schuster know about my *replacement*?"

"No. He was never involved in any of it and was upset about being made to abort the weapons law," Kaplan replied.

"Good. I like him and I'd like to continue to work with him."

"Up to you, Madam President," the CIA director said. "Although he did illegally purchase an organ from Rothschild."

"To save his son."

"But it remains illegal to—"

"Thank you, gentlemen. I take it we have nothing further to discuss?" she said, dismissing them.

Both men nodded.

"Thank you for your time, Madam President." Kaplan extended his hand. "I'm glad we could clear up this…misunderstanding."

CHAPTER THIRTY-NINE

Penrose, Colorado
A week later, March 16

As promised, the CIA had given Ryden a new identity and moved her into a furnished condo in Penrose, Colorado, an agriculture-based town with all the necessities but too small to have a traffic light. So far, the locals seemed to be paying no heed to her likeness to the president. She'd shed the brown contacts and tried to minimize the resemblance by lightening her hair and getting it cut in a new style. She was also happy to shed the designer suits and high heels for jeans, T-shirts, and sneakers, which helped with the transformation. Part of her wanted to believe she'd heard and seen the last of TQ—she'd seen her ushered away by the feds with her own eyes, after all—but Ryden couldn't help but look over her shoulder whenever she left the apartment.

She'd started applying for jobs right away and, five days into her new life, landed a position at the local no-kill animal shelter. She knew the work would be gratifying, and she might even have an opportunity here to resume her candle making. She'd spotted a little gift shop that day in town that she thought might be interested in selling her work on commission.

So, all in all, she couldn't have asked for a better resolution to her ordeal—a good job, a comfortable home with a splendid view of the Rocky Mountains, and a modest bank account to get her started.

But she was lonely in a way she'd never been in her entire life.

The CIA had said her new identity forbade any ties to her past life, so now, here she was, moving furniture in an effort to forget Harper and make the new, unfamiliar environment hers.

The intercom by the door chimed and she stared at it in disbelief. No one knew where she lived and she didn't know anyone in town yet. She slowly walked toward the panel and pushed the button. "Who's there?"

"Harper."

Her depression lifted in an instant, replaced by euphoric excitement. Ryden buzzed her in, opened the door, and dashed into the bedroom to check herself in the mirror.

Less than a minute later, Harper came through the doorway.

Ryden wanted to play it cool, but she flung herself into Harper's arms as soon as she shut the door. "I thought you were gone...forever." Ryden squeezed her tight and Harper returned the embrace, but with less enthusiasm. She felt the distance and pulled away. "I'm sorry. I was just so happy to see you."

"I'm happy to see you, too," Harper said halfheartedly.

"Have a seat," Ryden said.

"I'm fine." Harper moved to the middle of the room.

"It's not much, but it's home," Ryden said, looking around.

"It's...nice," Harper replied dryly.

"I still can't believe they let me go."

"My employer had a lot to do with that."

"He hardly knows me."

"I asked him to."

"I...thank you." She fidgeted with her pockets, wanting to show her gratitude but not sure how. "I read about Moore's...accident."

Harper nodded. "He got the worst end of the deal."

"He drove his car over a cliff."

"A tragedy."

"The CIA took care of him?" Ryden asked.

The corner of Harper's mouth twitched as she suppressed a smile and looked down at her feet. "I can't talk about that."

"I see. I can't say I'll miss him." Ryden grinned, but the smile quickly faded. "Rothschild is still out there, though."

"They told you."

"Not really much more than she was let go and that was part of the reason for my relocation."

"They led her to believe you had an accident, similar to Moore's," Harper said. "But with TQ, you can never be sure of anything."

"I wouldn't want to risk it, either." Ryden shivered at the thought of TQ suspecting she was still alive. "Why did they let her go? Couldn't they make her disappear, too?"

"She had power lawyers pounding down the door by the time they brought her in for questioning that night," Harper replied. "The attorneys stayed on the case even after she was led to CIA headquarters, and they pulled every political, fed, and—dare I admit—CIA string they had."

"But she's an arms dealer and a terrorist."

"Among other things. But she also owns people in high places, either because she knows their dirty big secrets or because they owe her money or favors or simply fear for their life."

"But she doesn't own the president," Ryden said. "Thomas could have decided TQ's fate."

"Not officially. As you know, Thomas chose to sweep it under the carpet to save face and protect her own family."

"How can TQ have so much power?"

Harper shrugged. "She bought the right people."

"So, she just gets away with everything?"

"Life has a way of turning the tables," Harper said. "I'm sure she'll one day get what's coming to her. The question is, how many more people will she destroy until then?"

Ryden wanted to stop thinking about TQ and focus on the fact that Harper was here with her. "Please," she said. "Why don't you sit?"

"I can't. I…I have to go." Harper took a step toward the door.

"You just got here."

"I leave for Europe in a few hours."

Ryden felt like someone had pulled the floor from under her. "Tuscany."

"Yes."

"When will you be back?"

"Not any time soon."

"Oh." Ryden hugged herself. "I…I thought…you'd stick around for a while."

"I can't. I have a business to run and we have to stay away from each other. It's not safe for you."

"But…"

"TQ knows I work for the EOO. If she starts looking for me—"

"She wouldn't. She's terrified of Pierce."

"I know, but she's a disturbed individual. If she starts looking for trouble again and finds me, she'll find you as well. That woman doesn't forgive or forget."

"I don't care. Let her come after me. I refuse to let that bitch dictate my life."

"I do care, Ryden. I can't risk your safety."

"So, what are you saying? You're just going to walk away?"

Harper stared at her like she wanted to say something but couldn't. A sad helplessness was etched on her face. "I have to."

"This is so unfair," Ryden said, her frustration boiling over. "I never thought I'd find someone like you, someone I can lo—"

"Please don't."

"You can control what you do but not what I say." She was pissed. "I'm in love with—"

Harper grabbed her and sealed her mouth with her own, kissing her long and hard until both ran out of breath. "I don't want to leave." Harper sighed. "But I can't stay."

Tears streamed down Ryden's face. "I want you to."

Harper turned around and grabbed the doorknob. "You're a beautiful woman, Ryden Wagner, inside and out, then and now." She opened the door. "Don't ever forget that," she said in parting. Then she was gone.

Ryden leaned against the door as the sound of Harper's footsteps receded down the hallway. She refused to believe she'd lost the only person she'd ever loved, until the long silence that followed confirmed Harper wasn't coming back. She finally let herself slide to the floor, where she cried for hours.

Southwestern Colorado

"Why can't I just go home?" Jack asked Cass. They'd released her from the hospital after five days, but only with the agreement that she receive appropriate after-care. The bandages on her leg needed to be changed regularly and her vitals closely monitored because of the swelling to her brain.

"The doctor said it's a wonder you don't have permanent brain damage," Cass replied sternly.

"I'm fine." Jack winced when she tried to sit up. Her broken ribs made it tough even to breathe normally.

"Obviously," Cass said.

"You're beautiful even when you're sarcastic."

"Flattery won't help you, Harding."

Jack looked around at the cozy bedroom, which she had to admit was more conducive to a quick recovery than the sterile hospital ward. "Why did he bring me here?" She couldn't fathom why Pierce and Grant had moved her into their home near the EOO campus.

"Because he wants to keep an eye on you."

"What for?"

"Because he cares."

"Why?"

"Ask him," Cass said.

"It's guilt."

"If that's so, then he has his reasons for feeling that way."

"Isn't he afraid I'll strangle him in the middle of the night?" Jack joked.

"I guess he's willing to roll those dice." Cass smiled. "In your condition, I doubt you'd make it to the door."

"You're sexy even when you underestimate me. I'll have you know I can make it to the bathroom on my own since this morning. Should've avoided the mirror, by the way."

"Look at you, all on fire." Cass avoided any comment on Jack's swollen and stitched-in-places face.

"Hey, it's all the way down the hall." Jack smiled.

Cass gently brushed a loose strand of hair from Jack's face. "I'm proud of you, baby."

"You're patronizing me."

"You find that sexy, too?"

"Damn straight I do." Jack winked.

"What am I going to do with you?"

"Give me a day or two and I'll tell you exactly what to do with me."

Cass kissed Jack softly on her swollen mouth. "I'll be back for more sexual harassment in a couple of hours. Now, get some rest."

"Okay, sexy."

Cass walked sensually to the door. "Later."

Jack tried to sleep but her swollen bladder kept getting in the way. "Damn." She slowly rose and got out of bed, wincing at the pain. Holding on to the walls for balance, she limped down the hall, passing the living room. "Anyone there?" she called out. No one replied, so she continued down the hall to the bathroom.

With an empty bladder and not ready to go back to bed, she took her time walking back, sticking her head in the rooms she passed. "Not bad, Pierce." The home was cozy and tastefully decorated, with colorful prints on the walls, modern but comfortable furniture, and subdued lighting.

Jack came to a closed door and started to pass by it, but curiosity got the better of her. She knocked first, and when no one answered, she turned the knob and looked inside. Pierce and Grant's bedroom, evidently. Near the king-sized bed, Pierce's trousers were hung over a plush armchair and Grant's skirt was draped next to it. Like the rest of the rooms, the décor and furnishings were stylish but minimal. The bedside tables were bare except for lamps and a solitary framed photo on one. Interested in what Pierce or Grant considered frame-worthy when the rest of the house was devoid of any pictures at all, Jack entered the room and went to the nightstand.

She couldn't bend over to look at it because of her ribs and the pounding in her head, so she picked up the photo and turned it toward the sunlight streaming in through the window.

Jack stared in disbelief, turning it this way and that. It was the same exact picture her mother had shown her: Jack as a baby, on her first birthday, covered in chocolate cake. "What the fu—"

"That's what happens when you open closed doors."

Jack turned to find Pierce staring at her. She held up the photo. "Where did you get this?"

"From your mother."

"Why?"

Pierce walked over to the closet and removed a small metal box from the top shelf. He continued to the desk to retrieve a small key. "Why don't you sit?" He took a seat at the edge of the bed.

"What the hell's going on?" Jack didn't know if it was the concussion or the situation that was this confusing. Maybe her mind wasn't registering something it should.

"I wanted to wait until you were better," Pierce said, "but…it's too late now."

"Wait for what?" Jack asked with trepidation.

He opened the box and pulled out handfuls of pictures, spreading them across the quilt. "Take a look."

Jack eyed the pictures from a distance. She didn't need to look hard or very long to see they were pictures of herself at all stages of her life. Many were the same as those her mother, Celeste, had shown her, and quite a few had been taken in recent years, after Pierce found out she was alive. "Where did you get these?" she asked quietly.

"The earlier ones are from Celeste. The later were taken here."

"I can see that. Celeste has some of the later ones as well. She said my father would occasionally mail pictures to her up until…I disappeared."

"That's correct."

"That still doesn't explain what *you* are doing with them."

"They're mine."

"What am I not getting?" Jack asked suspiciously.

"Jaclyn..." Pierce ran his hands through his hair and took a deep breath.

"Well?" Jack was angry Pierce had once again invaded her private life. "Do you collect pictures of all of us and alternate at your bedside?"

"No. Just my daughter's."

Jack didn't...*couldn't* register what Pierce had just said. "What?"

"Jaclyn, you're my daughter."

Jack let this sink in for a moment, her eyes going from Pierce to the scattered pictures. "No. That's not true." Her mind flashed back five months earlier, when she'd stumbled upon the mother she never knew, still alive and residing in Sainte-Maxime, France. Celeste had filled her in on the circumstances of her birth and had provided some details about the father who came to claim her when she was three. "My father was an American soldier stationed in France. That's where he met Celeste and got her pregnant."

"Correct."

"No," Jack shouted. "He dumped her when she got pregnant. She...she was a prostitute and not good enough for him."

"I liked Celeste a lot, but I was never in love with her," Pierce said. "I never counted on her getting pregnant, and when she told me she'd given birth to my child I went to get you. I couldn't let you grow up in a brothel. Celeste loved you more than life, but I couldn't let my child grow up like that."

Jack opened her mouth but nothing came out.

"I was young and had needs when Celeste came along," he continued quietly, "but I've only ever loved one woman. Joanne. I've loved her since we were children, pretty much like you did Cassady." Pierce started to collect the photos. "Things were different, then. We couldn't have relationships or marry, let alone father children. We were married to the organization, and any other relationship would have compromised our dedication and loyalty, or so they told us. This company, our work, came first, and anything or anyone who stood in the way or became a priority was destroyed or taken away. They would have taken *you* away, Jaclyn, if they knew you were mine."

"You could have told me."

"I wanted to when you were older and I could trust you to keep the secret, but…I didn't have the nerve. I started to so many times but never followed through. I kept telling myself you were better off without a father rather than someone who could never live up to the expectations of one. If you had known the truth, you would have expected me to treat you differently and I would have, and that would have gotten us both killed."

"Why the hell tell me now, now that I don't need a damn father?"

"I have a bad heart, Jaclyn, and…I think my time is running out. I can't take this secret with me."

"So this confession is all about you clearing your conscience so you can rest in peace."

"I'm telling you because you deserve the truth."

"I deserved the truth a long time ago, not now because it's convenient for you."

"I know." Pierce sighed. "I'm sorry, Jaclyn, I…"

Jack nodded vehemently. "If you were my father, you never would have treated me like dirt. You pushed and pushed me to be someone you wanted. My father would've given me a normal life, not raised me like a soldier and turned his back on me when I almost died in Israel. No father does that."

"I wanted to tell you to come back," he said. "Hell, I wanted to come get you, but…"

"But what?" Jack shouted, ignoring the increasing pain in her head.

"The decision wasn't mine. The three of us had to agree to it, and back then, Joanne and Arthur didn't know you were my daughter. They outvoted my decision to pull you completely from any further missions."

"I barely made it out alive. What did it matter whose daughter I was?"

"Not that it'll make any difference, but I found and killed Amzi myself. Buried him alive for what he did to you."

"You're right. It doesn't make one shit of a difference, because all you wanted me to do was go on with the job while I could barely stand long enough to talk to you on the pay phone."

"You…" Pierce paused and busied himself with piling pictures. "You were too damn good. One of the best ops this place has ever seen. They argued they couldn't afford to pull you off duty, and they…*we*… clearly didn't understand how badly you were hurt."

"One of the best?" Jack plucked the pictures from his hands and threw them against the wall. "You're a fucking liar. If I'm one of the best, that means you picked me because I showed promise like the rest of the kids you bring here. If I was your daughter, I'd have ended up here because of pity, not skills."

"I couldn't raise you here as my child, and I couldn't leave this place, either. Of course I feared I'd never be able to bring you up to the other children's standards, but I didn't take into consideration how much the same we are. You were born for this work like I was. Call it genetic or whatever modern science calls it nowadays, but you only had to try half as hard as the rest."

"Why do I remember trying twice as hard to keep up?" Jack refused to believe a word Pierce said.

"Because I demanded twice as much from you. Your abilities were...*are*...exceptional. It didn't take long for me to realize even I didn't have half the talent you did."

Jack covered her ears. "No."

"I've done everything in my power to get close to you ever since I found out you were alive. I lost my mind when TQ took you. I couldn't lose you just when I had found you. I know you don't want to hear this but..." Pierce wiped his eyes. "I'm sorry for everything. Please, give us a chance before it's too late."

"You're not my father," Jack shouted again.

"Please try to understand that I am," Pierce said calmly.

"Never. I could never hate you this much if you were my father."

Pierce rummaged in the steel box for something and got up. He walked over to Jack and she flinched at the closeness. "And I could never love you this much if you weren't my daughter," he said. He dropped something into the pocket of her robe and left the room.

Still stunned and furious, Jack put her hand in the pocket and pulled out what Pierce had put there. She let the tears fall when she recognized it. A delicate angel, three inches long, handcrafted from braided gold wire.

They had appeared to her all her life in dreams—comforting golden angels, suspended above her head. The puzzle had been solved when Celeste showed her the mobile from her crib, kept as a memento all these years. But it had been missing one piece. One angel.

Her mother had told her that her father had taken it with him.

CHAPTER FORTY

Tuscany, Italy
Three weeks later, April 7

A month had passed since Harper's return to her beloved home and country, yet the comfort she expected to find wasn't there. She spent her days in the vineyards until late in the evening and would return home exhausted.

Monica would stop by on occasion to keep her company and distract her, but Harper would beg off early after staring silently into the flames of the outdoor fireplace. Her good friend and sex partner caught on very quickly that something was wrong. The first time she'd showed up to welcome her back, Harper had been pleased to see her but kept her distance. Monica had simply and silently understood. She'd asked if there was something she could do, and when Harper didn't answer, she'd said she hoped this woman was worthy of her.

Monica, however, did start to worry and fuss over her when Harper refused to eat or have her traditional glass of wine at night. She'd show up with containers of ready-cooked meals and place them in front of Harper. To be polite, Harper would play with her food for a while, then beg off to bed.

Ever since her return, all she wanted to do was spend every moment working in the fields. It was the only time she could stop thinking about Ryden for longer than an hour. She had been tempted to call her every day that passed, but her voice would only make Harper hurt more, and it wouldn't be fair to Ryden.

"Signorina Harper," one of her hands called out from halfway across the vineyard.

Harper looked up and found him signaling her to walk over. She removed her gloves, brushed the soil from her pants, and went over to meet him.

"Someone here to see you," he said in Italian when Harper

neared.

"My appointment isn't for another hour." A new wine buyer was coming for a tour of her property and equipment. "Just show them the way," Harper said indifferently. Normally, she couldn't wait to escort potential buyers and friends through her vineyard, but she just wasn't in the mood for conversation and business. "I'll be over there." She gestured to the new vines she had been working on before returning to them.

She'd intended to change her clothes for the clients, but right now she couldn't care less. Her cargos were comfy and it was too hot to wear anything other than a tank top. She was stooped over, absorbed with the vine, when she felt someone staring at her. When she straightened and turned to look, she gazed straight into Ryden's beautiful green eyes.

Ryden stood looking at her bemusedly, hands folded at her belt. She was wearing jeans and a red button-down shirt, and she looked amazing.

Resting her hands on her hips, Harper looked slowly from Ryden's eyes to the very deep cleavage revealed by her shirt.

"I didn't want to miss you anymore," Ryden said. "So I looked up your vineyard and came to find you."

Harper smiled. "You look great."

"Don't let the foundation fool you. I have circles blacker than tar under my eyes."

Harper walked the few steps to her, not daring to take her eyes off Ryden, afraid that if she blinked Ryden would disappear like a dream. She gently placed a stray lock of hair behind Ryden's ear. "Beautiful is what you are."

"It's how I feel when you look at me."

"Breathless is how you leave me." Harper caressed her ear.

"I've never felt like this before."

"Like what?"

"I can't explain it, but when I'm with you, everything is perfect. I come alive."

Harper craved those lips. She leaned forward as Ryden closed her eyes, but a shout from her foreman interrupted them.

"Signorina Harper, your next appointment is here."

Both of them looked in his direction. Harper felt like she was in a trance.

"I'd better leave." Ryden was breathing heavily.

"Please, stay. I'm going to give a potential customer a tour of the vineyard, and I'd like you to join us."

"I'd like that, too."

"After they leave," Harper said, "I'd like to take you to my home and cook for us."

"I didn't know you cook."

"Then it's about time we got to know each other."

Once she'd toured the cozy Tuscany farmhouse, Ryden went to sit in the garden with a cold glass of iced tea while Harper jumped under the shower.

She couldn't get enough of the magnificent panoramic view: the lush, eye-popping green of the vineyard, carved into terraces that cascaded down the side of the mountain to the rich, multi-hued blues of the sea below. The terra-cotta rooftops of a village etched into the cliffs along the distant water's edge caught the sunlight, while above, a massive flock of seagulls rode the air currents in a spectacular and seemingly choreographed display of aerial acrobatics. Here and there, small plumes of smoke rose from the greenery, where hired hands burned off dead trimmings from the vines. If the planet had one perfect spot where beauty met serenity, this was it.

She heard noise from inside the farmhouse, so she slipped into the kitchen through a side screen door that adjoined the garden. Harper stood hunched over a chopping board, her back turned. She made no sign she'd heard Ryden come in, so Ryden used the opportunity to study her from the doorway.

Not only did Harper look comfortable cooking, she appeared well versed in the fundamentals of Italian cuisine. She'd told Ryden that Italians believed the magic lay in the simplicity and freshness of the ingredients, so tonight's angel-hair pasta would be accompanied by a sauce made from sun-ripened tomatoes, scallions, basil, olive oil, and regional cheeses.

Captivated, she watched the easy, sensual way Harper moved, fluid grace in every motion, with no wasted step or gesture as she chopped ingredients and tossed them into a wide saucepan. Ryden couldn't take her eyes off Harper's ass, perfectly defined by the light linen trousers she'd changed into, and realized for the first time why men spent so much of their life checking out women and thinking about sex.

"Enjoying the view or the smells?" Harper asked, her back still turned.

"Both," Ryden replied with confidence, actually glad she'd been caught appreciating Harper.

"I'm glad." Harper looked at her with those penetrating blue eyes.

"Can I do something?" Ryden asked, relieved she could form a sentence in the face of such enticing temptation.

"You're going to have to be more specific before I answer that." Harper stared at her mouth.

How could this woman turn her on with just one look or sentence? "Can I help you in the kitchen?" Ryden asked.

"Are you being deliberately vague?"

Her cheeks burned with the insinuation. "I'd like to help you prepare dinner."

Harper smiled. "You're fun to tease. Here..." She placed a knife on the counter. "Why don't you work on the salad?"

Ryden stood next to her, slicing tomatoes, peppers, cucumbers, and red onion, while Harper cooked.

"Almost ready." Harper dipped her finger in the sauce and was about to taste it when Ryden stopped her hand.

"Let me," Ryden said.

Harper let Ryden guide her finger to Ryden's mouth.

She slowly licked off the sauce, playing her tongue provocatively around Harper's finger, never taking her eyes off Harper's. "Delicious," she whispered.

Harper swallowed.

"You're fun to tease." *Touché*, Ryden thought, with a satisfied smile.

"I love to be *teased*," Harper replied, "in the kitchen and every other room."

Ryden had to put some space between them before she embarrassed herself. She took a step back. "I'll set the table."

They ate at the rough-hewn table by the outdoor fireplace, sitting side by side on a bench that faced the spectacular view. As they talked about Italy and drank Harper's divine red wine, Ryden found herself torn between staring at the view—spectacular in the setting sun—and Harper's equally compelling profile, her bronzed skin shining in the amber light, eyes sparkling in pride at her vineyard, and her inviting, lush lips.

After they finished their food and cleared the table, they poured a second glass and returned to sit in comfortable canvas chairs by the fireplace.

"You never told me why that special-edition wine I drank was so important," Ryden said.

"Pepo—the founder of the vineyard—gave it to me before he died. It was a fifty-five-year-old wine, the first to be produced."

Ryden gasped. "Oh my G...I'm so sorry. I had no idea."

"Clearly." Harper smiled.

"No wonder you got so upset. I thought it was because it was expensive."

"It was priceless because it was given to me by the only father I ever knew. He was my family."

Ryden sat there shaking her head. How could she have been so stupid and insensitive?

"Hey, what's done is done." Harper touched her hand. "It was about time someone drank it."

"Maybe, but not me. I can hardly tell the difference between wine and Sprite."

Harper laughed. "That's not true."

"But you know what I mean." Ryden couldn't even look at her.

"If it makes you feel any better, I kept the bottle."

"Should it? Because it doesn't."

Harper sat back in the chair. "I guess it was always about the bottle, since I never intended to drink the wine. The bottle is what I looked at whenever I missed home and the grapes. So, now it's empty." Harper shrugged. "Only means it's lighter to carry around."

"You're too kind. I'll have to accept your reasoning since I can't replace it."

"I mean it," Harper said.

"Why did you choose Angelo as a name for your wine?"

"Pepo was obsessed with his dog," Harper replied, her voice tinged with a bittersweet sadness at the memory. "This house and vineyard have never been without an Angelo, even after he died and I took over."

Ryden looked around.

"He died a month and a half ago," Harper explained quietly. "I buried him up there."

Ryden ached to ease the pain in Harper's voice. "You must miss him."

"Like crazy."

"Will you get another?"

"Of course. I can't imagine life without a dog."

"But not yet."

"I've been waiting for the right moment."

"A particular litter?"

Harper shook her head. "I don't believe in buying expensive certified breeds when the shelter here is full of strays that desperately need a home."

"I totally agree, especially after having worked for a shelter for the past month. You won't believe how many people dump their dog because it's no longer a fuzzy, cute puppy the kids want to play with."

"It's ridiculously sad. I don't see how anyone can decide to get rid of a living creature because it's no longer convenient. You wouldn't do that to your child."

"So the right moment depends on, what?" Ryden asked.

"I just know. The same way I know which dog to pick. It's a personal moment for me and something I do alone, so that I know the animal is mine and I'm his, no one else in between. It's silly, I know, but—"

"But you want to know *you've* been chosen. You, exclusively, and without a doubt or hesitation."

Harper smiled. "Yeah."

"I've been tempted to take at least ten dogs home in the past month."

"Nothing yet?"

"I keep putting it off. But who knows? Maybe when I get back."

Harper's smile disappeared. "When do you go back?"

"The day after tomorrow. I wanted to take a week off, but...I'm new, so I had to beg for the three days. I told them I had a family emergency back home. I never said I was going to Italy."

"Good thinking." Harper got up to tend to the fire.

"One of the few perks of being able to reinvent yourself is that you get to be someone with a loving, fully functional family who needs you to rush home."

"I guess," Harper said flippantly.

"Don't you miss it? Having a family?"

"Not really." Harper sat back down. "Not in the traditional sense, anyway. What I miss is someone I can call family. I've never wasted my time with *what ifs* because I can't miss a mom or dad when I've never had to lose them. But what I can miss is a sense of belonging, a mutual feeling of being needed and wanted." Harper took a sip of wine.

"Now, *that* I miss."

"She hurt you a lot."

"I'm no expert, but there's no bigger hurt than that of betrayal," Harper said. "To find out you loved what was never there, loved someone who couldn't or wouldn't give herself...because who she wanted, what she needed, wasn't what you had to offer."

Ryden wanted the mountains to echo the desperate screams of her heart. She'd never intended to deceive Harper; duplicity was not who she was or could ever be, and she desperately wanted this woman to believe and forgive her. But her decisions, and her new life, allowed for nothing more than a glimpse of what could have been.

She had made the trip because she had to see Harper, and tell her she was sorry, and prove what she felt had nothing to do with Moore or money. But fate had sealed the deal for her. This wonderful, hurt woman could never trust her, and the worst part was, she couldn't blame her. The bottom line was, she had lied about who she was, what she did, and even what she looked like, and nothing she could say or do in the very limited time they had together would make Harper believe her intentions were honest and her feelings true.

Ryden didn't know what to do. The fact that Harper, a woman completely out of her league, found her attractive was flattering and exciting, but what Ryden felt went above and beyond a mere weekend to remember. Would she spend the rest of her life regretting what could have been or regretting the memory of a beautiful mistake?

"I lied...to you." Ryden shifted in her chair. "I hurt you and...I almost got you killed." She stopped and both stared at the flames.

She took a deep breath. "I can say I'm sorry, say I never meant for any of it, but the simple fact is I...I can't erase what I did, the same way you can't erase your regrets for having trusted me."

Harper sat listening, saying nothing, either because she didn't want to interrupt or because she didn't have anything to add to the indisputable truth.

"I wish I could say that if I could turn back time, I'd make different choices, but...I'd be lying. I took this job to save my life and I lied to you to protect yours."

"I know."

Ryden nodded. "But that doesn't change the fact that I deceived you, does it?"

"No."

"I didn't think so." Her heart sank in disappointment.

"But what bothers me most..." Harper sat forward, "is that you were so quick to give up who you were: your life, face, identity, to become someone else."

"It didn't seem like a sacrifice, then."

"How could you so easily reject who you are? Who you'd become?" Harper sounded aggravated.

"Because I couldn't appreciate what I had. I couldn't see what life had given, just the things it had taken from me."

"I can understand not being happy with how life sent you off, what it deprived you of. But, on the other hand, look at what it gave you. It made you a fighter, a woman capable of fending for herself and finding ways out when there were no doors."

Ryden nodded. "That it did."

"It made you the most beautiful kind of woman, the kind that's too busy surviving to realize just how attractive she is," Harper said. "Trust me, no amount of makeup or surgery can create beauty that isn't there."

"Thank you," Ryden said halfheartedly. "I'm glad you think of me in those terms."

"But?" Harper obviously caught the unenthusiastic undertone.

"The fact remains that you don't trust me, and I'm in a witness-protection program that prohibits me from seeing you." Ryden exhaled loudly. "An added stigma, another permanent reminder of everything I've done." She got up. "My only regret about this ludicrous period is that I met you during it. I wish you'd come along before I sold myself. I wish you could have met the real Ryden, the one incapable of lies and worth trusting."

When Harper didn't react, she walked the few steps to the house. "I'm going to take a shower and retire for the night. Thank you for the lovely day and evening." She opened the door and turned to look at Harper, who was lost in thought, staring at the dying flames.

"It's funny," Ryden said, "how life can give us insight into our alternate future, as if to rub in our faces how much we screwed up at the crossroads." Forlorn, she entered the house and shut the door to what could have been.

Harper moved mechanically as she extinguished the fire and gathered up the dessert plates and wineglasses. She couldn't stand to see Ryden hurt, and she didn't know how to deal with the finality of the situation.

Whether Ryden was trustworthy or not was not for her to judge, since Harper barely knew her, but what she did know was that this woman had thrown herself forward to take a bullet.

Ryden possessed a certain virtuousness and naïveté for a woman of her age that Harper had never witnessed. Life might have been hard for Ryden, but contrary to the way that most who traveled a rocky path reacted, she hadn't become hard, and her purity was a genetic disposition, not an acquisition.

Harper could feel how much Ryden regretted having to lie to her, as well as the consequences of those lies, and she believed Ryden when she said she'd wanted to protect her. It would have been so easy for Ryden to confess what she'd gotten herself in to and ask for Harper's help to get her out of a dangerous game, but Ryden had put Harper's safety above her own.

The problem was, Harper didn't want to believe she was ready or willing to trust another woman after Carmen, and another straight one at that. She'd given her heart before, and it had taken her years to come to terms with her own blindness and self-delusions.

She was incredibly attracted to Ryden; she'd struggled with that desire from the moment she'd first seen her. But she was too old and too burned to let attraction dictate her more profound need for an unconditional bond.

Stolen moments with a woman she was forbidden to contact was not Harper's idea of a foundation to build on.

She heard Ryden moving around upstairs. Probably just getting out of the shower, since the guest bath was just above her head. Frustrated, she kicked the door to the dishwasher shut. Why the hell did this woman have to walk into her life? And why couldn't Harper walk away from this condemned situation?

Was life testing her? Was she at a crossroads of her own, where her alternate future was being constructed as she stood in the kitchen picturing Ryden exiting her life for good?

Harper locked the door and switched off the lights. Years from now, would a potential glimpse into an alternate life fill her with remorse or relief?

Distraught, Harper walked quietly up the stairs and stopped at Ryden's room, where she rested her hand on the closed door and silently bid her farewell, chastising herself for the decision she knew she would regret.

CHAPTER FORTY-ONE

Ryden got out of bed when Harper stopped moving around downstairs. Certain Harper had gone to bed, and too upset to sleep, she wanted to go outside to feel the warm breeze and look at the stars. She went to the door and listened closely to make sure she couldn't hear Harper and, when she didn't hear any noise, turned the knob and opened it.

She jumped when she saw Harper standing there, three or four feet away. "Harper!"

Harper stood like a statue, saying nothing, her arms at her sides and a desolate expression on her face.

"Are you all right?" Ryden asked.

Still Harper didn't move, but her eyes did. Ryden stood there as Harper's gaze languidly descended, from her eyes, to her lips, neck, breasts—lingering there, before continuing to the rest of her body.

She should've felt exposed, in her snug T-shirt and bikini panties, but she didn't. Ryden let Harper take her in, as she observed Harper's face change from sad to...

Her thoughts stopped, together with her breath, when Harper took the remaining step into her room.

They stood silently facing each other as Harper's mixed expressions reflected Ryden's own turmoil of emotions. "I want the impossible," Ryden finally whispered. "Even if I never see you again, I want the impossible."

"What do you want?" Harper's voice was deep.

"To erase your doubts, make you understand how I feel...but..." Ryden looked at the floor, blinking hard as tears formed. "I don't know how."

With gentle fingers, Harper lifted Ryden's head and wiped her tears with her thumb.

"Show me," Harper said, and brought Ryden's mouth to within an inch of her own.

Trembling, Ryden wrapped her arms around Harper's neck and pulled Harper to her, kissing her with a passion she hadn't known she possessed. Harper moaned and moved into her, her thigh between Ryden's legs, and Ryden immediately buckled, her body unable to control the new sensations.

She let go of Harper and stepped back, breathing hard. "I have to take it slow." Grasping Harper's hand, she led her to the bed. Then, with a mixture of shyness and arousal, she slowly lifted her T-shirt and removed it. She'd never before stood exposed like this in front of anyone, but then again, no one had ever made her feel as sexy and wanted.

Harper took her nakedness in, slowly and thoroughly, her arousal apparent by the twin peaks straining her tailored white shirt.

Ryden, flustered by Harper's painfully hard nipples, hoped she could contain the fire she'd started.

As though Harper sensed her insecurity, she took Ryden's hand and placed it on her breast. She gasped at the feel of Harper's firm arousal, her anxieties quickly turning into a distant memory as she confidently played with one nipple.

Harper covered Ryden's hand with her own, urging her to increase the pressure, and she thought she might lose her mind at the sensation.

"I want more," she said, as she unbuttoned the top button of Harper's shirt.

"I need more." Harper groaned.

She unbuttoned the rest of Harper's shirt and let it drop, then removed her sheer white bra. She openly admired the taut, tan body until she could hold back no longer. She attacked Harper, hard on the mouth, as she wrapped her arms around Harper and stroked her back. As she brought her hands forward to cover Harper's breasts, she kissed and licked her mouth and neck.

Harper gasped and took her in her arms. "If I have to go slow much longer, I'm going to burst."

"I can't get enough of you." Ryden sounded drunk even to herself. "Tell me what you want." She unbuckled Harper's pants.

Harper removed the rest of her clothes, took Ryden in her arms, and they fell back onto the bed, with Harper's warm body covering hers. That first, full-length touch of each other's skin—breast to breast, pelvis to pelvis, legs entwined—made both of them pause.

"You feel perfect," Harper said as she began to move against her.

"I've never felt this...turned on."

Harper's sexy, lopsided smile almost stopped Ryden's heart. Was it possible she'd never really made love until this very moment?

Harper kissed her passionately, and when she ran her fingers down the side of Ryden's body, Ryden involuntarily writhed beneath her, sensations she'd never experienced flooding every fiber of her.

Harper felt Ryden shiver under her touch. She wanted to go slow, like Ryden had asked, but for the first time, she had to struggle to comply. Although she wanted to savor this woman, and the night, her need for Ryden was painfully strong. She had to clench her legs to fight the impending orgasm that tortured her.

She kissed her way down Ryden's neck to her perfect breasts and licked her nipples, stroking them teasingly with her tongue. Ryden's hand entwined in her hair, guiding her from one breast to the other and back, until Harper finally sucked hard on one nipple as she pinched the other.

"Yes." Ryden dug her nails into Harper's back.

Harper, no longer in control of her own body, pressed her center against Ryden's. Both moaned in unison and rocked together until Harper felt helpless to stop the wave about to devour her. She took Ryden's hand and guided it between her legs.

"So wet," Ryden said, stroking Harper slowly before entering her.

Harper eased on top of her, in tune with Ryden's hand. "So perfect." She kissed Ryden, neither breaking the taunting rhythm, until she couldn't hold back any more. Harper practically felt herself levitate as she climaxed longer and stronger than she ever had.

"That was amazing." Ryden's voice was hoarse. "I felt you come."

Harper remained on top of her, kissing Ryden's neck. "I thought I'd never stop."

Ryden slowly pulled out of her, brought her hand to her mouth, and licked her fingers. "Beautiful."

Harper licked Ryden's mouth, tasting herself there. "You drive me crazy. Always have." She kissed her way down Ryden's body, stroking and licking every inch of it.

Ryden reacted with sighs and gasps to every caress from her mouth and hands. "Your touch, kisses…everything about you, is…" She half sat up, leaning back on her elbows. "I don't recognize myself or my body."

"I want to taste you." She kissed Ryden just above her center.

"Every drop."

Ryden fell back with a moan and grabbed the sheets.

Harper licked her slowly until Ryden cried out, "God, what's happening to me?"

Harper entered her with two fingers as she continued to lick and suck.

"Oh, my…yes." Ryden moved her body against Harper's tongue. "God, I can't stop coming." She pulled the sheets so hard Harper thought they were going to tear.

Harper penetrated her harder and harder, until Ryden screamed something unintelligible and fell back limp on the bed.

Harper kissed her way up to her and lay next to Ryden, caressing her face. "Are you all right?"

"I think so." Ryden lay with her eyes shut. "I've never come like that. So powerful."

Harper smiled. "Tired?"

"Insatiable." Ryden climbed on top of her.

"You're pretty amazing for someone who's never done this before." Harper smiled. "You sure you're new at this?"

"In every way." Ryden kissed her. "In every single way."

They made love all night, occasionally stopping to watch the moon crawl across the sky and fade in the morning light. Finally, they dozed, and when Harper awoke and checked the clock, it was nine a.m. They couldn't have slept more than a couple of hours.

Ryden stretched and caressed Harper's abdomen. "Morning."

"Hey." Harper kissed her. "Big day today."

"Oh, yeah. That." Ryden's blissful expression faded, replaced by sadness. "One more day together before I leave."

"That's not what I mean." Harper kissed her again. "Today's the day I get Angelo."

"That's great." Ryden sat up. "You decided to get a new dog."

"Almost right." Harper kissed Ryden's shoulder. "We're going together. If you want to," she added shyly.

"But you said you go alone. You want the dog to bond with you, as its only master and friend."

"I changed my mind."

"Why?"

"Because I want you to stay with me and I want Angelo to be ours." Harper sat up when she saw Ryden tear up.

"But I have to go back."

"No, you don't."

"What?" Ryden asked with a shocked expression.

"I'll talk to Pierce. I'm sure we can work something out."

Ryden tossed the sheets aside and threw herself into Harper's arms. "Are you sure?" She had never looked happier.

"As I watched you sleep, I got a glimpse of my alternate future."

"And?"

"I don't want to live with remorse." Harper kissed Ryden soundly on the lips.

EPILOGUE

Halkidiki, Greece
Fourteen months later

The sleek, 440-foot-long Fincantiere superyacht was a study in luxurious excesses, with seven decks, two helicopter landing pads—one with a hangar—a huge indoor seawater swimming pool, and storage for a large submarine. Noted naval architect Espen Oeino had designed the *Pegasus* to comply with the maximum safety international regulations, while still providing its billionaire owner with a breathtaking profile. The largest yacht ever built in Italy, it currently ranked ninth in the world, but its state-of-the-art technological advancements and sophisticated splendor set it apart from even the bigger mega yachts.

The internal space of the superyacht measured more than forty-eight thousand square feet, twenty-nine thousand of which was devoted to ultra-luxury designed by the renowned Pascale Reymond from Reymond Langton Design. Twelve elite cabins could accommodate twenty-four guests in extreme comfort, while additional living space below housed the ship's fifty-two-person crew.

TQ's host, Greek shipping magnate Konstantinos "Kostas" Lykourgos, had given her a richly appointed stateroom more impressive than any hotel she'd ever stayed in, but she rarely spent any time there. The rich blue waters of the Aegean, the perfect weather, and the panoramic views all beckoned her topside. This particular morning, Kostas had promised her a spectacle surpassing any they'd seen thus far, so she dressed in a flowing printed kaftan and broad sun hat and went to breakfast with a rare sense of delightful anticipation. Her time in Greece had been the perfect way to put the frustration and disappointment of last year behind her.

"*Kalimera*, Theodora." Lykourgos stood when he spotted her from the aft second-tier deck, where a table for three was laid with the finest china and crystal. Side tables held a variety of breakfast fare: fresh fruit, cheeses, croissants, and honeyed yogurt, strong Greek coffee and juices, and sterling-silver warming trays with lids. "I hope you slept well." He pulled out a chair for her.

"Good morning." TQ looked from Kostas to his beautiful, twenty-six-year-old daughter, Ariadne.

"I was just leaving. Enjoy your morning." Ariadne got up. "My friends will be picking me up shortly." She kissed her father's head and disappeared inside.

TQ had met the young woman yesterday for the first time, and although the girl struck her as immaculately groomed, exceptionally educated and bright—in other words, a worthy successor to her father's multi-million-dollar business—TQ didn't like the way Ariadne scrutinized her, as if waiting for TQ to falter and expose her less-impressive background. Maybe mutual antipathy was inevitable between two strong women.

The day was already warm and the sun was barely up, but the steady sea breeze made it comfortable on the boat. "May I assume the promised land isn't far off?" she asked her host. Lykourgos had invited her on his yacht with the purpose of a business proposition. TQ couldn't wait to hear what kind of business this Greek tycoon wanted with her. So far, he had been vague, but something told her it would be big.

"*Agio Oros,*" he replied. "Mount Athos. The most splendid view in Halkidiki and home to some of the world's most magnificent ancient treasures."

His description got her full attention. "What kind of treasures?" she asked.

"There are twenty monasteries on the Holy Mountain," he said, "the oldest dating back more than a thousand years. They contain an abundance of medieval art, richly drawn icons, ancient manuscripts, religious objects like chalices, holy relics, and elaborate codices. Some of the icons are believed to work miracles. An effort to catalogue and preserve the treasures has been under way for some thirty years or more, but the sheer magnitude of the collection is so vast, it will take many more decades to complete."

"I can't wait to see some of them," TQ replied, already calculating how she might acquire a few choice pieces for her own collection.

"That will be impossible, I'm afraid." Lykourgos frowned apologetically. "Women are prohibited from entering the mountain. Even for men, it is difficult and requires a special visa, signed by four of the secretaries of the leading monasteries. Although part of the Greek state, Agio Oros is self-governed, with its own rules."

"Surely an exception can be made," TQ said, and sipped her coffee. "We merely need to provide the good monks with the proper incentive."

Lykourgos's deep laugh made him even more attractive. "I have heard that you do not take no for an answer, Theodora. But I assure you, even my money can't get you in."

"I doubt there's anything money can't do, but that aside, why are you taking me to a place I'm not allowed to enter?" The sexist prohibition already irritated TQ.

"Come," he said, extending his hand. "We are getting close now. Let me show you."

They were momentarily distracted by the approach of a much smaller, but also luxurious, yacht. "Ariadne, your friends are here," Lykourgos called out.

The young woman reemerged from below, wearing a turquoise bikini that matched her eyes and showed off her long, lean body. She said something in Greek to her father and gave TQ a cold stare before she made her way to the lower-deck stairs. From there, she jumped into the water and swam to the waiting yacht, where a group of five young women waited for her.

"She is my most precious achievement," Lykourgos said.

"She looks very much like you." TQ tried to sound respectful of his adoration for his irksome daughter.

"Only on the outside. She's sharper and tougher than I'll ever be. She is already thriving in the company."

"Good for her." TQ shrugged. "Now, back to what interests me."

He led her forward, six levels up, to the sundeck. There they had a 360-degree view, but the sight ahead demanded their full attention.

Mount Athos rose dramatically from the sea, an enormous sharp-peaked pinnacle that appeared a deep, dark blue against the azure Aegean. A magnificent spectacle all on its own, and made the sight of a lifetime with the addition of the enormous monastery perched atop an enormous stone cliff just ahead. It towered over them, more than a thousand feet in the air.

"There were once three hundred monasteries on the Holy Mountain," Lykourgos said. "This is the Simonopetra Monastery, or Simon's Rock. It was founded in the thirteenth century by Simon the Athonite and is still in use. Its choir is world renowned."

"Breathtaking," TQ had to admit.

"Indeed."

TQ took the view in a while longer, then turned to her host. "Now, tell me why we're here."

"This sacred and very secretive monastery possesses some of the world's most priceless antiquities."

"You mentioned." TQ couldn't wait for the pronouncement she was sure was going to make this particular business deal the finest of her life.

"Everyone knows, or at least suspects, that the monastery hides and protects artifacts the world has never heard of nor considers missing."

"Yes, yes," TQ said, eager for him to continue. "I own similar relics."

"A high-ranking monk of another monastery is a close friend who has had the honor of acquainting himself with some of these missing relics."

TQ's rich background in rare antiques, after years in the auction business, was screaming for an answer. "Which? I'm sure I've heard of them."

"A solid-gold icon that dates back to the twelfth century and depicts—"

"Theotokos." TQ nearly yelped. "The mother of Christ."

He nodded. "Not many know about the existence of this icon."

"I'm not *many*."

"Are you a religious woman, Theodora?"

"Don't be ridiculous," she replied. "Such asinine beliefs are for the simple masses."

"I happen to have such asinine beliefs," he said quietly, "but that's another matter."

"One I'm sure will bore me."

"It is said that, aside from being priceless, the icon possesses the power to heal."

"Pish posh. But if the idea thrills you…" She shrugged.

"I want that icon," Lykourgos said.

"May I ask why? I'm sure you have plenty of priceless goods already decorating your walls or in a safety-deposit box."

"I'm sick," he replied. "And the best doctors in the world can't do anything more than they already have."

"And you think the icon will heal you."

"I do, Theodora."

"How quaint."

"I'm willing to pay five hundred million euros."

The Greek had more money than God. TQ laughed. "I hardly think money will convince these God-fearing pathological worshippers."

"No one, Theodora, is immune to money, as you know. These people, however, cover their greed very convincingly."

"If you think you can bribe the robes, I'm sure the amount you mentioned will do the trick, especially since this country's economy is beyond repair."

"The monks will never feel the economic or social hit Greece has taken. They are a country of their own, and a very wealthy one at that, very much like the Vatican. The amount I mentioned is for *you*."

TQ pulled at the brim of her sun hat to shield her eyes from the glare as she looked at him. "Do explain," she said coquettishly.

"Your track record of acquisitions speaks for itself. If anyone can…get it, it's you."

"I'm flattered that you estimate me accordingly, but my reputation is based on the fact I have always known the precise location of the object I'm after." TQ thought the man's sickness, whatever it was, had gone to his head. As appealing as the idea of owning the Theotokos was, the fortress was not only impenetrable, but it would also be impossible to find the icon in this small city without the knowledge of where it was being kept.

"I know where they hide it," he said.

TQ tried not to gasp. "You what?"

"You have a renowned reputation in very private circles for trading in appropriated, priceless artifacts. I can lead you to it."

She couldn't believe the Greek would willingly lead her to one of the world's most invaluable treasures. Oh, she would do it, all right.

"In return," he said, "I will give you—"

TQ didn't hear the rest. *In return, I will walk away with the Theotokos and you will never see it again.* She smiled. "We have a deal."

About the Authors

KIM BALDWIN (kimbaldwin.com), a former network news executive, has made her living as a writer for more than three decades. In addition to the Elite Operatives Series she is co-authoring with Xenia Alexiou, she has published seven solo romantic adventure novels: *Hunter's Pursuit, Force of Nature, Whitewater Rendezvous, Flight Risk, Focus of Desire, Breaking the Ice,* and *High Impact.* She's also had several short stories published in BSB anthologies. A 2012 Lambda Literary Award winner and 2011 Lambda finalist, she is also the recipient of a 2011 Rainbow Award For Excellence, a 2010 Independent Publisher Book Award, three Golden Crown Literary Society Awards, eight Lesbian Fiction Readers' Choice Awards, and an Alice B. Readers Appreciation Award for her body of work. She has recorded audiobooks of her own novel *Breaking the Ice,* and the Rose Beecham mystery *Grave Silence.* Kim lives in Michigan but keeps her laptop, camera, and passport handy to travel whenever possible. She can be reached at baldwinkim@gmail.com.

XENIA ALEXIOU (xeniaalexiou.com) lives in Greece. An avid reader and knowledge junkie, she likes to travel all over the globe and take pictures of the wonderful and interesting people that represent different cultures. Trying to see the world through their eyes has been her most challenging yet rewarding pursuit so far. These travels have inspired countless stories, and it's these stories that she has decided to write about. *The Gemini Deception* is her sixth novel, following *Demons are Forever, Dying to Live, Missing Lynx, Thief of Always,* and *Lethal Affairs.* She is a 2012 Lambda Literary winner, 2011 Lambda finalist, has received three Rainbow Award Honorable mentions, and is the recipient of three Golden Crown Literary Society Awards and six Lesbian Fiction Readers' Choice Awards. Xenia is currently at work on the seventh and final book in the Elite Operatives Series. For more information, contact her at xeniaalexiou007@gmail.com.

Lethal Affairs, Thief of Always, and *Missing Lynx* have been translated into Dutch, and the first two books are also available in Russian. In 2010, *Dubbel Doelwit (Lethal Affairs)* won second place among Dutch readers in their vote for best all-time Lesbian International (translated) book.

Books Available From Bold Strokes Books

The Princess Affair by Nell Stark. Rhodes Scholar Kerry Donovan arrives at Oxford ready to focus on her studies, but her life and her priorities are thrown into chaos when she catches the eye of Her Royal Highness Princess Sasha. (978-1-60282-858-2)

The Chase by Jesse J. Thoma. When Isabelle Rochat's life is threatened, she receives the unwelcome protection and attention of bounty hunter Holt Lasher who vows to keep Isabelle safe at all costs. (978-1-60282-859-9)

The Lone Hunt by L.L. Raand. In a world where humans and Praeterns conspire for the ultimate power, violence is a way of life…and death. A Midnight Hunters novel. (978-1-60282-860-5)

The Supernatural Detective by Crin Claxton. Tony Carson sees dead people. With a drag queen for a spirit guide and a devastatingly attractive herbalist for a client, she's about to discover the spirit world can be a very dangerous world indeed. (978-1-60282-861-2)

Beloved Gomorrah by Justine Saracen. Undersea artists creating their own City on the Plain uncover the truth about Sodom and Gomorrah, whose "one righteous man" is a murderer, rapist, and conspirator in genocide. (978-1-60282-862-9)

The Left Hand of Justice by Jess Faraday. A kidnapped heiress, a heretical cult, a corrupt police chief, and an accused witch. Paris is burning, and the only one who can put out the fire is Detective Inspector Elise Corbeau...whose boss wants her dead. (978-1-60282-863-6)

Cut to the Chase by Lisa Girolami. Careful and methodical author Paige Cornish falls for brash and wild Hollywood actress Avalon Randolph, but can these opposites find a happy middle ground in a town that never lives in the middle? (978-1-60282-783-7)

Every Second Counts by D. Jackson Leigh. Every second counts in Bridgette LeRoy's desperate mission to protect her heart and stop Marc Ryder's suicidal return to riding rodeo bulls. (978-1-60282-785-1)

More Than Friends by Erin Dutton. Evelyn Fisher thinks she has the perfect role model for a long-term relationship, until her best friends, Kendall and Melanie, split up and all three women must reevaluate their lives and their relationships. (978-1-60282-784-4)

Dirty Money by Ashley Bartlett. Vivian Cooper and Reese DiGiovanni just found out that falling in love is hard. It's even harder when you're running for your life. (978-1-60282-786-8)

Sea Glass Inn by Karis Walsh. When Melinda Andrews commissions a series of mosaics by Pamela Whitford for her new inn, she doesn't expect to be more captivated by the artist than by the paintings. (978-1-60282-771-4)

The Awakening: A Sisterhood of Spirits novel by Yvonne Heidt. Sunny Skye has interacted with spirits her entire life, but when she runs into Officer Jordan Lawson during a ghost investigation, she discovers more than just facts in a missing girl's cold case file. (978-1-60282-772-1)

Murphy's Law by Yolanda Wallace. No matter how high you climb, you can't escape your past. (978-1-60282-773-8)

Blacker Than Blue by Rebekah Weatherspoon. Threatened with losing her first love to a powerful demon, vampire Cleo Jones is willing to break the ultimate law of the undead to rebuild the family she has lost. (978-1-60282-774-5)

Silver Collar by Gill McKnight. Werewolf Luc Garoul is outlawed and out of control, but can her family track her down before a sinister predator gets there first? Fourth in the Garoul series. (978-1-60282-764-6)

The Dragon Tree Legacy by Ali Vali. For Aubrey Tarver time hasn't dulled the pain of losing her first love Wiley Gremillion, but she has to set that aside when her choices put her life and her family's lives in real danger. (978-1-60282-765-3)

The Midnight Room by Ronica Black. After a chance encounter with the mysterious and brooding Lillian Gray in the "midnight room" of The Griffin, a local lesbian bar, confident and gorgeous Audrey McCarthy learns that her bad-girl behavior isn't bulletproof. (978-1-60282-766-0)